THE HIDDEN DEAD

THE HIDDEN DEAD

DAVID PENNY

HEREFORDSHIRE, ENGLAND

JUNE 1502

ONE

"Pa, Will says you have to come." Amal Berrington tugged at her father's hand. "There is something wrong with one of the graves we opened."

Thomas Berrington came slowly back to the present. It was a long way back. Almost fifty years, and in his memory the house that now stood in ruins in front of him was whole. His mother, his father, and his brother had all been alive.

Now, on this first day of June in the year 1502, Thomas, his son and his daughter had left their new home in Burway a little after dawn to come to this ruined house on the hillside above Lemster. At this time of year, dawn came early. St Lawrence's church bells had struck four times as they rode around the walls of Ludlow and crossed Ludford bridge over the Teme.

Others could have accompanied them, but Thomas had told them this was Berrington work and only Berringtons could do it. Besides, he knew that Jorge had an aversion to bones; even long-buried ones. Both Silva and Bel had wanted to come, but Thomas had told them no, even though he could not exactly say why he wanted it to be only the three of them. Himself, Will and Amal. Berringtons.

He gave a shake of his head and turned to his daughter. "What is it, my sweet?"

Amal pulled a face at being called my sweet. Her face was dirt-streaked, the dried clay paler than her skin.

"Will has found something that should not be in the grave." She consulted a sheet of paper in her hand. "My grandmother's grave."

Many other fourteen-year-old girls would have been troubled at digging up the remains of their ancestors, but not Amal. As for her brother, five years older, little daunted Will Berrington.

"What about it?" Thomas's mind was still half in the past. This house had once been his. Well ... his father's. Now in ruins, it lacked the importance he felt it should have. He had memories buried within its walls, though the memories had survived better than the walls.

"I told you," said Amal. "There is something that should not be there."

"Has it been disturbed by animals?"

"If you come and look instead of standing there like you have lost your wits you will see for yourself." Amal tugged again at his hand and Thomas finally let the tangled memories blow away into nothing in the warm breeze.

He followed his daughter around the house to where

the ground rose towards the crest of Eaton Hill. Five excavations had already been made in the hard soil, only two of which Thomas had contributed to. His son, Will, had dug most of the rest, even Amal doing more than her father.

"Show me," Thomas said.

She went to one of the opened graves — though grave was too fine a word for what was little more than a shallow trench holding bones. Thomas had first dug this one when he was a lad of thirteen years. It held, if his memory was accurate, which he was sometimes less sure of these days than he had once been, his mother, Catherine Berrington. Taken too soon by a pestilence that scoured the district. A shallow mound indicated a second grave beyond it, as yet unopened. The mound puzzled Thomas for a moment. So many years had passed he would have expected the grave to have settled more. It would contain the remains of Thomas's brother, John Berrington. John, like his father of the same name, had been a bully and a braggart, as well as strong as an ox. None of those attributes had saved him from an invisible enemy.

Thomas stood on the edge of the excavation and looked down at a jumble of bones. They were less disturbed than he expected and he put that down to Amal being the one to expose them.

Will tackled each hole with a spade, then stopped when he came across any sign of remains and allowed his sister to complete the work. So far they had made a good team.

Thomas's gaze scanned the bones, measuring, analysing. He had studied bones and the bodies containing them for more years than he cared to recall. It seemed today was becoming a day for memories.

He gave a shake of his head. "What am I looking for?" As his eyes tracked what lay in the bottom of the shallow grave it came to him there were more bones than could be accounted for by a single body.

Amal came past him and dropped into the grave. She reached down and withdrew one bone from among those lying there before holding it out. "This, Pa. Does this bone belong to my grandmother?"

Thomas took the thigh bone and turned it over in his hand.

"No," he said. "Show me exactly where it was."

Amal knelt and pointed. "And there are more, Pa. A full set, near enough. Was she with child when she died?"

"There was no sign, and these remains are from something older than an unborn infant."

"So why are they here?" Amal stared up at her father, her eyes narrowed against the brightness of the sky.

Thomas looked at the bone in his hand then dropped it back into the grave, causing Amal to frown because now she would have to separate it out again.

"I do not know, Ami. Did you find anything in the other graves?"

"Nothing that was not expected. Three females and two males. All adults, though short for adults."

"Where did you put the bones?"

"Inside what is left of the house, as you told us. Each

is laid out on a sack because I knew you would want to see them before we take them home. I will bring these out and arrange them too."

Thomas turned and walked into the house that seemed much diminished from the one in his memory. There was no need to open a door because most of the wall on the side facing the hill had fallen in after a fire.

Amal had cleared a space and set out seven sacks. On five of them lay the skeletons of Thomas's ancestors. He had written a name on a sheet of paper for each, which lay atop the bones to identify whose they were. Grandma Elizabeth. Grandpa John. Great-uncle Paul, Cousins Alice and Mary. They had been laid in their graves many years before Thomas had been born, but his mother had told him who each plot belonged to. She had come to Lemster from Wales to marry Squire John Berrington. She claimed he had been quite a catch. He wondered how long it had taken before she realised her mistake.

Thomas knelt and stared at the bones, not touching them yet. He heard Amal behind him, but she said nothing. She stood to one side, waiting.

Eventually, Thomas turned to her.

"Go and ask Will to open the last grave."

"Already being done, Pa. There is nothing unusual about the other bones, is there?"

Thomas rose to his feet. "No, nothing I can see."

Amal opened the sack she held and emptied the bones onto the remains of the tiled floor before going to her knees and separating them into two piles. Thomas looked back through the collapsed wall to where Will continued to dig.

When he turned back he saw something, sure Amal had not yet noticed it.

"What's wrong, Pa?" Amal looked up at him.

"Take another look at the bones, Ami," Thomas said. "Tell me what you see."

Amal made a sound of impatience. Thomas stood back until he saw her shoulders. She tapped her head, and he nodded.

"Did we miss it? Is it still buried?"

"We both looked in her grave. We missed nothing."

Thomas glanced to where Will was still digging. "Are you close yet, Will?" he called out.

"I'm already deeper than the last one but nothing yet. Can you remember if you dug them the same depth, Pa?"

"No, I cannot. I had thirteen years and had lost half my family in a single day, so of course I do not remember. Make room, I'll come to help."

"Stay where you are. We will only get in each other's way if you come down here."

Thomas knew Will was right, but an urgency ran through him it was hard to ignore. He tried his best, which he knew was not always good enough. All the same, he stood and watched as the muscles in Will's back and shoulders flexed. Each strike of his spade brought out four times as much soil as Thomas would have. He felt a hand slip inside his.

"It is all right, Pa. We will find Grandma's head, I am sure."

Thomas was not, but he said nothing. The sun beat down on their heads, and sweat ran down Will's flank to dampen the soil he dug until, finally, he straightened.

"There is something here." He pulled himself from the hole so his father could take his place.

Thomas held a hand out, and Amal threw a trowel to him. He began to scrape the earth away from bones that lay beneath the surface. Even before he pulled the first out, he knew it did not belong to his brother. John had been strong at eighteen, a skilled archer able to draw a longbow. That built muscle, but it also built bone if the practice of it started young enough. It had been the same for Thomas. He recalled drawing a shorter bow when he was eight years of age. At first, he could not pull it, but as the weeks passed he learned. By the time he was thirteen, he could almost draw a three-quarter-sized longbow. He had done so at the battle of Castillon when his father took him to France.

Thomas looked up at Amal. "Fetch two sacks."

Once she had run off, Will leaned in to look at what had been revealed.

"Is it your brother, Pa?"

"Another interloper."

"Why?" said Will.

"If I knew that I would..." But Thomas did not know.

It was clear someone, or more than one person, had opened the graves and added a body to each. Only one, it appeared, but Thomas was aware they had not brought out all the bones yet. He redoubled his efforts, exposing bone after bone, each of them small. When he sat up to catch his breath, he found Amal squatting beside the grave, her eyes on what he had revealed. Two sacks lay on the grass beside her.

"The cuckoo bones were mixed in with those of your mother," she said. "These are the same. There were no bones in the other graves, were there? Why is that?"

"Wrong question, Ami. You should ask why there is an excess of bones in any of the graves. I suspect the answer is that these are more recent, so they were possibly easier to open. Or there were only two bodies that needed to be hidden."

"Why hide a body in an old grave, Pa? The skeletons are of children. Young children. Less than a year in age for the first, I would say. Would it not have been easier to..." Amal waved a hand. "...to burn the bodies? Or bury them somewhere else? Even leave them in the woods for animals to take. Why here? Why the graves of your family?"

"I do not know, Ami."

"But you are going to find out."

Thomas looked up at his daughter. "Why do these things keep happening to me?"

Amal laughed, the sound sweet in the warm June air. "Because you are Thomas Berrington, Pa, and sometimes things that are wrong need to be fixed. That is what you do. Trouble finds those who can fix it, that is all."

"Well, I wish it would stop. Now, lay out these bones while I hand them up. And tell Will he can start filling in the empty graves and make the ground good. I would not want anyone to come this way and fall into one. That would cause more trouble."

It was gone noon before John Berrington's grave lay empty, and Thomas stared down at his remains. Most of his remains. Like his mother, the skull of his brother was missing. Amal is right, he thought; trouble finds me whether I want it or not.

But was this trouble? As he stared at the small skeletons that should not be there, he suspected it was. Some manner of trouble, anyway. Not as bad as some that had affected him. Perhaps only a small mystery, which would soon be solved, he hoped.

He told Amal to take the bones into the remains of his old home and went to help Will shovel the soil back into the graves.

Amal had placed the bones into separate sacks by the time they were finished. Nine sacks rather than the seven expected, and Thomas was glad they had brought extra with them even though he had been sure they would not be needed.

"Can you take them back to Burway without me?" he asked Will and Amal.

"Of course we can," said Will. "Where are you going, Pa?"

"Lemster. I need to talk to Prior Bernard about the extra bones."

Thomas watched his son and daughter mount their horses. The sacks of bones draped across their saddles looked innocent enough. They might have contained straw or wood. Once they were gone from sight, Thomas mounted Ferrant and turned the horse down the slope to where Lemster lay in a curve of the river Lugge. The priory sat solidly on the eastern edge of the town, surrounded by stone walls beyond which the sun glittered silver from carp ponds fed with clear water from the Kenwater.

Bones, Thomas thought. Bones that had no place in the graves of his family.

TWO

Thomas tied Ferrant to a post beside the gate to Lemster Priory and asked a brother to tell Prior Bernard he wanted to speak with him.

"The Prior already has visitors, sir. You can sit and wait if you wish. I will bring water."

"How long will he be?"

"I do not know, sir. His visitors have been with him some time, but they can be all day once they become engrossed in talk of relics."

"Relics?"

"Yes, sir, relics. Lemster Priory has only a small selection, but all are exquisite."

The brother turned away and moved off in that slow gait all men of God acquire after a short time within the walls of a priory, church, or abbey.

Thomas sat on a stone bench and watched the robed brothers move through the grounds as they performed their daily tasks. He knew the priory was almost a town within a town, as well as the largest landowner in the district. Most people in Lemster would be tied to it in some way. They rented houses and land from it. Sold their produce when the priory could not grow it themselves. At least one son from most families would be sent to add to the number of brothers. The subject had never been raised in Thomas's family, but that might have been because John Berrington was squire to the Earl of Shrewsbury and considered himself above the rules of ordinary people. Or perhaps Thomas had been considered too young, though he knew of other boys of thirteen years who were sent into the Church. It seemed odd to consider how his life might have been had he joined the ranks of those he watched. He had believed in God then and might not have put up much resistance. Though there was the matter of Bel Brickenden and what they had done in the room above her parents' barn. Brothers were meant to abstain from all such temptations, though Thomas knew the truth was often different. Abbots, priors and priests were known to take lovers, even wives, and to father children. But not Prior Bernard. Thomas knew the man would take his vow of celibacy seriously, as he took most things seriously. Was that the same for the brothers he watched move around the courtyard? Thomas knew his companion Jorge would no doubt be able to tell those who sinned from those who did not. Except Jorge would not call it sin. Jorge did not believe in such a thing as sin. There were times Thomas believed Jorge might even welcome more of it into his life.

Thinking of sin made Thomas smile, for Bel Brickenden now lived under his roof and lay in his bed beside him every night. He had never considered what they did all those years ago a sin and certainly did not consider it one now. They had found each other again as if it had been fated ... and perhaps it was.

"What are you doing out here, Tom?"

Prior Bernard stood with the sun behind him so it formed a halo around his greying hair. He was accompanied by two men, both strangers to Thomas. One was tall and thin, and his face carried a scowl, but whether permanent or caused by Thomas's presence, he did not know. The other was shorter than Prior Bernard but strongly built. He too wore a scowl, as well as a white robe marking him as a Benedictine. He ignored Thomas.

"I will leave you, Prior, but do not forget what we spoke of. Abbot Haylewith will want an answer before long." The man turned and strode off.

"I hope I did not interrupt anything," Thomas said. "I was content to wait."

"As you can see, I have been in discussions, but am never too busy for you, Tom. This is Brother Ambrose." Prior Bernard introduced the man at his side, who offered a brief nod in return. "The man who left is Prior Madoc. He serves under Abbot Haylewith at Hindwell Abbey." The words were plain enough, but Thomas sensed a tension in Bernard as he spoke them.

"You are Thomas Berrington?" asked Brother Ambrose.

"I am."

"Tom saved the life of Catherine of Aragon," said Prior Bernard.

"But not Prince Arthur," said Brother Ambrose.

"No, not the Prince. Sometimes God takes the good as well as the wicked, as we both know." Prior Bernard looked back at Thomas. "Brother Ambrose is the authenticator of relics for the Marches."

Thomas had no idea what an authenticator of relics did, but noted the man stood more erect when his title was offered. Presumably, then, he was someone important. And the Marches covered much of the borderlands between England and Wales, running from sea to sea.

"What is it you want of me, Tom?" asked Prior Bernard.

Thomas hesitated, unsure if he wanted to state his problem in front of the stranger, but it was not as if he had done anything in secret.

"I have moved the bodies of my relatives from the land on Eaton Hill, so you can assign the lease to someone else now."

"You came to tell me that? Are you sure you do not want the land yourself? You have a fine house in Burway, but land is land and much coveted. I will wait before deciding who might take the lease in case you change your mind."

Prior Bernard started to turn away, but Thomas said, "We found something unexpected when we opened the graves."

Prior Bernard stopped and turned back. He glanced at Brother Ambrose, who was now taking an interest.

"I take it something that has brought you here to speak with me?" said Bernard.

"As well as the bones of my mother and brother, we discovered something else in the graves. Other bones. Those of children. No more than a year old, I would say, probably younger."

"How can you be so sure?" It was Brother Ambrose who spoke, a note of accusation in his voice.

"Tom is a physician," said Prior Bernard. "Perhaps the most skilled physician in the Marches. If anyone can tell it will be him. Were these extra bodies recent or old, Tom?"

"I would say they have been in the ground at least eight years, most likely longer. And there is something else..."

"State it."

"The skulls of my mother and brother are missing. Taken, I assume, when the extra bodies were added to the graves. Have you heard of anything like this before, Bernard?"

Thomas realised his mistake when he saw Brother Ambrose scowl and wondered if he had shocked the man.

"I have," said Prior Bernard, for once ignoring the lack of respect, perhaps knowing he would always have Thomas's respect. "Not often, but I know of what you speak. Not the missing skulls, but children who die in childbirth or soon after are sometimes ... disposed of in such a manner."

"It is claimed children who die unbaptised are tainted with sin," said Brother Ambrose. "But Prior Bernard will tell you he does not believe that, and neither do I. All children are born immaculate, proof of God's goodness. But not all believe as we do. The Prior is right in that some might want evidence of their sins hidden."

Thomas glanced at Bernard, but it seemed Ambrose had spoken for him as well.

"It is the theft of your ancestors' skulls that concerns me most," said Bernard. "You need to consult someone who knows of such things, but I am afraid that person is not me." Prior Bernard glanced at brother Ambrose, and Thomas knew he wanted to say more but could not speak in front of the man, to whom he turned. "Will you stay and pray with us at Vespers?"

"I wish I could, Prior, but I have another engagement today, and it will take me two hours to reach my destination. Another time, I hope."

"Indeed. Another time."

Prior Bernard started to walk towards the main gate, but Brother Ambrose remained where he was.

"These bones," he said. "The extra ones, not those of your family. Where are they now?"

"Being taken to my house in Burway."

"That is a shame. I would have liked to see them."

"Bones of infants?" Thomas said. "What interest would you have in them?"

"A man never knows where he might find God," said Brother Ambrose. "My calling burdens me with curiosity. I am drawn to examine things that often are not easy to examine. Such as bones. The detritus of this world. God may reside in any object, and my skill lies in finding him. No matter, perhaps another time." He turned away without any farewell and walked after Prior Bernard, moving faster than was seemly in such company.

Thomas watched him go, puzzled. He had never heard of an authenticator of relics, but then he had never possessed much interest in the trappings of religion. He remained where he was for some time, knowing Prior Bernard would return when he could. Which he did a good quarter hour later.

"Ah, Tom, you are still here. I thought you might have gone."

"I sensed you wanted to say more but could not in company."

"You did, did you? Have you been taking lessons from that friend of yours, the eunuch?"

"No, but I have lived in his company long enough that a small part of his skill may have rubbed off on me. What did you want to say?"

Prior Bernard glanced around at the bucolic scene. "You have missed dining with us but come to my office, and I will ask for something to be brought. I doubt you have eaten, have you?"

"I intended to once I reached home."

"Then go to my office, and we can talk. You know the way, and I will go ask a brother to bring bread and cheese. And wine. It is our own, and fine too. Unless claiming so is immodest. I am meant to set an example, but sometimes it comes hard. And now I am complaining." Prior Bernard lightly slapped his own face. "Perhaps

I have already spent too long in your company, and your immodesty is rubbing off on me."

Thomas followed the cloister to its end and entered Prior Bernard's office. There was a deep desk, lamps and candles, and painted panels, most depicting images of Jesus, but some of saints Thomas did not know the names of or what their protections were. The Church seemed to have a surfeit of saints, each with the ability to cure some ailment or other or bestow protection. Rarely riches, unless it was riches for the Church, which it already had an excess of.

Thomas sat in a comfortable wooden chair and closed his eyes for a moment. Dawn seemed a long way in the past, and the digging on Eaton Hill had been hard. Though the children's skeletons were a mystery, they were most likely unimportant. What mattered were the bones of his family, in particular those of his mother. He tried to conjure her face in his mind, but all he saw was that of his sister, Agnes.

Thomas rose when the door opened.

"Food and wine are coming, Tom."

"My thanks, Bernard."

"You may forgo my title here when it is but the two of us, but try not to forget it when we have company. You did so in front of Brother Ambrose, and I saw his reaction. I would not want him to think you and I are too close. I am meant to have a position here in Lemster and in the Church. Or perhaps I should call you Sir Thomas or Duke, and you can always call me Prior Bernard."

"If it came to being called sir or duke, I would rather always call you Bernard."

The Prior smiled, all well between them as it had been both long ago and also now.

"What could you not say to me in front of Brother Ambrose?" Thomas asked.

"You heard my reluctance, did you? Ambrose, despite his refusal to take higher office, is well-respected but is ... well, he has firm opinions on certain matters. One of them, perhaps the prime opinion other than his worship of God, is his belief in his own abilities. He is immodest and difficult to like at times, but I believe you might find common ground with the man. He believes in science and analysis. Other authenticators of relics are less diligent. Some take payment to declare a relic genuine. Others do not care and seek other ways to be rewarded. Ways I will not go into."

"Is that what you wanted me to know?"

Prior Bernard gave a soft laugh. "No, it was not. But you deserve to know about Ambrose. I was going to tell you to speak with Silva Taylor about the bones. She lives with your son now, does she not?"

"She does, and it surprises me you say I should consult her. Does what she offers not go against everything you believe in?"

"Does it, Tom? I believe in God in all his glory, yet where is the proof of him? I have faith, and that is all I need. Faith is the most powerful thing of all. More powerful than a sword or a bow. More powerful than any man — even one as strong as that son of yours. People have faith in what Silva can do. Perhaps that is enough. Though I am surprised you believe in her talents. I would have thought you too rational a man."

"I am, but my rationality is based on science, on evidence, and I have seen evidence of what Silva can do."

"You have faith as well, then," said Prior Bernard.

"In some things, yes. Why was that other man here? He had a face like thunder. Do you have problems here?"

"A few, as all holy houses do, but Lemster Priory is in general well-behaved. Prior Madoc was indeed angry when he left me."

"It is not like you to anger anyone," Thomas said.

Prior Bernard smiled. "Then you do not know me as well as you think, though it was not me who angered Madoc but Brother Ambrose. Though if I am honest, Ambrose reflected my own feelings on the matter."

"A matter I am not allowed to be privy to, I take it."

"There is no reason why not. Madoc will shout it to the rafters every chance he gets if I know him. You are aware Abbot John is old and unwell?"

"I am."

"Prior Madoc is visiting all the holy houses petitioning for his Abbot, Abbot Haylewith, to replace Abbot John when the time comes. Madoc is also searching for something his master wants, which is why he was talking with Brother Ambrose."

"What does he seek, or can you not tell me?"

Prior Bernard smiled. "A dream. A fantasy. Abbot Haylewith has become convinced the true Grail exists and is hidden somewhere nearby."

Thomas laughed. "I have heard similar tales in most of the places I have lived. The Christian places, anyway."

"As have I. Abbot Haylewith is a man with great ambition. Whether he believes the Grail exists or not he uses the possibility it might to further those ambitions. One of which is to sit as Abbot at Wigmore."

"Abbot John is not yet dead."

"This year will be his last. You have not seen him in some time. He has grown weak."

"Do you not want his position when it becomes vacant?"

"I am content here, but no doubt my name will be put forward, as will those of others. In most abbeys and priories it is the brothers and sisters who appoint a new Abbot, but Wigmore is no ordinary abbey. It controls the district. North, south, east and west. Who rules there will be chosen by a conclave when the time comes." Prior Bernard scowled. "Madoc is seeding the ground for his master. As much for himself, I suspect, as for Abbot Haylewith. Madoc would like to become Abbot at Hindwell if Haylewith is assigned to Wigmore." Bernard shook his head. "My life used to be one of quiet contemplation and prayer. Now politics are involved. The death of Prince Arthur, and the diminution of Ludlow Castle, have changed things. Ambitious men now reach out greedy fingers to grab whatever power and wealth they can. Tread carefully, Tom, for you are part of their world now."

"Brother Ambrose is ambitious too?"

Prior Bernard laughed. "Ambrose has not a single

ambitious bone in his skinny body. But the mention of him brings to mind one more thing I wanted to tell you. If you want to know more about the stray bones left in the graves behind your house, you should talk to Ambrose. He travels everywhere and sees everything. Whether he is willing to speak with you might be another matter, but you can try. If anyone knows who is opening graves to leave children's bodies in them Ambrose might."

"Where will I find him? I assume he has a place in one of the holy houses close by."

"He does not. Ambrose moves from one to the other, but he spends more of his time at Elmbrook Priory than any other. It is possible you might find him there if you go within a few days. After that it could be Hindwell Abbey or even further west."

"Are you going to explain why it would benefit me to talk with him?"

"I cannot, for what little I do know has been told to me in confidence. But you are a man who finds things out. I trust you to do so. You are also a man who believes in justice."

THREE

It was late by the time Thomas arrived at Burway, where the lowering sun cast a golden light over the house. He had stayed with Prior Bernard longer than intended but was now aware of some of the sins the man claimed to have committed when he served his God in battle. Even though Thomas knew he was not the right man to absolve them he did so, knowing Bernard could not confess them to anyone else. When he left, the Prior had embraced him and kissed both cheeks, then made the sign of the cross on Thomas's forehead. He felt no different for it.

He found Amal in his workshop. She was laying out the bones on the table to examine them. Outside, a stack of nine rough-hewn coffins awaited, two of them smaller than the others. Will, Thomas and Jorge would dig graves for the remains of his family in the morning. Thomas had asked Prior Bernard if he would come in the afternoon to speak words over them when the coffins were lowered, and he said he would. He needed to visit Wigmore Abbey in any case, and it would require little in the way of a diversion.

"You were a long time in Lemster, Pa," said Amal as Thomas entered.

"Prior Bernard wanted to talk."

"About the skeletons?"

"About many things, some of which I cannot speak of, but it was important I stay. He says he will come tomorrow when we place the bones in the ground."

"What about the other two?" asked Amal. "Do we dig graves for them as well?"

Thomas had not considered that. "I do not know, my sweet. I will ask Bernard about it when he comes. I suspect he will tell us to bury them in Ludlow, or more likely Lemster. Does Will know we have work to do in the morning?"

"He does. He has gone with Silva, who was sent for to treat a woman. Will went to provide protection."

"I do not believe Silva requires much in the way of protection."

Amal smiled. "No, likely not, but Will likes to offer all the same. They have been gone most of the afternoon so should return soon."

"I want Silva to examine the bones of the infants," Thomas said. "To see if she can glean anything from them."

"Do you believe in her now, Pa?"

"Prior Bernard told me he believes in her, which surprised me. I did not expect him to."

"Is that one of the things you are not meant to tell me?"

"Possibly. You know I believe in what I can see and measure. Silva has an ability I do not understand, but I see evidence of what she can do. I want to think there is some rational explanation for it, but whether there is or not, she is undoubtedly skilled."

"We have talked about it, the three of us."

"Three of you?"

"Belia, me and Bel. You know Belia has talents other than herbs, and Silva told us that Bel has some small talent as well. Silva even said the same about me, but I do not feel anything in the way she does."

"Perhaps as you grow older," Thomas said. "Women change when their bleeding comes."

Amal laughed, a sweet sound in the warm air of the workshop. "I already bleed, Pa."

"I am sorry, I did not know."

"Why should you? It is my body, and Belia told me what to do."

Thomas hesitated, then asked because that is what he did. "Since when?"

"Eight months, soon after we arrived in England. Do not concern yourself with trying to analyse it, Pa. It is what we women do. Bel told me the bleeding stops once we reach a certain age, but I already knew that." Amal smiled. "I read your books, Pa. There is everything in them. I am sure some people might accuse me of knowing too much, just as they do you."

"There is much that is not in books, Ami. Much we do

not yet know, but one day we will. I hope many wonders lie in wait."

Thomas leaned over the bones on the table, as much to end the conversation as to examine them. They could wait until the morning, he knew.

One of the strips of paper he had written names on identified the first set of bones as belonging to cousin Alice. Thomas had no idea at what age she had died or even any knowledge of who she was. The bones were fully formed but slim, and he suspected she had died young. Possibly in childbirth. In which case he might have expected her child's bones to be laid with hers, but there had been none in her grave. He was aware of how little he knew of these people and wondered if Agnes might know more. She had been too young when Thomas left her in Ludlow, but her aunt might have had knowledge of the Berringtons and passed it on to her. He made a mental note to ask when he went to see her, but it would not be tomorrow. The day after, perhaps, and he would take Amal with him. She and Agnes's daughters, Rose and Jilly, had become firm friends and often had their heads together whispering. About boys, most likely. They were all of an age to have boys on their minds.

Thomas was only aware he had leaned closer to the bones when Amal lit a lamp. Outside the sun had set and the air grown thick.

"Those can wait until tomorrow," said Amal. "You need to eat and then you need to sleep."

Just like her mother, Thomas thought. But he knew

she was right. The bones were going nowhere. Their time had come and gone.

Inside the house, the big kitchen was a chaos of cooking and children, while Jorge sat and watched with an expression of joy. Amal went to help Belia at the stove, while Thomas sat on the floor as he tried to help Bel gather Jorge's children, who were also his, into some semblance of order. Which is when Will and Silva entered the room, and the three children ran to embrace their legs. Thomas sat back on the floor and laughed until Bel offered a hand to help him up.

"Amal told me you have your ancestors' bones now. Do you feel better knowing they will lie in ground you own?"

"I would feel better if the skeletons were whole."

Bel looked into his eyes. "Amal did not tell me that. Have animals disturbed the graves? The woods come almost down to your old house, and Eaton Hill has several sounders of boar. They will dig anything up."

"Not boar. Did Amal also tell you about the bones we found that were not expected?"

Bel frowned. "No, she did not. It is your family, Tom, so it is your business. There is no need to tell me unless you want to."

"There is no reason not to. The bones are not of my family. Cuckoos, Amal called them, and in that she is close to the truth. Young cuckoos. Someone opened two of the graves and placed the bodies of young children in them."

Bel touched his arm. "Oh, Tom, who would do such a thing?"

"Who indeed…"

"Do you intend to find out?"

Thomas considered the question. "I went to Bernard to tell him of the children. He said such things are known of, but he never wanted to discover who might have done such a thing. He said they are no doubt fatherless children who died young and best forgotten about."

"That sounds a harsh judgement coming from Prior Bernard," said Bel. "I am aware of many priests who would refuse to bury such foundlings near their church, particularly if they were not baptised, but the Prior is not one of them."

"What would their baptism have to do with it?" Thomas asked. "Does everyone not deserve a Christian burial?"

"You have been away from England too long. Many in the Church hold harsh views of the newly born. They believe all children are born in sin, and baptism is how that sin is expelled."

"Baptism is an exorcism?" Thomas had never heard of such, but he knew Bel would be right. He had been a stranger to England for too long and had forgotten its customs if he had ever known them. He had lived among the Moors of al-Andalus who held to different beliefs. They performed the ceremony of Shahadah on a newborn child. It had been done for Amal, torn from her mother's belly. But there was no expulsion of sin through Shahadah. Thomas would not have had it performed on

Amal, but Belia insisted, even though her Gods were different to those of the Moors. She told Thomas he had to do it because Amal had held the faith and would want her daughter brought into it, as she had been. Now, Thomas was unsure what Amal believed in, if anything.

"Of course it is," said Bel. "All children are born with sin. It must be driven from them by the act of baptism."

"You believe this?" Thomas regretted the words as soon as he spoke them. The love rekindled between him and Bel felt strong, but there was still much that chafed in their relationship. They were mature men and women now and had pasts that formed them. When they were young everything had been heat and want and need. Some of that remained, but they were different people now from what they were.

"The Church tells it to me, so yes, I believe it." There was a coolness to Bel's words.

Thomas knew he had said too much, so stood and lifted six-year-old Leila into the air and swung her around, making her squeal with laughter. He had done it, he thought, to please her. But as he swung her he realised there was another reason. The children he had gifted Jorge and Belia had never been baptised, never been subject to Shahadah. They were innocent. Untouched by religion. In the eyes of the Catholic Church they must therefore be creatures of sin, but holding Leila, Thomas knew that as a falsehood. Amal, Leila, Saman and Jahan were perfect children. They were wicked at times but never sinful. It only reinforced Thomas's view of the Church he had turned his back on. When he looked at Bel she was staring at him, a frown troubling her brow. Was she thinking the same as him?

Thomas set Leila down, but she asked to be picked up again.

"Ask Will," Thomas said. "He can lift you even higher than me."

"I banged my head when he did that. Will lifts me too high, Uncle Thomas."

"Then tell him not to. He does not know his own strength. I want to talk with Silva."

Leila stayed where she was as Thomas moved away and he felt a moment of guilt, which he tried to ignore. He approached Silva, who greeted him with a kiss on both cheeks. It was something Thomas still found unsettling but had grown more used to.

"Will told me you want me to examine the bones you found," she said. "Shall we do it tonight or can it wait until tomorrow?" She stared at his face before nodding. "Tonight, then."

"It can wait if you prefer," Thomas said.

"No, let us do it tonight, Tom. Besides, the veil is thinner at night, particularly at this time of year." She reached out and took his hand. "Come, show me, then we can eat. This will not take long."

She kept her hand around his as they walked into the wide courtyard and out through the gates at the end, where she released it. Enough light remained in the sky, so no torch was needed to see the workshop. Inside Thomas lit candles and a lamp, then set the two small sacks on a side table and opened the first.

"Go stand in a corner, Tom," said Silva.

She touched the bones, at one point raising a rib to her face and sniffing it. She ran her fingers along several before turning to the second sack and repeating her actions.

"Will said these were on top of the bones of your ancestors, yes?"

"They were. Do you sense anything?"

Silva smiled. "You do not doubt me as much now, do you?"

"I have seen the evidence of what you can do, so no, I no longer doubt you."

"But you do not know how I do it, and that worries you."

Thomas did not want this conversation, so tried to change the subject. "What did you glean from the bones?"

"Little, which in itself also tells me a lot." Silva laughed when she saw his expression. "I am not teasing you, Tom. These are the bones of young children, so they did not experience much before they died. Which means there is little for me to sense. But even a newborn experiences the pain of being born, and it would be held in its bones. I sensed only a little of that, which makes me think they were less than a year old but more than half a year."

"I agree."

"That is what your science tells you?"

"It does."

"Then we believe the same thing but by different

means. Good."

"Did you..." Thomas took a breath. "Did you sense any sin in them?"

"Sin?"

"I had a conversation with Bel about baptism and sin."

"Ah, I see. No, I sensed no sin."

"Can you?"

"Sense sin?"

"Yes."

"Of course, though it is a little different to the hexes I found in your house. Sin is strong, as are anger and betrayal. Many emotions are strong, like love. But I sensed no love in the bones."

"Which means?"

"The children were not wanted."

"Could you tell if they were murdered?"

"That depends."

"On what?"

"On whether they died quickly or slowly and in pain. If the latter I would sense it. But they might have been killed swiftly and not seen death coming, in which case I would be unlikely to feel it. I sensed no violence in their deaths. Most likely they died of sickness. Children do, you know."

"Yes, I know."

"Of course you do. Is there anything else, Tom?"

"Nothing for now."

Silva came to him. She kissed his cheeks again then left. Thomas returned the small bones to their sacks and snuffed out the candles. He took the lamp with him to light his way. He did not need it but felt unsettled by Silva. By her beauty. Her talent. Her power. He wanted to disbelieve in her but could not.

FOUR

Thomas was in bed when he heard someone shout his name from outside. Beside him, Bel stirred, mumbled, complained and rolled onto her front. Thomas rose and padded to the window. Below, he saw a cart led by a donkey. Standing beside it were Prior Bernard and Brother Ambrose.

"Who is it?"

Thomas turned back to Bel. "Bernard and a brother by the name of Ambrose. He is the authenticator of relics for the area. I knew they were going to call, but they must have left before dawn."

"Tell them to go away and come back to bed." Bel offered a coquettish smile that sent a thrill through him.

"Keep whatever thought you have in mind until later. I had best go down to them."

Thomas dressed hurriedly and descended the stairs.

Ambrose stood looking around at the rectangular

courtyard surrounded on four sides by accommodation. He glanced briefly at Thomas before returning to his study, no indication in his expression whether he approved of what he saw or not. It was, for England, certainly strange; better suited to a Moorish town than Ludlow.

"You must have left Lemster at some ungodly hour," Thomas said when Prior Bernard approached, leaving Brother Ambrose to his analysis of the rill that ran the length of the courtyard.

"No hour is ungodly, Tom, as well you know. We attended Matins, then Brother Ambrose suggested we make a start. He is keen to view the remains you found, and we are expected at Wigmore by noon. They have some new relics they are keen to have validated, though they may not have counted on Brother Ambrose's dedication."

"He is not an easy man to warm to, is he?"

"He is not a man who would care whether you warm to him or not, but give him time and your opinion may change. I accept many believe him strange, but his work is exceptional. He is both honest and incorruptible. There are several religious houses who are less than open about their relics."

"Do you have many in the priory?"

"Less than other houses, but some, certainly. All authenticated by Brother Ambrose."

Thomas glanced at the man to discover he had stopped examining the courtyard and now spoke with

Jorge, who had come out to see who the visitors were. It might make for an interesting conversation. Perhaps too interesting, which sent Thomas to join them. As he came close, he heard the end of what Jorge was saying and hoped he had not revealed too much.

"... and I owe Thomas everything. My life, my children, my place in the world."

"You are Spanish? I hear an accent in your voice, and Thomas also has something similar. Yet Prior Bernard tells me he was born in Lemster."

"Spanish, yes," said Jorge. "Though in my later years perhaps Moorish rather than Spanish. I was a eunuch in the Sultan's harem in the palace of al-Hamra."

Thomas half-expected Brother Ambrose to show surprise. Instead, he cocked his head to one side, the gesture oddly bird-like.

"But the whole of Spain is a Catholic country now, yes?"

"So it is claimed," said Jorge. "How did you come into your position? Are there many authenticators of relics in England?"

"I am the only one in the three counties, but some places such as London will have several. And I think the role found me rather than I found it. I was taken under the wing of the last holder of the post who helped train me."

"Only one trainee?"

"There was another, but he did not prove suitable."

"What kind of skill does it take?" asked Jorge. "Is the training hard?"

"No special skill," said Ambrose, "other than a commitment to the truth and an eye for authenticity."

Jorge smiled. "In that case you ought to get on well with Thomas. You and he sound like brothers."

Ambrose glanced across at Thomas. "He is too old to be my brother."

Which made Jorge laugh.

Belia appeared in the doorway and walked across to join them. Thomas saw Brother Ambrose switch his attention to her as she approached.

"We are about to put food on the table, Thomas. Do your friends wish to break their fasts with us?"

"Ask them."

Brother Ambrose avoided looking in her direction until Belia had gone, then turned to Thomas.

"You have a most impressive home and appear fortunate in your friends. Would it be possible to examine the bones you found before we eat?"

"Of course, they are in my workshop." Thomas glanced at Prior Bernard. "Do you want to see them as well?"

"I would rather not unless you need me to."

Thomas shook his head. "No, I think I can manage."

"Prior Bernard tells me you designed this house yourself," said Brother Ambrose as they left the courtyard and made their way towards the workshop set on a spur of higher ground above the river.

"I told Edward, James and Michael Brickenden what I wanted, and they passed the information on to the masons. My contribution is questionable at best."

"I do not believe I have ever seen the like in England."

"That is because it is based on the palace of al-Hamra, where Jorge served as a eunuch, and these buildings are a poor copy of its beauty."

"Your friend is very handsome. He does not look like a eunuch."

"Which he would be pleased to hear on both counts."

"He told me he has children?"

"Two boys and a girl."

"How unusual."

"Indeed, but then Jorge is an unusual man. The bones you wish to see are in here." Thomas opened the door of the workshop. Tall windows set on two walls faced south and west, filling the interior with light.

"And the others? The bones of your family?"

"Are lying in new coffins ready to be buried. We intend to dig the graves this morning."

"You plan to bury them here, in unconsecrated ground?"

"They have lain in unconsecrated ground behind my old house all these years, so it will not matter."

"You are not the arbiter of that, Thomas Berrington. I will speak to Prior Bernard and Abbot John about it and seek their opinion."

"Prior Bernard knows this land belonged to the Church before it was sold to me. It is possible this ground remains consecrated. If it does, I am sure Wigmore Abbey will have a record of it."

"I will still ask for a ruling, as well as any papers they might have. Now, these other remains..."

Thomas drew out the two wooden boxes from beneath a bench and set them on the table in the centre of the room. He removed the lids.

"I doubt you need to examine whether they are relics or not."

"You may be right, but I will be a better judge of that. Sometimes miracles can be found in the most inauspicious of places."

Thomas tried to work out if he had been put in his place or not. He took a step back and watched Brother Ambrose work. The man drew a glass from beneath his robe and used it to examine the bones as his thin frame swayed. After some time, he made a sound which might have been approval and reached for one specific bone. Thomas leaned closer to see it was a tooth, so from the older skeleton as the other, the infant, lacked them.

Brother Ambrose turned to show it.

"Does this look a different colour to the other teeth?"

Thomas held out his hand, waiting, and the glass was passed to him. He examined the tooth, then chose two others.

"Perhaps, but there are several reasons why it may be so. Minerals in the soil, the cloth the bodies were wrapped in or not. What the person ate, and what the cause of death was. It is too long ago now for us to even guess."

"You appear to have knowledge of such things."

"I trained four years at the infirmary in Malaka, then practiced ten times that. I am, foremost, a physician."

"But I suspect not the kind that pulls teeth." Brother Ambrose almost smiled.

"No, not that kind. I take it these bones may now be given the last rites and interred in the churchyard of St Laurence?"

"There is nothing here for me, so yes, do as you wish with them."

"Can I ask you something?"

Brother Ambrose met Thomas's eyes. His own showed nothing. "Of course."

"How do you decide if a relic is authentic or not?"

"I pray, of course, and God guides me."

"So there is no science to it?"

"Only faith, which is stronger than any science."

Thomas considered whether a rational discussion of the matter would be worthwhile before deciding not.

"I expect there is food on the table by now. Shall we break our fasts?"

"My thanks. And then we must leave for Wigmore. They have a chest of relics arrived fresh from the Holy Land and I am impatient to see them."

Over an hour passed before Thomas watched Prior Bernard and Brother Ambrose cross the Teme at a shallows and climb the steep slope of Dinham Wood on their way to Wigmore Abbey. Amal stood at his side, Jorge and Belia on the other, and after a while Will and Silva joined them.

At the crest of the hill Prior Bernard turned and waved. Brother Ambrose continued on without looking back.

"There is something strange about that man," said Silva. "And he is keeping a secret. A big secret."

"Do your abilities tell you that?"

She gave a shake of the head. "Being a woman tells me."

"Do you know what his secret is? He is a monk, so I might be able to make a guess as to what it is."

Silva slapped Thomas's arm. "It is nothing like that, Tom. Ambrose likes women, but his admiration is pure. Ask Belia and she will agree with me. As for the secret, I have no idea. It must be something important to him for me to be able to sense it." She glanced at Belia. "Do you agree?"

She frowned. "About his secret?"

"About him liking women."

"Oh, that. Yes, I agree. I know little about England but even in Spain a monk liking women in the way you suggest was frowned upon."

"But it happens there, and I am sure it also happens here," Thomas said.

"Of course it does," said Silva. "But I do not believe Ambrose is one who would act on any desires he has. There is a softness, an innocence about him."

Thomas glanced at Amal, but if she had any opinion she kept it to herself. He looked at Bel, but she also showed nothing. He thought for a moment about what Silva had said then dismissed it. For Brother Ambrose, being confronted by the beauty of the four women would be something he was unused to. It would no doubt unsettle him.

"As soon as we have dug the graves I want to go into Ludlow to talk with whoever deals with burials at St Laurence's Church."

"Can I come with you, Pa?" said Amal. "I like the church, and we can call and see Aunt Agnes and my cousins when we are finished."

"I know the priest," said Bel. "It will make it easier if I am there. You are not the most diplomatic of men, Tom."

"I thought I had got better."

Bel smiled. "Think what you like. I take it only the remains of the children need to be found a place?"

"They do, though I believe I antagonised Brother Ambrose when I told him the others would be buried here."

Amal accompanied them to the church, but once inside left them to walk to a front bench. She sat and looked up at the gilded cross, the wooden Jesus hanging in agony, the candlesticks and censers, the goblets and plates. Multi-hued light fell across her face from one of the many stained-glass windows. It masked her expression, so Thomas did not know what she thought of all the pomp. Or whether she might believe in it. She had shown some interest in Islam at one time, but that had been in Spain. Now ... now he did not know what she believed. It was one more conversation he had neglected to have.

"Has Ami talked to you about religion?" Thomas

asked Bel as he looked around the gilded interior. The high arched ceiling echoed the sound of the organ being played by a lone man, the only other person within the church.

"She came here with me once or twice, but she had no questions. I think she likes the stillness, the oration of the priest. Does she understand Latin?"

"She does. For a practitioner of medicine it is expected."

Bel touched the back of Thomas's hand, a fleeting stroke. "I like that you have become so clever, Tom. Shall I ask John Perche if he knows where the priest is?"

"Who is John Perche?" Thomas took Bel's hand and turned it over against his own. The touch felt illicit within the church.

"You are listening to John Perche playing the organ," said Bel. "He will know where Father Yorke is. Most likely in his house at this time of day."

"Why not go directly to his house?" Thomas asked.

"Because John Perche has noticed us and will wonder what business we have. You stay here while I talk to him. He knows me."

Thomas considered sitting on one of the benches while he waited, then decided against it. It would look as though he was here on God's business and he had no wish to create such an impression.

The sound of the organ stopped abruptly, and the seated man rose and embraced Bel. Thomas felt a small pang of jealousy before dismissing it. If he grew jealous of every man Bel knew he would drive himself mad. He thought of how they had settled into domestic life at Burway, like an old married couple. And perhaps they were, but with a gap of forty-five years between first love and second. Thomas wondered what Bel's answer would be if he asked her to marry him. It felt like the right thing to do. The completion of the circle that had started in the barn beside her house. The house Edward Brickenden now lived in with his wife and their children. It meant something, he thought, that Bel had passed it on to her son. She must consider Burway her home now.

"Father Yorke is in his house. John thinks he will see us if we go now, before his dinner." Bel took Thomas's hand and led him outside.

"I have a mind to ask you something," he said as they made their way along a narrow path between gravestones.

"Oh, yes?"

"Yes."

They reached a wooden gate and passed through into a grassed area beyond which sat a fine black and white house with two floors. The chimney curled smoke into the still air. Beyond, smaller houses jostled cheek to jowl.

The door was answered by a woman in a smock. She smiled and embraced Bel, then admitted them without asking their business.

Father Yorke did not embrace Bel but welcomed her well enough before turning to Thomas.

"I know who you are, sir, and wondered how long before you came to visit."

Thomas was about to ask why he should have done so but Bel saved him the bother.

"Thomas has been far too busy, Malton. He prays at his new house in Burway."

"I expect that is acceptable. You do know a small church once stood there?"

"I did not," said Bel. "And if I did not then Tom will not either."

"It fell into ruins over a century ago. The stone was used to build a house on the site, but that too fell into ruins. Perhaps the land is cursed."

"I hope not," said Bel, "for that is where I now live."

"Does that mean the ground remains consecrated?" Thomas asked.

"Usually a building is deconsecrated if it is no longer intended as a church, but oftentimes it is forgotten about. Why?"

"I asked permission of Prior Bernard of Lemster to move the bodies of my ancestors from behind my old home to my new one. I want them buried in ground I own. I was warned this morning I could not unless the ground was consecrated."

"Do not take my word for it. All I know are the rumours. No doubt Wigmore Abbey will have a record of its status. You should go there to confirm whether you can do as you want. Was that the reason you came to me?"

"I have another matter. When we opened the graves we found two additional sets of bones. Children. I came to ask if they can be buried in the churchyard of St Laurence's."

"Do these children have names?"

"They may well have, but if so I do not know what they are."

"Were they baptised?"

"I do not know that either."

"If you can provide me with names then they are most likely also baptised. Without names, I cannot help you. Toss the bones into the river and forget you ever found them."

"I intend to discover who they are, Father, and when I do, I will bring their names to you. Until then I will hold their remains at Burway, where they will be made welcome."

"I thought men of God were meant to be compassionate." Thomas stood beside Bel in the cemetery surrounding St Laurence's Church, leaving the priest as soon as they could make their excuses. "Throw the bones in the river? Where is the compassion in that?"

"The Reverend Martyn Yorke is not a compassionate man. In his own mind, at least, he believes he is right. Unbaptised children cannot receive a Christian burial, but you would not know that."

"I am beginning to think there is a great deal I do not know."

Bel smiled. "I can scarce believe I heard you utter

those words, Tom Berrington. Come on, let us go to your sister's house. Amal is no doubt already there."

"And the bones?"

"Fear not, we will find a solution," said Bel, "but they will not go into the river."

FIVE

The hour was late as Thomas sat in the large kitchen at Burway and drank wine he had bought after visiting Agnes and her daughters. Food had been consumed, and for perhaps the first time that day he felt himself relax. At least as relaxed as he ever became.

Jorge slumped in a padded chair, also with a beaker of wine in his hand. Will and Silva sat together, their arms and legs entwined. Belia had taken the children to bed and not returned. Amal too had gone to her bed, as had Bel.

"I want to ask you something," Thomas said to Silva, making her turn from staring into Will's eyes.

"Ask her, and she will say yes."

Thomas frowned. "Ask who what?"

Silva smiled. "Bel. Ask, and she will say yes. That is what is on your mind, is it not?"

"It was earlier, but not now. I want your advice on

something else. But first, how did you know? Can you see into my mind?"

"Of course not. I am merely an adept, like Jorge. And you are so easy to read."

"He is," said Jorge, who rose to refill his glass. "And Thomas will ask Bel in his own good time, as always. He never rushes such things."

"She wants you to," said Silva, "but Jorge is right. It is your decision alone, but do not leave it too long. Now, what is the other thing you want?"

"Would you come to Lemster with me tomorrow? I want you to see the ground where my ancestors lay and the house that is now in ruins."

"Why?"

"Because I do not know enough about what happened and hope you might offer some insight."

"Because I am strange?"

"Because you are skilled."

Silva smiled. "In that case I will come with you."

"And me," said Will.

"And me," said Jorge.

Thomas sighed. "We might as well all go then."

"Not the children. They want to chase fish in the river, and Belia will stay with them. But yes, the rest of us should go. I have not seen this old house of yours and am curious."

"Afterwards we can eat dinner in The Star."

The morning saw six of them travel south through a low-lying mist that burned off the fields before they reached Eaton Hill.

"What do you need from me?" asked Silva when they arrived at Thomas's old house.

"I want you to examine the graves we opened. They are all filled in again now, but perhaps you can tell me if you sense anything odd about them. And then perhaps the house itself." He glanced at his old home, recognising little about it now. "Do you need to do this alone? And ... you know..."

Silva laughed. "I have no need to disrobe, and I can do this in company. I want you with me in any case. You have memories of this place, and they will help me form a picture. I want to start with the graves first, if that is all right?"

"You are the expert," Thomas said as he dismounted after Bel had let herself to the ground from where she sat behind him.

Will lifted Silva down even though there was no need, but Thomas could not blame him for the opportunity to hold her for a moment. They tied their horses to a fallen tree that lay almost horizontal and went to where the refilled graves lay beyond the house.

Silva stood at the foot of each, starting with the oldest. She spent several minutes with each. There were no ornate movements. She stared at the ground, her expression placid. Thomas wondered what she saw. The here and now, or the past?

When Silva came to the grave of his brother she went

50

to her knees and buried her fingers in the soft soil which mounded the ground. She closed her eyes and made a soft humming sound. She spent longer there but eventually rose and moved to the final grave. She repeated the same process. She started to sit up then stopped. She pushed her hands deeper into the soil, burrowing down until she pulled free a small object. Only then did she rise.

"What have you found?"

Silva held her hand out, palm up. Cradled there was something coated in soil so Thomas could not make it out.

"Take it, Tom. It is safe. Tell me if you recognise it."

Thomas took the object and brushed the soil from it until a small cross was exposed. A fine chain fashioned of silver had broken, and the clasp was missing.

"Is it your mother's?" asked Silva.

"I do not think so. She wore a cross, and I buried her with it around her neck, but this is not it." He turned to Amal. "Did you find anything among the bones that might be a crucifix? It would be more ornate than this, fashioned in the Welsh manner."

"There were objects," said Amal. "I placed them in the sacks with the bones they were found with. They are still in there, I expect. I thought nothing of them. Buttons, coins, a clasp. Things that do not rot away. But I have no memory of another cross."

"No matter. I will have another fashioned and a cross of the same to stand as her headstone." Thomas frowned. "I am not sure what to put on the stones. I know the year John was born and died, and the year my mother died, but am unsure what age she was. As for the others..." He shrugged, dismissing the thought for now, then asked Silva, "Did you sense anything?"

"I sensed you," she said. "This ground is where you were raised, so it knows you. Other than that, the first five graves offered little. They are older, and such things fade with time. Your brother's grave gave me a small sense of him and all I can say is I am glad Will is like you and not his uncle. He was not a good man."

"I never got on with him, but sometimes brothers do not. He used to hit me without cause. He was a Berrington, so believed he had a right to do whatever he wanted."

"You are also a Berrington but you are not like that, Tom."

"Perhaps I am more like my mother, then. As is Agnes. She could be her in both looks and temperament."

"Yes, I believe you are like your mother. I also gained a sense of the interlopers in the two graves."

"Were they good or not?" Thomas asked.

"They were nothing. The sense of them was barely there at all, and if I had not touched the first graves I might have missed it altogether. They were too young to have developed a sense of themselves."

"You felt no evil?"

"None."

"No sin?"

Silva laughed. "No, Tom. No sin. But I did sense something, though it confused me. There was a pull to the west, which I assume is where they came from. And a feeling of movement, though what that means, I do not know." Silva shook her head as if unused to such uncertainty. "Can I go into the house now? I want you to come with me, but everyone else must stay outside. I would like to hold your hand as well if I am allowed."

This time Thomas laughed. "You had better ask Will and Bel if you can do that, not me."

As they crossed the threshold, Silva took his hand. Thomas looked around at what had once been one large room. The chimney stack remained in place, as did an iron fireplace, but the stairs had collapsed long ago. Much of the wooden spars which supported the walls were blackened from fire.

Silva led him around the space, moving slowly.

"Tell me what it was like to live here."

"Ordinary. It is where I was raised, so I never thought about it."

"There is love still in these walls, but also anger."

"I told you, my brother was a bully, and my father had enough anger for a dozen men."

"Often with men like that their anger is directed against themselves. You have none of that. Neither does Will. As for Jorge..." Silva laughed.

"There is no room in Jorge's heart, it is so filled with love for Belia and his children."

"And you, Tom. Jorge loves you a great deal. But you already know that."

"Many years ago Jorge offered me his wisdom on love. I did not understand it when he told me, but now I do. Jorge claims love is infinite and can never be restrained. I expect hate can also be the same. I know it was that way for Philippa Gale — all of it directed against me."

"But now she is gone," said Silva.

"Yes. Now she is gone."

"Your soul is lighter as a result. Do you feel it?"

"I am relieved she is dead. As for my soul, I am unsure I even possess one."

"We all have a soul, but it is not a gift from any God. Our soul holds the essence of who we are. Just as an object can also have a soul. An essence." Silva looked around. "Like this house. It senses you. It recognises you. It wants to be yours."

"I already have a fine house."

"You do, but can you not have more than one? This house wants to be a Berrington house."

"And if I ignore it?"

Silva raised her shoulder in a shrug. "Then it will moulder away and eventually forget, but it will be a sad end."

Thomas laughed. "Am I meant to feel guilty?"

"No, you are not that manner of man. But I thought you should know." Silva released his hand, and the sudden loss of her grip felt like a jolt. "Now leave me for a while. There is something hidden here. It calls to me, and I would seek it out. To do so, I need—"

"To remove your clothes." Thomas finished for her. "Why do you do that?" He considered it an affectation.

"Because without cloth between me and the air I am more open to whatever resonates in a place. I can feel the vibrations when clothed, but they are clearer when I am naked. So go, unless you want to stay and watch. I should tell you I am not shy. Not at all."

Thomas turned and walked outside. He sat on the slope beside Bel and the others and stared down at Lemster, almost surrounded by running water. The Lugge and Kenwater to the north and east, the Arrow to the south. The advantage of height allowed him to see beyond the town to where banks of hills faded away into Wales. He lay back and closed his eyes, the soft murmur of conversation between the others lulling him into a doze.

He woke when something touched his flank. When he opened his eyes, Silva stood over him.

"Did you find anything?"

"Come with me and you will see. It needs to be you who retrieves it."

"Only me?"

Silva thought for a moment. "No, you can all come."

Will offered his hand. Thomas took it, getting to his feet.

"Are you happy to come inside?" he asked Bel and Jorge.

"I have always been curious about what your house looked like," said Bel.

"Nothing like it does now."

Amal took his left hand, Will his right, and they went into the house.

Silva stood near the remains of the fireplace.

"You must do the next part, Tom. There is something concealed here and it wants to be found."

Thomas's reservations were sparked by her words. He had grown to accept Silva's talents, but there were moments when she did or said something that seemed irrational, as she had now. When he made no move she came and stood in front of him, her face turned up.

"You must turn your mind off if you are to do this."

"Do you know what this thing is?"

"Of course."

"Then you can get it."

"It is not mine. It wants you. It wants a Berrington."

Thomas started to turn away, but Silva grabbed his arm to stop him.

"This is important, Tom. You will know when you uncover it."

"I will do it," said Amal, starting towards the fireplace.

"No," said Silva, still staring at Thomas. "It has to be Tom."

He let loose a great sigh and moved to the fireplace if only to humour her. He glanced back. "Where do I start?"

"Let your mind empty and you will know."

Thomas almost turned away again, then decided that if Silva thought this so important the least he could do was try. So he knelt at the fireplace and tried to still his mind. It was not something he was used to, and it came hard. By nature he observed, analysed and questioned.

Thomas tried to picture the fireplace when it had been complete. His mother standing in front of it stirring a pot of mutton pottage rich with barley and herbs. He imagined the two of them together in the room on the ground floor, his brother out carousing with his father. Agnes would be in bed. He would be reading a book, which he could not see, and then he did. It was a Bible. The family Bible, and he was reading the Gospel of Matthew because it was the most exciting. He liked books with stories rather than preaching.

"Your father and John will be home soon, Tom," his mother had said. "Do not let them catch you reading."

Thomas nodded, twelve years old and unlike his brother or father. He finished the page, closed the Bible and handed it to his mother. She loosened a stone to the side of the fireplace and slid the Bible into its place. He recalled asking her once why she needed to hide it, but she would not tell him.

Now Thomas returned to the present. He leaned forward, brushing his fingers across the remains of the wall until he found what he was looking for. A loose stone. He smiled and almost laughed. All the stones in this ruin were loose, but this particular one was what he was looking for. He expected the Bible to be gone, but it was not. He reached in and drew it out. It was stained with dust and covered with cobwebs. He brushed off some detritus.

When he turned Silva's eyes were on him, and she nodded.

"Now you will know the names of your ancestors."

It was mid-afternoon by the time they came out from The Star with bellies full of good food. The finding of his family Bible had felt like a good omen, and Thomas had drunk more ale than was good for him. He hung onto Ferrant for a while before trying to lift himself into the saddle.

Bel put her arms around him.

"Are you all right, Tom?"

"A little drunk," he said. "And the sight of the priory reminds me that I have not acted on Bernard's advice yet."

"What advice is that?"

"If I want to know more about the burial of bodies in the graves of others, I should speak with Ambrose, and the most likely place to find him is Elmbrook Priory."

"Did you not ask him when he visited yesterday?"

"I tried, but he was more interested in the bones we found. When I pressed he remembered a more important meeting he was late for. Perhaps he is protecting someone."

"Perhaps he is," said Bel. "I have seen him about now and again. He keeps to himself. Does his job. If something underhand is going on I doubt Ambrose has anything to do with it. Do you have suspicions about the bodies, Tom?"

"I am trying not to, because if the children did not die natural deaths the meaning is almost too much to think about."

"Do you mean if they were killed? Why would they be?"

"We both know there are people who need little reason to kill. My concern is why they chose the graves of my family to bury them in. There were no Berringtons in Lemster after I left with my father so it cannot have been a message for us."

"Except nobody knew you would not return for over forty years," said Bel.

"Which is why I go to speak with Ambrose if he is at this priory."

Elmbrook is a strange place," said Bel, "and its Prioress, Felicia Hughden, has a reputation for being even stranger, but also of being kind. She cares for her flock. All of them. Take Jorge with you when you go. He will understand the place better than you. You could probably reach it in a few hours from here."

"Not today. I need a clear head before I go there. In the morning, perhaps. Do we need to take care?"

Bel smiled and kissed Thomas's cheek. "No, you are not the kind of man to be drawn by what is on offer there."

"Now you are being mysterious."

"Good. We women are meant to be mysterious. Now, do you want me to help you into the saddle or can you manage on your own?"

Thomas managed on his own.

SIX

As they rode south the next morning Thomas and Jorge stopped for a mug of ale at Richards Castle and asked the puller if he knew the direction to Elmbrook Priory. Before they left he had asked Bel if she knew where it was, and she said of course, had she not told him the day before? Which is why they rode south. They had left Burway later than Thomas wanted, but he knew Jorge could never be rushed. It was a philosophy of life Thomas might have envied if he could make himself act the same way, but knew he could not.

"Where did you come from, sirs?" the puller asked as he placed two rough-hewn pots on the lintel that separated his house and business from the roadway.

It seemed a strange question to Thomas after he had asked directions to where they were going, but he said, "Ludlow," in the expectation the man would not know where Burway was.

"So why come this way?"

"Because I thought it was the right way." Thomas tried to keep annoyance from his voice.

"It would be if you wanted to go to Lemster, but Elmbrook is over that way." He pointed beyond the road to where rounded hills rose. Thomas assumed it was towards the west. The puller smirked. "Are you going there for any particular reason?"

"No reason."

The puller's smirk remained. "That's what all the gentlemen say."

"How long will it take us?"

The man appeared to give the question some consideration before answering.

"A while."

It seemed that was as accurate as time was measured here. The pace of life in this village could be counted off by sunrise and sunset, the passage of hours driven by how high the sun might rise before starting to sink again. Now it was almost midsummer, so the time between those markers would be long and filled with work.

Thomas thanked the puller, paid him and rode west with Jorge. As he did so he recognised landmarks that had once been familiar to him as a thirteen-year-old. After less than a mile, he turned to climb Brightall Common. From the ridge, the land undulated towards Wales, each hill higher than the last until in the distance they rose to become mountains.

They descended and crossed the Lugge, narrower and shallower here than at Lemster as it cut its way through the surrounding slopes. Thomas was aware he was close to the limit of his knowledge of this countryside. He had visited these hills as a boy but recalled little of them. Earlier in the year, he had come this way in search of a debtor who had tried to flee his debts. He had found him in a village a few miles further on, and the memory of the name came to him. Elmbrook. And there had been a church building he had ignored.

While waiting for Jorge to rise, Thomas had asked Amal if she could search the records for any mention of Elmbrook Priory. It had taken her an hour, but she came back with several documents. One told him the priory housed fifty-nine nuns and raised an annual income of £675 16s 7¾ d — which was a sizeable sum for such an out-of-the-way priory holding so few nuns. He would not have recalled the amount except Amal had pointed it out, asking if he thought it a mistake. The figure was greater than that of Lemster Priory and most other religious houses in the county, only exceeded by Wigmore Abbey.

The valley they rode through widened a little where a stream twisted on its way to add to the waters of the Lugge. The cluster of houses, most little more than wattle and daub with rush roofs, brought back a memory of arresting the debtor but Thomas had no recall of what had happened to the man.

The priory sat at the foot of a slope beyond the stream, a chest-high stone wall surrounding it with a single gate offering entry. The gate was open, but Thomas made no move in that direction. Nuns in grey robes moved slowly through the grounds, which were extensive and held a stew pond and large vegetable garden. The priory itself was smaller than the one at Lemster, but sufficient for the number of those who lived within its walls. A substantial stone building was set to one side, half within the priory grounds and half outside.

"We should watch for a while to judge the lie of the land," Thomas said to Jorge.

"I am always content to sit in the sun and watch beautiful women."

"You may be out of luck. These are nuns we will be observing."

"All women are beautiful in one way or another. And you know I am now content to do no more than watch."

Thomas did not, but was sure Jorge believed so. The man saw beauty in everything he set his gaze on, but had grown content with Belia and needed no one else anymore.

Thomas bullied Ferrant up the slope on the opposite bank until they entered a sparse woodland dotted with the occasional oak, but mostly pine and birch. He let Ferrant and Jorge's horse roam, knowing they would not wander far, then settled against the trunk of a tree to watch the priory. Late afternoon sunlight caught the grey stone and gave it an air of welcome it would lack in the midst of winter. Thomas could make out nuns working the gardens. He also saw a figure that surprised him. Madoc, who he had last met at Lemster Priory when the man had argued with Prior Bernard. Madoc approached a tall nun dressed differently from the other sisters, and Thomas wondered if she was Prioress Felicia that Bel had told him about. She embraced Madoc warmly, which surprised Thomas, then turned and led Madoc inside. Was this friendship? A tryst? Thomas knew too little of the mores of religious orders to know its subtleties but was almost certain that relations between nuns and monks were forbidden. At least according to the edicts of the Church. But Thomas knew of many men and women of God who bore children, married, and carried on as if their religious role had nothing to do with their secular one. It reminded him of an abbot he once had to kill who had fathered a child he had also been forced to kill. Corruption on corruption.

Was that what was going on at Elmbrook Priory? Was there more to Bernard's mention of it than as a place Ambrose spent more of his time?

Thomas was continuing to watch the work of the nuns when two men appeared leading a cart pulled by a single ox.

He waited.

The men were greeted warmly and the nuns began to unload the cart, which held rolled fleeces sheared from sheep. No doubt they would be teased out and spun to make into cloth. Some for the priory, some to be sold on. Is this how they earned their unrealistic income?

"Some of those nuns are exquisite," said Jorge.

Thomas made no response, watching as the work of emptying the cart continued. When it was done, the two men turned and led the ox and cart back onto the road. They turned left, which would take them past Wigmore Abbey, but Thomas knew he was spinning connections from thin air. Not everything had to mean something.

Thomas narrowed his eyes and glanced up to judge the position of the sun. A good five hours before it set. A scattering of clouds hung over the hills of Wales, but he judged the night would be dry and not too chilled. He had to make a decision soon. Stay where they were and sleep beneath the stars, or ride home. Two hours would take them there now he had some idea of the way. He could afford to spend another two or three hours observing the priory but doubted Jorge would be happy to amuse himself for that length of time.

Thomas knew from Prior Bernard what the hours of prayer were and estimated the nuns would need to file inside before long to offer praise for their Lord. Would Madoc join them or not? Or if he left where would he go? Wigmore Abbey, back to Lemster Priory, or to Hindwell Abbey that Prior Bernard had told him about?

Time passed, and Thomas fought to stay awake, but Jorge succumbed, a soft snore coming from his parted lips. In the end Thomas stood so he would not doze off. Ferrant came and nudged him, perhaps wondering why they had stayed in this place so long. Thomas patted his neck and pushed him away.

Still none of the women below had been called to prayer, and Thomas was sure they should have been. It made him wonder if this strange manner of running a priory was one reason Bernard had sent him here. So far there had been no glimpse of Ambrose, nor the cart he used.

More movement on the roadway drew Thomas's attention and he straightened, taking a few deep breaths.

Three horses approached ridden, as their appearance suggested, by gentlemen. They were no one Thomas knew, but he supposed the region around Ludlow and Lemster was not short of supposed gentlemen. He assumed they would continue east towards Lemster, but instead they rode to the priory where their horses were taken by a man who came from the stable. Five of the nuns approached, and Thomas wished he was close enough to hear the conversation.

There was still no sign of Madoc or the Prioress.

Jorge mumbled and woke. He offered a hand so Thomas could pull him to his feet.

"What is happening? Anything interesting, or more of the same?"

"The priory has visitors."

Despite the distance, the breeze carried the sound of laughter up the hillside. Thomas leaned forward when he saw one of the men slip his arms around the waists of two of the nuns. Then a second man did the same. The last grabbed the remaining woman and kissed her hard on the mouth. More laughter followed, an undercurrent to it now that Thomas had not heard since he had been in the company of soldiers availing themselves of women who followed an army. More embraces were exchanged. More kisses. Distance made the spectacle unreal, the actions of those involved making it even more so.

"Is this how nuns act in England?" asked Jorge. "If so my opinion of your country has increased tenfold."

"I am sorry to disappoint, but this is not how they are meant to act."

Jorge shrugged as if this was exactly as he expected.

After a while, the men were led inside a stone building set apart from the main priory. The remaining women continued to work, but they gathered more closely together, and it was clear a conversation was taking place. Were they as shocked at what they had witnessed as Thomas? Or were they wondering why they had not been chosen?

If what he witnessed was true, Thomas understood how the income of the priory might be as healthy as recorded. Such a sum would attract suspicion. And suspicion should have brought attention. Attention would have uncovered what appeared to be happening here. Which would mean ... Thomas was not sure. That someone knew and allowed it to continue? Because payment was made for their silence? Or payment in a way other than silver? And if so, who would that be? Elmbrook Priory was isolated here in a far western corner of the county, but it was almost on the doorstep of Wigmore Abbey. Which meant Abbot John must know what went on here. It was impossible to suppose he did not.

Neither could Thomas see Bernard turning a blind eye to whatever wickedness took place in the stone building below. Was that why he had suggested Thomas came to Elmbrook Priory? That it had nothing to do with Ambrose?

He wondered if all the nuns were involved. Did they take turns, or did some men have favourites?

Thomas turned to speak to Jorge to ask his advice,

knowing there was no one better in England to offer it. As he did so he found Jorge facing away from him, staring at a group of people who must have ascended the far side of the slope.

Madoc stood forty paces away on the edge of the woods, and Thomas was annoyed at himself for not hearing his approach. Neither Madoc, the two men standing behind him, nor the tall Prioress.

"What are you doing here, Berrington? Spying? Or come to get your wick dipped?" Madoc gave a coarse laugh.

"A man can go where he pleases in this land. We are on our way to Wigmore Abbey and stopped to rest our horses. What are we meant to be spying on?"

For a moment Madoc said nothing, then came forwards, the two men shadowing him. Thomas judged them as ex-soldiers. He knew many returned from wars abroad and took up the cloth, perhaps to escape from the memories of what they had seen. No doubt these were a guard for the priory to protect the business being carried out. Beyond them, the Prioress remained where she was, but Thomas caught a brightness in her eyes that disturbed him. Was it caused by the possibility of violence?

Thomas's weapons were still strapped to Ferrant, who stood at a distance.

"Did that prig Bernard send you? I expect he did. Not brave enough to come himself in case he was seduced into sampling the charms on offer." Madoc glanced at Jorge, who stood relaxed at Thomas's side. "Your friend looks like a man who would not say no to a little seduction."

"He has been known to indulge."

"Unlike yourself. Word is you are also a prig like Bernard."

"Then word is wrong." Thomas wondered why he even bothered to respond. "What are you doing here? I thought your home was at Hindwell."

"Which is only a small distance away. Hindwell Abbey and Elmbrook Priory share many things. It is essential out here close to the borderless lands of Wales. We look out for each other. Question strangers when they turn up uninvited."

The Prioress walked towards Thomas. As she did so Madoc and his two men moved away, then stopped to watch. Felicia Hughden was not young, but her skin was flawless and the figure covered by her robe offered a promise her position suggested she should not be able to meet. Her hair was long and dark but had streaks of grey running through it. When Thomas looked into her light-grey eyes he saw her pupils were blown wide.

"I hear you live with Bel Brickenden these days," she said. "Yes, I know who you are. And I know Bel Brickenden who is no better than her mother, who was a whore."

"I knew Joan Brickenden and admired her. She was the best whore in Lemster. And if you know Bel, then you also know she never followed her mother into that profession."

"You were away a long time. How can you be so sure?"

"Because I know Bel."

The Prioress laughed and came forward until she was inches from Thomas. He could smell her scent. Something dark, musky and unsettling. When he looked at her face he saw small lines around her eyes.

"Would you like to come down to our house of sin and partake of what is on offer there?"

"My thanks, but no. We must get on, we have business to attend to."

"I promise you will enjoy the experience. Both of you. And no payment is required. Not in silver, anyway. A favour asked in the future, perhaps."

Thomas walked past her without speaking and called Ferrant to him. After he mounted he turned to look back. Madoc was moving away, believing he had done his job.

Felicia Hughden remained where Thomas had left her.

She smiled. "Return any time you wish, Thomas Berrington. Rumour has it you are a clever man with an interesting past. There are too few such men around these parts. I would welcome conversation ... or more."

Jorge said nothing as they climbed the track away from Elmbrook. It allowed Thomas to think, but was too good to last.

"Is it not blatant for a Prioress to offer what she did?" asked Jorge. "You know I see things in people, and what I saw in her confused me. She wanted you to believe she wanted to seduce you, but there was something else beneath the surface. She is afraid." Jorge smiled. "Perhaps she sees you as a saviour."

"Bernard sent me here for a reason. He told me I might find Ambrose and that he in turn might know something about the bodies left behind my old house."

"Do you think Bernard knew Ambrose would not be here and sent you for some other reason?"

"He may have wanted me to know the priory is running a bordel, though what that has to do with what happened to me is another matter. Or perhaps..." Thomas waved a hand. "Or perhaps I am talking nonsense. Spinning conspiracies from nothing."

"You have done that before," said Jorge. "Though you have also uncovered conspiracies as well. Is that what we have here? A conspiracy?"

"I do not know enough yet to decide. Elmbrook is not what I would expect to find in a priory; far from it. Whether it is more than that I will have to wait and see. But it does not answer the question of the bodies. That is something we must do for ourselves."

"How?"

"I need to know if the orphaned bones left on Eaton Hill were a message for me or a part of something wider. The only way to find that out is to see if it has happened elsewhere. When we return, I intend to speak with the others. We should ride out tomorrow to ask questions."

"And if it brings trouble down on us? Often your questions do that, you know."

"And when they do, we always meet it head on. But I expect no trouble. I am not even sure whether I expect to find any answers, but if there is nothing to find, it answers one question at least."

"Which is?"

"The message was meant for me. How, or why, I do not know."

"But you will find out," said Jorge.

"Yes. I will find out."

SEVEN

Thomas rode north astride Ferrant while Bel rode beside him on a short horse she had borrowed from Agnes that morning. Their packs held fresh bread, cheese, and two flagons of ale, though Thomas expected ale would be easy enough to come by. Every village and hamlet possessed at least one house where you could buy a pot. Mist hung along the rivers and streams as they descended from Ludlow through Linney Gate then turned a little to the east as they followed the tree-shrouded Corfe.

"Do you expect us to find anything, Tom?" asked Bel.

"I do not know. If we do then it means the children buried in my family's graves were not a message to me."

"Why would they send you a message? You left Lemster many years ago with no expectation you would ever return."

"The Berringtons, then. I would rather we find other instances. It would ease my mind a little."

"If they are there to be found you will find them. I know you. Resourceful and stubborn."

"Am I stubborn?"

Bel said nothing, but she did smile.

To their right, the ground rose to a low hill. Ahead, the river wound through verdant fields where crops grew and sheep grazed the meadows. A heron rose from the corfe, wide wings whistling as it crossed a few feet above their heads.

They rode on in companionable silence as the sun warmed the air. Thomas thought about how he and Bel had grown used to each other so easily. It was almost as if they had married young and lived together for all the time they had spent apart. It told him that perhaps she was a destiny he had turned away from. Except he knew there had been others who were also a part of it, and he did not regret most of what he had done with his life.

As they approached Stanton Lacey the square tower and squat building of St Peter's Church appeared through a stand of tall elm trees. Closer, they saw a short, sturdy man in the field next to it, digging what could only be a grave. On the far side lay two sacks, on them two long metal devices Thomas did not know the purpose of, but no doubt were part of the process being undertaken.

The field was ordinary, backing up against the stone churchyard wall. No markers. No crosses. But it could be nothing but a graveyard. Whoever this grave was for would be poor — only the rich could afford to lie within the boundary wall of the church itself.

Thomas dismounted and greeted the man.

"Good morrow, sir. Can I speak with you?"

"As long as you do not stop me from working. Is it another pit you want digging?"

"It is not. A question only. Do you dig all the graves in this plot?"

"And those within the walls. We have not enough people, or death, in Stanton Lacey to employ another gravedigger. You are not from these parts are you, sir?"

"Not for some time, no, but my companion is."

"Aye, I know Bel Brickenden."

Bel nodded at the man and smiled. He smiled back as he continued to dig. He stood up to his chest in the hole, and soon it would be deep enough.

"How do you know where to dig?" Thomas asked. It was not the question he had intended, but curiosity was not something he could turn away from when it came.

The man stopped digging long enough to tap his temple with a gnarled finger. "I know where all the graves are here and mostly who lies in them. This one was Goodwife Carslow's until today, and tomorrow it will be home to her sister. I try to keep things in the family if I can, but it is not always possible."

The man's shovel hit on something hollow, and he looked up at Thomas. "Are you a man of sensibilities or might you be willing to help an honest workman lift what lies here?"

"I can help," Thomas said. He removed his jacket and looked into the grave. At the bottom lay a pine coffin, the surface scarred. It had clearly been used more than the once, as was often the case. "I take it you will want it opening, too?"

"Of course. You would help with that as well? Most gentlemen would turn their back at such work."

"He is no gentleman," said Bel, which made the man chuckle.

Thomas offered his hand, and the man took it to be pulled up.

"Have you done this work before, sir?" he asked.

"Not the opening, but the digging and laying a shrouded body in a grave, yes."

"Then perhaps you will not throw up at the work." The man picked up one of the metal devices. "You will not know of this either, then. I will show you how to use it at this end if you take the other one."

Thomas picked the metal object up to discover it jointed in the middle and cumbersome. He went to the far end of the open grave as instructed, then watched the man slide the metal sides of his own device on either side of the coffin before pushing the ends in his hands together. It was a clever contraption, and when Thomas did the same with his he was surprised at how easily it gripped the underside of the coffin.

"It will not be heavy, sir. Nothing but bones in there now. Lift on my count, but try not to jerk."

"How would you have managed had I not come along?" Thomas asked.

"I would have had to get down there and use my hands, but no doubt someone else would have passed by before long."

Thomas watched the man, lifting when he did, and the coffin rose, scattering soil from itself as it elevated. Once it was clear of the hole they moved sideways and set it on the ground beyond the sacks, which Thomas now knew the purpose of.

The man used an iron peg to prise the coffin lid open and peered inside before removing it. All that lay within were bones and a few scraps of cloth. Thomas scanned them, but the skull remained in place and there appeared to be no unexpected bones. The sight reminded Thomas of why he had come here and why he had stopped to speak with the gravedigger.

"Do you ever find bones you do not expect?" he asked as he held open one of the sacks so the man could place the bones in it.

"I told you, I know every grave in this field and the churchyard, so no."

"No stray bones?"

"None, sir. Why do you ask?"

"I had reason to open some graves recently and discovered bones had been set in them that did not belong."

"That would not happen here, sir. I always remove the bones of the previous occupant before I place a new body in their place. I expect some diggers are not as diligent as me. Though any gravedigger who wants to keep his job would never do such a thing, as I am sure you know. What church was this?"

The bones were all in the sack now, and the man set the lid back on the coffin and brushed it clean.

"These will lie in the charnel house?" Thomas asked.

"Of course. It is set to one side of the crypt beneath the church."

"And you never find stray bones there?"

"You ask mighty strange questions if I can say so, sir. What is your interest in these bones?"

"The graves I opened belonged to my family, and within were bones that belonged to a child. Two sets of them. And when I found the remains of my brother and mother their skulls had been taken."

The man stared at Thomas before crossing himself. "Bad goings on, it sounds like. Not Christian doings, I wager. There are still those around these parts who follow the old ways." He inclined his head towards Bel, who had come to stand beside Thomas. "I expect Bel here knows that well enough."

"I do," she said.

"If you should hear of anything strange as I have described, could you send a message to me?"

"If I knew who you were, I might."

"My name is Thomas Berrington, and I live in the new house at Burway."

"I heard your name and heard about your house." The man pursed his lips as if he intended to say more, then thought better of it.

Later, as Thomas and Bel rode on Thomas said, "What did the gravedigger not say?"

"You do not need me to tell you, Tom. You know full well the rumours that swirl around you."

"From people like Cornwell and others?"

"And ordinary folk. They think you strange, and a fool for your honesty and diligence. But they find it amusing rather than a threat like some others do. That gravedigger will have his own opinion about you now because you helped him, and he will tell others you did so."

"I am surprised he knew nothing about additional bones in graves."

"You are assuming there are other cases, Tom. What if it was something aimed at only your family?"

"Felicia Hughden hinted at something like that, but why would someone do that? There were no Berringtons left other than Agnes."

"Your father was not liked."

"My father was not buried there, but you are right, he was not. Neither was John, so perhaps it is something he did." A thought occurred to Thomas. "He could never resist the temptation of a pretty girl. Often times he did not even need them to be pretty, only buxom. What if he set a child in one of them and it died? Would someone have opened his grave and placed the body in it, do you think?"

"He tried for me at one time and I punched him on the nose." Bel smiled at the memory. "Punched him hard. Broke it, I reckon, and he never tried again. But I suppose you might be right. It is a possibility, but if so where did the other body come from? Another girl? Twins?"

"The bones were not from children the same age, so it does not work."

"Perhaps the gravedigger knew something he did not

tell you. What if he was the one putting bodies in the ground? He would have the perfect job for it, after all."

Thomas twisted to look back but knew there were holes in Bel's logic.

"If he was doing that his cemetery would be full of other bodies. Besides, I believed him."

Bel smiled. "Sometimes you are too trusting. Are we going home tonight or must we sleep on hard ground?"

"We will be out longer than a day, but I have made arrangements."

"Where?"

"You will see."

Which she did many hours later as the sun lowered to the hills in the west. They were following a different river now, the Onny, and had visited more than a dozen hamlets and villages, all to the same effect. The Haytons both Lower and Upper; the Suttons both Great and Little; Lawton, Peaton and Munslow; Dinchope, Wistanstow and Halford. None had heard of stray bones deposited in graves. Now the last rays of the sun caught in the turrets of what appeared to be a cross between a stone manor house and a small castle. Stokesay. Thomas had never visited before but had been invited to call at any time by its owner, Thomas Vernon, who he had met at Ludlow Castle several times while Prince Arthur remained alive.

A short woman of indeterminate years opened the door when Thomas knocked and cocked her head to one side.

"I am Thomas Berrington, and your master has offered

me a bed for the night. I wrote to him and asked if we could stay a week ago, but did not know the exact day. I heard nothing back but am aware squire Vernon is a busy man."

"And away at his holdings in Derbyshire at the moment, but come in, sir. I opened your letter so knew to expect you, but you made no mention of a wife."

Thomas opened his mouth to say Bel was not his wife then closed it again.

"I am Bel, of Lemster. This is a fine house. Do you look after it alone?"

"I have men and women come in during the day, but it is all mine after dark. Have you eaten? I can probably find something if you have not, but it will be meagre fare."

"We took food at the inn at Wistanstow."

"Ale then? Or would you prefer wine?"

"Ale suits us both, madam."

"I will put it in the master's garden room, then will be to my bed. I rise early and need my sleep. As will you. There is a bed made up for guests next to the garden room, so you will not have far to wander, which is a good thing."

"We would never go where we are not allowed," said Bel.

"Oh, wander where you wish, my lady. I was thinking of the ghosts. I would not wish them to set a fright in you. I am used to them, as is the master, but strangers can find them off-putting." She smiled as if pleased at the thought, then left to fetch the ale.

"This is a fine house you have brought me to, Tom. Did you not think to build one like this?"

"Do you not like what I have built?" Thomas looked around at the garden room, which did indeed open to a garden that led down to the fast-flowing river, the sound of a small waterfall sweetening the air.

"I like your house well enough, but a good solid one like this would send a message you are an important man."

"I would rather be an ordinary man."

"That you will never be, Tom Berrington." Bel reached up to kiss him, their embrace interrupted by the return of the housekeeper, who set a jug of ale and two cups on the table and left without a word.

Later, ale drunk and love made in the comfortable bed, Bel said, "Do you think the others will have found anything?" She lay naked inside the crook of his arm, her skin warm against his.

"I hope they might have learned more than us."

"And if there is nothing to find? If it is only your graves that were desecrated?"

"Then I believe I will have to assume they were a message meant to me — or rather, my family."

"It could not be for you, Tom," said Bel. "Everyone believed you were dead, like your father. Word reached us of the battle you fought alongside John Talbot. A lot of English men died on that French field, it is said."

"On both sides, but it was the French who triumphed."

"You never talk of it."

"And I never will." He drew Bel tighter against himself. "So if not a message for me, then who?"

"Let us see if the others have found anything," said Bel. "Do not concern yourself with something that might be nothing." She ran a finger across his brow as if wanting to smooth his worries away. "Now sleep, Tom, and tomorrow we may know more."

EIGHT

The following morning Thomas and Bel stayed late in bed until the presence of two men outside trimming a yew hedge forced them to rise and dress. They were at home before noon after calling at a string of churches and graveyards on their way south, but found out no more than they had as they travelled north.

Jorge had returned the evening before after riding east in the company of Jack Pook, who he appeared to have taken a liking to. Will and Silva had returned only that morning after travelling west, but Amal and Usaden, who had gone south, were not yet back.

"Should we ride out to see if we can find them?" Thomas asked Will, knowing there was little point in consulting Jorge on such matters.

"We are as likely to miss them as find them, Pa. They will have stayed at an inn for the night or slept under the stars. Ami will be safe with Usaden."

"I have no doubt of it, but can we start to discuss our findings — or lack of them — without them?"

"I do not see why not," said Will. "If they are not back by the time we have heard each other's news, then we can consider looking for them, but there is no point in going yet." Will looked around at each of them, waiting until each indicated their agreement until only Thomas remained.

"I expect you are right," Thomas said. "Apart from what we discovered will take little telling. Nobody knew about stray bones, and we visited every hamlet and village as far north as Newton and as far along the corfe as Munslow. We learned nothing. What about you?"

"Let us hear from Jorge first. What did you find out?"

"Not me, Jack," said Jorge. "He knew every dip and hollow and hedgerow we came across, almost every person we met, but it did us little good. We heard nothing, either. But it sounds to me as if you did, Will. Is that why you are being so coy?"

"As you all know we rode west and did the same as you appear to have done. At every place where bodies are buried, we stopped. We went further than we should have and were about to turn back when Silva met an old man she had helped at one time. After pleasantries were exchanged, he told us that a grave at Tref-y-Clawdd had been disturbed. The surface of it, in any case. So we rode there. It was further than we intended but I considered it worth the time."

"What did you find?" Thomas asked.

"I will get to that. We went to the graveyard and were

fortunate to find two men digging a new grave, and they told us which plot had been disturbed. One of them offered to show Silva where it was if I helped with the digging, so that is what we did."

"Was the grave disturbed?"

"Not as far as I could tell," said Silva, "but the man said the disturbance had been a month before, and he had smoothed the surface down again since. I asked if he had thought to check nothing had been taken from the grave and he said no, it was only the surface that had been dug and he would know if the grave had been opened. I believed him."

"Did you think to ask why they did not do more than repair the damage?" Thomas asked.

"Of course," said Will. "I knew you would want to know. They told me it was not unusual. The graveyard is open and lacks high walls. It could have been dogs, boar, even people searching for coin or jewels. They said they could not investigate every disturbance or the dead would remain unburied."

"Did you see the grave?"

"I did more than that. I stayed until the grave they were opening was deep enough and helped lift an old coffin out. Silva blessed the bones before they took them to the ossuary at the local church. I borrowed one of their spades and Silva showed me where this other grave was. It did not take long. We found the body of a young boy. He had been in the ground no more than six weeks, I would say, and stank worse than a badger's arse."

Thomas smiled. Will had taken to using a number of

local expressions since coming to Ludlow, but he had not heard that one before.

"Did you dig further to see if the skull of the original inhabitant had been taken?"

"The boy was laid atop the coffin. I was about to open it but had no chance because the men returned and saw what we had done. They asked if we had killed the lad and I do not think they believed us when we said we had not. One of them stayed while the other went to find the priest and a constable, but we left before they returned. The body remained where it was. Sorry, Pa, I could not think what else to do."

"They would not know who you are, but what about Silva? You said the old man knew who she was."

"That was a few miles east of the town, and the gravediggers did not know her. I doubt they will send anyone looking for us. I suspect they might simply rebury the boy's body and forget we were ever there."

"Which might have been what happened before when these cuckoos were found," Thomas said. "Is it worth us riding back that way to ask more questions?"

"It might be," said Will. "But not today. I need to wash the stink of death from me first. We both bathed in the Teme, which runs through the town, but it is not the same as hot water."

Once Will and Silva had gone to bathe, Bel went with Belia into Ludlow to fetch food for their evening meal. Thomas tried to suppress his concerns over Amal but could not. He rose and walked down to the river where he tossed pebbles into the water, half his attention listening for the sound of approaching horses. After a while he realised he was being stupid. The rustle of the swift-running Teme would mask any faint sound of Amal's return, so he threw the last of his stones into the water and returned to wait at the tall gate. He was still there when Will came to join him, smelling of the soap they'd purchased from a local woman, his hair still wet.

"I will saddle my horse and yours, Pa. We will go and see if we can find them."

"Usaden will allow no harm to come to her."

"I know, but you still want to go, so that is what we will do." Will turned away.

Thomas continued to stare south, a pointless exercise because trees obscured the view more than a hundred paces away. They had grown closer before the house was built, but Thomas had cut some down to leave an open area that could more easily be defended. It had been needed more than once. The felled trees had been sawn up and some used in the fences that enclosed the meadow where the horses grazed. Others had been sold to local landowners. Thomas had grown aware of how commerce and the connections of mutual trade had crept up on them as a family. They were accepted in the local area and beyond. The coming of Bel to Burway had forged stronger links with Lemster. The relationship between Will and Silva forged even more because Silva was well-respected both as a healer and mage. And then there was Thomas's sister, Agnes, and her daughters who baked bread and pies in Ludlow. All connected. Those connections were both good as well as bad, for Thomas had also made enemies. It was those he was worried about when he thought of Amal. Except he knew Will was right. Amal was with Usaden, and Usaden would die before he allowed any harm to come to her. Yet one more debt of loyalty and love.

Will returned astride his stallion, leading Ferrant. Thomas pulled himself up into the saddle and they started south.

"Did you tell anyone we were going?" Thomas asked.

"There was no need. Bel and Jorge sent me out to you. They know you will not rest until Ami is safe at home."

"I am sorry if I have given the impression I am unhappy about you and Silva."

"You have a little, but it is no matter, Pa. I understand why, and so does Silva. She tells me she knows you are a good man, an honest man, and likes you all the more for it."

Thomas said nothing, even though Will's words surprised him.

They waded the Teme where it swung east beyond Ludlow then picked up the track south. Usaden and Amal would have taken this road as well, and no doubt would take it on their return. They continued on to Lemster without seeing any sign of either, by which time noon had come and gone.

Will reined in his horse and turned to his father. "Would they have stopped at the town on their way south or back?"

"I told them not to bother. If anything untoward had occurred in Lemster, Bernard would know of it, and when

I asked him he did not. I told Amal to go no further south than Hereford and to concentrate on the smaller villages and hamlets, the isolated burial fields and churches. Whoever is burying these children, and for whatever reason, will not want to be seen doing so."

"So they could be almost anywhere," said Will.

"They could."

"If that is the case we might never find them, not the two of us even if we split up, and then you would have me to worry about."

"I have no need to worry about you."

Will smiled. "Then I will worry about you. We should return to Burway and organise the others. You and me to search separate areas. Jorge and Jack again, Bel and Silva; we can even recruit Agnes's daughters. Both ride well and are trustworthy."

Thomas sat astride Ferrant, staring at the bulk of Lemster Priory but not seeing it.

"Rose and Jilly would need a man with them."

"I am sure Agnes knows somebody she trusts."

Thomas knew Will's plan made sense, so he nodded and turned Ferrant north. Searching for Amal would be easier with more people.

Thomas wondered how he had managed to raise such a sage son, then realised it was almost certainly more Jorge's doing than his. The thought made him smile as he recalled all the years he and Jorge had spent with each other. Not all of them were good, but there was a connection between them that only they shared. Jorge would be worried about Amal as if she was his own daughter.

But as they approached Ludlow a short figure astride a short horse came riding towards them.

Usaden reined in and waited for them to reach him.

"Where is Amal?" Thomas experienced a surge of fear because Usaden showed no expression.

"At your house. Jorge told me you were looking for us so I came to find you."

"We came to find you but you managed to evade us."

"It is what I do, but in this instance not on purpose," said Usaden. "We returned a little to the west and came down from Dinham Hill. Amal was never in any danger. We did discover something, but she wants to tell you about it herself."

Thomas urged Ferrant into a canter. When he looked back Usaden remained where he was, talking with Will.

He found Amal in the courtyard. She had bathed, and her long, dark hair hung damp across her shoulders. She wore a fresh robe from the dozen she had, all almost identical, only the colour of each distinguishing them.

She rose and embraced him, clinging to him for a moment.

"Jorge told me you were worried about me and went looking," she said as she unwound her arms from around him.

"I did."

"You know there was no need. I was with Usaden."

"I was still worried. Usaden told me you found something."

"We did." Amal retook her seat.

Thomas sat across from her. From inside the house he

could hear the laughter of Jorge's children, of Belia telling them not to be so silly, then laughing herself. It was all normal. And Amal had come home. Still, a tension ran through him and try as he might he could not altogether dismiss it.

He leaned closer. "Tell me."

"I thought we would return with nothing. It was most likely a mistake sending us together. Everyone we met thought we were husband and wife and had come from a foreign land."

"Part of that is right, at least," Thomas said, and Amal smiled.

"They were suspicious of us. We went to every place of burial we could find, but people were unwilling to talk. Most were polite enough, but it was clear they did not trust us even if they knew something. That was until we met a young woman returning from cleaning a small church in the hamlet of Garway. She was open with us." Amal smiled again. "I think she liked Usaden, perhaps thinking him exotic."

"He is exotic in this land. As are you."

"But she was not interested in me. There are girls who are, but she was not one of that kind. Do you want to hear about what we discovered or not, Pa?"

Thomas was about to say it was not he who had strayed from the topic but knew it would be the wrong thing, so nodded.

"She told us several graves had been disturbed in the churchyard of Saint Michael's several years before, but no one had done anything about them. The damage was covered over and nothing more was said about it. She also said there were rumours of other graves in the district that had been disturbed, but she did not know where those were. She only knew about some of these because it happened shortly after she started to clean the church."

"You said she was young?"

Amal nodded.

"So how long ago was this disturbance? Did she start working there as a child?"

"I did not ask her, but most likely she did. You know it happens. Not all girls or boys are as lucky as me and Will, or Aunt Agnes's girls. Many families around here have little and must send their children out to work as soon as they are strong enough."

"Did you find the grave?"

"We did, but as the girl said, it was several years since it was disturbed and there was no sign of it now. I wanted to dig into it, but Usaden persuaded me to be patient. He said we needed to come back and ask you what to do. Did you or the others find anything?"

"Will and Silva, and they did dig into the grave because the disturbance there was recent. They found a body that had been in the ground for only a month or two."

"Where was it?"

"A long way to the west. Further than they intended to go but, like you, someone told them of the desecration so they went to investigate. You did right coming back. If you had been caught opening the grave the constables would have arrested you."

"That is what Usaden said, and I realised I was being hasty. But I wanted to find out if there was a stray body in there, Pa."

Thomas realised Amal was too much like him. He knew he would have wanted to do the same and most likely would have done so.

"You did the right thing. Where does this Garway lie?"

"South of Hereford, which we did not enter. Usaden said larger towns are less likely to be the target of these burials and I believe he is right."

"So do I. I take it this Garway is small?"

"Barely a few houses," said Amal, "and the church is cradled all around by hills. A good place to open a grave and bury something not meant to be there."

Thomas thought about what Amal had said. The hamlet of Garway was south of Hereford. Tref-y-Clawdd, where Will and Silva had discovered the recent burial, was to the west. Both places lay along the borderlands of Herefordshire. Did that mean there were no bodies closer? Those left at his old house were to the east of Lemster, but they were also isolated. It made sense they would be, all of them.

"Are you going to open the grave, Pa?" asked Amal.

"The one you found, and the one Will and Silva found. I need to know if a second body has been buried, and I need to know if the skull of the original inhabitant has been taken. Why it would have been I do not know, but if it has there must be some significance to it. I will write to the Coroner today and ask his permission to open the grave in Garway. This Tref-y-Clawdd may be outside his jurisdiction, but I can ask for that as well. I will ask him for a quick decision, so come morning we may be able to discover more." Thomas looked into his daughter's dark eyes. "You did well."

"We both did well," she said.

NINE

Kin lay on the stone slabs in the courtyard, panting while he slept. His long body twitched and his legs paddled as he dreamed. Thomas sat in a comfortable round-backed chair with a beaker of average wine. Will had ale in his own beaker. Usaden had gone to the river to wash, refusing the offer of the baths in the house. Thomas had written his note to the Coroner and despatched it for delivery. Food had been promised but not yet appeared. The air had grown soft with the coming of evening so the sound of approaching horses came loud.

Thomas rose and walked to the gateway. Two men rode towards the opening, and with a sinking heart he recognised both. Slightly ahead, because that was his nature despite his lower rank, rode Amos Mapp, assistant to the Coroner. A little behind came Lyman d'Alston, the Coroner for south Shropshire and north Herefordshire, who also took responsibility for west Worcestershire on occasion because of its proximity to Ludlow.

Their presence did not auger well for the response to his message. They must have started out only moments after receiving it. Lyman d'Alston lived in a large black and white beamed house set only a few streets east of the Market Square in Ludlow, so their journey would not have taken long.

The two men reined in their horses and slid to the ground. Thomas started forward to stable them, but Usaden was faster and took the reins to lead the horses away. Amos Mapp watched him go with a scowl on his face, no doubt wondering what a Moorish servant was doing in the house; unaware, of course, that Usaden was no servant.

"I have fresh wine if you have thirst," Thomas said.

"Wine would be most acceptable. We are here about the message you sent." It was Amos Mapp who spoke while the Coroner stood a few paces behind him.

"There is food as well if you have hunger," Thomas said. "We can eat inside, or out here in the last of the sunshine. I assume you have come to discuss my request."

"Not discuss," said Lyman d'Alston as he finally passed Amos Mapp and took a seat. He reached for an empty beaker and waited for Mapp to fill it. "I am here to tell you to stop investigating matters that are my jurisdiction, not yours."

"I am investigating no deaths, Lyman." Thomas glanced at Jack Pool. "Would you tell Belia we have guests? Another two plates of food and more wine. I think we may need it."

"Another chair as well, Tom?"

"Yes, one more." Thomas knew Jack would glean his meaning. The conversation would consist of three men, not four. Jack would not mind, but he might stand inside the door and eavesdrop, as Thomas hoped Jorge would also do.

Thomas stood because Amos Mapp had now taken the chair he had been using. He lifted the beaker Thomas had also used and sniffed before pouring the wine onto the slabs. Thomas suppressed his annoyance.

"I hear you want to bury unbaptised remains in the churchyard at St Laurence's."

That had not been what Thomas expected. "I take it Malton Yorke came to you." He stood facing the two men, his back to the lowering sun, so they had to narrow their eyes. It was a petty victory, but a victory all the same.

"He is concerned you intend to investigate where these bones came from and who they belong to. And now you send me a note saying that is exactly what you plan to do. Where did you discover these stray bones?"

"They were buried atop the remains of my mother and brother on Eaton Hill."

"The disposition of such remains falls under the jurisprudence of the Coroner, as well you know."

"They were old bones, Lyman." Thomas saw a flash of annoyance at his use of the man's given name and hid a smile. "I believe they must have lain in the ground for at least twenty years or more. My son also found more recent remains only yesterday."

"So you have already begun an investigation even before consulting me?"

"The original bones were found on land my father once owned, so yes, I started to ask questions. I believed it was my responsibility to do so."

"You should have come to me."

"And you would have done what? Got Amos to write a script and file it, then forget all about the matter? What would you do with the bones?"

"I would not bury them at St Laurence's. The Reverend Malton Yorke is correct when he says they are no doubt unbaptised, and as such cannot be allowed to desecrate the churchyard of true Christians."

"What would you do — burn them? Discard them on the roadside like the remains of a meal for the dogs to chew on? Whoever they may be they deserve justice, the same as everyone else."

"Which it is my responsibility to dispense."

"Are you telling me to stop?"

"I am."

"And if I refuse?"

"I will have no alternative but to arrest you."

Thomas laughed. "Ludlow Castle is abandoned, Prince Arthur is dead, and Sir Richard Pole and Gruffydd ap Rhys have returned to their holdings. Who do you intend to help you with this arrest?"

"The King, of course."

"As if he would concern himself with such a trifling matter. Apart from which he knows me and what I do. I pursue bad people, whether you believe they are your responsibility or not."

"King Henry has advisors who deal with matters such as the breaking of protocol and responsibility. Without both, we have only chaos, and the King will not stand for that. Has not stood for it. He takes action. He has men hanged."

Thomas laughed again, louder this time. "You would have me hanged for trying to find out who buried the bodies of children in my mother's grave and stole her skull? Since when has that been a hanging offence?"

"You would be surprised what is a hanging offence, Berrington."

"Then surprise me." Thomas walked to the doorway. "Jack, tell Belia there are no guests after all." He turned back. "I want you to leave now. Both of you."

"Do not make an enemy of me, Berrington. I have influence in three counties."

"And I am Justice of the Peace."

"Which is barely a position at all. Unlike mine. Take heed, I write to the King this very day."

"Then best you get Amos to do the writing if you want him to be able to read it." Thomas glanced at Amos Mapp. "Make sure you spell my name right."

Thomas stood with arms folded, waiting. Lyman d'Alston stared back, as did Amos Mapp. Thomas knew if it came to it he could forcibly expel them, but that would only increase their enmity. He wondered if he cared enough not to do it. Then he thought about what he had become. A man with a position in the district. Men such as that did not fight other men of equal or higher positions. And the Coroner was, he accepted, a more senior position than Justice of the Peace. Even if Lyman d'Alston was a corrupt Coroner. But such would not come as a surprise to anyone. The surprise was that Thomas was not a corrupt Justice as the last one had been, and no doubt the one before that.

D'Alston finally rose, Amos Mapp following his example.

"You will not hear the last of this, Berrington," said d'Alston.

Amos caught Thomas's eyes and offered a barely perceptible shrug as if apologising for his master's attitude.

Thomas watched until they turned beyond the gate. He hoped Usaden would note their expressions and leave them to saddle their own horses.

"Are you sure you wanted to do that, Tom?" asked Jack Pook, as he came out of the house.

"I take it you listened?"

"Did you not want me to?"

"No, it is fine."

"They threatened you. I am witness to it."

"As if that would make a difference."

"To folks around here it would," said Jack. "Not the high and mighties perhaps, but the common folk who farm the land and raise sheep, cattle and pigs. It would make a difference to the people that keep everyone fed and the world working."

"And since when have the common people had a say in the way the world works?" Thomas said.

"I agree they are not listened to, but hunger soon convinces a man. It would not be the first time common men have risen up against their masters, and I do not suppose it would be the last."

"It always ends in bloodshed, and nothing ever changes."

"One day," said Jack, his voice soft. "One day it might. What are you going to do if they write to the King?"

"Henry knows me. I expect he knows d'Alston, too, and the King is no fool. He recognises those who steal from him and those who do not."

"You state that as if he might judge between those two states," said Jack, all at once sounding less like himself than Thomas had ever heard. "I hear the King likes to line his own pockets when he can. Perhaps he admires others who do the same. Or more likely takes a tax from each to allow them to continue stealing."

"So I am an honest fool?" Thomas asked.

"You are no fool, and I would not like you as much if you were not honest. Neither would Bel. But you need to know how things work, Tom. Both Justice of the Peace and Coroner are unpaid posts. A man must either be exceedingly rich to want to attain either position or be corrupt. Looking at your house, I would say you are rich. I know that Lyman d'Alston is not."

"So he is corrupt?"

Jack laughed. "You say that with such surprise, as if you have never considered it before. Of course d'Alston is corrupt, though I admit Amos Mapp may be less so. Do you know he sometimes works with Brother Ambrose?"

"How would I know that? Is it significant?"

Jack laughed again. "Do not ask me about significance, Tom, I leave such things to you. Mapp sells relics and that brings him into contact with Ambrose now and then."

Thomas stared at Jack, trying to work out if he was saying something or not. He was still staring when Amal came out with a flagon of wine and plates holding slices of ham, cabbage, carrots and sauce. She set them on the table.

"Are you sure you want to eat out here, Pa? Everyone else is inside."

"Jack and I are having a talk."

Thomas sat in the comfortable chair and Jack took the other.

"Where does Mapp get these relics from?" he asked.

"Here and there. I suspect some of them are fake, but I expect one or two are the real thing. There is only so much of the true cross that exists, but every priory and abbey in the land seems to have a piece of it. And that is just England. I expect all of Christendom claims the same. That must have been some big old cross He died on."

"I met Brother Ambrose recently," Thomas said. "He did not strike me as someone who would allow Mapp to pass off fake relics to the Church."

"Neither would I, but that is not what is happening. Ambrose identifies false relics and Mapp destroys them.

He provides the Church with documentation to say so. The two are not exactly friends but they rub along well enough. They make use of each other."

Jack cut his meat and chewed, making a sound of pleasure. He drank some wine and nodded his approval.

"Does Prior Bernard and Abbot John know of this arrangement?"

"I would assume they must, but they are not responsible for Ambrose. Hereford Cathedral is. Now, this food is too good to waste by talking and eating at the same time."

Amal came out with a chair and sat beside Thomas but said nothing.

Once the food was finished, Thomas gathered the plates and took them inside before Amal could do so. He brought a fresh flagon of wine out, aware he and Jack had almost finished the first. He also brought an extra beaker for Amal, who liked to take a little wine thinned with water. When he emerged Amal had taken a chair and she and Jack were talking.

"Jack tells me you have made an enemy of the Coroner," she said after Thomas had put the flagon on the table and sat.

"I am not sure we were ever friends, or even associates."

"Can he cause trouble for you?"

Thomas looked beyond Amal to Jack. "What do you think?"

"D'Alston is always happy to cause trouble for those he dislikes, and it appears he dislikes you a great deal.

You are an honest man in a sea of corruption, so yes, he will try to cause trouble. But you have dealt with such men before and are still here."

"There are many honest men and women in Ludlow and Lemster, Jack. You for one."

Jack laughed softly. "If I am your judge of honest men then no wonder you believe there are a lot of them. I am a poacher, Tom, you know I am."

"But an honest poacher. You told me only today you only take rabbits, hares and boar and leave the master's deer alone."

"Perhaps I value my neck is all."

Amal rose and lit the three lamps that hung from the walls. The air had thickened and darkness was falling. A faint red line to the west augured another fine day in the morning, and Thomas wondered what he would do. The Quarter Sessions were not due until the end of June, and Amal took care of the submissions. Thomas had appointed her as Clerk of the Peace, which raised some eyebrows because she was the only female ever to hold the post. It also came with a fee for each session, which Amal kept for herself. Thomas knew most clerks passed their responsibilities on to someone else, but that would not be Amal's way. It was usual for the position to be in the gift of the Justice of the Peace and most appointed a member of their family, which is why Thomas had done so for Amal. He wondered if others considered it as corruption, which did not sit well with the conversation he was having with Jack Pook. But Thomas would trust no one but Amal to carry out the task.

"What are you going to do about the Coroner, Pa?"

"Nothing, unless he acts on his threats, but I suspect the man is all bluster. He will not write to the King. Even if he does, it will not be Henry who reads the letter. It will be filed away and forgotten."

"He is part of the local gentry," said Jack. "And they are all corrupt. They stick together and include some of the richest landowners in the three counties, as well as members of the Church."

"But not Prior Bernard," Thomas said.

"I agree, Prior Bernard is incorruptible. But Abbot John is one of them, as are most of the other heads of religious houses in the area. The Church, after all, is the biggest landowner and landlord of all. Wigmore Abbey has grown soft under Abbot John's watch, and there is always be resistance to change." Jack stood, stretched. "Well, I thank you for the fine food and wine, but the woods are calling me."

"You are not going back with Usaden to his house?" Amal asked.

"Not tonight." Jack walked away, his steps soundless.

"What about you, Pa?" asked Amal, as she poured a little more wine for both herself and her father.

"Am I going to sleep in the woods? No, though I have done often enough in the past. My bones grow weary these days."

Amal smiled. "Always you say you are growing old, but you are still hale and strong if only you stop pretending to yourself."

"Why are you so clever, Ami?"

"We have had this conversation before, Pa. Both me and Will are who we are because of you."

"And Olaf, and your mother, and Jorge, too, I expect."

"But mostly because of you." Amal reached across and squeezed his hand.

"Tomorrow I intend to go to Bernard and find out what he knows about what is happening here. There are too many links to holy houses. If anyone can tell me about what is going on he can. Perhaps there is nothing and I can forget about everything other than my own family and friends."

"If you go to Lemster, take Will with you if he is back from Silva's cottage. Otherwise Usaden. Better still, take them both, and Jorge, too. You know he judges people better than anyone else."

"There is no need to judge Bernard. I have known him since I was a boy and trust him better than almost anyone."

TEN

Thomas had no need to go to Prior Bernard because the man came to him. Thomas was in his workshop labelling bottles of herbs imported from Spain when he heard voices outside but continued his work. He had written to a friend in Granada asking for hemp and poppy, then almost forgotten he had done so until a man arrived with a box on the back of a cart and a demand for payment. Amal had done most of the work of separating out and bottling the contents of the parcel, but it soothed Thomas to write the labels and then gum them to the glass. His mind had stilled with the familiar scents and repetition of the work when he was jarred back to the present when someone called his name. When he went out to see what the urgency was, he found Prior Bernard standing beside a tall grey. Bel and Will had already come from the house, and Thomas ran across to join them.

"I need you with me, Tom," said the Prior. "A

messenger came to tell me that Abbot John is fading fast. I trust only you to ease his passing."

"I will get my bag. Will, saddle Ferrant and bring him here." Thomas ran back to the workshop and pulled his leather satchel from beneath a bench, then filled it with everything he might need. Most of it consisted of herbs, but he added a little of the fresh poppy and hashish he had been sent, then added a canvas roll that held his instruments. By the time he came out Will was holding Ferrant, and he mounted and rode out beside Prior Bernard.

Rather than go to Dinham Bridge they bullied their horses directly across the Teme and urged them through the woods flanking Dinham Hill. Wigmore Abbey lay three leagues west of Ludlow. The direct route required them to pass over several high hills, but Prior Bernard assured Thomas it was the fastest way. Descending to the wide plain that stretched to Wigmore, beyond which more hills rose, the two men urged their horses into a gallop.

They left their mounts to be taken care of by a brother before entering the abbey, where they were taken to the Abbot's chambers and ushered inside.

"You can leave us," said Prior Bernard to the brother who had accompanied them. The man appeared reluctant, but the Prior stared at him until he turned and left.

Thomas moved to the wide bed and pulled aside the heavy drapes cloaking it. The smell of imminent death reached him and he knew there was nothing he could do.

Abbot John lay propped on a stack of pillows, thick blankets covering him. His face was pale and waxy, his expression a grimace of pain. When Thomas touched his neck to feel the pulse he also felt the warmth of his body and asked Prior Bernard to remove some of the blankets.

"Can you do anything?" asked the Prior, his voice low.

"I cannot save him if that is what you mean, but I can ease his pain." Thomas leaned closer. "Do you have much pain, Abbot?"

The faintest of nods came, and Abbot John closed his fist and placed it over his chest. "Here. Bad pain."

"When did it start?"

"This ... this morning, when I..." His words trailed off as he panted, his mouth compressed in a line, his lips with a blue tint.

Thomas moved away and set his satchel on a table standing in front of a tall window which looked across the cloister. He took out bottles, then looked around for a cup. All he could see was a wine glass with liquid still in it. He tipped the contents out onto the floor and began to prepare a mixture of poppy.

"What ails him, Tom?" The Prior stood beside him, far enough away to allow Thomas to work.

"His heart is failing. I am only surprised he has lived this long. He is fat enough for three and no longer a young man."

"It was not always that way. I recall when he came to Wigmore Abbey as a novice. He was slim, handsome and urbane. But time erodes us all. Is there anything you can do for him?"

"Not now. A year ago I might have been able to offer him something to ease the strain on his heart, to advise him to eat less and take exercise, even if only a daily walk around the cloister. Now it is too late. All I can do is ease his passing."

"How long?"

Thomas stoppered two of the bottles. He set one aside, which he would use if the pain grew too much. The other he poured into the empty wine glass.

"It would surprise me if he sees the sunset." He looked around. "There must be more wine somewhere."

"Abbot John usually keeps some in here." Prior Bernard opened a cabinet and took out a dark bottle. He eased the cork loose before passing the bottle to Thomas, who measured a little into his mixture before swirling it around.

"Help me sit him up. This will ease his pain, but it is no cure."

"And the other bottle?" asked Prior Bernard as he supported the Abbot's weight so Thomas could pour the contents of the glass, little by little, into his mouth.

"For when the pain grows too fierce."

"You would end his life? That is a foul sin, Tom, and beneath you."

"I will not kill him. His failing heart will do that. The other bottle is the same, only stronger. It will send him deep, but not kill him unless I have lost all my skill."

"I will need to call others in to pray over him. He would want it, as would I."

"Fetch them, then. They can do no harm, and hearing their prayers will soothe his passing."

Prior Bernard scowled. "Sometimes I question why I like you so much."

After the Prior had gone, Thomas stood watching the Abbot. Slowly the grimace left his face and his breathing grew shallower. He opened his eyes and stared up at Thomas, who thought he was not recognised until the Abbot spoke.

"I remember you. You were here when Peter Gifforde tried to kill me."

"I was."

"And now death comes for me in any case. It is a relentless foe and will not be denied."

"It comes for us all in the end," Thomas said.

"What did you give me? I am sorry, I have forgotten your name."

"Thomas. And I gave you something to ease your pain."

"Then I thank you, as does God. Has Bernard gone to fetch some of my flock?"

"He has."

"Then God will take me to sit at His side." His eyes met Thomas's. "How long?"

"I cannot say for certain, but today I suspect."

"Good. I look forward to eternal life." The Abbot's eyes closed and he fell into a shallow sleep. His fingers moved, twitching and curling against the covers.

Prior Bernard returned with eight monks, two carrying a censer already lit, another holding a bottle of holy water. The Abbot roused enough to see them then drifted away again.

"If you are going to sing your dirges and burn incense, I will take a walk outside."

"Do not go far, Tom. He may need you again."

"And he may not. I will stay close, but I would rather not witness this."

Prior Bernard turned away, failing to chastise Thomas for his lack of faith. In truth, it was not faith Thomas lacked. Rather, it was an inability to accept the trappings of religion. God, if He existed, would not require it. If He had truly sent his son to earth, then that son also would not ask it. According to the Bible Thomas had read, memorising much of it, Jesus had lived a modest life and turned his back on silver and gold. Which the abbey contained a great deal of.

Thomas walked out into the working areas of the abbey. Four monks had raised their habits and tied them at their waists as they attempted to net carp from the stew ponds. It would be hours until Abbot John passed away and Thomas did not want to return to the fetid room filled with incense and prayer. He made his way towards a gate that would lead him to the slopes beyond the abbey. He felt in need of clean air and expansive views. He knew he could find Ferrant and ride, but using his own two feet felt right, and the climb would exercise his body. Beyond the abbey wall he found a narrow track that led up through woods and followed it. The air was cooler beneath the trees, sharp with the scent of wild garlic. Thomas passed a pile of stones which might once have been a house. If so it had been small. Perhaps somewhere a shepherd might shelter on long winter nights when lambs were being born. At the crest of the hill the trees grew sparse and he came out onto a wider track that ran away along the ridge ahead, descending in the other direction back to the village of Wigmore. He also discovered he was not the only person using it.

Brother Ambrose appeared, only the top of his head at first as he climbed from the village, then the donkey he was leading, and finally the small cart it pulled. He saw Thomas but gave no sign of recognition or greeting as he approached, but he did slow.

"What are you doing here, Thomas Berrington? This is a long way from Burway."

"If you have come from the abbey you should know why I am here."

"I did not visit the abbey today, only passed through the village and took my dinner there. I am heading into Wales to study more relics."

Thomas glanced at the cart, the contents of which were covered with sacking. Boxes, it looked like. Perhaps Brother Ambrose's possessions. He wondered if the man had a base or did his life consist of continual travel between holy houses.

"I will not keep you, then," Thomas said.

"You are not. I need to catch my breath after the climb." Ambrose looked around. "You can see God's wonder from up here, can you not? See His hand in all we survey."

Thomas made no comment.

"I enquired about the status of your land at Burway," said Ambrose. "I told you I would and I am a man of his word. The ground was consecrated when a church stood there and it appears that was never changed. So the bones of your family will lie in hallowed ground."

"My thanks." Thomas held his hand out, grateful to Ambrose, but the man only stared at it without responding and Thomas allowed it to drop to his side.

"Has something happened at the abbey that requires your presence?" asked Ambrose. "Why would the abbey need a Justice of the Peace?"

"I am not here as Justice but as a physician. Abbot John's long life is drawing to an end."

"Abbot John is dying?"

"He is."

Brother Ambrose appeared not to know what to do. He turned away, turned back.

"I must go to him. Who hears his confession?"

"Prior Bernard is with him."

"Good. Yes, that is good. But I will still go to him. Can you..." Brother Ambrose shook his head. "No, you cannot."

He turned the donkey and cart and started down the slope, descending faster than he had ascended. When he had disappeared Thomas stayed where he was, confused at Ambrose's actions. He was a brother, nothing more, but had acted as if only he could hear the confession of the Abbot. It was likely he would arrive too late in any case.

Finally, Thomas turned to descend the same track he

ELEVEN

In the end, Abbot John slipped away without waking, but there had been a short time as the first draught of poppy wore off and before Thomas administered the second when he roused.

"I need to make my confession," he said.

As the words came out the monks crowded around the bed stepped back, startled. Within moments they were gone.

"I will leave as well," Thomas said.

"No," said Abbot John. "Bernard is not my confessor. I need ... I need..."

"Brother Ambrose?" Thomas asked, scarcely able to believe what he was hearing.

"Yes ... Ambrose ... he hears my ... my confession each ... each time he calls. Send for him if there is time. If not ... Prior Bernard can hear it ... but I would like..."

"Ambrose may be here," Thomas said.

Prior Bernard stared at him. Already he had found the

items he needed. A rosary, a small bottle of holy water, and arranged them on a small table near the bed.

"I met him when I went out for some air," Thomas said. "He should be here somewhere. Shall I find him?"

"If you can."

It was Abbot John who spoke, and Thomas left in search of the strange brother. He found him sitting in the cloister, praying. As soon as Thomas told him what the Abbot wanted he nodded and rose.

Thomas and Prior Bernard left the two of them together but sat beyond the heavy oak door of the Abbot's room.

"How did you know Brother Ambrose was Abbot John's confessor, Tom?"

"I met him on the hill. I did not know it at the time, but he said something strange on the roadway. He asked who would hear Abbot John's confession. I told him most likely you, but I do not think he was completely satisfied with my answer." Thomas glanced at the Prior. "Is it normal practice for a brother to hear the confession of an abbot?"

"It is not, but it happens. There is meant to be a hierarchy. I hear the confessions of my flock at Lemster Priory, but I used to confess to Abbot John. There are few above an abbot in the district, so he could appoint someone of lower rank, which it appears he did. I was not aware of the arrangement, but it makes sense. Brother Ambrose visits Wigmore at least once a month."

"I do not suppose Abbot John has a great deal to confess."

"I would not know, and even if I did could never reveal it."

Thomas felt chastised.

"Who will take his place now?"

"Unfortunately, I suspect it may be me until someone more suitable can be found. An abbey the size of Wigmore cannot be left without a head for any length of time. I will need to ride to Hereford to consult Archdeacon Webb, but I can think of no one else who might preside here other than myself. At least it will only be until a permanent abbot can be appointed."

"What will happen at Lemster Priory?"

"I will put one of the senior brothers in my place until I can return. There are two or three suitable candidates who will be willing to do the work without wanting to usurp my position."

"Will Abbot John be buried here?" Thomas asked.

"He will. I suspect he had already chosen a spot, as have I."

"You have?"

"Of course. A shaded corner in the grounds of the priory where I can reset for all eternity. I have asked for no stone to be set. I prefer to be ignored."

"Speaking of stones, can you recommend a good mason to make headstones for my family? I would like my mother's to be a Celtic cross."

"Do you know all their names? And the year of birth and death would be useful but not essential."

Thomas leaned down and lifted his satchel, which he had not wanted to leave in the room with Brother

Ambrose. He did not trust the man not to look inside it, and some of the contents could be dangerous in the wrong hands.

He drew out the family Bible Silva had led him to. It had been cleaned but was still fragile and in need of attention.

"I found this at my old house. It is our family Bible and has every name going back centuries, even if most of them would never be able to read any of the content itself."

"Latin?" asked Prior Bernard before shaking his head. "Of course it is." He held out his hand. "May I?"

Thomas passed it across. "Be careful, it is old and fragile."

Prior Bernard nodded, turned the Bible over without opening it. "If you will allow me there is a skilled book-binder at the priory who can effect repairs." He eased the cover open and consulted the first three pages. Different hands had written in a minute script a list of names and dates. The Berringtons, as well as the Watkins from his mother's side. A list of births, deaths and marriages. Thomas had studied them the night before, and later Amal copied the list to new sheets of paper so they could be consulted without having to risk more damage to the Bible. She had also added her own and Will's name, as well as that of her mother, Lubna. By the time Thomas had finished telling her about his life, more names had been added. Olaf Torvaldsson and Olaf's wife Fatima. Helena, the daughter of Olaf's first wife who died in childbirth. Thomas and Lubna's daughter Bahja, who had died at birth. Agnes was already listed, but not her daughters, so Amal had added them. And then Thomas asked her to add Jorge, Belia, Jahan, Samar and Leila. It was, Thomas hoped, a list that would grow down the years.

Prior Bernard handed the Bible back to Thomas.

"Bring it to the priory, or leave it with me and I will have it repaired. I recall I taught you how to read Latin many years ago. Have you read this book?"

"I like Matthew," Thomas said.

Prior Bernard smiled. "Yes, that was one of my favourites when I was a boy. But there is much wisdom here, Tom. Even for those who do not believe."

The door to the Abbot's chamber opened and Brother Ambrose stepped out.

"He is gone." He showed no expression. "I will continue my journey." He turned and walked away.

"He is a strange man," Thomas said when they were alone. "Am I allowed to say that?"

"Yes, he is strange, but knows more of relics than any other man in England. You and he ought to get along, for you are both men of rare intellect. Though I will admit, Ambrose is also a man of strong views on a great many things."

"I noticed," Thomas said as they entered the Abbot's chamber.

He stood over the corpulent body. It looked little different from the last time he had seen it, when Abbot John still breathed. He wondered whether he had made his confession or not, and if he had what manner of sins he might have confessed. Small ones, no doubt. Gluttony, perhaps. Thomas would never know.

"Will the brothers take care of him?" he asked Prior Bernard, who came to stand at his side.

"Of course. He looks peaceful. There can have been no pain at the end." He patted Thomas on the back. "Your doing, Tom."

"I expect this will mean you are going to be busy. I will find someone else to speak the words over my family when we inter them."

"Yes, I will have many calls on my time. I have to return to Lemster to arrange for someone to take over my duties until I am finished here. Perhaps we can ride together and call at Burway. Nothing is going to happen quickly. I will send a message to the Archdeacon at Hereford. He will need to officiate at Abbot John's funeral mass, so there is time if you still want me to speak some words."

"I would like that, Bernard. Stay the night, and we can bury them in the morning."

"I may do that. It will help me summon my strength for what is to come. There will be politics involved."

"Even in the Church?"

Bernard laughed. "Particularly in the Church."

"Did you think you would ever rise as high as you have?" Thomas asked.

"I did not. And when it became clear I might, I prayed for it not to happen. It seems I did not pray hard enough."

"Or God wanted you to be the Prior at Lemster. He wanted a good man."

"For an unbeliever, Tom, there are times you speak a great deal of truth about the Church. We should leave and let the brothers prepare Abbot John. Perhaps we can ride to your house in time for supper."

They were a mile beyond Wigmore when Thomas's mind turned once more to the skeletons.

"There is no one to hear us now, Bernard," he said, "so may I speak bluntly with you?"

"If this is about Abbot John or Brother Ambrose, then no."

"It is neither. At least I do not think so. It is the bones. Two issues. The first is the foundlings buried in the graves and what to do with them. The second is the missing skulls."

"If you ask it I will take the bones of the children and lay them in the grounds of the priory."

"Reverend Yorke told me he could not bury them at St Laurence's Church without names."

"Then we will give them names. They deserve to rest in peace, Tom. What about the skulls?"

"Have you ever heard of such a thing happening before? Heads missing from bodies?"

"I have not, but it has the taste of sin to it. I assume you are aware that when burial grounds grow too full the graves are opened and the bones placed in an ossuary?" When Thomas nodded, Bernard continued. "If there is space the bones are stacked with others. If not the skull and a thigh bone might be separated out and the rest discarded."

"Why keep them at all?"

"It is claimed by some that when judgement day comes the dead will rise up. So they will need a leg to stand on and a head to hold high."

"Do you believe that?"

Bernard glanced at Thomas. "I believe in judgement ... but no, not literally. We are more than our bodies. More than our bones. It is our souls that ascend, nothing else."

"I knew a man once — an evil man — who spent half his life searching for the location of the soul."

"Did he ever find it?"

"No."

"Perhaps he has by now, but if so I believe everyone would know of it."

"He died," Thomas said. "He thought he could fly."

"Did you play a part in his fate?"

"I did. It seems, looking back, I played a part in the fate of many, but it was never of my choosing."

"But you were chosen. And you rose to the challenge, which is why you are here riding beside me. No doubt you will do the same again."

"I had hoped to put all such things behind me."

"That is not in your nature. It was not as a boy and even less so now. You hunted down the killer of that miller lad not long since. It is what you do. Who you are. You will pick and pick at this mystery until you uncover the truth. And then you will pass your own judgement. You should talk with Brother Ambrose about the missing skulls. He travels everywhere in the region, and if such things were happening, I am sure he would hear of them. I will ask him to call on you next time I see him. It is possible one of the other priories, abbeys or churches have had the experience of something similar. If so, Ambrose will know of it, for he visits them all."

"Is that not unusual for Ambrose to hear the Abbot's confession? I am no longer familiar with such things, but you told me not long since that you confessed to Abbot John. Why would he confess to Ambrose who is but a lowly monk?"

"They have a history."

Thomas waited, but when Bernard did not go on, he said, "And this history is a secret?"

"It is to me, but I suspect was not to Abbot John. When Ambrose comes to you, ask him about it if you want."

"Will he tell it to me?"

Bernard smiled. "It will depend on what mood he is in when you ask. He might, he might not."

"Is this secret history important?"

"How can I know that when I have no knowledge of it? Abbot John mentioned it in passing, nothing more. I have a mind to stay at your house for a week to avoid the politics that will follow Abbot John's death, but know I will not be allowed."

"You are always welcome, Bernard."

Bernard only smiled at Thomas's continued lack of protocol.

TWELVE

Prior Bernard was still at Thomas's house the following morning when a messenger arrived. Bernard took the note, opened it and walked into the courtyard while he read it. When he finished he came back to Thomas.

"I need you to return to Wigmore with me, Tom. A conclave has been called to appoint the next Abbot. It is unlike the Church to act in such haste. I fear they may choose me as abbot and I do not want it. I am content in Lemster. It is where I have always believed my bones will lie when God takes me."

"You told me the appointment would not be made for some time yet," Thomas said.

"Which is usually the case, but not this time. You need to attend as Justice of the Peace. You are mentioned in this note, though it was sent to Lemster Priory in the first instance. There may be people who do not welcome your presence, but all the more reason for you to be there. You will not be allowed to vote on who becomes the next abbot, but you can offer an opinion; though nothing more. Croft and Cornwell will represent the Marcher Lords. Coroner d'Alston will represent the lay members of the district."

"Then I know of at least two people who will not welcome my presence. I thought the choice of a new abbot would be a Church matter."

"And in most places it would, but here the Marcher Lords are a powerful presence, so they or their representatives are allowed to express an opinion."

"Are Croft and Cornwell Marcher Lords?" Thomas asked.

"Of course they are. I am surprised you did not know. They are powerful men whose influence spreads far and wide. But we can talk more as we ride; I am already late."

As they ascended Dinham Hill, Thomas said, "D'Alston called on me three days since and warned me to stop looking into the stray bones being buried in graves. I suspect he hopes they will be forgotten about if he does nothing — and nothing is what I am sure he will do."

"I understand why you cannot let it lie, Tom. Two of those foundlings were found in the graves of your family, but I have heard of no others so perhaps d'Alston, while being wrong, may also be right. There is no mystery to be uncovered here."

"I believe there is. We recently rode out in four different directions to ask questions and look at burial sites. Amal and Usaden discovered evidence of a disturbed grave. Will and Silva found even more in a town by the name of Tref-y-Clawdd. They dug into a grave that showed signs of disturbance and found the body of a child. It had been in the ground no more than six weeks."

"And what did they do with this body?"

"They had to leave it. Two gravediggers saw what they had done and sent for the priest and a constable. Will and Silva left before they arrived."

"Will is easily recognised, Tom. Who do you think this body would be reported to?"

"I assume not d'Alston. He is Coroner for Hereford, Shropshire and western Worcestershire. This town was in the borderland between England and Wales."

"Lyman d'Alston's territory is extensive and reaches west to beyond that town. Exactly how far west is a mystery to me and, I suspect, d'Alston also."

"West," Thomas said. "There is a connection here with the west. The grave Amal and Usaden discovered was at Garway, which is south and west of Hereford, but unlike Will they did not attempt to open it. I sent a note to d'Alston asking if I could do so but he warned me off. He made it clear there would be trouble if I tried."

"Yet here you are explaining all of this to me. And if I know you, Tom, you will continue to look into these bones."

"I do not even know if the owners of them died at the hand of someone or not. The ones I know about are all young, less than a year old, I estimate, and we both know the first year of a child's life is the most dangerous."

"I agree, and if the children had been killed word would have spread. A missing child would be noticed."

"So why were these not?" Thomas asked.

"That I do not know, but if you ever discover the answer let me know because I am curious. Not curious enough to investigate myself, but curious all the same."

"Who else will attend this conclave?" Thomas believed he had gone as far as he could with what he knew about the bones for now, and he had a curiosity about where they were headed.

"John Martyn, the Archdeacon of Salop; William Webb, the Archdeacon of Hereford; Prioress Felicia Hughden; Abbot Owain Haylewith; Sir Thomas Cornwell, as Sheriff of Shropshire; Sir Richard Croft as a past Sheriff of Hereford; Coroner d'Alston, of course; also a brother from the abbey, though his presence has little meaning. No doubt he will already have been told how he must vote by Webb."

"And you will be there," Thomas said.

"Yes. I will be there. When it is time to vote you will have to leave the chamber. There must be a minimum of five souls for a conclave to be held, but no upper number as long as it is odd."

"Is there always a conclave?" Thomas asked.

"No, and it is unusual one has been called in this instance. I suspect there is some reason for it, but if so it has not been communicated to me. In most instances the Abbot is appointed by the monks of an abbey, as I was appointed Prior by the brothers at Lemster. A conclave is called when there is no clear person to elect, or there is a political need. In this instance, I suspect the latter. Wigmore Abbey controls much of Herefordshire and south Shropshire, as well as west Worcestershire. The Abbot must be a person of substance."

"You said you feared you might be appointed."

"Much as I do not wish to say it, I am a person of substance in the area and do not see anyone else who might be suitable. I pray I am wrong."

"Will you still be my friend if you are made Abbot, Bernard?"

"Of course not. I will be far too important. Unless you promise to remember my title now and again."

Thomas changed the subject so Bernard did not have to think about his pending change of status, and he would not have to think of bones. Instead he spoke of his life as a lad, when he and Bernard had wandered The Marsh in search of medicinal herbs. He also told of how he came to study medicine in the infirmaries of Malaga. Bernard listened without comment and, Thomas suspected, without hearing his words, either.

As they approached the outer stone walls of Wigmore Abbey six mounted men barred their way. They were dressed as soldiers and armed like soldiers. They wore dark padded jackets on the front of which were sewn red crosses. The same manner of men who had been with Madoc at Elmbrook Priory.

"You know me," said Bernard.

"We do. We also know Thomas Berrington. You are welcome to pass but must leave your weapons with us."

"I have no weapon," said Bernard.

"But I am sure Berrington has. I see a sword strapped to his saddle."

The man held a hand out. Thomas unsheathed the sword and handed it hilt first to him. He reached inside his jacket and withdrew two knives: one long, the other short; both wickedly honed.

Once the soldiers parted Thomas and Bernard rode through the gap. Beyond the outer gate, monks took their horses, and Thomas followed Bernard into the cool interior where a tall stranger greeted them.

"It is a pleasure to see you again, Prior."

The man embraced Bernard before turning to Thomas. He was of medium height, with dark hair, dressed in ordinary clothes of hose, leather shoes and a linen shirt, but over them he wore a black habit. A cross hung around his neck, not ornate but small and fashioned of silver.

"Archdeacon Webb, this is Thomas Berrington, Justice of the Peace for the district," said Prior Bernard.

The man offered his hand. Thomas shook it, receiving a strong grip in return, the kind one man uses to judge another's their measure. The Archdeacon offered a faint smile at the strength returned. No doubt he would also have felt the calloused palm from years of wielding a sword.

"You are welcome," said the Archdeacon. "I trust acting Abbot Bernard has informed you of the process? You can attend our discussions but must vacate the room before we vote."

"He knows, Your Eminence."

The Archdeacon laughed. "I think eminence is too mighty a title for one such as me. I am but an ordinary man who finds himself in an extraordinary position. I am only here on sufferance because the Bishop of Hereford remains in Italy, though I am sure he will cross the sea before long to take up his post. Come, there is food and drink in the chamber. Everyone else is here so we can start."

Thomas tried to hear some note of criticism in the Archdeacon's words at their tardiness but detected none. Perhaps the man was all he claimed.

As they entered a large room which looked into the quadrangle, heads turned, though their entrance must have been expected. Thomas saw Sir Thomas Cornwell, whose features remained without expression. In contrast, Sir Richard Croft crossed to Thomas and shook his hand.

Thomas acknowledged the others, receiving a smile from Prioress Felicia Hughden. Her grey robe covered her from neck to toe but the hood was thrown back to display her luxuriant hair and beautiful face. The smile she offered carried a sultry undertone which was out of place. No doubt it was meant to remind Thomas of their previous encounter. A short man with a balding head stood beside her, their conversation interrupted by their entrance. By his dress and manner, Thomas assumed this was the other Archdeacon, that of Salop, John Martyn. A saintly man according to Bernard, but perhaps too much not of this world.

Unlike Lyman d'Alston, who took two paces towards them.

"What is Berrington doing here?"

His words elicited a smile from Amos Mapp, who

stood at his side, master and servant rarely straying far from each other.

"He was invited to observe as Justice of the Peace," said Bernard. "Just as you are invited as Coroner."

"I asked Prior Bernard to bring Thomas because he has a reputation as an honest and intelligent man," said Archdeacon Webb. "We need as many of those as we can find." There was a subtle insinuation in the words, implying that d'Alston might not meet those criteria himself. They brought a brief scowl to his face before he regained control of himself.

Thomas wondered exactly why Bernard had brought him to the meeting. He knew nothing of canon law, even less of the machinations of Church politics. He suspected he had been brought only to make some of the others uncomfortable. If so the ploy appeared to be working.

The remaining man Thomas did not know but assumed must be Abbot Haylewith of Hindwell Abbey. He was tall, skeletally thin, with greying hair that hung past his shoulders and a long white beard. He was dressed in a white robe that marked him as a Benedictine. When he approached he held his left hand out, and Thomas hesitated, unsure what he wanted him to do. He glanced at Bernard, who pursed his lips. Thomas gripped the Abbot's hand lightly and touched his lips to his ring of office.

"As the Deacon has already made clear, you are welcome here Thomas Berrington." The man's voice was cultured but carried a light patina of the accent of Wales.

Thomas took a seat to one side and listened as the

others spoke. On occasion one or other would turn and ask his opinion, which he offered without trying to expose his ignorance. As the discussion continued, it was obvious to him that Bernard's antipathy to being appointed was clear. To him, at least, but Thomas was unsure it was communicated strongly enough to the others.

Abbot Haylewith on the other hand indicated he would relish the position as head of Wigmore Abbey.

At one point Prioress Felicia said she would also be willing to serve as abbess of a combined male and female abbey by merging her own priory with Wigmore. Thomas was shocked at the brazenness of her approach.

Haylewith rose and dismissed the Prioress's claim, once more putting his own name forward.

"These are lawless times," he said. "Even more so in these borderlands. As Abbot of Hindwell, I have experience of the Welsh and their raids. They call themselves Christians, but it is a poor example of their faith when they raid and rape wherever they go. I have fought for God in Spain and the Holy Land. This abbey needs a strong hand. A strong master."

"And who will be abbot in your place?" asked Bernard.

"I propose appointing Madoc before I leave Hindwell. He is popular with the monks and a man who fought beside me when we defeated the heathen Moors." He glanced at Thomas, making it obvious he had heard of his past and found it wanting.

"You are quiet, Prior Bernard," said Archdeacon Webb. "Do you have a case to make for yourself?"

"Only that Wigmore is an old house, an exalted house, and deserves an abbot of unimpeachable honesty and holiness. Whether that is me or someone else, I leave it up to this conclave to decide. I am here to serve both you and God, nothing more."

The Archdeacon inclined his head in acknowledgement. "If there are no more names put forward I suggest we call for a vote at once. I propose two names only. Prior Bernard and Abbot Haylewith." The Deacon glanced at Prioress Felicia. "I am sorry, my dear, but much as your suggestion has merit, a man must rule at Wigmore. Thomas and Amos may leave us now, but do not stray far. Once we have concluded our discussions and voted, I will call you back to count the papers."

"Wigmore Abbey will be all the better for either man being appointed abbot," said Amos Mapp as they walked into the quadrangle.

"I know nothing of Abbot Haylewith. What is he like?" asked Thomas.

"Pious enough. He has some strange ideas but would be a good leader here."

Thomas was about to ask what the strange ideas were when Mapp strode off as a familiar figure entered through the gate. Brother Ambrose led his donkey and cart into the quadrangle. Mapp spoke briefly with him before moving on.

Ambrose saw Thomas but offered no indication of

welcome, which Thomas ignored as he crossed the grass to intercept the man.

"Your work went well?" he asked. "It was Hindwell you were visiting, was it not?"

"You have a good memory," said Ambrose.

"It was no more than three days since. I would like to believe I can recall events that far back. Can I ask you something which you may not answer if you prefer?"

Ambrose said nothing, which Thomas took as permission to continue.

"What is your opinion of Abbot Haylewith? I take it you are aware he and Prior Bernard are the two candidates for the position here at Wigmore?"

"I did not, because as you know I have been busy validating relics at both Hindwell and Elmbrook. Abbot Haylewith is a godly man, though stricter than Abbot John. Prior Bernard is also godly and strict in his own way, but he is not as hard-edged as Abbot Haylewith."

"Amos told me Haylewith has strange ideas. Do you know their nature?"

"I do not, but even if I did, it is not my place to reveal them to a lay person such as yourself."

Thomas believe himself chastised but pushed on anyway.

"And Prioress Felicia?"

Brother Ambrose stared at Thomas. "She could never be an Abbot."

"I am aware of that. I was asking your opinion of her. Is she also godly?"

"She is the Prioress of Elmbrook, so of course she is."

Thomas believed Ambrose was not saying everything he knew, but whatever opinion he withheld was unlikely to be forthcoming.

"How did your work go? Did you find authentic relics or not?"

"You do not believe, do you?" said Ambrose.

"I believe that someone claimed as the son of God may have died on a cross in the Holy Land, but what I cannot believe is how many pieces of that cross are held in abbeys, priories and churches through all of Christendom."

"And yet some will be part of the true cross. It is my job to authenticate the genuine and reject those that are not. England is fortunate in the number of relics it possesses." Brother Ambrose glanced around. "Come, I will show you something that may change your mind."

"And your cart?"

Brother Ambrose offered a smile, the first Thomas had seen on his face, and for a moment it softened him. "No one will touch my cart. It is safe here."

He strode away, and Thomas followed. They entered the main body of the church, where Ambrose turned and entered a narrow alcove where a heavy wooden door barred their way. He drew a key from his robe and opened the door. They entered a room where high windows allowed sunlight to spill in and illuminate a small altar on which lay glass cases. Within them, Thomas glimpsed bone, stone, wood and cloth. Ambrose approached with reverence. When he looked back his face shone with some inner exaltation.

"These two are the jewels in the crown of Wigmore Abbey's small collection of relics." He put his hand close to one of the glass cases but did not touch it. "This is a piece — a very small piece, I admit — of the one true cross on which our saviour died before rising again. The cross you claim does not exist."

Thomas leaned closer. The sliver of wood was more than a splinter, but not by much.

"I did not say it did not exist, only that it appears to have shattered into ten-thousand shards. Did you authenticate this?"

"I did, but not only me. Other authenticators agree with me. There are papers that confirm its authenticity in Rome and Jerusalem."

"And the other?" Thomas saw a small metal object in the case beside the sliver of the cross.

"It is the tip of a spear point that still bears the blood of Christ. Come closer, Thomas. Prior Bernard tells me you are a trained medical man so this may interest you."

Thomas peered at the object. Old and rusted, it looked ordinary, but he accepted it could have come from the tip of a spear. As for the rest of the claim ... he did not believe any of it, even if Brother Ambrose did.

"Every year on Easter Friday this is taken out and placed on the altar of the church. Every year drops of blood gather on the tip and drip into a bowl. Christ's blood, Thomas. Sacred blood. You must come and witness this miracle next year. Perhaps it will convert you, for I hear you have lived among the heathen too long to retain your faith. This will bring it back. One more miracle from God Almighty. You will come?"

Thomas considered only a moment before nodding. "Yes, I will come. Next Easter, you say?"

"Next Easter."

"What do you do when you discover relics that are false?"

"I take them to be checked by another authenticator. There is a man in Hereford who does the same work I do, though his is not as good as mine."

"And if he agrees?"

"Then they are destroyed. Metal is melted down. Wood is burned in a furnace. Bones are ground to dust."

The mention of bone sparked another question. "You know about the bones of children we discovered in the grave of my family when we opened them, but have you ever heard of anything similar in your travels? A man such as you, crisscrossing these borderlands, would be bound to hear of such a thing, would you not?"

Thomas saw Brother Ambrose's exaltation drain away, and once more he watched him close down his emotions and become the controlled individual he had first met. His words were stilted when he replied.

"If these children were buried in the graves of others then yes, I would. But I have not. I suspect someone wants to send a message to you. One only you might understand. Now, I wish to stay here and pray in the presence of God."

Thomas heard someone call his name and left Ambrose to his worship. He found Sir Richard Croft looking for him and followed him back inside. He was handed a small pot holding slips of paper, and went through them slowly. He handed each to Amos Mapp, who placed votes for Bernard to the right and votes for Haylewith to the left until all nine had been counted and Thomas knew he was wrong.

"I count five votes for Abbot Haylewith, four for Prior Bernard," said Thomas. "Do you concur, Amos?"

Mapp nodded in agreement.

"Pass me the papers," said Archdeacon Webb, who checked the numbers before nodding. "In that case, Abbot Haylewith is now Abbot of Wigmore Abbey." Archdeacon Webb turned to Bernard. "I ask a favour before you return to Lemster. It will take a few days for Abbot Haylewith to ensure continuity at Hindwell, so I would like you to remain as acting Abbot until he arrives. Do you agree?"

"As I said, William, I am here to serve. It would be my honour."

Once he had handed the papers to the Archdeacon, Thomas watched Abbot Haylewith, disturbed at the expression of exultation on his face, and knew Wigmore Abbey would never be the same again.

THIRTEEN

Thomas, Archdeacon John Martyn and Archdeacon William Webb remained in the room after the others left.

"Prior Bernard told me you have a matter you wish to discuss with me while I am here," said Webb.

Thomas had been thinking about riding home, his mind on the journey so that he frowned at the question.

"Something to do with bones placed in graves before their time?"

"Of course. My thanks."

"Do not thank us yet. John, will you stay? This may affect Shropshire as well as Herefordshire."

"I will be glad to. I was planning to stay tonight in any case. It is a goodly ride to Salop from here and the day is more than half gone already."

"In that case we should both stay. We will pray in the abbey church and talk over a good meal tonight."

"We may need to find somewhere else to eat. I recall how bland the food is here. Now, Thomas, let us find somewhere less ostentatious, and you can tell us what you want."

As Archdeacon Webb led the way, Thomas realised they were heading to the Abbot's office, surprised they regarded it as less ostentatious. Before entering, Archdeacon Webb asked a brother to bring wine and a little food. Once inside the room he took the Abbot's old chair, leaving John Martyn to pull a round-backed chair up to one side so that both he and William Webb were on the far side of the desk. Thomas remained standing.

"Tell us about these bones," said Archdeacon Webb. "And I suggest we use our names rather than titles. I always find it confusing when in John's company and we are both referred to as Archdeacon." He smiled. "So I am William. John is John, of course. And you, we know, are Thomas." Another smile. "Bernard also told us you are not much for the formalities and frequently forget to use his title. We have time to spare, and I find the reports of some of your actions rather amusing."

Thomas wondered what those reports might be and who had made them. But as he had been offered an opening, he decided to raise another matter first.

"Are either of you aware of the presence of a whorehouse at Elmbrook Priory?"

Both men stared at him, and then William Webb laughed. "Did you think we would not be? Of course we know of it and, to some extent, condone its presence. Even if we cannot be seen to do so. I take it our confession will not be broadcast beyond this room?"

"It will not," Thomas said. "But I am confused. I

always thought members of the church were meant to practice celibacy."

"Indeed we are. But you are a man of the world and know how men and women act. Women are temptresses and men weak. We have all been tempted. I know I have, and I am sure John has also. And you, Thomas? Have you ever lain with whores? For that is what we are speaking of, is it not?"

"It is, and yes I have on occasion, but not for some time now. It was in Spain and long ago, and the women never seemed like whores to me."

"Yet I expect you paid them."

"I did."

"And received a service in return."

Thomas nodded.

"Was this when you lived among the heathen?" asked John Martyn.

"When I lived among the Moors, but I would not call them heathen. I found them enlightened."

"They follow a false God, but you may harbour your opinion if you wish so long as you do not spread it in these parts. Now, these—" The Archdeacon broke off as a monk entered carrying wine, bread and hard cheese which he set on the desk before withdrawing.

Once the wine had been poured, Webb continued. "Tell us about the bones."

"What has Bernard told you already?"

"That you found remains in the graves of your brother and mother that should not have been there. He also told us he considers you a good friend."

"I have known him since I was a child. As for the bones, my companions and I have visited many places of burial within a day's ride and discovered two similar instances. Graves opened before their time and the bodies of children placed in them. My son discovered the body of a young boy who had lain in the ground no more than six weeks. My daughter knows of a grave that has been tampered with, and I would like to open it to see if foreign bones also lie there. I also seek advice on what to do with the bones we found on Eaton Hill. I asked the priest at Ludlow if he could find a resting place for them but he refused."

"Because they are, no doubt, unbaptised," said John Martyn.

"I do not know that for certain, but he claimed it would be the case. That the children were sinners and died before they could be baptised. But some of them were older than infants, I am sure. Are children not baptised as soon as possible?"

"If they are raised as Christians, then yes, but the old ways hold strong in some parts of this wild borderland. Tell us exactly what you want of us. I make no promise, but we will discuss it between ourselves and give you an answer later today if we can."

"I want two things. To open the grave Amal found in Garway, and to have permission — a note of authority would be best — to ask questions so I can search for any other instances."

"Did you say Garway?" asked William Webb. "I take it you refer to the church of St Michael there?"

Thomas gave a nod. "I believe that is what Amal called it. She says there is a small cemetery at the church and a burial ground nearby, but the disturbed grave is within the bounds of the churchyard. Do you know of this place?"

"I am Archdeacon of Hereford, so of course I know of it. As well as the rumours that swirl about it."

"Rumours of buried orphans?"

Webb smiled. "If only it were that simple. The Templars built St Michael's Church. If you visit there you will see what I mean. It is unlike any other church in Herefordshire, perhaps even in England."

"And the rumours?" Thomas asked.

"What do you know of the Templars?"

"Perhaps more than some, and with less fashioning of tales around them. There were many in Spain at one time. I even heard some lived as I did among the Moors. But they were disbanded over a century ago."

"They had grown too powerful and became a threat to Church authority." William Webb smiled. "It amuses me you use the word disbanded. They were destroyed. Hunted down and killed. One of the rumours about St Michael's is that the church was one of their last redoubts. Others refer to relics the Templars were believed to own."

"If you refer to the Grail," Thomas said, "I have never believed it existed; unlike some."

"Oh, it existed, of that there is no doubt. Whether it still does so is another matter. So yes, these rumours claim the Templars hid the Grail somewhere within the church or the grounds of St Michael's."

"This Grail would overshadow all other relics, would it not?" Thomas said. "Brother Ambrose showed me one today he says is a fragment of the true cross."

"Wigmore has a fine collection. But if these rumours regarding Garway are true — and I admit I do not believe them — but if they are, then whatever lies there, if it is ever uncovered, will be taken to Rome." William Webb shifted in his seat. "Now, we will ask you to withdraw while we discuss your request. Give us an hour, at least."

Thomas did not want to wait an hour for their deliberations but knew he had to. He had hoped to return home before dark, but already the day was fading towards an evening that glowed with a soft light. God's light, Brother Ambrose would claim, as would almost everyone within the confines of Wigmore Abbey. Thomas felt constrained by the holiness surrounding him, so went out through the gate, noting Brother Ambrose's cart remained where he had left it. And as promised it was untouched. In fact, Thomas noted most of the brothers made a point of avoiding it, even going out of their way to do so.

Beyond the abbey walls, Thomas strolled into the village which lay strung along the road that led from Hereford to Bishop's Castle and onward into north Powys. It was not as well-used as the road from Hereford to Lemster and Ludlow, but used well enough to have spawned inns and taverns along its route. Thomas went into the first and looked around before leaving. It was not suitable. He entered three others before he found what he was looking for: one that could host a pair of Archdeacons. Thomas's reason for doing this escaped him, but it amused him to think of their disparate group gathered together. He realised he had eaten nothing since he broke his fast that morning, so he sat and ordered bread with pork and a flagon of ale, which was sweet tasting.

As Thomas picked at his food, he thought of what the Archdeacons had revealed to him about St Michael's Church at Garway. He did not believe a word of it, but that did not mean others would not. And when the rumours concerned bones, Thomas wondered if they might also explain the theft of the skulls. He knew he needed the Archdeacons' permissions to continue his search. If the ideas forming in his mind bore any sense he would expect almost all of the graves at Garway to have been opened in search of what might lie there. It was not the fact of the cuckoo bones themselves as what they implied. Death. Deliberate, accidental or natural. And if deliberate, then he needed to know who had caused it. And then there was the matter of the missing skulls of his family.

He wanted to talk to Ambrose about what he had heard. Would someone such as him be able to authenticate the Grail? It would be fifteen hundred years old if it ever existed. Thomas did not believe such a thing could have survived through all those years. He looked up, wanting a distraction from his thoughts.

There were few others in the wide main room because most of the locals would work their fields until sunset. Then they were more likely to return to their own homes rather than spend money on food they could grow themselves. When he finished his ale, Thomas asked the goodwife if there was a private room which could be used to dine in and was told there was, but it would cost him dear, to which he slipped her a silver penny and received a smirk in return.

The hour had passed before he returned to the abbey where William Webb and John Martyn remained.

"I am afraid we have not reached a decision yet," said Webb. "We would like to speak more with you about what you believe is happening with these bones and who you suspect may be responsible for the burials. But it is growing late, and we both have a fierce hunger and thirst. Perhaps you can join us and we can talk over dinner. We have a few additional questions for you."

"I have found somewhere you can dine beyond the confines of the abbey if you wish it," Thomas said. "A fine inn only a short walk away at which I have made arrangements. I sampled a little of the food and ale, and they are good."

William Webb glanced at John Martyn. "It would be pleasant to breathe uncloistered air for an hour or two, yes?"

John Martyn nodded his assent. "Prior Bernard has told us a little of your past, but I would welcome hearing more. He tells us you are a confidant of the Spanish King and Queen."

"I know them, but confidant may be pressing our relationship too far. But I will be glad to tell you what I know." Thomas knew it would be a mistake to tell these men quite how close he was to Queen Isabel of Castile, but perhaps he could persuade them that the Moors were not the heathens they believed.

"Let us hear your tales while we eat," said John Martyn. "But first, a question that puzzles us both. It is one thing to discover bones left in graves that do not belong there. Another to want to investigate where they came from and who might have buried them." The man's eyes met Thomas's. "Why do you make this your business?"

It was a good question, and one Thomas had not given much thought to. It is what he did. Pick away at mysteries until he unravelled them to find their core.

"Partly it is personal," he said. "The first bones were left in the graves of my family. But then I grew curious about what they were doing there. The explanation may be innocent, but it has a feeling of aberration to it. And secrecy. Perhaps even of murder. So I intend to pick until I either have my answer or can pick no more."

"And if you uncover something you would rather have left lie?" asked John Martyn. "That whoever is behind this does what they do for innocent motives?"

"Then I will have my answer and can let the matter rest."

"Very well. Now let us eat for we both have great hunger."

Thomas was surprised at how quickly the time passed, and at what pleasant company both men were. They had removed their robes of office before leaving the abbey, so were regarded only as gentlemen at the inn, their faces unfamiliar. The evening turned sour when six people entered, saw them and approached.

"We went to the abbey for you, but they told us you had come here to eat." Lyman d'Alston looked around the room. "Is the food good?" Standing at his side was Prioress Felicia Hughden, who stood half a foot taller than him. A little behind, Amos Mapp stood next to Abbot Haylewith. At the rear were Sir Richard Croft and Sir Thomas Cornwell. Thomas assumed they had left the abbey but they could not have done. Only Prior Bernard was missing from the members of the conclave.

"Better fare than the abbey's," said Archdeacon Webb. "Will you join us? Thomas was about to leave, and I am sure the goodwife can find more chairs."

Thomas had said nothing about leaving, but assumed the eight of them wanted to speak together, so he made his farewells and went out into the night to discover that while they had been eating rain had arrived. It was not heavy but hinted that it might become so before dawn.

He saw no one else as he made his way to the abbey, where he enquired about his sleeping arrangements. Thomas found himself assigned to a single cell with a narrow bed, a bowl to wash with and a pot of water. A small bucket stood at the foot of the bed in case he needed to relieve himself. The window was narrow and unglazed, and when Thomas lay on the cot he listened to the fall of rain, allowing it to lull him into a dreamless sleep from which he was jerked awake by the sound of shouting and wailing, followed a moment later by the door to his cell being thrown wide.

A brother entered holding a wavering candle.

"The Abbot needs you to come at once. A brother has been killed."

Thomas rose and pulled his clothes on.

"Who?" he asked as he followed the man, hopping as he pulled his boots on.

"Brother Ambrose."

FOURTEEN

The brother who had fetched him pointed to an open doorway twenty paces distant, but the corridor was blocked by a seething mass of bodies which Thomas had to push through. He barely heard the chatter of suspicions, claims and counter-claims concerning who the killer might be. At the door, Thomas was relieved to discover only two people within. One of them was Prior Bernard. The other was dead, his body covered head to foot with a rough blanket. A lantern hung from a hook on the wall and a thin light entered through the single window to indicate dawn was not far off.

"Thank the Lord you are here, Tom. Close the door and come examine Ambrose."

"Who found him?" Thomas asked once the door was shut, cutting out the noise from beyond.

"Brother Caradoc, one of our Welsh brethren."

"Do you mention he comes from Wales for any specific reason?" Thomas asked.

Prior Bernard turned to look at him. "No, not at all. I merely..." Bernard shook his head. "I have no idea why I said it. Where he comes from is irrelevant."

"Where is he now?"

"I knew you would ask, and why, so he is locked in a cell with two brothers guarding the door. He is under no suspicion, but you can question him later if you want."

"My thanks. I will examine Ambrose now."

"I warn you, he is not a pretty sight."

"I am sure I have seen worse." Thomas crossed to the narrow bed. "You do not have to stay."

"I owe it to him." But Prior Bernard stepped back to a corner so he was as far from the body as he could get short of leaving the room.

Thomas drew the blanket aside and took a moment to study the damage done. As Prior Bernard had warned, it was not a pretty sight. Far from it.

"He would have made a great deal of noise," Thomas said without turning.

"Perhaps he did, but if so, no one admits to hearing it."

"Whoever did this would have been covered in blood when they left. I assume this Brother Caradoc was not?"

"You are correct."

"I still want to talk to him to find out what he heard and if he saw anyone else, and why he came to Ambrose's room in the middle of the night." Thomas looked around at the evidence of the attack. Blood on the walls, the cot, the floor. Some had even sprayed far enough to stain the small table beneath the window.

Thomas studied the wounds on Ambrose's body, trying to discern which might have been made first, but could not. However, it was clear which must have been made last — the one to his throat. It was deep, and would have brought death almost instantly. Which might explain the lack of noise. It was also, without doubt, the source of much of the blood that had sprayed everywhere. Thomas could not understand how such wounds had been made to Ambrose without him screaming. Ambrose's stomach had been cut open, spilling his organs out. Even viler, his manhood had been removed and pushed into his mouth.

"Is this significant?" Thomas asked without taking his eyes off Ambrose.

"I assume you mean his cock?"

Thomas nodded. "Do you think someone is trying to tell us Ambrose liked to do the same to other monks?" He turned to look at Prior Bernard, who was pale. "I assume such acts go on in an enclosed order such as an abbey or priory?"

"They have been known to, yes. Whether here or not I do not know, but I will not countenance it at Lemster and would be surprised to learn Ambrose practiced such deviancy."

"I imagine you would, but you and everyone else must know such things happen. I barely knew Ambrose, but I would not suspect him of such acts. Though he would be aware of most of the sins in the houses he visited, would he not?"

"He is ... was an intelligent man."

"How many monks reside at Wigmore Abbey?"

"In excess of three hundred, plus the same number of lay brothers and sisters."

"And there were guests staying the night?"

"There were, as well you know, because you dined with some of them."

"Only the two Archdeacons, both of whom I would call civilised men. When the others came I was dismissed. I suspect they wanted to discuss your position now."

"I already know my position, Tom. I am a caretaker here for a week, two at most, then return to Lemster Priory. For which I will be profoundly grateful. Do you think you can find out who killed Ambrose?"

"I can try but will need help. Send a message to Burway to ask Jorge to come. He can speak with this Caradoc when he arrives, but almost certainly the man is innocent. Tell Will to accompany Jorge. If he is not there, send for Usaden. Either will keep him safe on the journey if anyone learns he has been sent for."

"Why would he be in danger? I have never met a more amenable man in my life."

"Whoever killed Ambrose will not want to be found out, and if there is one thing Jorge excels at above all else, it is the teasing out of a lie from a man or woman."

"He always told me he excelled at more amatory arts."

"One often leads to the other. I have never seen a woman Jorge has not perturbed. It is because he sees into their very souls and listens to what remains unsaid between their words. If there is anything to be found out, he will uncover it."

"I take it you do not believe a woman could do this?"

"It is unlikely, but I take it Prioress Felicia stayed?"

"She did, also the others with her. Even the Coroner and Mapp, though their home is but a few hours ride away."

"Except it was dark, and rain had come."

"Do you suspect any of them? I know Felicia is unusual, but she is no killer."

"I suspect this is the work of either a brother or a lay brother," Thomas said. "The damage done and the nature of it would lead me to believe it was done out of jealousy. A lover's quarrel, perhaps, or a jilted lover's revenge."

"You talk of blasphemous acts, and I have told you Ambrose was not like that."

"The evidence of his injuries would indicate otherwise. They also point to these acts taking place either here or in one of the other houses. Do you have any other guests staying from them?"

"I would not know, but I will have the guest master check his rolls and let you know. With God's good grace, it will be a stranger who did this and it is nothing to do with what you accuse Ambrose of."

"Perhaps," Thomas said. "Was anything taken from this room before I arrived?"

"Nothing."

"Then who took Ambrose's robe? It is not here. There is nothing here other than the body, and whoever killed him took the knife away. It would be worth setting some brothers to search the abbey and grounds to see if it can be found." Thomas walked the room, examining the blood stains. He spent some time at the door, searching for any sign of a handprint. Whoever had killed Ambrose might have left some sign, but he found nothing.

"I would like to examine his cart. Do you know where it is?"

"I do not, but I expect it will be in the stables. Unless it has stood out in the rain all night, but someone will have taken care of his donkey and no doubt the cart as well."

"There is nothing more I can do here, so I will go and see if I can find the cart. What will happen to Ambrose now?"

"He will be prepared and laid to rest here at Wigmore."

"He had no home abbey or priory?"

"He was born in the village of Elmbrook, but his place was here. Did you not know that?"

"How could I? But it is good he will lie in a place he belongs. I will cover him again. You must ensure no one looks beneath the blanket when they take him out."

"I will have a litter brought. And when you are done, come and find me. I have something for you."

"Send that message to Jorge," Thomas said, before turning to leave.

Brother Ambrose's cart was in the stables where he expected to find it, his donkey standing with eyes open but fast asleep. Thomas wondered if he would miss his master or not. Wondered if Ambrose had been a good master. The man had appeared to him as if made of sharp edges and hard-held views, with no bend in him. That did not sit well with him showing love, even if it was love for his own kind. No doubt Jorge would be able to explain everything to him when he arrived.

Thomas climbed to the bed of the cart and perched on the side, the leather bindings creaking as he did so. The boxes he had observed when he met Ambrose on the road to Hindwell remained neatly stacked. He had been curious about their contents but not asked. Now there was no one to stop him, so he leaned over and examined one of the smaller boxes. It was closed with a catch but had no lock. Thomas opened the box and peered inside. There were small pieces of bone, a tooth, two toenails, and a small metal nail almost rusted away. Relics, or false relics? There was no indication on the box which they might be, but Thomas assumed them false for Ambrose to have taken them away from whichever abbey or priory he had found them at. As Thomas went to close the lid he stopped, noticing a small wooden panel on one side. He used his fingernails to ease it open and drew out a tiny slip of paper. When he turned it over he saw the single word: *Hindwell*, written in a meticulous script.

So, he thought, false relics Ambrose had failed to validate. He slipped the paper back behind the panel and snapped it shut, then closed the box before moving to one of the larger ones, wondering what relic would warrant something its size. When he opened it, he felt the breath leave him because what he saw there was the body of a young girl wrapped in linen. He reached out to touch her face, then drew back. It felt too much like sacrilege to do so. He took a breath, steadied himself and tried again. He needed to know. When he lifted her arm by the wrist he found no resistance, which meant rigor had come and gone. The girl had been alive less than two days ago. Thomas estimated her age at less than a year but more than nine months. She would have survived the dangers of childbirth and the first few months, and been on the cusp of becoming her own person. Even in death she was pretty, and he wiped tears from his eyes at the waste of such a life. Despite his reluctance, he checked her carefully, then turned her over, but found no signs of violence. Her death had come about through natural causes. It answered one question about the bones he had found — that the deaths might all be of natural causes.

Only as Thomas arranged the young girl back in the box did he notice the small silver crucifix hung on a silver chain around her neck. It sparked a memory that he had to search for. It came to him only slowly, and even then he was unsure. He thought Amal had shown him a similar cross which had been in the grave of his mother on Eaton Hill. Thomas stared at the cross for a moment, unsure whether it was significant or not. In the end, he decided it was impossible to know without further information, which he might never have.

He ran his fingers around the edges of the box but found no hidden compartment which might hold a scrap of paper identifying who she was and where she had come from. Not that he needed either to know that Brother Ambrose was the person, perhaps the only person, taking the bodies of children and burying them in the graves of others. But was he the cause of death of the children, or only the person tasked with their disposal?

Thomas opened another of the larger boxes but found it empty. Did that mean it awaited another body? Did it mean Ambrose might, on occasion, dispose of two bodies at the same time? Is that what he had done behind Thomas's old house on Eaton Hill? Except as the idea came to him, he dismissed it as impossible. Those bones had lain in the ground longer than Ambrose had been alive. Had there been someone before him? Was it a task passed down through the generations, and if so, how and why?

Thomas sat up, aware of a deep ache in his body. His sleep had been disturbed again, and although he had solved the mystery of who was burying the bodies, it only raised several more. Someone had murdered Ambrose. Had his death been connected to the bodies he had disposed of, or was there another reason? Could it be both? The placing of his cock in his own mouth hinted at a darker motive, unless that was meant to lead them in the wrong direction.

Thomas knew he needed Jorge.

He dropped from the cart, snuffed out the lamp and returned to the abbey buildings, hoping Prior Bernard might have returned to the Abbot's office because he needed to tell him what Ambrose had been doing and judge his reaction.

FIFTEEN

Thomas found Bernard on the far side of the abbey where a group of monks were struggling to raise a heavy stone slab. A wooden coffin sat on the damp grass to one side, presumably holding Ambrose's body. Felicia Hughden stared down at it, her face contorted with grief. Abbot Haylewith stood beside her, one arm around her shoulder as he offered words of comfort.

"I have found something on Ambrose's cart you need to see," Thomas said to Bernard, his voice low so no one else could hear.

"What?"

When Thomas told him Prior Bernard said, "I do not believe you."

"I can show you if you are finished here."

Prior Bernard looked at the brothers struggling to raise the thick stone slab that sealed the grave and suppressed a smile. "I expect I am finished now. One of the few advantages of higher office is you avoid the heavy lifting. I also have something Ambrose left me to give to you."

"Why would he want me to have something of his?"

"It is a sealed letter, so I have no idea of its contents, but it is addressed to you. You can read it once you have shown me what you think you have found."

Thomas led the way across the cloister and out towards the stables. As they passed, brothers each nodded their head at the temporary Abbot in a sign of respect.

"They like you," Thomas said. "Will they welcome Abbot Haylewith in the same manner?"

"They barely know me. Their respect is for the position, not the man, and they will offer the same to the new Abbot as they do to me."

As they entered the stable Thomas stopped so fast that Prior Bernard walked into him.

"It is gone," Thomas said. "When I left, the cart was in the middle of the stable, and now it is gone." He glanced into the stalls. "Together with Ambrose's donkey." Thomas looked around but there was no one else in the stable.

"What was it you wanted to show me?" asked Bernard.

"I found the body of a young girl in a wooden casket on the back of Ambrose's cart."

Bernard stared at Thomas. "Are you absolutely sure of this? Perhaps it was some joke being played on you."

"It is in poor taste if it was when the cart's owner lay dead with his guts spilling out."

"I am sorry, Tom, but I find it hard to believe. Are you implying Ambrose had something to do with this girl's death?"

"Do you believe that I saw what I did?"

"I know you as an honest man, but I also knew Ambrose as an honest man. A good man. I believe none of what is implied here. Not what the killer did with his cock. Not the presence of a corpse on his cart. They are attempts to accuse him of unnatural acts."

"Attempts by his killer to taint his reputation?" Thomas said. "How long has Ambrose served in his role as an authenticator of relics?"

Bernard frowned at the question. "Twenty years. He had fifteen years when he started his training."

"Who trained him? You?"

"Of course not. The previous holder of the post did so."

"And who was that?"

"A brother by the name of Gareth Anwyn. He had been an authenticator for forty-five years. Who trained him I do not know. You may even have met him at the priory when you were a lad. He was a frequent visitor."

"Was Ambrose his only student?"

"There was one other."

"Who?"

Bernard stared at Thomas for a moment before saying, "Father Owain Haylewith. He was a parish priest at the time."

"Who is now the new Abbot of Wigmore."

Bernard nodded.

"Both were trained to authenticate relics?"

"They started their training at the same time, though Haylewith was the older by more than ten years. He had returned from fighting in Spain. It soon became clear he was not suited to the job. He was too impatient. Too quick to say something was real when it was not. Ambrose was different. Not an easy man to like, driven by his work, but no one doubted the authenticity of what he approved."

"And unambitious?" Thomas said.

"He was content in what he did and never sought advancement. Unlike Haylewith. But I believe there was always a connection between the two of them despite the difference in their positions. Perhaps it came from those early months when they trained together."

"Did Haylewith come from Wales, like Madoc?" Thomas asked. "Owain is not an English name."

"He did, but his first position in the county was at St Michael's Church in Garway. This was after he failed as an authenticator."

"The Templar church?" Thomas tried not to make a connection in his mind, but it was hard not to after what Archdeacon Wells had told him over their meal.

"At one time, yes, but that was a century ago and the Templars no longer exist. I have heard rumours about the church but dismiss them. There are always rumours."

"Do you think Haylewith believed them?"

"Ask him, not me."

"He and Madoc are close, are they not?"

"He brought Madoc to Hindwell a few years after he

was appointed Abbot there. I heard they fought together, despite Madoc being younger. Do you see some conspiracy here, Tom? Because if so you are wrong. Haylewith is strange, but a good abbot. Madoc can be harsh and believes the Church too soft, but he is no killer."

"He was unwelcoming when I visited Elmbrook."

"Madoc has a tendency to bully people, but never carries through on his threats."

"Some of those men dressed as soldiers were with him. What is their purpose?"

"They protect the Church. They impose order, but are not the only such group of men. You know I fought for my God, as did Haylewith and Madoc. As well as many others who became priests, priors, abbots and bishops if they lived to return home."

"Which you three did." Thomas looked past Bernard, trying to conjure some connection between these men and the death of Ambrose, but if one existed it was beyond his wit to find it. Perhaps it was nothing more than it appeared. A lover's quarrel taken too far. But if so it did nothing to help Thomas's search for the skull of his mother. With Ambrose gone the trail was broken.

"You are angry now, Tom? I can see it on your face. You want to hit somebody or something."

"Ambrose is dead, and he was the link to the buried orphans and missing skulls. I was too late in discovering his involvement, and now there is nothing for me to pursue. So yes, I want to punch something. But not you."

"Good. Then let us go inside and I will give you

Ambrose's message. Perhaps there will be something in it to help you."

"Soon," Thomas said. "Go inside, Bernard. I want to stay here a little longer to make sure there is nothing I have missed. I will find you when I am done."

When he was alone, Thomas moved slowly through the stables. He saw where Ambrose's cart had sat overnight from the indentations made on the floor. He tried to recall which stall the donkey had been housed in but could not decide between the three empty ones. He went to his hands and knees and put his cheek against the ground, which smelled of straw and dung. He could make out depressions where the cart had been led away, but when he rose and went outside he lost all trace of them.

He was still standing there when a man came towards the stable, a lay brother from his clothing.

"What are you doing?"

"Do you work in the stable?" Thomas asked.

"I do."

"And did you see the cart Ambrose brought in here?"

"I would soon lose my job if I did not notice something as obvious as that."

"And you notice it is now gone?"

"Have I not already told you I am not an idiot?"

"Did you move it?"

"Not me. That was the Coroner and Amos Mapp. They came in after all the fuss about Brother Ambrose's death. I heard the Coroner tell Amos Mapp to take the cart back to Lemster as evidence."

"Did you not try to stop him?"

"Why would I do that? Lyman d'Alston is not the kind of man someone such as me questions. And Amos Mapp can be a hard man. I stayed where I was in the corner and hoped they did not know I was there."

Thomas wondered what Amos Mapp was doing taking the cart. Had he also opened the casket and discovered its contents, or was he merely removing the cart of a dead man? Thomas thought of his meeting with Ambrose on the hill above Wigmore. He wished he had taken more notice of what lay in the bed of his cart then, but at that time had no suspicion of the man. Now he believed Ambrose was the means by which the dead children were distributed throughout the district. It made Thomas question who else might know of what he had been doing. If others did, might that be the reason the man was killed? But to find that out Thomas would first need to know who they were. There were too many questions, but he was determined to start seeking out answers as soon as he was finished at Wigmore.

Thomas offered his thanks to the lay brother and turned back to the abbey, which sat confidently at the foot of the hills that rose to the west. A place of refuge, worship and wealth. He hoped Prior Bernard would be in his office and walked faster, curious about what Ambrose's note might contain.

Thomas caught sight of Prior Bernard returning to the cloister from the cemetery and trotted to catch him up.

"Amos Mapp was seen taking Ambrose's cart from the stables. Can you think of any reason why he would do such a thing?"

"I told you they were friends, of a sort, also colleagues, of a sort. Perhaps Amos wanted to protect Ambrose's reputation."

"What manner of colleagues?" Thomas asked.

"Do you ever cease asking questions, Tom?"

"Only when I know everything I need to, and I never seem to reach that point."

"Ambrose, as you know, was the validator of relics in the district. Amos Mapp forged a relationship with him for two reasons. The first was that he sold relics and used Ambrose to validate them. A note of authenticity from him meant he could charge more for them."

"You said two reasons. What was the other?"

"Amos destroyed the relics Ambrose rejected. He burned what he could and melted down what he could not. Then he provided documents stating what measures he had taken so they could never be sold again."

"Archdeacon Webb told me about the destruction of fake relics but did not say who destroyed them. Did anyone check Mapp actually did what he was meant to?" Thomas asked.

"The Coroner did. He would observe this destruction from time to time and apply his own seal to Amos's documents to prove he had done so. It was all perfectly valid."

"Do you think Mapp knew of Ambrose's other activities?"

"I doubt it. If I did not then I am sure Amos Mapp would not either. I still cannot believe what you accuse Ambrose of."

"Then perhaps I am wrong, but the evidence is now missing, taken by Amos Mapp who, as you say, had a working relationship with him. If he took the cart it might not have been to protect evidence but to hide it. I intend to go and ask him as soon as Jorge arrives and I can finish up here. You did send the message I asked you to?"

"If I were a man allowed to curse, Tom, I would be cursing you now. Do you think I would forget? I sent it at once and expect your companion is at this moment reading it."

"My thanks, Bernard, and my apologies. These are not easy times for you, I know."

They passed from the cloister and turned into the door that led to the Abbot's quarters.

"I apologise as well, Tom. You are right, these are not easy times, and I have allowed my thoughts to stray from God. I did not think I wanted to be Abbot, but was surprised when I was not chosen. It is immodest of me to think that way, I know, and it has filled my head with why I should have felt disappointment."

"Might it be something to do with who has been made Abbot?"

"Neither would it be modest of me to reply to your question. Here we are." Prior Bernard opened the door to the Abbot's rooms, familiar to Thomas now but somehow diminished without its original inhabitant. "Now, where did I put that note?" Prior Bernard started searching through stacks of papers on the desk. "Ah, here it is." He held a single folded sheet of paper out to Thomas.

There was a blob of wax closing it, but it lacked the adornment of a seal. Thomas assumed the Abbot of Wigmore would have his own; Prior Bernard, too.

Thomas stared at the unopened paper, unsure what he expected to find. "When did he give you this?"

"Do you recall when we were with Abbot John as he faded and he sent for Brother Ambrose to hear his confession?"

"You do not think the two deaths are connected, do you?"

"Of course not. You know Abbot John died of natural causes. But the day after hearing Abbot John's confession brother Ambrose came to Lemster Priory and handed me that note. He told me not to open it but to give it to you under one condition, and one condition only. His death. But not any ordinary death. I could pass the letter to you only if he died at the hand of someone else."

"Why me?" Thomas asked.

"He knew what you do, Tom. You hunt down killers. You punish them, through the law or otherwise."

"Ambrose barely knew me. It was only yesterday I had the longest conversation with him I have ever had."

"I may have spoken of you to him. He asked who you were after that first time you met and why I was so forgiving of your obvious sins."

"I have no sins," Thomas said.

"I expect you are not aware of them, but it is no matter, for they are all small sins and soon forgiven once you allow the light of God into your heart. Open it but not here. I do not want to know what it contains. If it points to Ambrose's killer I will have to act, and I have no wish to do that. You are better at retribution than me."

"I prefer to think of it as justice," Thomas said.

"Justice, then. Read the note, do what you are best at and find out who killed Ambrose. I will leave you alone while you do so." Prior Bernard started for the door.

"No, stay. I can read the note without you seeing it, and if there is something you should know it will save me having to find you again."

Prior Bernard took the comfortable chair behind the Abbot's desk. "I will close my eyes so I cannot see."

"Try not to fall asleep."

"I cannot promise that."

Thomas twisted the paper to break the wax and unfolded it. He expected tiny writing that might fill the page. Instead, he saw only a few words, but the hand was clearly the same as the small note Thomas had found attached to the box on the cart.

He read them then looked up to find Prior Bernard's eyes open.

"Do you have any idea what he has written here?"

"None at all. Is it about the Abbot?"

"Yes and no. It refers to the confession he heard, which surprises me, but it also contains his own."

"If Ambrose has told you what the Abbot confessed

then perhaps he deserved to die. The sanctity of confession is one of the cornerstones of the Catholic Church, and whatever is spoken can never be told to anyone. Only God hears."

"It does not say anything about what Abbot John confessed, only that he sinned greatly." Thomas waved the paper. "No more than that."

"I expect Ambrose trusted you to find out what manner of sin that might be."

"Perhaps. This is more than anything Ambrose's confession, and why he did not speak it to you I do not know."

"If it truly is his confession, then you cannot speak it to me, either, Tom."

"Except I do not believe in confession, not of that kind. Let me call this an admittance of guilt."

"In which case, perhaps I can hear what is written there."

It was clear Prior Bernard was curious, but he might be disappointed.

"Ambrose admits to disposing of the bodies of dead children but claims to be innocent of killing them. He buried them to save their souls. He does not say who is responsible for their deaths but tells me to look to the west. To question Prioress Felicia Hughden if I want to know what happened to them, and why he was chosen to do what he did. He tells me Abbot John also knew about them, which was the nature of his confession. Ambrose asks to be absolved."

"Abbot John lies in his tomb now. I spoke the words

of prayer over him, so he is absolved of any sin. But if Ambrose spoke the truth he is guilty of sin whether he killed the children or not. He should have come to me and confessed his actions."

"And what would you have done?"

"I truly do not know. Do you plan to speak to the Prioress? Should I come with you?"

"Do you want to? Is she still in the abbey?"

"I believe she left with Abbot Haylewith and Madoc once Ambrose was interred. But I will accompany you to Elmbrook if I can be of any use. Abbott Haylewith will take up his position here soon and I will return to Lemster Priory. Before that happens, I would like to find out what lies behind Ambrose's death. We can leave today as soon as your friend arrives and you have told him what needs to be done."

"I want Jorge to speak with every brother and lay brother who was here and judge if any of them killed Ambrose or knew of who might have wanted to."

"You trust him to do this without your presence?"

"More than any man in the world."

SIXTEEN

Thomas went to speak with Brother Caradoc, unable to wait until Jorge arrived. He was shown to the cell where he was kept, one of Madoc's warrior monks standing over him as he sat on the narrow cot. He glanced up as Thomas entered, his face grey with fatigue and worry.

"You can leave us now," Thomas said to the guard.

"I was told to stay with him."

"And I am telling you to leave. Do you not trust me to keep him captive?"

The man opened his mouth to object again then snapped it shut. He turned and left the room, leaving the door open. Thomas crossed and shut it before pulling up a three-legged stood and sat in front of Caradoc.

"Why am I being held prisoner?" said the man. "I did not kill Ambrose."

"I am not saying you did, but you found him and I have questions for you. Answer them truthfully and you can return to your life of quiet contemplation."

Caradoc said nothing, waiting for whatever questions Thomas had.

"Why did you go to his cell?"

"Because of the noise. I heard a raised voice. A scream."

"It woke you?"

"I was already awake. I needed to piss. I was on my way back when I heard the noise and went to find out what was going on. Sometimes brothers have night-mares. I thought it might be that and I could help."

Thomas stared at Caradoc, thoughts sparking through his mind, most of them senseless.

"He was alone when you found him?"

Caradoc nodded.

"Did you see anyone else when you went to his cell?"

Caradoc shook his head.

"Was Ambrose dead when you reached him?"

Caradoc nodded. Thomas was growing tired of his lack of a verbal response so asked a question that required one.

"Tell me what you saw when you entered the cell."

"I saw Ambrose, of course. And blood. A great deal of blood."

"Was there a knife?"

Caradoc started to shake his head, then saw Thomas's expression. "I did not see one."

"Or his robe?"

This time Cardoc could not stop himself and shook his head.

"Did you put his cock in his mouth?"

Caradoc's eyes widened in shock. "Of course not! It was already there when I arrived."

"You said you heard a voice and screams."

"One scream," said Caradoc.

"The same voice, or a different one? Did you recognise it?"

"No. But I believe it was Ambrose who screamed. Do not ask why I think so because I am unable to say, but it makes sense, does it not, considering what was done to him?"

"You knew Ambrose?"

"Everyone knows Ambrose."

"Did you like him?"

Caradoc frowned at the question. "He was Ambrose," he said. "He was a difficult man to like, but also not unlikeable. Did you know him, sir?"

"Not well, but I think I understand what you mean. You are sure you saw no one at all? Perhaps someone as you went to the privy?"

"Nobody at all, sir."

"How soon after you called out did someone arrive?"

Caradoc looked off into the air as he thought. "Almost at once. Madoc was first, then one of his soldiers, and then ... I think then Prior Bernard."

Thomas could think of nothing else for the moment so told the man he could go, but not to stray far from Wigmore Abbey.

"Where would I stray to, sir?" said Caradoc before he left the room.

Thomas stayed a moment longer. He examined the

cot Caradoc had been sitting on, then turned the mattress over, but found no trace of blood. He believed the man innocent, and fortunate not to have arrived sooner or he might also lie dead.

It was mid-morning before Jorge arrived and Thomas could brief him, by which time Prior Bernard had changed from his habit and wore clothes more suited to the soldier he had once been. Perhaps, Thomas thought, they were indeed the clothes he had worn when he fought in the Holy Land and Spain.

Will had accompanied Jorge, and Thomas told him to stay close in case whoever killed Ambrose tried to attack Jorge. They left for Elmbrook Priory as fresh rain threatened from the west and blustery winds tugged at their jackets. Bernard rode a sturdy grey that looked capable of good speed if required. Thomas rode Ferrant but knew he might have to replace him with a younger horse before long. Ferrant could live out what time was left to him grazing on lush riverside grass in the meadow at Burway. There were times Thomas wondered if he should be put out to pasture as well and pass the reins over to Will and Amal. But not while he did not yet feel his years.

"Do you know Elmbrook well?" Thomas asked. He was wondering if going there was the right thing to do at the moment. He wanted to question Amos Mapp to find out why the man had taken Ambrose's cart. He also wanted to talk to Madoc, wondering how he had managed to be the first to respond. But Ambrose's letter felt the more important. Unless it only seemed that way because the man was dead.

"It falls within the view of Wigmore, as does Lemster Priory, but so do many other holy houses. But yes, I know it well enough, of course."

"You have visited?"

"On occasion."

Thomas tried to hear some trace of deception in Bernard's response but found none. He suspected he would have to be blunter to elicit more.

"And Prioress Felicia?"

"Yes, I know her, which should come as no surprise."

"When I first met her she had consumed the mushrooms that open the mind."

"For a woman of the Church, Felicia has some strange notions. I am afraid I may have told her of the mushrooms, as I did you when you were a lad. I did not know she would come to love them as much as she does."

"Do you know why that is?" Thomas asked. "Most people never experience their effect. Those that do repeat it only occasionally. Someone who uses them often might be trying to escape from something. Do you have any idea what that might be?"

"Assuming you are right in your assumptions, Tom, perhaps she regrets having the bordel at Elmbrook."

"It surprises me you say that."

"I was merely trying to offer you an answer, but it would also surprise me if that was the reason. The Church sanctions what goes on there, so I keep my opinion to myself."

"Archdeacon Webb told me he believes Elmbrook provides a much-needed service."

Prior Bernard laughed. "I had forgotten you were now best friends with both of the Archdeacons."

"Hardly friends. They sent me away as soon as their real friends arrived, which included Felicia Hughden, Abbot Haylewith and Madoc, Cornwell and Croft, as well as the Coroner and Amos Mapp. All of whom spent the night at Wigmore Abbey, I assume."

"They were given rooms in the guest house. It is more comfortable than the cell you were assigned."

"And separate from the main building?"

"It is set within the village, so yes. Are you implying something?"

"Only that whoever killed Ambrose would have been nearby. It did not have to be someone from within the abbey grounds itself. Caradoc told me the first person to respond to his shout was Madoc. Which would mean he was closer than the guest house."

"Obviously. But it could have been some passing stranger. You cannot suspect anyone who was at the conclave?"

"I see no motive for any of them to want Ambrose dead. What was done indicates rage. Rage at Ambrose. Tell me more about him if you can."

"Ambrose was a private man — as private as a monk can be when we live cheek by jowl with their brothers. He was clever and diligent, as I told you, but kept very much to himself. All the more reason why I believe what was done to him was intended to lead us wrong."

"I agree with you. Jorge met him briefly when you and he visited, so I asked him about it before we left today. If anyone could tell Ambrose's true nature Jorge would be that man. He told me neither men nor women beguiled Ambrose. I take it he validated the relics you have at Lemster Priory?"

"The ones we acquired since he took up his post, yes. He also rejected some of those authenticated by the previous holder of his post."

"Do you know who selected him?"

"It would have been the Archbishop of Hereford. At that time, it was a man by the name of Thomas Mylling."

Prior Bernard looked across the hills again and Thomas allowed him the time to examine his memories. They were following the roadway where Thomas had met Ambrose leading his cart. Had he been coming from Elmbrook Priory or further west? As far west as Hindwell Abbey, the home of Abbot Haylewith? Thomas wondered if he was doing no more than plucking suspects from empty air.

The valley they followed narrowed. To the left, a sheep-dotted hillside rose to a rounded crest. To their right, the higher peak of Woodhampton Hill rose, also grazed by sheep which no doubt belonged to Wigmore Abbey and were the source for much of its wealth. The promised rain offered its first kiss as a sharp squall scurried along the valley. Whether it was that which prompted Prior Bernard to speak or he had reached some internal conclusion, Thomas did not know.

"Thomas Mylling was unusual as a bishop in that he was previously an abbot, which is a rare promotion. Perhaps even a demotion, I am not sure. But he was a scholar and an honest man. I met him several times, and we got on well together. It is he who would have chosen Ambrose and Haylewith to train as authenticators. He died ten years ago to be replaced by Edmund Audley, who was also a good man but less of a scholar. He would have known Ambrose but had little to do with him. When he died, the current incumbent was installed. An Italian by the name of Adriano Castellesi, who has never visited the city. It seems he prefers to dabble in the politics of Rome and gather appointments to himself. Which is why William Webb attended the conclave. He would also know Ambrose, as would all the other members of the Church who were there. I think you can safely rule both Archdeacons Webb and Martyn out of your list of suspects, Tom."

"As I can you."

"I am so relieved." Prior Bernard smiled as more rain arrived, more than a squall this time, and he raised the hood of his cloak, but they were riding into it and it did little good. Thomas did not bother, accepting the weather for what it was. A sign he now lived in England.

"That still leaves too many suspects for my liking," Thomas said. "I would be minded to exclude Felicia Hughden as well, but as you say she is strange, and I would not rule her out altogether."

"Felicia will not have killed Ambrose."

"I saw she was upset at his graveside when I came to find you. Haylewith was comforting her, which seemed a strange thing for him to do."

"They have always been close, and Ambrose's death

was taken hard by Felicia. At least her grief rules her out from suspicion. There are three-hundred-odd brothers under my temporary stewardship at Wigmore. Almost any one of them might have killed him. Until we know the *why* we will not know the *who*."

"Which is why Jorge is now speaking to every one of them."

"He will not finish that task today," said Bernard.

"He will not. I hope you can provide him with a bed for the night."

"He and your son can use the guest accommodation. I can hardly put any of you in the cell Ambrose was in, can I?"

"Jorge may have already found our culprit," Thomas said.

"I hope he has. From what was done to him, it would seem likely it is someone from the abbey."

"But not a lover's argument."

"Merely an argument," said Prior Bernard. "Which, if true, makes me sad at the triviality of his death."

"I believe what Jorge told me, but are such liaisons common within an enclosed house?"

"They happen, of course they do. Jorge would tell you the same. I hear he regaled Richard Croft with tales of the harem in Granada, much of which concerned the love lives of the concubines."

"I once lived with a concubine," Thomas said, aware he had been distracted, but they still had half their journey left to draw the conversation back to what he wanted to discuss.

Prior Bernard glanced sharply at him. "That must have been a pleasurable experience."

"In the physical sense, yes, but not in companionship. I believe I told you I married her half-sister."

"Ah, yes, I think you did, but not that one of them was a concubine. Or were they both?"

"Only the one."

"Do you suspect any of those who stayed in the guest house last night could be guilty of murder?" asked Prior Bernard.

"It would be a mistake to rule any of them out, but I consider it unlikely. The manner of Ambrose's death, as you say, hints at someone close to him, both emotionally and physically."

"You said Madoc was the first to respond when Caradoc called out. Do you suspect him?"

"In your opinion, is he capable?"

"I do not like the man. Never have. Never will. But being unlikeable is no admission of guilt. But I do wonder what he was doing close by. It might be completely innocent, and most likely is. I cannot confront him, but you might be able to find what he was doing there."

"I will need to wait for him to be alone, with none of his warrior monks around him."

Bernard laughed. "I think you more than capable of handling them, even without the help of your son and Usaden."

They were ascending Deepmore Hill now, and from its brow they looked down on Elmbrook Priory. Small.

Compact. Nestled around with hills which seemed to embrace it.

"You told me Ambrose was born at Elmbrook," Thomas said. "In the village, or in the priory?"

"How would I know that?" said Bernard.

Except when they reached the priory, it was to be informed that Prioress Felicia was resting. Apparently, the sister informed them, she had been disturbed during the night. She stared at Bernard as she told them, as if perhaps he was to blame. It was clear, despite him being dressed as an ordinary man, she knew who he was. Thomas too, and he wondered if she had been one of the sisters he had met on his previous visit, or even one of those who sold their bodies.

"Did Abbot Haylewith and Madoc accompany the Prioress when she returned?" Thomas asked.

"They did, then the Abbot went on his way. The road from Wigmore to Hindwell passes Elmbrook and he is a frequent visitor. I believe Prior Madoc may have stayed."

Once more, Thomas tried to find something more beneath her words or in the way she held herself, but there was nothing. Jorge would have seen it if there was, but he was not Jorge.

"Do you know how long before the Prioress might see us?"

"I do not, sir, but suspect it will be at least several hours. She asked not to be disturbed. Shall I fetch someone to care for your horses? I can arrange for food and mead if you wish. Or something else, perhaps?"

Now the message came across clearly.

"Just the horses and the food."

"You are both welcome to join us for Vespers once you have refreshed yourselves. I will arrange for a private room you can use."

With that, the sister strode away across the grass.

"You did hear what she offered us," Thomas said.

"Of course. She was blatant with it, too, but that is not surprising here."

"Perhaps both Jorge and I are wrong," Thomas said. "Ambrose may have partaken of the temptations on offer here, and what was done to him was merely cruel and had no message."

"Oh, I think you are correct in your initial thinking, Tom. I told you I had no suspicion regarding Ambrose's nature. Whoever killed him and for whatever reason is still a mystery. But it feels connected to this place, so it is good we came, and so soon after his death."

"Is that what Ambrose meant in his note? That we would find his killer here?"

"Except when he wrote that note he did not know he would be murdered. Yes, he might have been seeking absolution for his sins, whatever they were, but if so he would have confessed them to Abbot John, or me, rather than..." Prior Bernard's voice trailed off.

"What is it?" Thomas asked.

"Perhaps it was not only Abbot John who confessed, but Ambrose who gave his own confession in return."

"Who else would know more about Ambrose than Abbot John or you?"

Prior Bernard offered a smile lacking any softness. "She may."

"The Prioress? Do you think she is capable of killing Ambrose?"

"I believe Felicia capable of almost anything."

"For what reason?"

"Ambrose may have known something about her she did not want to be revealed. I doubt he would have confronted her with it, he was not that kind of man. But he might have let something slip that told her he knew her secrets."

"What secrets?" Thomas was aware of a frustration building in him. There was too much he did not understand. Too many people conspiring to achieve something hidden from him.

"That is what we need to find out." Prior Bernard turned and started to walk. "We go to see her now."

SEVENTEEN

Several of the sisters tried to block their way, but Prior Bernard pushed them aside, and for those he missed Thomas did not. It appeared Bernard knew exactly where Felicia Hughden would be because he entered a cloister and crossed to the far end until, after following a corridor he opened a door without knocking. They were confronted by a half-naked Felicia Hughden cowering in a corner while Madoc had his hand raised to strike her.

Thomas pushed past Bernard and grasped the man's wrist just as his fist began to descend.

Felicia Hughden flinched, then slid sideways as Madoc turned his anger against whoever had interrupted him.

"You again," he said, his face twisted with rage. "Can you not mind your own business?"

"When I see a woman being beaten I make it my business."

Thomas still had his hand around Madoc's wrist. His

grip was firm, but Madoc used his left hand to reach down to his belt to draw a dagger. Thomas jerked aside as it came at him, then released his hold and punched Madoc as hard as he could on the side of his face. His head snapped around and his knees went. He sank back onto the bed which presumably belonged to Felicia Hughden.

"I cannot have anything to do with this, Tom," said Bernard. "Can you manage him on your own?"

"What do you think?"

Madoc was half a foot shorter than Thomas, but strong. Even so, Thomas knew he would prevail. What to do with the man was another matter. One more enemy to add to a growing list.

Bernard reached out a hand to Felicia, who arranged her torn habit so her breasts were covered.

"Come with me. I believe your office is next door, yes?"

She nodded, and as she did so Thomas noticed the bruising on her cheek, a dribble of blood from her nose, the swollen lips. Thomas patted Madoc's body, retrieving another dagger. He tossed both into a far corner then sat the man up as he began to come around.

"You hit me," said Madoc, shaking his head. "You attacked a member of the Holy Church. This is a hanging offence, Berrington, and I will laugh as I watch you drop."

"Do you want me to hit you again?"

"You would not dare."

Thomas hit him.

He went to the door Bernard had taken Felicia

through and checked on events there, knowing Madoc would be out for some time yet. He flexed his fist and rubbed it.

Felicia sat on a round-backed wooden chair behind a large desk. Bernard held her chin, turning her head to examine her bruises.

"Has he gone?" Felicia asked, slowly returning to herself.

Thomas looked into her eyes, relieved they were normal.

"He is taking a nap," he said. "Does he hit you often?"

"He is a man much given to getting his own way, and I would not let him have his way with me. Could not let him."

"Were your nuns not good enough for him today?" Thomas knew his question cruel but anger still sang in his blood.

"I would not allow him, which is why he came to me. Tried to take me." Her gaze met Thomas's. "There are things I need to tell you," she said.

"Now?"

"Best to do it before my courage leaves me." She glanced at Bernard. "You may not want to hear any of what I intend to say to Thomas." She looked back at him. "What do you intend to do with Madoc?"

"I have no idea."

Felicia nodded. "He will be angry when he wakes. It might be better if you kill him before he does."

Thomas stared at her, saw she was serious.

"I will go to him and wait, then take him outside,"

said Bernard. "Lock the doors so he cannot send his men for you, Felicia. If we are lucky, Tom hit him hard enough to addle his wits and he will forget what happened here."

"Madoc forgets nothing," said Felicia, but she rose and embraced Bernard, which seemed to unsettle him.

When he had gone, she turned the heavy keys in both doors, the one leading to her bed chamber, the other to the corridor, then retook her seat. She nodded at a chair on the other side of the desk.

"Bring that around so we are closer together. No one will overhear us, but I need the comfort of your presence. You are a brave man but may have acted in haste."

Thomas brought the chair around and sat. "I could not allow him to strike you again. I do not regret my actions."

"I pray you do not come to do so." Felicia reached out and took both his hands in hers as tears came to her eyes.

"What is going on?" Thomas asked. "I saw Abbot Haylewith comforting you at Ambrose's graveside. You were crying then, too."

"As you would expect when you watch your only son being laid to rest."

Felicia's voice broke as she spoke the words and her fingers tightened around Thomas's. It might have been an intimate moment. Felicia was a beautiful woman, her scent heady, but she was distraught.

Thomas thought about what she had revealed to him. The implications of it. If Ambrose was her son it might explain some of what he did. A noise came from the next room and they both turned to look at the door. Felicia's face showed fear.

"You are safe with me," Thomas said, and she smiled.

"Yes, I believe I am."

Voices were raised, then a door slammed. Someone tried the door to the corridor then went on when they found it locked.

"He will come back," said Felicia. "You cannot stay here forever, much as I would welcome it."

"Tell me about Ambrose. And you. Did you work in the bordel here? Is that how you came to fall pregnant?"

Felica shook her head, her eyes downcast as if she needed to look back in time.

"I was in love." She gave a soft laugh. "At least I believed I was in love. He was so handsome. So strong. So powerful. Three days we had together. Only three days. But they were enough." Her gaze rose. "I had fifteen years. Ambrose was born as I turned sixteen." Another smile, which showed love.

"You were a nun here?"

Felicia nodded. "I was never part of the bordel. I was innocent, had never lain with a man, but Edward was like a strike of lightning the moment I saw him."

"Was he a local man?" Thomas asked, and Felicia laughed.

"I have said enough. If you want to know more about him ask Sir Richard Croft. I hear you and he are friends. I also hear he respects you, which is unusual for Richard."

"Ambrose grew up here?"

"In the village. A family looked after him, but he

always knew I was his mother. I wanted him to know because I loved him. I still love him. He has taken a part of my heart with him."

"So why did you treat him as you did? It was you who asked him to bury the children, was it not?"

When Felicia met Thomas's eyes tears streamed from her own. "Because I loved them all."

"They were born of your nuns?"

She nodded. "And lived short lives."

"Why not bury them here? Not in the priory grounds perhaps, but nearby. Why get Ambrose to open graves and add them?"

Felicia stared into space for some time before giving a small jerk. "At first … at first it was shame. And yes, in the beginning some of them were buried in a field behind the priory, but it was Ambrose's idea. He was a good man. A pious man. He knew unbaptised children could not lie in consecrated ground but believed they did not hold any sin. You knew him a little. Did you think him a soft man or made of flint?"

"He struck me as someone with strong views on things, but my companion Jorge told me he had a kind heart. He sees such things."

"He was the man with you when you came here before?"

"He was."

"He is beautiful."

Thomas smiled. "Yes, he is." And then, because it had to be asked and he felt the conversation had drifted away from what he wanted to know, said, "Do you know who killed Ambrose?"

Felica sat up sharply. She wiped a hand across her face. "Do you think if I did I would be sitting here now? I would take a knife and kill them myself, even if I am a mere woman."

"You are no mere woman. Who might have killed him? Some believe he lay with other men and one of those did it."

"Ambrose would not do that. He had no urges for either men nor women. He loved God. He love the Church. And he loved me and this priory." She smiled. "And relics. I think he found comfort in them. They brought him even closer to God and His servants."

"Tell me why he stole the skulls," Thomas said. "Why did he bring you skulls from the graves he buried the children in?"

"What skulls? I have no idea what you are talking about. Ambrose brought me no skulls. Do you think me so wicked?"

Thomas stared into her eyes but saw no deception there, though whether he would see it was another matter. He knew he was not the best judge of such things.

"I buried my mother and brother behind the house I used to live in," he said. "I had thirteen years when I did so, and remember the day well. The house is mouldering away now, walls broken, the roof open to the sky. I wanted the bones of my ancestors on my land, so we dug them up. Two of the graves had been opened and children placed in them, but it was long ago. All that remained were bones. But something was also missing. The skull of my brother and the skull of my mother. I want them back."

"I am sorry for your pain, Thomas, but I do not have the skulls. It does not sound like something Ambrose would do. Are you sure it was him?"

"If he buried the children then he must have taken the skulls. It makes no sense otherwise."

"Or someone worked alongside him and it was they who stole the skulls."

Thomas only stared at Felicia until she could no longer meet his gaze.

"I do not rule out he had help. Digging down six feet is hard work, particularly if the grave is old, though Ambrose was strong."

"Because of who his father was."

Was? Thomas thought. *Not is?*

"Which you are not going to tell me."

Felicia hid a smile that appeared and went almost at once.

"Ambrose developed a friendship with Owain Haylewith. They trained together as authenticators of relics."

"Archdeacon Webb told me of that," Thomas said. "Are you trying to say their friendship was significant in what happened to him?"

"I do not know why he had to die. I leave discovering that to you. Everyone says you are the best man to find it out. But you might benefit from knowing more about Owain. When he first came to Hindwell from Garway he was filled with ambition. Also filled with desires which

Elmbrook could satisfy. Which made the friendship between the two of them even stranger. I believe Ambrose wanted to bring Owain back to his own vision of God."

"I take it that never happened."

Felicia Hughden shook her head. "There were times I thought Owain might have drawn Ambrose to his own worldview instead. But most likely his belief only hardened, as steel plunged into water. Owain Haylewith's deviancy made Ambrose's creed all the stronger."

"What manner of deviancy do you mean? The nuns here, or something else?"

"The nuns here, yes, but it is more than that. Owain and Madoc both fought in God's army in the Holy Land and Spain. The same as Bernard did, but they returned with strange ideas. Have you heard the rumours of Garway, the Templars and the Grail?"

"Bernard told me Haylewith was obsessed with it. Convinced it lies hidden somewhere in the county. Is it that you refer to?"

"That and other matters, not all of which I know of. A word spoken here and there. Owain's beliefs owe less to the Christian Church and more to the one that it replaced. He follows Pagan ways."

"Yet he is Abbot of Hindwell. What do the Archdeacons think of that?"

"As I said, a word here and there, but nothing specific. If Owain is confronted, he can deny everything. But there is a celebration at midsummer on the hill behind his abbey which is not Christian. It worships older gods. I have attended in the past, and Madoc always comes for some of my nuns. Besides, this land is on the edge of England, far from the King in London. What goes on here passes unnoticed. Apart from by you. Which is why you are the right man to uncover whatever wickedness is going on."

"I take it you mean apart from the wickedness of your bordel?"

Felicia Hughden laughed. "What have I done that is wrong? Nothing, other than operate a service for the district, one that is highly respected. On occasion that service resulted in lost lives, but none of the children were murdered. All deaths were natural. Ambrose travelled throughout these borderlands and knew every place of burial, both official and unofficial." She smiled. "He told me he used old graves behind a ruined house outside of Lemster, only later discovering it belonged to your family. Perhaps his confession to you was meant as some form of apology."

Thomas believed Felicia knew more, but he knew she would be unlikely to reveal it to him. He would do as she suggested. Speak with Sir Richard Croft. Investigate Madoc and Haylewith.

"Will you be safe here when we leave?" he asked.

"My girls will protect me. I will send word that he is not to be admitted again. I made a mistake in dining with them at Wigmore. It gave them the belief I was more available than I am." She stared at Thomas. "I am proud of the work we do here, and the services we offer. But it has nothing to do with what happened to my son. Find his killer, Thomas, and bring him to me so I can look into his eyes. I am even willing to wield the knife that kills him myself."

"I will not allow that. If I find him he will be punished, but the law will decide his fate."

"And if he is a member of the Church? Ask Bernard his opinion on that."

"I already know it." Thomas rose, unlocked the door and left Prioress Felicia Hughden to her grief.

He found Bernard standing by the gate, talking with three of the nuns.

"We need our horses."

"I will go to the stable and have them sent," said one of the nuns. The other two turned and wandered away.

"Madoc left?" Thomas asked.

"Not without much cursing, but he knows I also fought and am stronger than he is, despite my years. I am like you, Tom, age does not appear to affect me. If I am fortunate, one day I will die in my bed and rise to stand beside my God."

"Felica tells me he will not be admitted again, but it would be good to send some men here to ensure that is the case."

"You can recruit some, I am sure," said Bernard. "What did she want to tell you?"

"Did you know Ambrose was her son?"

Bernard stared at Thomas so long the nun had time to return leading their horses. Only after they had mounted and ridden from the priory did Bernard finally speak.

"I did not. I never even suspected it. She admitted this to you?"

"She did, but not who the father was. And she did say *was*, which makes me think he is now dead. She told me to speak to Sir Richard Croft, who might be willing to tell me who he was."

"Could it be important?"

"I do not know. It may not be significant, but now she has told me of it I would like to know. Felicia also told me she is proud of the work done in her bordel."

"I am not surprised. I would never use it, but I know of many who do. Do you know that the first house set up to service men in the same way as Elmbrook does was created at Southwark Cathedral south of the Thames, many centuries ago? It was done at the behest of the King at that time as a necessary measure." Bernard shook his head. "Perhaps the Church is wrong to expect us to turn our backs on our natures as men and women. It demands celibacy, then herds us together in dormitories cheek by jowl with others of our own sex."

"You do not share a dormitory now," Thomas said. "Neither does Felicia Hughden, William Webb or John Martyn."

"When I was a young monk I did. I am aware of what happens even if I did not partake myself. But I feel urges as other men do. As do we all. It is not natural to ignore them, but it is what we must do. Resist. Refrain. Obey. I am in accord with Ambrose on that."

"You are stronger than other men. Stronger than me."

"Am I a fool, Tom, to have forsaken the pleasures of

an ordinary life to serve God? I could have had a wife, children, grandchildren by now. And for what? A Church that turns its gaze away from what sits here for all to see. It is regarded as a necessary evil, but there are times I wonder what it is we are meant to worship; God or Mammon?"

"There are laws in this land," Thomas said. "Laws set out by kings and better men than me."

"It is not illegal to operate a brothel, not even in a priory or abbey. No law has been broken."

"The children, then. I will go to the Coroner and tell him what Ambrose did and on whose behalf. He will have to take action."

"I wish you luck with that." When Bernard looked ahead, he said, "I believe we are about to have company."

When Thomas followed Bernard's gaze he saw ten men sitting on horseback. He had seen their like before the first time he came to Elmbrook Priory. Sitting at their head was Madoc, his sword drawn.

"They dare not attack us," he said.

"Do you really think so, after the insult we gave him back there?" Prior Bernard looked around. "I see no witnesses other than members of Prioress Felicia's flock. We should turn aside and ride as hard as we can."

"They will catch us. Your steed may outrun them but Ferrant will not." Thomas reached down and drew his own sword. He held it out to Bernard. "Take this if you want. Otherwise, I will wield two, but it is going to come to a fight."

"I have not used a sword in over fifty years. I doubt I even recognise one end from the other."

"The pointy end does the damage. It is as simple as that."

"Stay here, Tom. I will ride and talk to them. If they kill me then you can fight, but I do not think much of the odds despite your reputation."

Thomas started to object, but Prior Bernard had already urged his horse forward.

If it comes to it, I will kill Madoc first, Thomas thought. It might discourage the others. It never occurred to him he could not defeat Madoc. The others, he was even more sure of. Ten men should be too many, but he had seen their like before. Not all would press the fight once one or two had been injured.

He sat and waited, stilling his mind. Then Bernard turned and rode back. The men rode away to the west, all except Madoc who went past them into the grounds of the priory.

EIGHTEEN

Thomas and Bernard reached a pass between hills before speaking again, each with their own thoughts. Rain had come again and water ran down their faces. Thomas knew if he turned and looked back he might get a last glimpse of Elmbrook Priory, but he did not. He never wanted to see the place again.

"You did well back there," Thomas said.

"Madoc did not want to fight us. It was nothing more than hurt pride that drove him to threaten us."

"And those men who were with him?"

"They belong to Abbot Haylewith and are based at Hindwell Abbey, though I suspect he will bring them with him to Wigmore. They also have a base close to the church of St Michael's in Garway where Haylewith was once the priest. And you know of its link with the Templars. These monks fashion themselves after them but lack the Templars' discipline."

"Are they dangerous?"

Prior Bernard smiled. "Not today, it seems. Some of them have served God in the Holy Land and Spain. Others wish they could have. In sufficient numbers they might cause trouble, but most of the time they are little more than bluff, with their smart jerkins and crosses stitched on them. All the same, take care when you return home in case Madoc sends a few of them after you."

"It has been tried before and did not end well for those who attempted to attack me."

"You are not a man to make an enemy of, are you, Tom?"

"I would prefer it otherwise, but it is never me who starts the conflict."

"But it is you the conflict seems to find, and you who often puts an end to it. You might be wise to ignore most of what Felicia told you today. That Ambrose is her son surprises me, but less so when I think about it. As for who his father is, or was, is almost certainly irrelevant. Look for Ambrose's killer, Tom, but I suspect you will never discover who it is."

"After today I suspect Madoc. He was at Wigmore last night, and I expect some of his soldiers would not have been far away. He strikes me as a man happy to threaten a woman but less so a man who might fight back."

"Yes, look at Madoc. I cannot think any of the others there capable. Certainly not the Archdeacons, nor Lyman d'Alston or Amos Mapp. Not Owain Haylewith, either. He is odd, but no longer a killer. Besides, why would he kill

Ambrose the day after his elevation to Abbot of Wigmore?"

"I assume the Church will have to find a new authenticator of relics," Thomas said.

"It will."

"Do you know of anyone?"

"None like Ambrose. He was relentless in his pursuit of the truth. There are others who deal in relics, including Amos Mapp, but they lack the honesty the post requires. We may need to search outside the county to find someone, or even look overseas." Prior Bernard smiled. "Do you know of anyone in Spain who might suit?"

"An honest monk?" Thomas laughed and shook his head.

The rain grew lighter as they started to descend the hill. Wigmore Abbey appeared on the edge of the flat plain where a swollen Teme wound its way across the fields. Beyond, hills rose again, hiding Ludlow and Burway.

"You will be faster going straight on here, Tom. You should be home in an hour. I am sorry we could not do any better today."

"I know more than I did when we went so the time was not wasted. I promise you I will not rest until I find out who killed Ambrose. I admit he was not a man I warmed to, but I know you respected him and that is enough for me. You take care too, Bernard."

"Abbot Bernard, Tom. At least for the moment."

Thomas lost sight of Bernard as their paths diverged.

Later, as Ludlow loomed above him, instead of heading for Burway he crossed Dinham Bridge and climbed the steep roadway to the market square. The rain had stopped, but his hair hung in wet strands across his face as he tied Ferrant to a post outside Agnes's bakery and went inside to warm himself.

"Where have you been getting all wet, Uncle Thomas?" asked Rose as he passed the open hatch at the side of the building.

"Is your mother home?"

"She is in the bakery. You can help her knead the dough if you want, though you do look a little tired."

Thomas suspected Rose was right. He stole a small tart from her, laughing as she swatted him, and went inside. The inner room was warm from the open ovens where his sister Agnes stood over a large table, leaning into the kneading of the dough, her strong arms and fingers making light work of it. The scent of flour and bread filled the air, making his stomach growl.

"Have you been swimming, Tom? There is a cloth over there. Wipe yourself before coming near me."

"I have been trying to solve another murder."

"Who is dead this time?"

"Brother Ambrose."

Agnes stopped her work. "When? How?"

"The when was last night." As he spoke the words came as a surprise. It seemed much longer ago. "The how you do not want to know."

"Who did it?"

"If I knew that I would arrest them."

"Not you, the Coroner. He already tells everyone you are trying to usurp his position."

"Then he should perform his duties a little more diligently. Besides, I have no wish to become Coroner. The post seems to be even more corrupt than that of Justice of the Peace."

Agnes returned to her kneading and Thomas went to help, knowing she might have to redo his work before the loaves were fed into the oven where the embers of logs glowed.

"Except you are that rarity, an honest Justice. Perhaps you would be an honest Coroner."

"I do not believe the position is vacant."

"Oh, it is vacant. It simply has a man sitting in it at the moment who is failing to do his job. Who has solved all the recent killings in the district — you or Lyman d'Alston?"

"I intend to tell him what little I have discovered about Ambrose's death. He was there, by the way."

Agnes frowned, and the expression looked so much like their mother, Thomas felt a ripple of grief that she was no longer with them.

"Who was there?"

"D'Alston. Together with Amos Mapp and half a dozen others, some of whom I might suspect of wanting Ambrose dead. Bernard and I rode to Elmbrook Priory to confront the Prioress, but we both believe her innocent. Did you know Ambrose was her son?"

"Felicia's son?"

Thomas nodded.

"I did not, and I suspect few others did, either. I assume this information is not to be made public."

"That is a good point, sister. Perhaps if people knew it might stir things up, make them think about Ambrose in a different way."

"Or cause trouble," said Agnes.

"Yes, or cause trouble. Keep it to yourself for now."

"Do you expect the Coroner to do anything about Ambrose's death?"

"No, but it is his job, not mine, as you have reminded me. So I have to tell him what I know. But perhaps not about Felicia's secret. He should also know Madoc was threatening her when we went to Elmbrook."

"Then take care. I do not trust Lyman, and my girls tell me Amos Mapp looks at them with hunger in his eyes. I tell them to ignore him because most men like that do not have the courage to approach pretty girls."

"Most," Thomas said, "but not all. I suspect Madoc would be more than happy to approach pretty girls."

"Everyone knows they would have me to answer to if they tried anything with Rose or Jilly, not to mention you and Will. That should be enough to scare away any man. Both are of an age when they should be thinking about marriage, but it does not seem to be on their minds as yet."

Thomas leaned across and kissed his sister on the cheek. She patted his face, leaving a smear of flour which he wiped away as he went out into the square again.

Lyman d'Alston's house stood at the eastern end where

the roadway narrowed before descending the hill. It was three storeys tall, with all the windows containing leaded glass, even those of the servants' quarters lodged beneath the eaves. Wooden beams fashioned from elm crisscrossed between lime walls which were painted a faded red. The door was wide with metal insets meant to impress, which they would probably have done if Thomas was the kind of man to be impressed by such things. He knocked and waited, then after enough time had passed, knocked again.

When the door finally opened, he was confronted by a slim woman of about thirty, the top of whose head barely rose to his chin.

"I am here to speak with the Coroner. I am—"

"I know who you are. Wait here, I will see if he is free."

Thomas tried to think of what might be so pressing to prevent the woman from admitting him, but perhaps d'Alston did some work on occasion. When footsteps finally approached he saw they belonged to Amos Mapp, who beckoned him inside.

"Are you taking me to Lyman?" Thomas asked.

"Not yet. He asked me to find out what you want first. He is busy with matters more important than your obsessions."

"Matters such as the death of Brother Ambrose, I hope?"

"He considers that a matter for the Church in the first instance. He will agree to become involved only if a culprit is not found within the week. He believes, as I do, that it is a lover's argument between two of the brothers. It happens. Everyone knows it does."

"But how often does it lead to murder?" Thomas did not yet want to reveal what Ambrose had written to him, sure that Mapp would again claim that everyone knew about Elmbrook Priory and what went on there.

They followed a long corridor that ran through the middle of the substantial house. Closed doors stood to either side until they passed one that stood open and Thomas glimpsed a large kitchen. In it, the woman who had admitted him stood kneading pastry, an unplucked chicken and some vegetables sat to one side.

"Our dinner," said Mapp.

"Where are you taking me if not to see Lyman?"

"My workshop. I want to explain a few things to you first. I also want to sound you out over a certain matter."

"I thought you did not respect my opinion."

Mapp glanced at Thomas. "I respect those who prove they deserve respect. I admit that did not include you when you first came to Ludlow in the company of the Prince and his new bride. I considered you one more rich man who had used his wealth to gain a position, but it soon became clear you were not. I like your sister, too."

"Everyone likes Agnes."

"True. I know I am not the easiest man to get along with," said Mapp, "but I would like us to start our relationship over, particularly in light of what happened last night."

"You told me Ambrose's death is none of my concern."

"And it is not, but his death is my concern, which is what I want to talk to you about. Besides, I suspect you took no notice of my words, did you?" Amos Mapp opened a door at the rear of the house and went out into a large garden where shrubs grew against a low stone wall. A dovecot stood in the far corner, the sound of its inhabitants filling the air. In the opposite corner sat a wooden building, the door to it secured with a substantial lock which Amos Mapp opened with an equally substantial key he took from his pocket.

"Come into my realm, Thomas."

Thomas followed him inside, surprised to discover the interior immaculate. All wall space not taken up by the single window and the door was shelved to the roof, wooden boxes, each labelled, stacked on them. Two large tables almost filled the rest of the space, with more boxes on them, but these were open. Some bones were scattered across the surface, together with other objects Thomas had difficulty discerning the nature of.

"These are your relics?" he asked.

"Those I have at the moment, yes, but my relics also inhabit the abbeys, priories and churches of the Marches."

"I heard you were a seller of relics but did not appreciate how many you possessed. How do you obtain them?"

"If I told you that I would be revealing the secrets of my trade. I will say only that I have extensive contacts, both here and beyond the shores of England. There were relics in Spain, were there not?"

"Many."

"And elsewhere in Christendom. There are also places that fall beyond it where relics also exist. Our saviour was born and raised in a land where the true God was unknown. There are countries beyond Jerusalem that worship false gods, but Christ's servants travelled through many of them. So relics may exist anywhere." Mapp was warming to his subject. He leaned forward and picked up a small bone. "This was sold to me as the finger bone of Saint Peter."

"And did Ambrose validate it? Is that what he did for you?"

"He would have had he lived, I am sure. As he did for me many times in the past."

"May I?" Thomas held his hand out, palm up.

Mapp looked at it, then placed the bone in it. "Can you not feel the holiness flow through you?"

Thomas raised his hand and analysed the bone, wishing he had a lens to magnify it further. But even without a lens he recognised it for what it was. It was indeed a finger bone, but one from a child, either the index finger or the ring finger. It had certainly not belonged to Saint Peter, or any other saint.

"Yes, I feel the power of it," he said, handing the bone back. He wondered if Mapp knew the relic was false or not. He also questioned the truth of his claiming Brother Ambrose had validated others for him. It did not sound like the man he knew or the man Prior Bernard spoke of.

"Ambrose talked to me about his work. Talked enough that I believe I can take on his holy vocation and offer myself as the validator of relics for the three counties."

"How would that work when you are also a seller of relics?"

"Clearly, I would need to give up that trade."

"Does the position not require a monk to do it?"

"It always has, but who is to say it always must? Besides, I was a member of the cloth for several years before leaving the Church as a novice. I believe I may be accepted. Even more so if you would sponsor me with Prior Bernard, who is currently acting Abbot at Wigmore."

"Why would I do that?"

"Because you want my help in another matter. I expect you know I took Ambrose's cart away this morning."

"Of course. You were seen."

"I made no attempt not to be seen because I am an innocent man."

"Did you look inside the boxes on Ambrose's cart?"

"I am no fool, so of course I did."

"What do you intend to do with the young girl's body?"

"It has already been taken care of. Father Yorke buried her this morning. I told him she was a foundling discovered on the roadside, so Ambrose's secret is safe. I am sure Prior Bernard will not wish to sully Ambrose's reputation. Neither would I. You, however, are less of a known quantity."

"I will not tell any lies."

"But if you are not asked, is that the same as lying?"

"Are you aware of what was taken from the graves behind my old house and what was left there?"

Amos Mapp shook his head. "Only that you were investigating disturbed graves, which is what the Coroner warned you against."

"And you agreed with him."

"He is my employer."

"In addition to your business of selling relics."

"Lyman knows about that and does not object to my earning a small stipend outside of his service as long as I do my work to his satisfaction. I know you employ your children on retainers to assist you as Justice of the Peace. That is as expected. My having another form of income is also expected."

Thomas did not know what to make of Amos Mapp. He had not liked the man on first meeting him but believed that may have been a false start. Now he made a great deal of sense. And if he could offer some assistance it would be a deal worth making. Except what exactly was the deal they were working towards? Mapp had stated his side, but Thomas had not.

"When the children's bodies were left in the graves of my brother and mother, something was also taken from them. Their skulls. Why I do not know, nor do I know if the same was done at other graves that have been opened, but I intend to find out. The Coroner forbade me from investigating, but I am sure you can persuade him to allow me some leeway. It is a personal matter, after all."

"Let us see, shall we? And you will talk to Prior Bernard on my behalf?"

Thomas was still uneasy at the request but knew it would not be his decision whether Mapp was appointed or not.

"I will put your proposal to him the next time I see him, but the decision will be his. Or rather, I suspect not his, but his word will go a long way in assisting you."

"My thanks. The final decision will, of course, be with the Archdeacons of Hereford and Salop, but I know both men respect Prior Bernard above all others in the district. Let us go to see Lyman."

Thomas followed Mapp inside the house and back along the corridor until they reached one of the closed doors. Mapp knocked and entered without waiting to be invited.

"I told you I was not to be disturbed," said Lyman d'Alston from behind a polished desk. He saw Thomas and rose to his feet. "And what is he doing here?"

"He has a request, sir, one which I think you should consider. Thomas has told me it is a personal matter rather than one of law."

D'Alston glared at Thomas, who suspected he already knew the response he would receive. But he had been wrong before, and was wrong again on this occasion.

It took only a little time until Thomas accompanied Mapp out of the house.

"Ambrose did not kill that girl we found," Thomas said. "I spoke with Felicia Hughden earlier today, and she admitted the children were born to the nuns who staff her bordel. Both there and in other places. They were not killed but died of natural causes."

"Which is what she would want you to believe."

"You cannot truly believe Ambrose murdered them, can you?"

Mapp turned and re-entered the house, leaving Thomas's accusation hanging in the air.

NINETEEN

The letter of authority arrived early that evening while Thomas was standing beneath a fall of hot water in the bathhouse. Amal handed it to him when he emerged.

"I did not open it," she said. "It was addressed to you, and I saw the seal was that of the Coroner. You managed to see him, did you?"

"Surprisingly, yes. Even more surprisingly, Amos Mapp was helpful. If it had been left up to Lyman d'Alston I would have left empty-handed. But there will be a price to pay, which Mapp made clear."

"I do not like the man," said Amal. She stood in front of Thomas, short, exotic, beautiful in a way that scared most boys off.

"I cannot say I like him much myself, but today I found him reasonable. Other than his accusations against Brother Ambrose."

"What accusations?"

"He knows Ambrose was responsible for burying the

bodies. Felicia Hughden confirmed the same to me today. What Amos Mapp told me is that he believes Ambrose killed the children rather than their deaths being natural." Thomas had almost told Amal about Felicia being Ambrose's mother but decided against at the last moment. He could see no advantage to her knowing, and the truth might put her in danger until he exposed whoever had killed the man.

"Did you believe Mapp? I cannot say I warmed to Ambrose, but I had no sense he was dangerous. Women can tell such things about a man."

Thomas smiled at Amal. So young yet so wise.

"I believe Ambrose innocent of any crime other than loyalty to Elmbrook Priory. Amos also told me he wants Ambrose's position as the authenticator of relics."

"Does he have the qualifications?"

"He knows relics, so I have to assume he is able to tell the difference between a genuine one and a fake. Though not today." Thomas smiled. "He showed me a bone he claimed was from the finger of Saint Peter, but it was a child's."

"They should offer the job to Silva," said Amal. "She can tell if something is genuine or not just by touching it."

Thomas padded after her, aware he should dress because all he wore was a long cotton robe that almost touched the ground. It was the kind of garment he wore when he lived in Granada but less so in England. The weather was less favourable most of the time, but summer was with them now.

"I think some belief in the Christian God might be required," Thomas said as he caught up to Amal.

"How was Ambrose killed?"

"With a knife. I will spare you the details."

"You know I do not mind the details, but spare yourself the remembering of them. The details make him no less dead."

"They do not."

Thomas was aware of how Amal was changing. She had matured even if she had not grown any taller in the last year. Her mind had expanded, which was a good thing. She was hungry for knowledge and also experience, which he was less sure of. He had been the same at her age but was unsure if it had been a good thing or not. It had made him who he was, and he was content within himself most of the time. But there were times he wondered who or what he would have become if his young life had been different. The loss of his father on a battlefield had hardened him, casting him into a new life where he cared less for others. Even less for himself.

"Are you not going to open your letter?" asked Amal.

"I already know the contents. It is a letter of authority from d'Alston allowing me to look into the disturbed graves."

Amal stopped and turned to Thomas. "Why did he change his mind? Every time you asked before he forbade it."

"I told you, Amos proved useful in persuading him to my way of thinking. I believe it was granted in the end only because it meant less work for d'Alston. He showed me his workshop."

"The Coroner did?"

"No, Amos. You would like it. He has many things there that would intrigue you."

"Perhaps you can ask him if I can visit, but if I do I would like to take someone with me. Silva would be good because she would be able to judge what he showed us. Just as she found the hexes buried in the walls of this house. It is how she found your family Bible, which is fascinating by the way. She would make a good authenticator, but I accept a belief in God might be necessary, and that she does not have. Not in a Christian God, in any case."

They reached the big room where everyone gathered because the rain had returned and returned hard. Will and Silva were not there, and Thomas suspected they were at her cottage in the woods beyond. He would need Will in the morning, but they could ride that way and get him. It was not far out of their way if the destination was Garway, where Amal and Usaden had discovered the disturbed grave.

Jorge sat at the wide table with Leila asleep on his knee. There was no sign of Jahan or Saman, and Thomas assumed they had already gone to their room on the second floor.

"I see you found your way home without me, Jorge," Thomas said as he sat.

"I waited, but when Prior Bernard returned I knew you had forgotten all about me, so came home on my own. I even managed to find my way without getting lost."

"Did you manage to speak to all of the monks?"

"Every one of them. A task I hope you never ask me to do again. Most are very dull individuals, even duller as a multitude. How I find your friend Bernard interesting is a mystery to me."

"Tell me what you found out. Could any of them have killed Ambrose?"

Belia came to the table and held her hands out. "Let me take Leila upstairs if you are going to talk of murder. She might be asleep, but I am sure she can still hear." She took her daughter and cradled her against her shoulder before leaving.

Thomas looked at Amal. "Do you want to leave as well?"

"Why?"

"As you wish. So tell me, Jorge."

"As I said, they are dull, but some less so. However, none are killers, even if they are sinners."

"Explain."

"Do you need me to?" Jorge glanced at Amal.

"You do not need to spare me any details," she said. "I know about men who lie with other men. Just as women sometimes lie with women. I do not understand why there are so many rules about who you can and cannot love."

Thomas wondered how she knew of such things, but was aware there was much he did not know about Amal these days. She was not a stranger to him but had developed a life of her own in Ludlow, settling into the town far better than he had himself despite being born only a few miles south of it.

"How many does this apply to?" Thomas asked Jorge.

"Many more than a few. Which is not surprising, is it? Most are young, and as we both know the sap rises strong in young men."

"Even you when you were young."

Jorge smiled. "You might have tried to cut the root from me, but yes it did, and still does."

Amal laughed. "Perhaps I am hearing more than I want to after all. I will go to the workshop. I have some things I want to check on. What time do you want us to leave in the morning, Pa?"

"Early, if we have to pick up Will. As soon after dawn as we can make it."

"Then I will also need to sleep." Amal rose, kissed Jorge, then kissed her father before leaving.

"She will get soaked," Thomas said. "It is raining hard out there."

"And she will dry. Getting wet is not a permanent state. Not even here in England. I am sorry, I did not mean to upset her."

"I do not think you did, but she thought we might find it easier to talk openly if she was not here. Our conversation would not upset her, but she thinks we believe it might."

"She is clever that way," said Jorge.

"Yes, she is. So immoral activities are going on at the abbey?"

"Did you think they would not be?"

"No, but you hinted at a significant number of the monks being involved. Or did I hear that wrong?"

Jorge leaned across the table, his hands spread. "I did not know how common it is in a closed order such as they have there, so I spoke with Bernard when he returned and asked him about Lemster Priory. He told me he was aware such liaisons took place there, too, but they are few and far between. Less so than in Wigmore and Hindwell."

"Did he condemn them?" Thomas asked.

"He did not. Bernard is a man who has seen much of the world. When I told him the number I estimate indulge at Wigmore Abbey, I think he was shocked, but not surprised. He did mention — which I suspect he should not have done — that Abbot John had grown lax in his old age."

Jorge stopped talking but the expression on his face told Thomas he had not finished. That he knew something but was withholding it until asked.

So Thomas asked.

"What else did you discover? Is it to do with Caradoc?"

Jorge laughed. "Nothing to do with him, but at least he was not one of the monks who wander the corridors at night in search of sex. He had woken to a call of nature and was on his way back when he heard a scream." The humour drained from Jorge's face.

"Which is what he told me. Also that he did see anyone else."

Jorge nodded. "I heard the same story and believed him."

"How did he know to go to Ambrose's room?"

"He did not, but as he went in search of the scream he saw the door open. He went inside and then wished he had not."

"Was Ambrose dead?"

"He was."

Jorge's account matched what Caradoc had told Thomas, which told him it was undoubtedly true. It was difficult for a man to remember lies when time had passed between the telling of them.

"So the scream was his final act," Thomas said. "Which means the other wounds were made before the fatal blow." He looked at Jorge. "Some kind of torture?"

Jorge's expression showed distaste. "I leave such matters to you. I asked Caradoc if he saw the wounds but he said he was too shocked to notice much and I believed him. After I left him one of the monks brought something to show Bernard. It was Ambrose's robe. At least I think it was his robe. It was covered in blood, so most likely was, and you told me it was not in his room."

"His killer would also be soaked in blood," Thomas said. "Perhaps it belonged to him."

"Perhaps so, but when one thing is lost and the same thing is found it makes sense not to overcomplicate matters. You do that too often at times."

"So I have been told."

"Wrapped inside the cloak was a knife." Jorge rose. "It

is in the armoury if you want to see it, but it is an ordinary knife."

"Show me."

Thomas followed Jorge from the kitchen and into the next wing of the house. In the small armoury a single knife rested on the middle of the table. When Thomas approached, he saw blood on the blade, but most had been wiped off by the robe.

He picked it up, turning it over, but knew it could tell him little. Other than that the edge was honed to a wicked sharpness, and the blade not much longer than five inches. A tool that could inflict pain as well as kill. Which confirmed what he already suspected. Ambrose was tortured before he died. What Thomas did not know was what secret his killer sought and whether Ambrose had revealed it. He glanced at Jorge but decided he did not need to know more about the damage inflicted on Ambrose. He placed the knife back on the table.

"What did you discover at Elmbrook Priory?" asked Jorge as they made their way back.

"A little more than we already know. The most interesting is that Ambrose was born there, and is the son of Felicia Hughden, who is unapologetic about running the bordel. She was being threatened by Madoc when we arrived, but what about she did not tell me."

"What was Bernard's opinion?"

"He was surprised about her being Ambrose's mother, but told me it explains a lot about both of them. As for the bordel, you know he does not approve of what goes on there but can do nothing about it. It is condoned by the Church. Better to offer places where men and women can satisfy their lusts than have them driven mad by them and taint the reputation of the Church itself."

"So nothing will be done?"

"Nothing will be done. I have decided to forget about it. It is none of my business, but the bodies are. Though I now know where they come from."

"You believe the body Ambrose was transporting was one of them?" asked Jorge.

"I do."

"They are the children of the nun's liaisons," said Jorge.

"If you know that why have you not told me before?"

"Because I had not made the connection and could not believe the blatant nature of what was going on. Will it ever be stopped?"

"Not short of destroying every abbey and priory in the land, which will never happen."

"The Church could abandon their mindless policy of celibacy," said Jorge.

"That will also never happen. But as I said, that is not our business. The bodies are. And, more importantly, the missing skulls. I want those of my brother and mother returned to me so I can make their bodies whole where they lie in their graves. If we find skulls missing in the other graves then it means those at my old house are not isolated incidents. In which case, I hope there will be clues to what has happened to them."

"You already know Ambrose transported the bodies,"

said Jorge. "Do you think he also disposed of them? If so it makes sense he stole the skulls as well."

"I agree. His work took him over this entire area, so he would likely know where the recent graves were, but whether he had the time to open them to place small bodies in, I do not know. It is possible he had an accomplice. Or more than one."

"Even if it were him he would need help. You only had to look at him to see he was not a man used to digging the earth."

"So we need to search for these others as well. It is not the burying of these poor children that concerns me so much as the skulls, which has a feel of blasphemy to it. But we need to solve one part to solve the other. So in the morning I take Amal and Usaden with me, and once we pick up Will and Silva we go to Garway to open the grave they found. Then we go west to open the other at Tref-y-Clawdd."

"Do we still need to look for any others?" asked Jorge. "Should we not let the poor foundlings lie?"

"I am hoping to find something that will tell me where the skulls were taken to."

"What if they were discarded? Thrown away?"

"Whoever took the skulls will have done so for a reason. But if they were tossed aside there is nothing to be done and our task is at an end."

"No, it is not. You forget that these children will continue to die. Accidentally, through illness, in whatever manner, but their disposal in the way that has been used must stop." Jorge reached inside his shirt. "Your friend Bernard gave me this for you." He held out a sealed letter.

"What is it?"

"It is for you, not me. Apart from which he no doubt knew it would do me no good even if I did open it."

Thomas broke the seal, read the words and smiled.

"It is another note of authority, this one from the Church. It commands any priest to arrange for the burial of whatever remains I may pass into their care. Do you know what this means?"

"That you can now kill as many people as you want and the priests have to hide the evidence?"

"It means any children we uncover will lie in consecrated ground."

"Except you do not believe in God, or the trappings of religion."

"But others do. Now we have everything we need. Permission to open graves that have been disturbed, and permission to have whatever we find blessed and interred in holy ground."

"And those who are yet to die?" asked Jorge.

"Now the practice is revealed, proper measures must be taken for them. Each will have a place of their own to lie in for eternity."

TWENTY

They left a little after dawn, the grass wet with a heavy dew. The rain of the previous night had fled east and the sky was a pale, flawless blue, so cloudless it looked like the inside of an upturned bowl.

Thomas rode alongside Amal, aware the two of them had not ridden this way in some time. He had a lot of questions he wanted to ask but knew they were mostly inappropriate. He thought of what Agnes had told him about her daughters and knew he could not hold on to his own for ever. Could not protect her from breaking her heart over someone if that was what she wanted. Telling her would do no good. Everyone had to experience life for themselves, even if their parents wanted to protect them from it.

Usaden rode ahead with Jack Pook, who had been at Emma's house when Thomas and Amal called to ask if Usaden wanted to accompany them. Jack offered to come as well if they could find a horse for him, which was not a problem. He was a useful addition to their company because he knew every inch of the country they rode through. His presence might save them several detours. Now he led them along the flank of Ambrey Hill, away from the flat land bordering the Teme. Kin ran between their two groups, then raced ahead when he caught Will's scent, who came out of his cottage to greet them. He wore hose and nothing else. When Silva appeared behind him she was fully clothed.

"I take it you want me for something, Pa," said Will. Thomas had not seen him in a while and thought he looked even healthier than usual. He assumed that was Silva's doing. For the last several weeks she and Will had spent most of their time living in her cottage on Ambrey Hill.

"I have permission from Archdeacon Webb and Prior Bernard — Abbot Bernard for the moment — to open graves, so that is what we intend to do. We go to Garway first, but it is almost a day's ride. We will stay overnight at an inn then return through Tref-y-Clawdd and open the grave where you found the more recent body."

"Then why are we standing here talking?"

"You might want to get dressed," Amal said.

Will grinned. "I am dressed. I will not scare the sheep, I promise." But he went inside, and when he emerged he wore boots, carried a leather jerkin and two swords.

They went south, Jack Pook leading the way while Kin roamed ahead. Occasionally Usaden whistled to call him back if he started to follow the trail of some interesting scent, and he always returned, streaking across the ground to defy his years.

"I take it you have sacks for the bones, Pa?" Will rode beside Thomas with Silva perched behind him. They were becoming more than a couple. They were becoming one.

"Sacks will not be necessary. I have another note from Prior Bernard instructing any priest to inter the bones we uncover. We can do the same with the corpse you found in the west. I am more interested in discovering if other skulls have been stolen."

"What good will that do?"

"I was hoping you would not ask because I have no answer, only a yearning for one. I have to find the skulls of my brother and mother. Discovering if their theft was an isolated incident will tell me something, but I do not know exactly what that might be."

"The taking of a skull can be powerful magic, Tom," said Silva.

There had been a time Thomas would have ignored her comment, but that time was now in the past. Silva had proven herself to him more than once, and he could not deny she had a strange talent. One that might prove useful in their current task.

"I had a conversation with Bernard about the Grail and the skull of Jesus but did not believe a word of it."

"Is that why we go to Garway?" asked Silva. "There are rumours about the church there, which is strange and has a presence I can feel."

"We go to Garway because that is where Amal and

Usaden heard of disturbed graves. Tell me what use might be made of a stolen skull."

"That would depend on the mage, but most practitioners would lean towards the dark side rather than the light."

"I take it you represent the light?"

"I like to believe so."

"And this dark magic?"

Not that I believe in magic, Thomas thought, but he knew others did. He would take whatever assistance might help.

"If the skull is of a person known to them, some believe it may be used to summon their spirit from the grave." Silva smiled and shook her head to let him know she did not. "In your case, the skulls taken appear to be of strangers, so there are several uses that might be made of them. The most common would be as a totem within a place of darkness. As a crypt is dark, as a grave is dark, some believe a skull can gather darkness to itself. And to some, that is strong magic in itself. If we ever discover who took them we will almost certainly find they have their own twisted beliefs to justify their actions."

"So you have nothing in particular that might help?"

"I am afraid I do not. What I do have is the ability to sense if someone resides beyond the light. And if you showed me a dozen skulls I might be able to tell you which had been stolen from its resting place."

"That might be enough," Thomas said.

"And if not, Will can hit someone. He claims that usually works."

"It always has in the past," said Will, grinning.

There were still several hours of daylight left when they tied their horses up beyond the lynch gate to St Michael's Church at Garway and Thomas went in search of the priest. He found him in a cottage nearby set on a slope above the church. He told him what he intended to do, then before the man could object showed him his permissions.

The man read them and looked up. "This is highly unusual, but these papers show you have the right. Do you want me to find men to assist you?"

"We can do the work ourselves, but I will also request any misplaced bones we unearth be reinterred in a fresh grave. It will not need to be large nor particularly deep, but it must be done."

"Which again is unusual, but once more I will do as you ask. I will also send a letter to Archdeacon Webb asking for guidance on the burials."

"I know Archdeacon Webb," Thomas said. "He and I ate a fine dinner together only a few nights since. If you write to him send my regards. The name is Thomas Berrington."

After he left, Thomas wondered if he ought to feel guilt at how he had treated the priest, but did not. He was growing tired of the ways of the Church. He had not yet met a man of the cloth he respected, other than Prior Bernard, and questioned if there were any more in existence. If not, it boded ill for the future of England.

When he returned to the church he found that Will had not waited for the priest's permission. Amal had shown him the grave they had identified and Will had already dug down three feet.

"Let me do some of the work," Thomas said.

Will climbed from the hole and handed the spade to his father, who dropped into the hole and started to dig. The soil was harder that he expected and he soon began to sweat.

"Where are Usaden, Jack and Silva?" he asked Amal as he continued to work.

She sat to one side of the grave, her legs crossed as she watched him dig.

"Usaden is sitting on the churchyard wall watching for danger. Jack and Silva are examining the other graves. Silva claims if any have been disturbed she will be able to tell."

"I hope she does not find any or we will be here another day."

"The weather looks fine," said Amal. "We can always sleep under the stars. I did that when I came here with Usaden and enjoyed the experience."

"You are both younger than me."

Amal snorted a laugh.

Thomas stopped talking as his breath grew short. Each shovel of soil had to be lifted higher than the last. He was shoulder-deep in the excavation when he encountered something hard, and when he tapped it he heard a hollow sound.

"Will, I need your help," Thomas called out, and Will came across at once.

"Do you need the whole coffin out or not?" he asked,

squatting beside Amal.

"No, only the lid prised off, but it will be easier with the two of us."

"I am not so sure, but let us see." Will dropped in, took the spade from Thomas and banged it into the top end of the coffin. He levered it from side to side then, as some movement showed, handed the spade back and used his fingers. As he strained, the lid of the coffin rose at one end. Thomas stepped out as Will lifted it to stand at the end of the grave to reveal a scattering of bones and the remains of some clothing. Thomas went back and knelt to examine them, but it was clear there was only one skull present, which belonged to a child. What was also clear was the surfeit of bones.

"We are not the first to open this coffin," he said. "Why go to all the effort? And effort it would be." Thomas turned to Amal. "Go fetch Silva."

"They had a reason, which was the theft of the skull," said Will. "If whoever did it wanted only to hide the orphaned bones, they would have left them above the coffin." He glanced aside as Silva approached, then offered a hand so she could replace him. He stood at the side of the grave beside Amal and watched as Silva ran her hands over the bones without touching them.

"The adult skeleton is of a woman aged around twenty-five," she said as she straightened. "Died in child-birth. I think if you separate the bones, you will find those of her infant among them, but that skull has also been stolen. The third set of bones are from another child, but not hers." She offered her hand to Thomas, who grasped it and pulled her out. He half-expected some kind of shock as he gripped her, but it was nothing more than a hand.

"What should I do, Pa, bring the coffin out?" asked Will.

Thomas shook his head before turning to Amal. "Can you pick the spurious bones out from the others?"

"Of course I can." Amal dropped into the grave, her head not even reaching the top of it, and began to sort through the bones. She gathered several in one hand before laying them on the ground, then continued.

"When Amal is done we will put the top back on and fill the grave again. Let the poor woman and her babe rest in peace, if they can." He looked at Silva. "Will the bones have any memory of the theft?"

She smiled. "Now you are spinning ideas beyond even mine, Tom. No, they are bones, nothing more. All I sense is a distant echo of who they once belonged to. Just as a pear dipped in wine absorbs some of the liquor, so bones will absorb a little of those they belong to."

Amal climbed from the open grave. "I will put the other bones in a sack, Pa. They are of a young girl. We should give her a name."

"Why?"

"So you can tell it to the priest. Without a name he might be tempted to discard them. With a name, it will make it harder to do so. Let us call her Matilda."

Thomas smiled. "Why Matilda?"

Amal shrugged. "I met a girl in Ludlow by that name, a friend to Rose and Jilly. I liked both her and the name."

"Let it be Matilda, then. I will take the bones and inform the priest." Thomas glanced at Silva. "Did you and Jack find any other graves that had been disturbed?"

"Several," said Silva, "but I sensed nothing different about them as I did with this one."

"You can tell?"

Silva made no reply.

Jack said, "People come to Garway searching, Tom."

"For the Grail?"

Jack nodded. "They never find anything because there is nothing here, but they still keep coming. Likely always will."

"It was a Templar church," Thomas said. "They seek the mythic treasures associated with those men."

"Aye, but that was a hundred years ago. Now it is just a church in an out-of-the-way hamlet."

"I take it you have heard of this mythic Grail," Thomas said to Silva, and when she nodded continued. "If such a thing exists, and it is what it is claimed to be, would you be able to sense it?"

"The cup held by Christ?" said Silva, then laughed at Thomas's expression. "I know who Jesus Christ is, Tom, and even believe he existed. Whether he was the son of God, well ... perhaps. And supposing he was then yes, I would sense it. Just because I worship smaller gods does not mean I do not believe in others. The Christian God must have some power to have spread His influence so far and wide. I do not have to worship him to recognise that." She stared around for a moment. "There is something about this place, mind. Something ... other."

Thomas glanced at the small church. It was squat, the square tower rising no more than twice the height of the rest. The foundations of an older round tower showed where a previous building had once stood.

"Fill the grave in, Will. I am going to take a look inside."

As he walked away Silva ran to join him on one side, Amal on the other.

The door of the church was unlocked, as expected. What lay within was not.

Thomas stopped in his tracks. Amal's hand came out and found his.

"It is a little like Spain," she said.

Thomas nodded. Ahead of them, a brick arch separated the church from the nave. It could have been taken from al-Hamra. Thomas had arches like it in his own house, which were considered strange, yet here one stood in a small church on the edge of England. All thanks to the Templars. Thomas had listened to the talk and accepted that those soldiers of God had once lived and worshipped here, but only now did he feel what it must have been like when they did. These were men who had spent much of their lives away from the land of their birth. Men who had gone to distant lands to fight. Men like Bernard. Men like Haylewith and Madoc. Thomas too had travelled to strange lands, but not to fight for his God or any God. Their belief would have made them different to him. Harsh men, perhaps, with harsh belief.

Amal tugged at him. "Look, Pa — the carvings." She drew him to where strange symbols had been cut into the stone. He had seen similar in the cathedral in Córdoba, which had once been the great mosque. He had seen similar in other places converted from the worship of Allah to the worship of God. Except those who had made these marks worshipped God and fought against Allah.

Had that fighting changed them? Had the Templars brought back some of the things they had seen, some beliefs they had acquired? Thomas did not know. He doubted anyone knew, and the only men who ever did were now long dead.

He, Amal and Silva stayed in the church for a full hour, exploring and examining. A Green Man, which Silva explained to him. Scratchings in the shape of fish, animals, and geometric patterns. A heavy stone slab sat on piers to form an altar. Carved into the surface were five crosses. Only when Will came to tell them the day was drawing long did they leave.

Thomas had one more task, so sent the others on their way, promising to catch them up. Then he returned to the cottage beyond the church and spoke with the priest again.

Thomas caught up with the others half a mile beyond Garway where the landscape opened up ahead, a sharp-edged ridge descending to a flat plain. Behind, to left and right, hills rose. When he looked back the small church seemed cosseted within their embrace.

As they rode north away from Garway, Thomas's mind was filled with questions, but he did not know if he would ever find any answers. The talk of the Grail, of relics, felt more real to him now.

TWENTY-ONE

"There is a place ahead we might find a bed for the night," said Jack Pook as the last of the light was fading. He had led them so far, the only one who knew how to reach Tref-y-Clawdd from Garway. They had ridden along valleys where clear streams tumbled between the surrounding hills, and passed through small hamlets where most people had already closed their doors.

"It is an abbey," said Jack, "so will offer sanctuary to passing travellers, though the women will have to sleep separately."

"We can sleep under the stars," said Amal, who had clearly grown a liking for the practice.

Thomas glanced at the sky, then at Jack. "Is that possible, or will there be rain? I would prefer not to sleep in another holy house. I begin to grow tired of them and their morality."

"No rain tonight, but maybe tomorrow," said Jack. "In which case we are best to find a nice meadow next to the river so we can wash. Usaden and me will catch coneys for our dinner. You and Will find wood and build a fire."

"We are going to bathe while you are gone," said Silva. "So go over that way, all of you." She flicked her fingers at them, laughing as she and Amal turned away.

The fire was lit, the rabbits skinned and hanging above it by the time the women returned. Jack tested one of the rabbits and shook his head. Not yet ready.

"Do you know the land around here well?" Thomas asked him.

"Not as well as Lemster and Ludlow, but well enough. I have, after all, been alive a long time and love to wander."

"It feels different here," said Silva.

"Borderland," said Jack and Thomas almost at the same time, both laughing.

"More than that," said Silva. "It feels like a land set apart. Neither English nor Welsh, and almost set outside of time."

"What do you know of the abbey we passed?" Thomas asked Jack.

"Dore Abbey? It is small, quiet, and well-managed for the most part. But like many other of the holy houses around here, it holds to both the old ways and the new."

"Which are?"

"Silva can tell you more about them than me. You saw the Green Man at Garway, I take it?" When Thomas nodded Jack continued. "Well, there is one at Dore Abbey as well, and most of the churches around here, particularly in this valley. They hold strong to the old ways."

"He means Pagan ways," said Silva. She was enclosed within Will's arms and looked more content than Thomas had ever seen her. Safe. Protected. Loved. "The abbeys and churches worship Christ, of course, but it is a Christ mixed together with woodland sprites, the spirits of the rivers, hedgerows and orchards. And belief in the Green Man, who protects both the land and those who inhabit it."

"What do the Church authorities think of such practices?" Thomas asked.

"You would do better to ask your friend Bernard than me."

"Then perhaps that is what I will do. But I do not see what being both Christian and Pagan has to do with the burial of the children's bodies or the theft of skulls."

"What do you intend to do with whatever we discover on this journey?" asked Silva. "We have found one set of orphaned bones and know of another body at Tref-y-Clawdd. But all that does is confirm what you already know from the graves behind your old house. That is not enough on its own."

"I need to confirm whether the children died of natural causes, as I suspect. If they did not, then I need to know who is guilty of taking their lives. Felicia Hughden claimed all the deaths were natural, but I would expect her to do that if she is involved in some way." Thomas leaned forward, the firelight playing across his face so he looked like one of the spirits of the land. "We have knowledge of four deaths. Four sets of bones placed in the graves of another. What if there are ten times that?

Twenty times? What if there has been one hundred deaths and someone is taking the lives of these innocents? That will need to be stopped."

Silva offered a smile tinged with sadness. "Then you and Will are the ones to stop it. But what if you discover the deaths are not deliberate? Can you let it lie?"

It was a good question, but not one Thomas had an answer for.

In the morning they were all damp with dew which dried off as they rode north across rolling countryside where sheep grazed meadows marked by hedgerows and small hamlets dotted the landscape. Jack told them they were heading for Kingston, beyond which they would find a raised ditch he claimed once held back the invading Welsh. It would lead them to Tref-y-Clawdd, and the fresh body Will had found.

Jack dropped back from riding beside Usaden and fell in alongside Thomas. For a while he said nothing, forcing Thomas to speak if only to find out why he had done so.

"You said you didn't know this country as well as you do around Ludlow and Lemster."

"I am familiar with the hedgerows, the houses, the inns and taverns and churches as far north as Salop and as far south as Hereford. Gloster, too, if you push me, but it would be a push. Here I am on the edge of my knowledge."

"And east and west?" Thomas asked.

"West as far as this town we are heading for. It gets wilder the further you go. High mountains. Wild folk. Some pretty women, mind."

"So you know most of the places where people are buried," Thomas said, finally asking the question he wanted to, suspecting it was the reason Jack had come to ride with him.

"Pretty much every single one, including those that are private, like the graves behind your old house. I took a girl or two up there after you and your Pa left. It was still in one piece then. A good place for a bit of privacy. It even had beds."

Thomas laughed at the idea of Jack carousing on the bed his mother and father had used, and welcome to it.

"So if I wanted, you could take me to them all?"

"If you wanted, but you might not. There are lots of them, and this is not your fight, Tom. Lyman d'Alston is not always right in his judgements, but in this he is, much as it pains me to admit it. Besides, what you want to find are the skulls of your family. The bodies are only a means to an end. Accept it."

Thomas rode in silence for a while, absorbing Jack's words, not wanting to acknowledge the truth of them, but knowing they were right.

"How many of these foundlings do you reckon might be scattered throughout the area?"

"Did you not ask Felicia Hughden for a number? If I know anything about her she will have kept records."

"She claimed not," Thomas said. "But even if she had

I am not sure she would let me see them. Can I ask you about the skulls?"

"Ask away. Whether I can offer any help is another matter."

"You know more about what goes on around these parts than anyone else. Why would Ambrose steal them? The bodies laid in graves I can understand, but why take the skulls?"

"You are sure it was Ambrose who did it?" asked Jack.

"I am sure he was responsible for burying at least some of the bodies of children. It makes no sense someone else opened the same graves and took the skulls. So yes, Ambrose took them."

"I do not know why," said Jack. "What would he want them for? I heard the talk you had with Silva yesterday about what reasons someone might have to covet them, but Ambrose is not that person. I knew him well enough to say that. Driven, God-fearing, but not strange. Not in that way, anyway."

"In what way was he strange?" Thomas asked.

"His belief in God was plain to see, but what else he believed in was not. He was like an empty bowl. He revealed nothing about himself. Whether it was to hide something, or there was nothing there to hide, I do not know."

"Do you have any idea who might have wanted him dead?"

Jack shook his head. "Ambrose was too benign for anyone to kill him."

"Yet someone did."

"As you say, Tom, someone did. I leave it to you to find out who that is, and the reason for it. I cannot see Ambrose ever provoking murderous intent in anyone."

"It was not only a killing, Jack," Thomas said. "He was tortured first. He knew something someone wanted. I would like to know what that was."

"Is it not obvious? You spoke of it yourself at Garway."

"The Grail? That makes sense if you believe it actually exists, but I do not."

Jack laughed. "You and I have no need to believe it exists. Only whoever killed Ambrose needs to believe it does. Ambrose would not have been killed because he stole skulls. Every church in the land has those in their ossuaries. Does that not make it even stranger he stole them from opened graves?"

Thomas had not considered that question before, so he did now. He was still exploring the idea when ahead the land fell away to reveal a small town set around a river.

"Is that the Lugge?" Thomas asked.

"The Arrow," said Jack. "Good fishing. We cross the Hindwell Brook before another hour passes, and then after that the Lugge. Then we climb over Hengwm Hill and our destination stands on the banks of the Teme. A lot of rivers around here. But then we also get a lot of rain. Did you get much rain in this place you came from?"

"Spain," Thomas said. "The south of Spain. And no, not so much rain, but when it did come it was heavier than any rain you will have ever experienced in England.

But most of the time it is dry and hot. Hotter than England by far."

"I am surprised you stayed there so long." Jack showed no sign of growing tired of Thomas's company.

"I liked it. Liked the people and liked the land, not to mention the knowledge that resides there. At least it used to. When al-Andalus fell, most of the libraries and what they contained were destroyed."

"Is that where you got all those books you have, from these libraries?"

"Some of them, yes, but most were acquired from more distant lands. Can you think of any reason why Ambrose would have taken the skulls, and for what reason?"

"I thought you had forgotten my question, but Usaden tells me you forget nothing."

"Not true, but I admit to knowing a great deal. Not all of it useful. Just as you know every brook, field and house around here, though I suspect that might be more useful."

"It is for someone like me who finds his food in the wild. And I cannot think of any reason at all why Ambrose would want the skulls. Though if he disposed of the bodies, then I agree he must have taken them, but not for himself. Do you know there is a church somewhere up north that claims to have the skull of Saint Cuthbert?"

"I did not — but Spain also has an abundance of saints, and I expect they all had skulls at one time, even if some had them removed with an axe or broadsword." Thomas smiled because the idea of Ambrose stealing skulls to pass them off as those of saints made no sense, either. Even if Ambrose had been the kind of man to do such a thing, how many saints' skulls could be pass off as being genuine before people grew suspicious?

"Tell me, Tom," said Jack, "who do you think he might have been taking them for?"

"I had a conversation with the priest at Garway."

Jack frowned. "That is no answer."

"Patience; it will be. I asked who the priest was before him and he said—"

"Owain Haylewith," said Jack. "I could have told you that if you had asked me. It is no secret, but it does lie a ways back in the past."

"Bernard told me Haylewith was the priest there, but I did not realise he was replaced by the current incumbent. So I asked what he knew of the man."

"And?"

Ahead, the valley they were following narrowed and hills rose which they would need to cross, but Thomas knew their horses would barely notice the ascent. They were less sure on a descent, but going up their strong back legs did all the work.

"He told me information that confirms what others have said or hinted at. Haylewith is strange. He holds to the notions you spoke of that are rich in this borderland. He believes in both God and the spirits of the land. Christ and Pagan combined, and in Haylewith's mind, perhaps one and the same thing. The priest told me Haylewith was obsessed with finding the Grail."

"It does not exist, Tom. I thought we already decided that."

"I agree. But Haylewith believed, and still believes. He also believes an even stranger story. That the bones of Christ were brought to England by the Templars and lie buried somewhere close to Garway. It would explain why Ambrose took the skulls at the same time he buried the foundlings."

"It would surprise me if Ambrose believed such a thing."

"As it would me, but he was not collecting the skulls for himself but someone else. Who that is might be Owain Haylewith, who still searches for that one skull imbued with great meaning."

"The night Ambrose died Haylewith was meant to be sleeping in the guest house at Wigmore, which is beyond the grounds of the abbey, but he was seen crossing the cloister in the company of Madoc a half hour before Matins. One of the brothers told Jorge he saw them."

"Do you intend to confront him with this?"

"When the time is right."

"It would be better now before he takes his place at Wigmore. As Abbot there he will have great influence."

"He is already appointed Abbot, so it makes no difference now or a month from now. I would rather build a stronger case before confronting him. It is not as if he will be going anywhere."

Beyond Kingston they picked up the raised ditch. Ahead the land rose to high, rounded hills. To the west, more hills faded into the far distance. This land marked the edge of England, and it felt like a different place. Thomas barely noticed the landscape because he was working through the connections spun like a web in his mind. Garway. Elmbrook. Hindwell. Wigmore. Other places. Every church and burial ground in the area. Could all this be about nothing more than the irrational beliefs of one man? He did not believe Haylewith likely to have killed Ambrose himself, but Madoc was another matter.

TWENTY-TWO

Tref-y-Clawdd nestled between rounded hills, a small town with a church set beside the glistening waters of the Teme, narrow and shallower here than at Ludlow.

"The burial ground is next to the church," said Will, who had replaced Jack Pook at Thomas's side.

"We should speak with the priest first. Show him my letter of authority."

"If you can find him," said Will. "When we came here he was nowhere to be seen. The gravediggers said he spends a great deal of his time absent. They told me lay preachers often have to take the daily service. But I agree, it would be politic to see if he is at home. He has a house set close to the church."

They made their way through narrow streets clustered around a small market square. People buying produce, and the stallholders selling it, watched them pass without comment. When they reached the priest's house, Thomas dismounted while the others continued on to the graveyard. He knocked on the door but there was no response. He peeked through the window of one room and saw it sparsely furnished. An open grate showed no fire laid, but it was June and one might not be needed. Even so, the house had an air of abandonment.

"If you be looking for the priest, he be gone to Hindwell Abbey. Always goes there this time of year. Some special midsummer celebration. Not that I asked him, but he told me all the same." The speaker stood beyond the gate to the house. He was short, bow-legged, the top half of his face obscured with a wide-brimmed hat pulled low, the bottom half by a thick beard.

"My thanks," Thomas said.

"Who be you?"

"I am Justice of the Peace for the district and wanted to speak with the priest on a matter of law." Thomas was unsure if his jurisdiction extended this far west but suspected the man would not know that, either.

"Does not surprise me he has done summat wrong."

"He has done nothing, as far as I know. I am looking into the opening of graves."

The man coughed, then spat. "There were folks here not long since digging into graves. Blasphemy, I calls it."

"Are you one of the gravediggers?" Thomas asked.

"Not me, but my brother is. It was him told me about it. Big lad, they said, white hair." He grinned. "And a girl they would both have liked to tup, but she had eyes only for the tall one. Said they found summat that should not be there."

"I heard the gravediggers told the man and woman where the disturbed grave lay."

"I never heard that, but it is likely. Who knows a graveyard better than those who put people in it?"

Thomas reached into his jacket and removed his authorisation. "I have permission to open the grave if you wish to see it."

"Would do me no good, nor my brother, but you look like an honest man."

The man turned and walked away swaying, not from ale but from the wear on his body over many years. Thomas expected life in these hills could prove hard. He did not bother to mount Ferrant again but led him around the church until he found the others. Will stood at the far end of the gravesite, where he had already started to dig.

"I assumed you would get permission," he said.

"I was told the priest has gone to Hindwell Abbey to enquire about a midsummer festival. So we have no permission other than the one I carry."

"The Church celebrates the feast of St John the Baptist at midsummer," said Silva. "Perhaps they do that at this abbey, but if so, they have stolen the true meaning of the day from older times. There is an old hill fort near there where Pagans used to celebrate midsummer."

"Whatever the reason, he is not here," Thomas said. "So we dig."

"Someone has worked this soil since I came last," said Will.

"Open it and show me what you found. The rest of you do not need to come close."

Nobody moved away, which did not surprise Thomas, so he nodded at Will to carry on and went to stand on the edge of the grave. He raised his gaze to the hills, aware this was a good place for a body to rest. The sound of the river running over rapids could be heard, and the cries of kites and buzzards fell across the landscape. In the sunshine it was a pleasant spot, but would be less so in the dark and cold of winter. As most places would, he supposed.

After a while, Will stopped when he reached a well-used coffin.

"The body was laid on top of this, Pa. I should have uncovered it by now."

"Open the coffin. I want to see if the skull is missing."

Thomas dropped in beside Will and between them they levered the lid from the coffin. As at Garway, all that remained were stained bones, but no skull.

Thomas pushed the lid of the coffin back down then climbed out. He handed the spade to Will to start putting the soil back and went to stand next to Silva.

"What is it about the skulls?" he asked her. "At first I thought it might be a message to me when they took John's and my mother's, but every time they bury a foundling they take the skull of whoever lies in the grave."

Instead of answering directly, Silva asked a question of her own. "When you first knew me you did not believe in my abilities. Is that true?"

Thomas nodded.

Silva went on, "And now?"

"I have seen what you can do. I expect Will has told you how I am. I trained in the great infirmary of Malaka so believed only in what I could see and measure, in how a treatment affected a patient. You have changed me. I do not know how you do what you do, but I have seen the evidence of it. So yes, I believe in you."

Silva smiled. "Will told me you had changed but I wanted to hear it from you."

Beyond her, Thomas saw Usaden move suddenly and knew he had seen something he considered a danger. He looked around but saw nothing. A place of burial. A river. A small town. Hills on all sides and raptors hanging in the air.

"What is it?" asked Silva.

"Nothing. You spoke to me of skulls when we visited Garway. Have you given them any more thought?"

"I have. Someone may be trying to seek their wisdom. A skull holds the brain, and the brain holds a person's memories and knowledge. Some believe taking a skull gives them access to its owner's wisdom." She hesitated, and Thomas could see her making a decision. "I have two skulls on shelves in my cottage. One is my father's. The other belongs to my grandfather. They were both men of great wisdom. When I partake of the ecstasy the mushrooms bring, I feel closer to them and their knowledge. That may be why the skulls have been taken. Not for who they are but for what they possess. Whoever takes them seeks to drink deep of their knowledge, but it needs a special state of mind to do so."

"The kind the mushrooms bring," Thomas said.

"You seem to know of it."

"I have experienced that loss of my true mind, yes, but it has been many years since I did so." Thomas smiled. "It was Bernard who showed me the mushrooms here in England and warned me of their effect. And there were others in France and Spain."

"Did he warn you not to partake?"

Thomas shook his head. "He told me what might happen. That it could be good or it could be bad. In general, he tended to leave the final decision on such things to me, even if I was but a lad of thirteen years."

"He is a wise man," said Silva.

Thomas nodded. "The wisest man I know. It concerns me that the taking of the skulls is an erratic thing. What if the people they were taken from possessed little wisdom? I know my brother John would have possessed little."

"But suppose the theft was not random but deliberate? That whoever took them knew who they belonged to and wanted the knowledge they possessed when alive."

Thomas stared at Silva, wondering if she truly believed what she said.

"Who might seek this wisdom?"

"I am not saying it is possible. I do not believe the wisdom of my father and grandfather has been transferred to me, but whoever wants the skulls might believe they can access it. It may be someone who lacks wisdom and seeks it, or someone who possesses great wisdom already but lusts after more, just as a glutton lusts after food even as their belly is about to burst."

"Abbot John was a glutton, but also a wise man," Thomas said. "Might he have taken them?"

"I doubt it was anyone in the Church, not even some of those who do not follow the strict rules of it. If pressed, I would say it is someone who does not believe in the Christian God but a far older one."

"Which do you believe in?" Thomas asked.

Silva smiled. "I told you, I believe in the small gods. The gods of the hedgerows and woods. The gods of rivers and pastures, of valleys and hills and clouds, of rain and sun and mists, of light and darkness. I also half-believe in the Christian God because I have seen him cure people when nothing else can. Unless people who believe strongly enough can cure themselves."

Thomas experienced a new closeness to Silva, aware she had opened herself to him. He wondered how much of what she had spoken about had she also told to Will. He suspected all of it.

"So who should I be looking for?"

"You mean we."

"Who should we be looking for?"

Silva laughed. "You are better at that kind of thing than me, but know I can help if you need me. Look for someone similar to me, but who follows the old Gods and also the new."

Usaden returned and motioned Thomas to join him.

"There are a dozen men dressed as soldiers on the northern hillside. They think we cannot see them and are tucked away in a fold of the land now, but they were watching us. We should attack them and find out what they want."

"What if they do not want us?" Thomas asked.

"Then we let them go on their way."

"And if they fight and we kill some of them, even if they are innocent?"

Usaden made no response. No doubt he did not understand the logic of what Thomas had said.

Thomas glanced across to see Will had filled the grave in and was now stamping up and down to settle the ground. Amal did the same beside him but without as much success, and Thomas smiled.

"We should attempt to get back to Burway before dark." He glanced at the sky. "How long to ride there from here?"

"It took us almost four hours when we came back, but we rode directly to Burway. I suspect you will want to speak to your friend Bernard at Wigmore first."

"I would like to, yes. But you and the others can ride to Burway and I will go on alone."

Will nodded at the empty hillside. "Not with those men up there. I could see them as well as Usaden. We stick together. Which means we all ride to Wigmore." Will raised his voice. "Jack, how far from here to Wigmore Abbey?"

"On horseback, close to three hours, less if we push

the horses, but they have already had two long days, so three hours. Is that where we are going?"

"If you want to come with us," Thomas said.

"Where else have I got to go? And a free meal is a free meal."

As they rode out from Tref-y-Clawdd, the men Usaden had tracked appeared on the hillside across the valley of the Teme. Twelve men, as he had said. Dressed in jerkins marked with a red cross, bows and swords slung from their saddles. No doubt knives pushed into their boots. Thomas set his hand on the hilt of his own sword, but the men only tracked them for a mile before turning away.

"Who are they, and what interest do they have in us?" Thomas spoke to no one in particular nor expected any answer, but Jack Pook offered an opinion.

"They are the warrior monks of Hindwell Abbey, Tom. I see them now and again when I come out this way, which is not often. They think of themselves as soldiers of God, but I call them a pain in the arse with their airs and graces and prayers. They claim to offer protection to the holy houses this far west but spend most of their time at Felicia Hughden's bordel."

"I suppose you have never visited there," Thomas said.

"Every red-blooded man for twenty miles around knows about it, and the other places. And as you know, despite my age, I am a red-blooded man."

"Who now has a sweet woman of his own in Ludlow."

Jack grinned. "I did not say I had visited there recently. And those warrior monks were never a threat to us. You, Will and Usaden would have made short work of them. They think they can fight, but all they know is how to bully money out of people. They claim it is charity for the Church."

Thomas turned in his saddle to look back, but the men had disappeared. He had learned new facts over the last two days, facts and musings, and needed to talk with Bernard to see if he could help him make sense of them because Thomas was not sure he could do so himself.

TWENTY-THREE

As they descended towards Wigmore Abbey their shadows danced long ahead of them. Soon, the sun would sink below the western hills and darkness would cover the land. They were a quarter mile away when a lone rider came from the abbey and started south on the main track at speed.

"Is that your friend Bernard?" asked Will.

Thomas narrowed his eyes, but it was Jack who said, "Aye, that's Prior Bernard. Looks like he is in a hurry to get somewhere."

"The rest of you go on to Burway, or stay the night at Wigmore, it will be dark soon. I will ride after Bernard. He would not leave in such haste unless something was wrong." Thomas did not wait for any confirmation before encouraging Ferrant into a gallop. The horse responded readily enough but would be tired after the long days. Thomas felt guilty but knew he had to catch up with Bernard.

Which he did within a mile. Bernard glanced across to offer a nod of recognition but rode on.

"What is wrong?" Thomas shouted above the sound of their horses' hooves.

"What might be wrong, Tom. I ride to find out. I am glad to see you, even more so to see you armed. I might need your skill with a sword if what I hear is true."

"Which is?" Thomas was a little out of breath, Prior Bernard less so.

"You will find out when we get there. For now, Tom, ride."

Thomas urged more speed from Ferrant, who made an extra effort. Thomas hoped he was doing no harm to the horse, but feared what Prior Bernard was leading them towards.

Light leached from the sky and dusk came to cloak the fields and trees. They rode through hamlets and villages, some no more than a house or two. At each place people came out to see who the madmen were. By the time they reached Lemster night had come, and it was only the candles in house windows and torches set in sconces on the town wall that offered guidance. At the priory, they left their panting horses in the care of a brother and Prior Bernard strode inside with Thomas following behind. He knew weapons were not allowed within the stone walls but did not waste time removing his.

"Where is he?" said Prior Bernard to the first brother he came across.

"Where is who?"

Thomas noted the lack of name or title.

"You know who. Where is he!"

Cowed, the man lowered his head. "Where you would be if you were still Prior."

Bernard pushed past him hard, almost knocking the brother onto his back. Thomas followed, stifling an urge to kick him. They entered the priory, familiar to Thomas, and he knew where they were going. A long corridor, a turn, and they were at the office of the Prior.

Bernard made no effort to knock but slammed the door open.

The man seated behind the desk rose to his feet, his hand reaching beneath it for what could only be a weapon, but none appeared. Not yet.

"Do you wish to speak to me, Bernard?" The lack of title was a deliberate insult. "If so, kindly make an appointment and I will see if I can fit you into my busy schedule. Lemster Priory has been badly managed for some time now, and there is a great deal of work to do."

"Judas! What right do you have to sit in this room?"

"I see you are going to be unreasonable," said Madoc. "Very well. I am appointed by the Abbot of Wigmore. Both Hindwell Abbey and Lemster Priory now fall under my jurisdiction. Abbot Haylewith called me to Hindwell because he was concerned about rumours of transgressions at Lemster Priory." Madoc tilted his head to one side. He withdrew his hand from beneath the desk. It was empty. Perhaps he believed the moment of danger had passed and he was now in the ascendency. "He spoke with both the Archdeacons of

Hereford and Salop, and they agreed something must be done."

"He has not had time to do that," said Bernard.

"I believe he dined with them the day of the conclave, as did your friend who stands beside you."

"I was there only briefly," Thomas said. "Is that what they spoke about after I left — falsity?"

"You mean Bernard's falsity, then yes, I believe they did. It has come to their attention that he has exceeded his authority in several matters. I am sorry to say that most of them involve you, Berrington. I believe the investigation of disturbed graves was mentioned, amongst other things. Both of you know that to do such a thing is blasphemous. And then there is the matter of the death of Abbot John. It is known that only the two of you were in attendance when he died." Another tilt of the head. "Was that a coincidence, or does it have a more sinister meaning?"

"Brother Ambrose was also there. He took the Abbot's confession at the end."

"And now he too is dead. Another coincidence? What secrets and lies were in that note Ambrose sent you, Berrington?" A wave of the hand. "No matter. I expect it has been destroyed by now. You are both fortunate that the Abbot is a godly and forgiving man. There was talk of having you both arrested and tried for murder. That may still happen if either of you tries to make trouble."

"Did you say Abbot Haylewith appointed you to both houses?"

"He did."

"Except he is not Abbot yet. I am."

"Really? Are you sure?"

Bernard frowned. "I have come from Wigmore not two hours since. I was Abbot when I left."

"And now you are here. My information is that Abbot Haylewith has this day left to take up his position at Wigmore Abbey. Which means..." Madoc smiled and looked off into space as if searching for an answer. "...ah yes, you are now without a position. I expect you can become a lowly brother again, but not here and not at Wigmore. Or Thomas might offer you a post. He no doubt needs someone to pick up the horseshit from his meadows."

Bernard started towards Madoc, but Thomas grabbed him and pulled him back.

Madoc continued to smile.

"You have made one mistake," said Bernard. "In fact, more than one, but this is the most important. An Abbot, even of a large abbey such as Wigmore, cannot appoint people to posts himself. The Archdeacon of Hereford, perhaps, but not Abbot Haylewith. If you are to sit over both Lemster Priory and Hindwell Abbey the brothers of each will have to select you."

Madoc was no longer smiling.

"The brothers confirmed my elevation this morning."

"Because there was no alternative, am I right? And if we were to walk out among them now and ask who they want to be Prior would they choose you? I believe it is almost time for Compline. Let us announce you wish your appointment — not elevation — to be confirmed in the proper manner. Which, of course, will require two candidates. Now, who can there be who is qualified for the position? Oh, yes. Me."

Bernard turned and walked from the office. Distantly, the bell rang to call the brothers for worship.

"I would hurry and follow him if I were you," Thomas said. "Before he has a chance to put his case before his flock."

"There is no need. Bernard will not get as far as the chapel."

This time Thomas rushed from the office. As he entered the cloister, he discovered a dozen armed men clustered around Bernard. He saw Thomas and shook his head for him to stay back, but it did no good.

Thomas knew he could not draw a weapon within the precinct of the priory, though that did not appear to have been pointed out to the men around Bernard. They should have known because they belonged to the army of warrior monks who had tracked Thomas and the others when they left Tref-y-Clawdd. They might even be the same men.

Twelve, Thomas thought. Only twelve. And with luck Bernard might assist, even if he claimed to have turned his back on war.

As Thomas ran through the line of brothers moving towards the chapel they stopped to watch what was about to happen. One or two of the warrior monks caught his movement and turned, raising their weapons. Knives, mostly, which might be a mistake.

Thomas punched the first man before barrelling into

a second. Now only ten remained on their feet, and most of those were trying to move away from Bernard to face their attacker. Thomas felled three more, still without receiving a blow, but it could not last. He had moved in haste and allowed men to get behind him. Four faced him, but as he moved forwards arms grasped him, holding him back. Before he could move there came a sharp blow in his back, followed by a sudden weakness. He tried to pull free but no longer had the strength.

And so it ends... The thought passed through his mind. *And if it ends this way, let me make a good show of it.*

He jerked one arm free, turned and lashed out. One man jerked away, stumbled and fell on his backside. Thomas kicked him in the face then turned to his other side. Before he could lash out, Bernard moved past him and punched the man on the side of the head. Which left four men standing. Seeing the odds shortened, they backed away, then turned and fled. Two others climbed to their feet and followed them.

"You are hurt," said Bernard.

"Winded, that is all."

"No, hurt." Bernard raised his hand to show it covered in blood. "They stuck you, Tom. In the precinct of the priory. This is the end of Madoc and his ambitions. Here, lean on me. I will take you to the infirmary."

Thomas accepted the offer and Bernard supported him.

"Not here," he said. "Not where Madoc rules. I will never see the sun rise. Take me home."

For a moment Thomas thought Bernard would

object, then he firmed the grip around his waist and turned aside. Their horses remained beyond the priory gate, and Thomas had to try three times to lift himself into Ferrant's saddle. He reached beneath his jacket to find his side slick with his own blood. *How much have I lost? Too much?*

"Take me to Burway, Bernard. As fast as we can ride."

He nodded and reached out to grasp Ferrant's reins. "Hang on tight then, Tom. I intend to get you there alive."

Townsfolk scattered as they passed, and then they were out in the darkness, only the faint illumination of a quarter moon and stars in a cloudless sky to guide them, but Bernard knew the way, and so did Ferrant. Their hooves sounded loud to be swallowed by the dark, and then, slowly, darkness pressed closer to encompass Thomas and gather him within its cold grasp.

It is time.

His last thought.

TWENTY-FOUR

Amal had been about to climb the stairs to her room but decided she needed a book from her father's workshop, so when Prior Bernard rode hard into the courtyard she spun around at the cacophony to see her father slide from Ferrant's sweat-streaked body to fall in a heap on the stone slabs.

"He was alive when we left Lemster but I have not checked on him since. It was more important I get him here."

Amal went to her knees and turned her father over. His eyes were closed, his face pale in the flicker of the torches lighting the courtyard.

"How long?" she asked.

"Less than an hour."

"What happened?"

"I can tell you later. All you need to know now is he was stabbed in the back."

Amal nodded and rolled her father over. She pulled his

jacket up to find his shirt stained crimson and felt a deep fear roil through her. *This cannot be. Pa is invulnerable.*

Then the training that her father had given her from the first moment she could perch on his knee to see what he was doing, and which he later showed her how to do the same for herself, took over and she ripped his shirt to reveal a gash in his side which was bruised around.

When she pressed against it blood seeped out.

She wondered how much of it remained in her father.

"Once we have him in the workshop I want you to fetch the others. I need Belia, and possibly Silva, and Will must know." Amal worked as she talked. Prior Bernard helped, removing Thomas's boots and hose. He knelt and lifted Thomas, barely showing strain as he carried him to the workshop.

"Lie him on his front," said Amal.

Prior Bernard set his friend on the wide bench then left Amal to her work, aware Thomas's blood streaked his own clothes.

Amal put her hand flat on her father's back between his shoulder blades and waited. Waited some more. Then she felt his chest rise and fall.

She touched his throat and found the beat of his heart, fainter than she would like, but he still lived.

Her mind closed down the fear that threatened to engulf her as she turned to the side benches to find what she needed. No poppy or hemp yet, because he would feel nothing until he woke. If he woke! *No!* — that thought she consigned to the darkness beyond the workshop.

She barely noticed when the others arrived, except Will came too close so she pushed him away.

"There is nothing you can do. Let me work."

Amal probed the wound, looking for internal damage. She drew the edges apart and had Belia hold a lamp close so she could peer inside, using wet linen strips wrapped around wooden spills to clear the blood. She nodded when she found the blade had missed his bowel, kidney and liver. Good.

"Herbs," she said to Belia, only to see she had already brought them. Mixed together in a pot together with oil and water.

Amal took them in her fingers and pushed them into the wound where they would help prevent infection. More hope, but hope based on experience. It is what her father would do.

Amal threaded a needle with gut, drew the edges of the wound together and began to stitch it shut. Her lips compressed, and she did not hear the conversation that flowed around her until she was finished. She cut the end of the gut and examined her handiwork. Yes, good enough. Better than her father could do, which is what he always told her, so more than good enough. Only then did Amal allow what had been done to him to wash through her. She would have fallen to the floor but Will was there to catch her. Her big brother. Tall Will. Strong Will. He lifted her as if she weighed nothing and turned to carry her to the house.

"No. I stay here until he wakes. Put me down." Amal

punched Will's chest and he set her on her feet, but kept one strong arm around her waist. It was a comfort.

"I will fetch a cot," said Belia.

"Do the children know?" asked Amal.

"Not yet. I thought it better to let them sleep."

Amal nodded. Her strength was returning, and as it did she was aware of the fear fading. She knew now how her father felt when he did this work. It was the reason people called him butcher, because when he worked humanity left him. It was not possible to be gentle and also save the life of someone who would die without you.

When Amal looked up she stared into Jorge's eyes. Tears tracked his face to drip from his chin.

"Save him, Ami. I love him."

"He knows."

"I will stay with you if you allow me to."

"Of course. Talk to him. Talk to me. Tell me stories about the two of you I have not heard before."

Silva came close, hesitated.

"Can I touch him, Ami?"

Amal nodded.

Silva set her hands on Thomas's back and closed her eyes.

Where she went and what she experienced Amal did not know. What she did know is she trusted her. She knew her father found it difficult to accept what Silva did, but Amal found it easier. Perhaps because she was young and more open to strange ideas. She wondered if her father had been that way when he was her age. She knew he had left England when he was a year younger than she was now. His mind would be open to new experiences, but he had never spoken of what he had done then and spoke little of what he had done since.

There was nothing she could do but wait. And pray.

Amal frowned, wondering where that thought had come from.

She turned to see Bel standing beyond the doorway, as if she could not bring herself to enter. She had found Thomas again after many years, and now the two of them were together as they were always meant to be.

Amal went to her.

"Come and hold his hand. Pray for him. I will fetch Prior Bernard. If God will listen to anyone it should be him."

"Pray with me," said Bel.

"We will all pray, even those who do not believe."

Prior Bernard joined them, leading the prayers, his voice sonorous, his demeanour holy. Amal allowed the words to wash over her and through her. Something touched her, but what it was she did not know. Something *other*. Something not of this world. No doubt Silva would claim it was a wood sprite or a spirit of the river, but Amal did not know, nor did she care. It brought comfort, and hope.

It was late. Only she, Jorge and Prior Bernard remained, but he told her to call him Bernard because he was no longer sure he was Prior of anything.

"Your father saved me tonight," he said.

"It is what he does," said Jorge. "He is not even aware

of it, but he saves people. He saved you, and he saved me."

"I do not believe those men would have killed me, but I would have received a bad beating, I am sure."

"I would have died without Thomas," said Jorge, and Amal leaned forward. She had never heard the full tale of how her father had met Jorge, only that he had turned him into what he had become, but not the how, the when or the why. She wanted to ask him but it felt like too much effort. Everything seemed an effort to her. It was late and she needed sleep, but could not sleep until her father woke. He will wake, she told herself, because the alternative was too awful to consider.

"Tell me how Tom did that," said Bernard, not Prior anymore. "When did it happen?"

Jorge smiled. "A long time ago now. A very long time ago. It was ..." He stared into space. "... it must have been thirty-five years ago because I had fourteen years and believed I had killed my brother."

"Believed?"

"He fell from the old bridge in Córdoba. There was blood, and I thought him dead, so I ran. I was lost. Afraid. I walked for days until I came across a group of soldiers. Spanish soldiers. They had heard a band of Moors were close by and were searching for them. They took me in. And then we found the Moors."

Nobody spoke. Eventually, Jorge went on.

"There was a battle. I will not describe it other than to say it was terrible, it was bloody, and the Moors prevailed. They took prisoners, but only so they could make each man watch as they beheaded another. One after the other, until only one remained. Me.

"I am a handsome man, I know it, and I was a handsome boy. The Moors decided not to kill me. I was to be saved for something worse. And then Thomas came along.

"He had been treating the wounded, ending the lives of those who would die in agony hours or days later. I heard what they called him. Butcher. And I feared him. He was tall and magnificent, with long hair bleached by the sun, his face almost as dark as those he treated, but I could tell he was no Moor.

"And then the Sultan came to see what his men had done. He approved. He looked at me, his eyes dark and cold. I knew as they fell on me that I would die, but only after hours of agony as each of the men took me in turn. I tried to run but they caught me, laughing, pushing me from one to the other, touching me. Then Thomas intervened."

Amal reached out and touched her father's back, relieved to find him still alive. His breath came louder, and drool dripped from his open mouth. She took a cloth and wiped it away, then kissed his cheek. She thought of him as a younger man. Thirty-five years younger. Which would have made him twenty-seven. She tried to imagine him at that age but could not. All she saw was the father she knew and loved now.

"What did he do?" she asked.

"The only thing he could do. He stripped me naked and stood me in front of the Sultan. I tried to appear brave, for I thought Thomas was about to rape me, and I shook with fear.

"'Look at him,' he said. 'He is young. He is beautiful. He will make a wonderful eunuch for your harem. The women will love him.'"

"'Not too much, I trust,' said the Sultan, and Thomas laughed and said, 'Not by the time I have finished with him.'"

"'Keep his beauty if you can,' said the Sultan. 'And his manhood as well. It is fine indeed. But take that which will cause problems if you leave them, yes?'"

"'Yes,'" Thomas said.

"I will not go into the details. I am sure you would not wish to hear them."

"I would," said Amal. "Pa has always skirted around what he did to you, and I am curious."

"Then ask him," said Jorge. "Know only that he used poppy on me, he used hot water, and when he took my balls I felt nothing but a pressure in my stomach. There was blood, but not so much. And there was pain, but again not so much. And then I recovered and found ... well, it is a delicate matter, so I will not mention exactly what I discovered, only that I could still satisfy a woman." Jorge smiled. "And can still satisfy a woman. But only the one now."

"Yet you have three fine children," said Bernard.

"Again, thanks to Thomas."

Amal thought of the young Jorge, the same age as she was now, unmanned but saved from something worse than death. Just as she had been violated. A violation that still stalked her dreams and woke her in the night, but she fought against it. She did not want that act to diminish her. Just as Jorge had not allowed what her father had done to diminish him. Amal loved Jorge as if he was a second father, and, she liked to think, he loved her as if she was a second daughter.

Moths fluttered against the lamps. Some died. Some escaped.

Jorge rose and went into the house to lie beside Belia, but Amal doubted he would sleep.

Bernard stretched out on the floor and wrapped his robe of office around himself.

Amal tried to stay awake, but eventually sleep took her as well. The night was still, only the whisper of the river running across gravel and an occasional cry as an owl sought prey to break the silence. And Thomas Berrington slept the sleep of the drugged as he hung between life and death.

TWENTY-FIVE

Thomas came awake slowly, in fits and starts. He drifted towards the surface, grew aware of voices but unable to decipher the words, and then he would sink again. Eventually he began to feel his body. The hardness of the surface beneath him. A pain in his back. Low down on one side, and as he floated upwards a fragmented memory came to him.

"Bernard..."

The word drifted into the world. As it did so it conjured an image of a man. Tall, strong, dressed in a long, dark robe. Prior Bernard. A man of God. A holy man.

"Prior Bernard." Thomas's lips were dry, the words meaningless even to himself. Then something cold was placed against his lips, and he sucked on the offer of water.

"Slowly, Pa," came a voice, together with another name. Amal. His daughter.

"How..." Thomas started, but the effort of talking sapped his strength and nothing emerged.

"A night and almost a whole day," said the voice. Amal's voice. "You will live, I think."

Live? The concept meant nothing to Thomas. I am alive, so I live. What does Amal mean?

"Hurts," he mumbled.

"You were stuck with a knife. Fortunately not a long knife, and wielded by someone who did not know where to strike. Bernard saved you. He brought you here and I stitched your wound. Belia packed it with herbs and the..."

The voice drifted away. Too many words. Too much meaning.

Thomas sank into the comfort of the darkness again.

The next time he surfaced his eyes snapped open, memory flooding through him. What had happened and what the implications were.

Beyond the window, golden light filled the air as the sun lowered once again. He had lost a night and a day.

"Where is Bernard?"

"He went inside to sleep. He has sat beside you the whole time."

"And you?"

"What else would you expect me to do?"

"Help me get up, Ami."

Her hand pressed him down.

"Not yet. But if you can, sit up. I want to examine your wound before I let you do anything."

"You might need to help me." Thomas shifted and

looked down at himself. "And where are my clothes?" The effort of trying to move exhausted him.

"I cut them off you. They were covered in blood and we had to wash you."

"We?"

"Me, Bel and Belia." Amal smiled. "Prior Bernard stayed. He said it was a matter of propriety."

"I am not sure Bernard is a Prior anymore."

"Of course. Abbot Bernard."

"Not that either. It is the reason I was stabbed. Has he told you what happened?"

"Not yet. I think he wanted to see if you lived first."

"How is my back? Can I stand yet?"

"Your wound looks better than I expected, so yes, as long as one of us helps you."

"Then send for Will and Jorge, but let Bernard sleep. I want to talk to the others. And send a message for Usaden to come."

"No, Pa. You are not riding out in pursuit of vengeance. At least not until you are fully healed, which will be ten days or more. I will fetch Will and Jorge because they can help you inside, but you will not do what you always do."

It was sometime later, once Thomas had been helped — or rather mostly carried — inside and sat in a wide chair padded with blankets and cushions, before Amal asked, "Who were the men who attacked you, Pa?"

"Bernard and Jack call them warrior monks. Pretend soldiers, more like, for which I am profoundly grateful."

"Three inches to the left and it would have pierced

your liver," said Amal. "So perhaps not such pretend soldiers, after all."

"But it was not three inches to the left, was it."

"Eat," said Bel, putting a bowl in front of him.

Thomas sniffed. "What is it?"

"Good for you. Eat it."

Thomas suspected she was angry with him for getting injured. For letting himself be in a place that allowed him to be injured. But life — his life — was not like that. A man could live quietly, keep his head down and his mouth shut, and allow people to grind him into the dirt. Or he could stand up and fight for what he knew to be right.

Thomas could not be anything other than what he was.

He also knew Bel would not love him if he were that other kind of man, so he ate whatever was set before him and said it was delicious.

Later, Bel kissed his mouth and told him she was going to bed. Amal followed, after telling Thomas he could stay in the kitchen another hour. Jorge and Belia disappeared. Only Will remained so he could help Thomas upstairs when he was ready to go, but he looked tired.

"Has Silva gone back to her cottage?"

"She is upstairs, where I should be."

"Go if you want. I am sure I can manage the stairs on my own."

"Bel would never forgive me if I did that, let alone Ami."

"Then lie back and sleep. I need time to think."

"About who attacked you?"

"Among other things."

Thomas turned his head at the sound of footsteps to see Prior Bernard enter the room, washing his hands across his face.

"Is there anything to eat? I am famished."

"There is some stew on the stove. It is not too bad."

"You make it sound so enticing. Perhaps you should be a seller of relics. "

"I am not myself." Thomas glanced at Will. "You can go to bed now. Bernard will help me up the stairs if I need it."

Will nodded and rose. He kissed the top of his father's head and left.

Bernard spooned some of the lukewarm stew into a bowl and sat next to Thomas.

"I am surprised to see you sitting up, Tom."

"I am surprised to find myself sitting up." Thomas leaned across the table to offer his hand. "I have to thank you for my life, Bernard."

Bernard shook the hand. "I only did what you would have done for me."

"But you brought me here when I asked. To Amal. Other men would have taken me to the priory infirmary."

"That might not have been a good idea with Madoc as Prior." Bernard shook his head. "I still cannot believe what happened."

"What do you intend to do about it?" Thomas asked.

"What can I do? I am a servant of the Church, and it

appears my services are no longer required other than as a plain brother. If so, that is how I will continue to serve God. To do otherwise shows pride. This stew is good. Who made it?"

Thomas shrugged, then winced. "Most likely Bel. Belia's food has more spice even though it is hard to get in England."

"It is still good. But then I am more used to the plain fare of the priory."

"There is more to what happened to you than a decision by the Church." Thomas shifted in his seat. His wound was starting to ache, and he would have to try and find some willow bark if he wanted to sleep. Though sleep was a long way from his mind.

"That is how it was told to me, Tom, and I will have to adhere to the instruction. You, on the other hand... Tell me what is on your mind. I am curious to see if it is the same as on mine."

Thomas smiled. "So you do not intend to wear your habit and walk with downcast eyes after all?"

"I am supposed to do as expected of me, but I know you will not. And if you do as I believe you will, then it makes sense for me to offer you whatever help I can, while I can."

"You know you can stay under this roof as long as you wish."

"I do. Tell me what you believe."

"Madoc is Abbot Haylewith's man, yes?"

Bernard nodded. "Of course."

"And Abbot Haylewith has some hand in the bordel set up at Elmbrook Priory?"

Another nod. "I believe so."

"I learned some things about Haylewith while we were away, most of it from the priest at Garway, but I suspect you also know them. What I do not know is the involvement of the Archdeacons of Hereford and Salop. They were at the conclave, and it is my opinion at least one of them voted against you."

"Probably both. I suspect Haylewith voted for me so he could express his support if asked. He is, after all, a man of God and would consider it a sin to lie."

Thomas laughed. "Such a small sin amongst all his others."

"God takes the balance of our sins into account when our time draws near. Not that his draws near, nor Madoc's. Haylewith can give me twenty years, thirty in Madoc's case. As for the Archdeacons, I would say they are not involved in any plot to oust me. They have nothing to do with what goes on at Elmbrook Priory, other than occasionally taking advantage of the services offered there."

"Really?"

"They are men of God, but still men, with all our weaknesses. Especially when it comes to matters of the flesh. You told me you have taken advantage of such services yourself, and I admit the same. When I was younger, of course."

"Of course. My involvement in all this started with opening the graves behind my old house. And my thanks for permitting me to do that. The additional bodies I know more about now after speaking to Felicia Hughden. She admitted most belonged to children born of the women employed in the bordel."

"Women who are also nuns. Or were nuns. I grow confused over the validity of what happens. Whether a woman can lie with many men and remain a part of the sisterhood or not. But I can see that burying the dead progeny of their liaisons might seem the best way of hiding what they do."

"None of which is against the law. Or rather, it may be but is unlikely to be prosecuted. Particularly by Coroner d'Alston, who no doubt is also a client of Elmbrook. As will be Amos Mapp." Thomas met Bernard's eyes. "What about Ambrose?"

"Brother Ambrose was a man forged of iron and faith. But the evidence is clear. I believe you when you say he was taking a body to be buried in someone else's grave when he was killed. I have tried to think of a reason for him to do such a thing and cannot conjure one. Ambrose was not a man who could be bribed, because I know many tried in pursuit of a false authentication of their relics. So it would have to be something other than money. What occurs to you, Tom?"

"A man is usually bribed, as you say, with money. If not that, then his reputation, his life, or the lives of those close to him."

"Of which Ambrose had none that I know of."

"In that case, perhaps someone he loved," Thomas said.

"Also unlikely. Ambrose loved God and nothing else."

"He may have loved his mother," Thomas said.

Bernard met his gaze. "You revealed who that was to me as we left Elmbrook, and I admit it came as a surprise. I have thought on it since and it explains some of the strangeness in Ambrose, also some of the contradictions. If Felicia asked him to bury the bodies he would have done it. But did she ask him to steal the skulls?"

"She told me not. I asked her who might have done but she did not know."

"Ambrose would not take them for himself, I am sure of that."

"I did not know him well, so will take your word for that. So who did he take them for, and why? I have spoken with Silva about skulls and she has her own thoughts for why they were taken, which also make sense to me if I can manage to suspend my doubts. I think Ambrose stole them for Abbot Haylewith."

"I can think of no reason he would do that. Ambrose did not respect the man. He considered his faith in God weak, and I agree with him. Haylewith is ambitious for power, but not to serve God. His appointment at Wigmore is a mistake, but I dare say nothing, of course."

"I need to speak with Croft. Felicia says he knows who Ambrose's father is. Whether he is willing to tell that secret to me is another matter, but I will ask, even if only for confirmation."

Bernard frowned. "Are you suggesting what I think you are?"

"That depends what you are thinking," Thomas said.

"That Haylewith is Ambrose's father. It would explain why he stole skulls for him — if that is who he gave them to. I agree with you Haylewith's Christian beliefs are not deeply held, a fact which only depresses me the more."

"As you say, it explains a lot. Now all I need is confirmation."

"And if you get it? You cannot touch Haylewith, Tom. He is Abbot of Wigmore now."

"And if he killed Ambrose?"

An expression of disgust crossed Bernard's face. "His own son? No."

"Madoc then," Thomas said. "He is as close to Haylewith as a son, perhaps even closer. What if he killed Ambrose out of jealousy."

"Cain and Abel," said Bernard. "Do you remember the passage?"

"Not any longer."

"There is a part there that always makes me go cold. '*For whether you offer well, or whether you do not, at the tent flap sin crouches and you are its longing…*'. I may be spinning nothings from thin air, but for me it makes at least some sense. Madoc was jealous of Ambrose because Haylewith favoured him. We both know he is capable of killing to gain his own ends."

"You told me Haylewith is untouchable, but does that extend to Madoc?" Thomas asked.

Bernard took a deep breath before letting it go. "I am the wrong man to ask that of because I would have to say yes, he is. But you are not me, Tom. I leave it to you to uncover the truth, and to act on it. But I want to be with

TWENTY-SIX

Thomas favoured his left side as he followed Amal to his workshop where she said there was something she wanted to show him. A week had passed since he woke. His wound was knitting together but he still fatigued easily. Will and Silva had returned to her cottage. Prior Bernard remained at Burway and Thomas believed the man was unsure of what else to do. Perhaps he was searching for divine intervention. Whatever the reason he seemed content for the waiting to go on.

"What is it you want to show me?"

"Wait," said Amal.

She opened the door to the workshop, then crossed to a set of drawers beneath a desk. Above it sat shelves, each filled with books and papers which had been sent across land and sea from Thomas's house in Spain.

Amal drew out a wooden box and set it on the large table in the middle of the room before removing the lid.

Thomas looked in and saw bones. A central divider separated one set from another. On one side were animal bones, on the other human.

"What is this?"

"I have been doing experiments," said Amal. "Jack Pook helped me get the animal bones, rabbits mostly, but also a fox, a boar and a fawn."

"Where did he get that from?"

Amal smiled. "I thought it best not to ask."

"And the other bones — are they from one from the skeletons we dug up?"

"They are from the graves behind your old house and the one we opened in Garway."

"Tell me what you have been trying to do." Thomas pulled up a high stool and perched on it before leaning close to watch as Amal picked up one of the animal bones.

"I wanted to find out if anything had been done to the bones before they were added to the graves."

"I suspect they were buried as bodies," Thomas said. "Like the one I found on the back of Ambrose's cart, and Will found at Tref-y-Clawdd."

"I did not know that when I started."

"When did you start?"

"Almost as soon as we brought the remains from behind your old house." Amal stirred the human bones with her finger.

"Why?"

"I told you, I wanted to know how they degraded."

"In the earth, I imagine," Thomas said.

"I know that now, but I did not at the start. Were the experiments not worthwhile, Pa? You always tell me all knowledge is valuable."

"I am sorry, Ami. You are right. I should have thought of it myself."

"You cannot think of everything. I want to help and thought I was."

"You are, my sweet." Thomas ignored her scowl. "Tell me what you discovered."

For a moment he thought she was going to refuse, then she picked up one of the bones from the animal side. It was the foreleg of a rabbit. She held it between her fingers before snapping it in two. A tiny puff of dust accompanied the breaking.

"This one was burned on a charcoal fire. I did the same with other rabbits on a wood fire. I also boiled some and had Jack bring me others that had lain on the surface of the ground until all flesh had rotted from them, and others that had died in burrows underground. I made notes, so if we ever need to work out how a bone degraded in future we can do so."

Thomas stared at Amal, impressed.

"This is excellent work."

She tried to hide her smile but failed. "I thought so, but now I realise it may not be as useful as I hoped."

"Not at the moment, perhaps, but knowledge is never wasted. One day we might need to know how someone died. I can think of other experiments that could be done, but they might involve a degree of cruelty."

"So can I, and I do not want to kill anything that

already lives. Even if it does eat the vegetables in our garden."

"So what do you know about the bones from behind my old house?"

"Nothing exciting, Pa. I believe the body was set in the ground and rotted away there. A body left above ground is different from a buried one. The buried bones are less brittle. Only a little, and some of it may be my imagination, but I tried to build something with pulleys and wires to measure more accurately, and I think I am right. I suspect it is due to contact with the air, rain, and exposure to the sun."

"I was wrong," Thomas said. "This is more than excellent work."

This time Amal beamed. She came across and hugged Thomas until he winced, then kissed him.

"I hoped it was good," she said. "But it means less now we know that Ambrose took the children's bodies and buried them."

"I suspect, and Bernard agrees with me, that he may have had help from someone else to bury them. It would be too much work for one man alone."

"So now we have to find out who that was."

"We do. Most likely more than one person. There would have to be people in each district. But yes, as soon as I can ride I intend to go out and enquire."

"We can do that for you," said Amal. "I will send for Will and Usaden, and Jorge can also help. Perhaps even Bernard. I suspect he is starting to grow bored with nothing to do. He prays, and visits the church in Ludlow, but time is long on his hands." Amal smiled. "I think he finds it hard to live under the same roof as several women. Particularly Belia. I catch him staring at her sometimes, and then he sees me and looks away."

"I believe I know why," Thomas said. "He once told me he had a woman in the east. He even told me he suspected he might have fathered a child with her. I suspect Belia may remind him of that woman and what it was like to be a man rather than a monk."

"Are not monks also men, Pa?"

"Indeed they are. I will see if I can come up with a task for Bernard. I will be fit enough to ride soon and he knows all the priests in the area. He may be able to find out if they know of other disturbed graves. Not that we need to find them anymore because I suspect the discarded bodies are no more than a distraction to what else is going on. But we might also try to identify if anyone helped Ambrose." Thomas cocked his head at a disturbance outside.

He rose, looking for a weapon, but Amal was first to the door and he cursed himself for his slowness. When he emerged he saw Lyman d'Alston in the courtyard, Amos Mapp at his side, but of more concern were the half-dozen constables standing behind them; men of Ludlow recruited for the task.

Thomas made his way across to them, trying not to show his weakness.

"Do you need me for something?" He could think of

no reason for their presence other than there had been a death or injury and they wanted his advice.

Amos Mapp walked past him, saying nothing, and Amal followed him towards the workshop.

"Reports reached me that you have ignored my order and are still looking into bodies buried in the graves of others," said Lyman d'Alston. "Why is that?"

"You gave me permission to do so, unless you forget so easily. I also have a note from Abbot Bernard. I have your letter in the house if you want to be reminded of it."

"That permission was temporary, not permanent. This is a secular matter, not religious. Besides, Bernard is no longer Abbot or Prior. Whatever piece of paper you might have is no longer valid."

"Coroner, I have found something you need to see."

Thomas turned to see Amos Mapp in the doorway of his workshop. Amal had come outside, her expression worried.

The Coroner pushed past Thomas. "Do not let him move from where he is," he said to the constables, before going to join Mapp. Both men disappeared into the workshop but emerged soon enough. Mapp carried the wooden box holding the bones.

"And now we have evidence of your crimes, as well as witchcraft. Which of the women are practitioners, or need I even ask? I hear that Silva Taylor has taken up with your son. Has she influenced everyone else?"

"There is no witchcraft here, only science." Thomas saw Bernard emerge, no doubt to find out what all the noise was about. "Ask Prior Bernard. He will vouch for me."

"I told you, he is no longer Prior. He is nothing. Constables, arrest Thomas Berrington. His daughter too. Then two of you search the house and bring any women out. If you find Silva Taylor take care. It is said she can hex a man just by staring at him."

"She is not here," Thomas said. "And you are to leave the women alone."

"Bring them all," said the Coroner. "Bring every member of this household, including Bernard."

The constables looked uncertain, but Lyman d'Alston screamed his instructions again and four of them moved reluctantly towards the house. Another grasped Thomas's arm, yet another held Amal.

Thomas knew he could break free and run, but that would not help the others. Apart from which, he was unsure how fast and how far he could run before being caught. So he stood and considered the possibility of what might lie ahead and how dangerous it could prove for him and the others. He suspected d'Alston's threat against the women was a bluff to scare him, but could not be sure. He feared the man had become unhinged, because this was an overreaction to what Thomas had done. He saw no reason why d'Alston would withdraw his permission unless he had been pressured by someone else. The only people he could think of who might apply such pressure were Sir Richard Croft or Sir Thomas Cornwell. And of those two, Cornwell was the man Thomas trusted least.

As they were led away, he tried to think of some way of at least freeing the women, but nothing came to him. For once, there was nothing he could do, and he did not like the feeling of being helpless.

TWENTY-SEVEN

They took Thomas up the slope into Ludlow and then into the outer bailey of the castle. A row of stone cells was set hard against the wall and it was here he was led. None too gently he was thrown into a cell and the metal door clanged shut.

Thomas looked around, though he knew exactly what to expect. Not so long ago he had come to this cell to speak with a man who claimed to have killed his wife in self-defence. Except Thomas believed it had been cold-blooded, and so had Will. The man had been judged by a jury of townsfolk and hung the following morning.

The cell looked no different to that day. Only the occupant was new. A wooden bucket stood in one corner. It had received no more than a token cleaning since the last inhabitant used it. A single, barred window looked towards the bailey. The opposite wall was that of the castle, four feet thick. Someone had scraped at the lime plaster and dug several inches between two blocks, but going further would have proved impossible. The castle was all but abandoned now, only a token staff left to maintain the structure and protect what furnishings and weapons remained. At one time, Thomas and his family had used the guest quarters while the castle bustled with the retinue of the newly married Prince Arthur and Princess Catherine of Aragon. Now Arthur was four months dead and Catherine banished to London, where she was effectively as much a prisoner as Thomas.

The opening of the far door brought him to his feet to peer through the iron bars. His heart sank at the sight that greeted him. Guards led Jorge in, then behind came Amal, Belia and Bel. Prior Bernard and Usaden took up the rear. Thomas knew that if the man wanted to he could disable all six guards without raising sweat, but Usaden made no move.

"Stand back unless you want a club in your face."

Thomas stepped away until he reached the outer wall and could go no further.

The guard used a large key to unlock the gate, then stood back. As soon as Jorge and Usaden entered the cell the gate slammed shut behind them.

"They came for you, too?" Thomas asked Usaden.

"They wanted Jack as well but he has gone poaching. They tried to bring Emma, but as soon as they brought her from the house your sister and half the townsfolk stood in their way and they had to release her. It seems their loyalty does not extend as far as me. Why are we here, Thomas?"

"Lyman d'Alston has lost his wits or been put up to

this action by someone who does not want the truth about what has been going on around here coming out."

"The Church," said Jorge. "There is no royal presence in Ludlow anymore, so the next most important power is the Church. And you have been poking into their dealings. Exposing their secrets."

"Who is looking after the children?"

"Agnes sent her daughters to take them to the bakery. They will be safe there."

"Did they try to arrest them?" Thomas asked, appalled.

"I suspect they thought about it, but even they could not stoop so low." Jorge glanced at the door to the cell, beyond which the guards had now disappeared. "Do you want me to see if I can pick the lock?"

"And what then? The guards will still be outside. Besides, once word gets out Bernard is in here with us, someone will come and sort out this misunderstanding."

"Or call for our trial," said Jorge.

"I would not set too much hope on anyone caring about what happens to me, Tom," said Bernard. "It appears I am no longer in favour with the Church."

"That is only a misunderstanding."

"Is it? Everyone knows how close I am to you. Lyman d'Alston believes I did not have the authority to provide you with that letter of permission. But I consulted with Archdeacon Webb and he wrote back telling me to write the permission for you."

"Where is his letter now?" Thomas asked.

"At Lemster Priory, of course."

"Which is now under Madoc's control. He will have destroyed it. We are in trouble, Bernard. We are in deep trouble."

"Who is behind this? Does d'Alston hate you enough to conjure these charges from thin air?"

"He does not have spine enough for that. He has been ordered to do it. As he was ordered to retract the note of permission he gave me." Thomas met Bernard's gaze. "Think about it for a moment and you will know who is behind our plight."

"I barely need a moment," said Bernard. "Madoc, of course, but also the man he works for: Abbot Haylewith. What I cannot work out is why their anger is directed at the two of us." Bernard looked around the packed cell. "As for your family and friends, well ... they have pushed things too far by arresting them. As soon as Archdeacon Webb hears about this everything will be straightened out."

"Money is behind it," Thomas said. "Money and the lusts of men. Also greed and madness. Madoc and Haylewith will have heard of our visits to Garway and Tref-y-Clawdd and suspect we are getting closer to the truth of what has been happening."

"What is Felicia's part in all of this?"

"She is not innocent," Thomas said, "but I believe her innocent of what is happening now. The despatching of dead children for secret burial was a mistake, but that is not at the core of why someone wants us stopped. I have scratched at the surface of graves and uncovered their sins. Each of those children should have been afforded a place of their own and then, eventually, their bones placed in the ossuary at Elmbrook Priory. The bordel there has been running for a century or more. They must have acted properly to begin with but then something changed. I wonder what that was?"

"We may never know. Abbot John might have had knowledge of it, but he too is dead."

"Had he not been so corpulent or old I would wonder about his death," Thomas said. "Yes, he had a bad heart, and that is what killed him, but there are herbs that could hasten his end, as well you know."

"If he had known something about what you claim would he not have mentioned it in his confession to Ambrose?"

"Only if he regarded it as a sin. And if you recall, Ambrose made no mention of what Abbot John might have confessed, only that he had sinned greatly. Someone might have feared what was revealed to Ambrose and killed him to hide the secret."

"You are linking this to what goes on at Elmbrook, Tom, but that is no secret. Every man for miles around knows of it, and most visit there. The girls are both beautiful and willing."

"You mean the nuns."

"Of course I mean the sisters, but none have been coerced or I would know about it. Felicia Hughden is strange but she cares for her flock, each and every one of them. Just as I expect she cared for those poor children who did not survive long enough to grow into adults."

"Why were they not buried in consecrated ground at the priory?" Thomas asked.

"If the children had not been baptised they could not be. A place had to be found somewhere beyond the priory. I wonder if that was what she asked Ambrose to do? If she did, then perhaps putting them in the graves of strangers was his idea."

"Why did Felicia not have the children baptised? They could be buried at the priory then."

"I do not know why they were not, Tom. Custom is that a child is baptised on the day it is born. Felicia holds to some strange ideas, but she is still godly. She spoke to you before, perhaps she will again. You can ask her."

Thomas stared at the bars of their cell, thoughts swirling through his mind.

"Except Ambrose is dead, and with his death some of the answers are lost. Felicia appears to be under Haylewith's control and I suspect all of this has something to do with his obsessions. The Grail. Christ's bones. His skull in particular. Haylewith believes it heart and soul. He is searching for both, which is why the skulls are taken." Thomas looked into Bernard's eyes. "Suppose for a moment what he believes is true." He saw Bernard start to shake his head and hold up a hand. "Hear me out. I do not believe it, and neither do you, but Haylewith clearly does. What if the children were baptised, but the burial of their bodies was nothing more than an excuse to obtain the skulls. Somehow he convinced Felicia it had to be done. She in turn persuaded Ambrose."

Thomas watched as Bernard considered the question,

taking his time, no doubt examining his own beliefs and faith.

"What you suggest stretches belief beyond breaking point, Tom. *If* Haylewith lusted for His skull and cup, *if* it lies somewhere in England, *if* he could persuade Felicia and she in turn could persuade Ambrose." Bernard shook his head. "It makes no sense. You know it does not."

"You are right," Thomas said. "Any rational person knows it makes no sense. But are Haylewith and Felicia rational? If they believe the Grail or Christ's skull lies buried somewhere in England, somewhere in Hereford-shire, how would anyone be able to tell? Would His skull be any different to others?"

Bernard shook his head. "I have no idea, Tom. As a Christian I would like to say yes, that I would recognise His skull at once, but as a man who studies more than might be wise for him then I doubt anyone could tell one skull from another after all this time. But you already know who may be able to."

"Silva," Thomas said, and Bernard nodded.

"Yes, Silva. We do not agree on matters of faith, but there is no doubt she has an ability I do not comprehend."

"I have already spoken with her regarding skulls. She thinks if we could find that of my mother or brother she may be able to confirm they are theirs. If such is true then His skull would carry even more power." Thomas leaned against the wall, suddenly tired. "It is all senseless, though. The act is too haphazard. The idea too insane."

"That assumes Haylewith is sane, Tom," said

Bernard. "I have known him a long time and he has always been strange, always held to strange beliefs. The Grail and His skull among them. Only here in the borderlands would he have been allowed to rise to the position he now holds. This place, these Marches, are unlike any other in England. Silva will tell you the same."

"Then I need to look more closely at Haylewith. Madoc, too, and Felicia. The three of them are connected in some way I do not yet see. I will make it my task once we get out of here."

"If we ever get out of here."

Thomas patted Bernard on the shoulder before going to share a few words with each of the others. As they spoke a commotion came from beyond the wall. It was muted, and they could not make out any words, but there was shouting as if a multitude stood beyond the stone.

"Agnes and Emma have roused the townsfolk," said Usaden.

But then the sound faded, as if each of those beyond the castle wall had all exhaled at the same moment.

Thomas thought he knew the reason and turned back to the cell door. More voices sounded, closer now as the outer door was opened, and he squinted against a sudden wash of light. Three figures entered, but their faces were obscured by the brightness behind them. Thomas made out one man of medium height but more than medium girth, who he assumed was Lyman d'Alston. A second was taller and slimmer, but he did not think it was Amos Mapp. The third was the shortest, and also broad, though not as rotund as d'Alston.

It was the short man who approached the bars, and as he did so Thomas made out a familiar face, and any hope he might have harboured faded. Sir Thomas Cornwell was no friend to him or his family. Beyond him, Thomas saw Sir Richard Croft, who he might regard as more likely to offer assistance, but the man remained where he was. No doubt it was a matter of rank. Cornwell had been re-appointed as Sheriff of Salop earlier in the year. It was a position both men had held over the years, but it could have only one incumbent.

"Lyman tells me you have once again been poking your nose into matters that do not concern you." Cornwell's gaze moved from Thomas to scan the others in the cell. He half-turned and spoke to Lyman d'Alston. "Do all of these people have to be incarcerated with Berrington?"

"They are for the most part of the same family, so I considered it a sensible approach."

"There are women here, and a young girl. I know Bel Brickenden and she has not a wicked bone in her body. As for Prior Bernard, I can see no valid reason why he is here. Let them out and we can talk of Berrington, who has crossed me before."

No, Thomas thought, there would be no help from the man.

Was this the start of the process that would lead to his trial? He wondered if the opening of graves was considered a hanging offence. It did not seem it should be, but he knew men were hanged for less.

"It would be dangerous to let the others leave," said

d'Alston. "You saw the mob gathered outside. Let the women go and they will foster sedition."

Cornwell laughed. "There are times I wonder why we appointed you as Coroner, Lyman. The position requires a man of intelligence and, with luck, honesty. I am beginning to see you lack neither of those qualities." Cornwell's voice hardened and took on a tone Thomas had never heard him use before. "Let them out. Now."

Lyman d'Alston turned away, and for a moment Thomas thought he was fleeing, but he disappeared for only a moment to fetch the gaoler, who used his key to open the cell door.

Thomas saw Usaden tense and reached out to lay a hand on his shoulder, hoping the touch would be enough as the women filed out.

Amal turned back. "I will get you out, Pa."

"See?" said d'Alston, and he grabbed Amal's arm.

Beneath Thomas's hand, Usaden tensed even more, and Thomas knew if he decided to attack he could do nothing to prevent him. But the situation was saved by Bernard, who approached the open door.

"Take your hand off her if you wish to live," he said.

D'Alston glared at Bernard, but after a moment, his hand withdrew and Amal continued out after the others.

The cell door clanged shut.

"Now," said Cornwell, "what are we going to do with the rest of you?" He glanced at d'Alston. "What are the charges?"

"None as yet, Sir Thomas. Amos is drawing them up as we speak."

"Tell me why you arrested Berrington if you do not yet have charges?"

"He has been opening graves."

"Has he, by damn?" Cornwell turned back to study Thomas.

"With my permission," said Bernard.

"Bernard no longer holds a position in the Church," said d'Alston. "Whatever permission he claims to have given Berrington is not valid."

"I have a message from Archdeacon Webb of Hereford telling me to write the permission," said Bernard. "I believe he still holds a position."

"Indeed he does." Cornwell took a breath and released it before turning to d'Alston. "Tell me, who do you serve?"

"The King, of course."

"And who does the King serve?"

D'Alston frowned. "The people?"

Sir Thomas Cornwell laughed. "I see you are even more of an idiot than I thought. No, Lyman, the King serves God. He is His appointed servant on earth. And beneath the King, who else serves God?"

D'Alston's frown deepened, and Thomas saw he was struggling to find an answer.

Cornwell made him dangle a little longer before saying, "The Church, the head of which is the Holy Father in Rome. Beneath him are the archbishops, the bishops, the deans and archdeacons and abbots, the priors and priests. All the way down to the lowly brothers and sisters. Then come the civil appointments. Sheriffs such as myself appoint a Coroner, who in turn sits far down the hierarchy."

Cornwell stared at the man. "Do you consider these letters of permission Thomas Berrington holds are real?"

"He might have forged them. I hear his daughter is capable of such work."

Sir Thomas Cornwell shook his head in disappointment.

D'Alston seemed to pull himself more upright. "If I agree with your argument, Sir Thomas, then a Justice of the Peace falls even lower in this hierarchy than a Coroner. So Thomas Berrington serves me."

"And you, Lyman, serve me, and I tell you these papers may be genuine and need to be examined by myself and Croft. Release these men. Do it now."

Cornwell started to turn away, then stopped. "And if I discover you have anything at all to do with these spurious charges against Berrington then it will be more than your position you lose."

Thomas stared through the bars at Lyman d'Alston. He saw the internal struggle but knew only one course of action could be taken.

In the end, the man took it.

TWENTY-EIGHT

In the market square Thomas considered approaching Sir Richard Croft with the intention of asking if he could talk with him for a moment. Felicia Hughden had told him the man might be willing to tell him who Ambrose's father was. Thomas doubted the information was significant, but it would be one item he could remove from his constantly growing list of things to do. He waited as Croft and Cornwell stood talking, not wanting to interrupt them, nor to pose his question in front of Cornwell. He was still waiting when Amos Mapp approached them and all three went back into the castle.

Thomas crossed the square to his sister Agnes's bakery. Her two daughters were at their usual station where bread, pies and cakes were being sold, but both came out to hug him tight.

"Was it your mother's doing to raise the mob?" Thomas asked over their heads, unable to extricate himself from their arms. There seemed to be too many of them for only two girls.

"Of course. Emma came to tell us what happened and we gathered the townsfolk. They still remember what you and your family did when the Welsh attacked the town. Most owe you their lives."

Rose was the first to release him and looked up with a smile. "They were not sure about you when you arrived, Uncle Thomas, but most like you now."

"I am relieved to hear it. Is your mother inside?"

"She is." Rose lifted up for a kiss, and eventually Jilly released her hold and received the same.

As he went inside Thomas thought of what good girls they were and of how they favoured Agnes in their looks. He had missed his sister growing up because he had abandoned her in Ludlow when she was barely three years old. Not for the first time he wondered why he had not returned until now, but even as the thought came he knew he would not have changed anything. He had seen a world filled with wonder and learned even more of distant lands. He had lived among an alien culture and loved Isabel of Castile, Queen of Spain. He had loved other beautiful women. The most beautiful was Lubna, Amal's mother, who was blessed both in looks and temperament. And he had saved the life of his closest friend, Jorge. It had been an unusual life for a boy from the Marches, and he hoped he would live long enough to make a place for himself back where he started. And Agnes was a part of it.

"What are you doing, Tom? I'm covered in flour!" She

tried to push him away, but he continued to hug her tight, revelling in the scent of her, which was the scent of the room she worked in, with its jars of yeast slowly growing, sacks of flour, and the heat of four wood-fired ovens.

Eventually, he released her.

"I thank you, sister. I feared what might have happened had you not roused the town."

"I saw Croft and Cornwell enter the castle. I except it was they who freed you."

"Cornwell, yes, which surprises me."

"He is not a likeable man, but he does his duty diligently enough when he wants to. The King would not appoint him Sheriff so often if he did not. Though I would have thought Croft the more likely to let you out. Mind, he has no high position at the moment, even if he has more experience."

"He too has been Sheriff, has he not?"

"He has, but I suspect he is too soft for the King's liking, as well as fighting against the Tudors at the battle of Mortimer's Cross. Though he must have been forgiven now. Is the King as harsh as people say?"

"Kings and queens are not like you and me, sister. They cannot act as ordinary men and women do. They must always consider the best interests of the country rather than individuals. But I have seen a softer side to him when he is with his children. He dotes on his daughters, and worries about Prince Harry. He is the only male heir remaining, though I am sure both Henry and his wife are trying for more children."

"I had two girls," said Agnes, "and glad I did. Boys are harder to raise."

"Will was hard because he likes to fight. Always has. But you are right, girls are welcome as well."

"Amal is beautiful, or do you not see it?"

Thomas found something interesting to look at on the wall to hide a sudden dampness in his eyes. "She is her mother reborn, so yes, I see it. I see it every day, and it worries me."

"We cannot coddle them forever, Tom." Agnes put a hand on his arm, having heard the emotion in his voice. "Jilly and Rose giggle and swoon over boys, but there is not much choice in Ludlow. Perhaps you can take them to London with you and introduce them around."

"I suspect the kind of people I could introduce them to would not be appropriate."

"What is he like, the young Prince? Does he favour Arthur?"

Thomas laughed. "There could be no more different boys. You know what Arthur's nature was. Serious. Timid in some ways, but also brave. Henry is confident. Over-confident, I would say. And worldly. He has been raised among women and, young as he is, has tasted their favours."

Agnes laughed. "Oh, such a coy turn of phrase from you, brother. What age has he?"

"He has but twelve years. Not enough to act as he does, but it does not stop him. I blame the ladies for spoiling him."

"You hint at more than spoiling, Tom."

"He is a prince, and kings and princes do not behave in the same way as the rest of us. In Spain, some of the princesses were married before they were any older than Henry is now, and were expected to bear a child within the year. Preferably a male child. When did you first lie with a boy, sister?"

Agnes's face flushed. "What kind of question is that to ask of your sister, Tom?"

He smiled. "I am curious, that is all. I had no more than thirteen years when I first lay with Bel."

Agnes's flush darkened. "Now you tell me too much. But if you must know, I was older than you but not by so much. Now, I have loaves to take from the ovens. You can stay and help as long as there is no more talk of such things."

"I will try to behave myself." Thomas picked up a wooden peel and slid it beneath one of the loaves. He turned it onto the wide oak table and reached for a second. Beside him, Agnes did the same, the smell of the freshly baked loaves filling the air.

The hour Thomas spent with Agnes in that room was an interlude made sweeter by his freedom, and one he would remember long into old age. It ended when shouting sounded from outside. Thomas ran out, fearing Agnes's daughters were being attacked.

Instead he found Amos Mapp.

"Good, I was told you were here," said Mapp. "I need you to come with me."

"If this is another attempt to put me back in gaol under false charges you have not brought enough men with you." Thomas glanced across the market square to see what he had expected. Usaden had heard the ruckus as well and stood still as a statue in a doorway.

"I would be a fool to do that, and I am no fool. I need you to examine Lyman."

"Is he unwell?"

"If you consider being dead unwell then yes, he is."

Mapp looked past Thomas with hunger in his eyes as he surveyed Agnes and her daughters, and Thomas suspected the hunger was not for their wares.

Thomas offered a curt nod and stepped out into the street.

TWENTY-NINE

"Does the Coroner show any sign of injury?" Thomas asked Mapp as they crossed the market square towards the tall black and white house.

"I came for you to tell me whether Lyman has injuries or not, and to say how he died."

"Did you know of Lyman's death when you approached Croft and Cornwell?"

"Do you think I would have not told them, or you, if I had? I have been busy with my duties since early morning; carrying out Lyman's orders. Only after I left Sir Thomas and Sir Richard did I discover Lyman dead in his office."

Thomas wondered how Mapp knew this was murder. There were a number of diseases that could kill a man without leaving any sign. A bad heart was most common and, like Abbot John, d'Alston had been obese. D'Alston was a disagreeable man, but if that was grounds for murder half the population of Ludlow would be littering the streets with their throats cut.

If it was murder, did someone want d'Alston silenced? Which might indicate he knew something his killer wanted to remain a secret. Thomas was aware he knew too little.

What might d'Alston have recently learned that put him in danger? Was it because Thomas's enquiries threatened him? But if that was the case why had his killer not come after Thomas himself? Unless whoever was behind this had seen how he had responded in the past.

He wondered if Mapp might have killed his master. Thomas suspected he was an ambitious man, and ambitious men were not always put off by the prospect of danger. But Thomas considered him more likely to be innocent. Mapp would hardly commit murder then demand Thomas examine the corpse immediately.

As they approached the Coroner's house Thomas saw Bernard standing in the market square. So did Mapp, who indicated he should join them.

After he had explained the situation, Mapp said, "Perhaps you would come with us to read the last rites over Lyman."

"Once I have confirmed he is actually dead," Thomas said.

"Of course, but I think you will find he is."

The body of Lyman d'Alston, Coroner for Shropshire and Herefordshire, lay atop a daybed in a small room at the rear of the house.

"What is he doing here?" Thomas asked. "You told me you found him in his office."

"That is where I found him but I could not leave him there."

"Then that is where you will take me once I have examined him."

Thomas went to the bed and looked at d'Alston's face, paying particular attention to his lips and eyes. The lips held a faint blue tint, but death could do that. The eyes were closed.

Thomas pointed at them. "Is this how they were when he was found?"

"No, they were open. Wide open. I closed them when he was brought in here."

"He is not a light man. Did you carry him on your own?"

"Of course not. I sent for the constables and they moved him before I came for you."

Thomas thought of the timescale. Only a little more than an hour had passed since Sir Thomas Cornwell released them from the goal cell, and d'Alston had been alive and well then. But not now. Thomas leaned over and pulled back one of the eyelids. Faint tracings of blood vessels made the eye pink. He checked the other to be sure, but it was the same.

Next, he prised open d'Alston's mouth, which opened easily, indicating rigor had not yet set in. Which he already knew because he had seen the man recently.

Thomas ran his fingers around the inside of the mouth and found a little food residue. When he leaned close and sniffed he caught a faint scent but failed to recognise it. He glanced along the body and considered removing his clothes, but there was no sign of blood on his front. He rolled d'Alston to one side, then the other, checking for wounds but finding none.

"He is dead, then?" said Mapp.

"Of course he is. Show me where you found him."

Mapp led the way out. Bernard had found a Bible and went into the bedroom to read the last rites over the body, though Thomas knew the book was no more than a prop because the words would be etched into his memory from having spoken them a thousand times before.

The office was a good size with a table set in its centre that might seat four and a desk against one wall with a view out to the north. Bookshelves lined one wall. Thomas glanced at the titles to see most consisted of lawyers' tomes. The meal d'Alston had eaten had been cleared away, as had any glasses or bottles.

"Where was he when you found him?" Thomas asked.

"At the table. He had eaten a small meal and drunk a little wine. I had it cleared away after I found him."

"Who prepares his food?"

"His housekeeper, Mary."

"Does she live under this roof?"

"She has a small room in the eaves."

"I would speak with her."

After Mapp left in search of the housekeeper, Thomas considered the change of manner in him. Only a few hours before Mapp had been happy to see him incarcerated, no doubt even happier to see him hang. Now he was amenable, and the change confused Thomas. He heard the man ascend the stairs, his footsteps fading as he climbed higher. Faintly, Thomas heard Bernard's voice intoning in Latin. Then an angry shout sounded from above. Thomas was about to follow it when he heard Mapp descending, a second pair of steps behind him. When he entered the room Mapp's face was flushed.

"She was—" He broke off, as if unable to find the words, then found them anyway. "She was on the bed pleasuring herself. While her master lies dead downstairs!"

The housekeeper appeared in the doorway, adjusting her clothing. Her face was also red, but for a different reason. Thomas suspected he knew what it was. The scent he had detected in d'Alston's mouth came to him now, and it might explain the man's death. It could have been accidental, but it could also have been murder.

Thomas beckoned the housekeeper closer. "You are Mary?"

"I am, sir." She performed a little curtsey.

"Are you aware your master is dead?"

Mary stared at him, her eyes wide, then broke into tears. "Dead, sir? No, he cannot be dead. I was expecting him, but he did not call me down."

Thomas turned to Mapp. "Who discovered the body if not this woman?"

"I told you, I did."

"And you did not seek her out?"

"I sent a message for a doctor in case my master could be saved, then had the constables carry him to his daybed. Only then did I recall you claim some medical knowledge so came for you."

Thomas shook his head and turned to the housekeeper because he believed he knew what had happened.

"How often do you administer Spanish Fly for your master?"

"When he requests it, sir. Once a week, sometimes less. Lyman is not as demanding as he once was."

"And then you come to him?"

The housekeeper nodded. "I do, sir. When he feels the heat rise in him he calls me down to his daybed." The flush on her cheeks flared more ruby. "Not always the bed, though he is less adventurous these days."

"And you take a smaller dose yourself?"

A nod.

"Which is why you were doing what you were upstairs?"

"The sap rose hard in me, sir, harder than usual. I could not help myself. I can still feel it and can scarcely stand for the wanting of a man between my legs."

"How much did you administer to the Coroner?"

"The same as always, sir. Four drops, and two for myself."

Four drops of Spanish Fly would not be enough to kill a man. Thomas had prescribed it in the past when he lived in Granada, for men who found it difficult to become aroused. Four drops was a decent dose. He normally prescribed two, but four would not cause death. Ten might. Twenty certainly.

"You are sure you gave him only four drops?"

"I am, sir. He said he needed them today. He came home in a fine temper and I feared he might hit me. Sometimes he does, but he told me he only wanted some relief. Perhaps the new bottle is stronger than we are used to because it sorely affected me and I only took one from it."

"Show it to me."

Thomas followed the housekeeper from the room, aware Mapp was behind him. He wondered if Mapp still suspected him of some involvement and that was why he was not letting Thomas from his sight.

In the kitchen, the housekeeper reached for a small stoppered bottle containing a viscous liquid and handed it to Thomas. He pulled the stopper and sniffed. It was the same scent he had almost recognised on d'Alston's lips. He had never needed to resort to it himself but had supplied the tincture to the old Sultan in Granada when requested. There had been other clients, too, and they paid well. He had not thought of the substance since arriving in England and had half-expected they did not know of it. But he should have known better. The tincture was made from the shells of blister beetles, crushed and steeped in liquid before filtering. A tiny amount could arouse both men and women, but there was a fine line between arousal and death if too much was administered. Thomas did not know the strength of the bottle he held, but the housekeeper had told him she took two drops herself. Double that should have been safe.

"Is this the bottle you took your dose from?" he asked, surprised when she shook her head.

"Only one from that bottle, sir. There was a little left in the old one so I took one drop of that." She pointed to an empty bottle on a shelf. "There was not enough for the master, so I opened the new one and took another drop from it myself before mixing the master's dose."

Which might explain his death.

"Where did this bottle come from?"

"The master sends away for it. He has used it for many years after hearing about it from a man he met in London. A special tincture that would bring us both to blissful arousal. He made me take it, sir. Made me service him as well, though I did not mind so much when he was younger. His demands changed as he aged."

Thomas glanced at Mapp. "Did you know of this arrangement?"

"Lyman made no secret of it. I believe he was rather proud he could still perform as he did. He was a vain man." Mapp looked at the housekeeper. "Tell me, Mary, did you truly administer only four drops to Lyman, as you claim?"

"I would swear it on the holy Bible, master Mapp."

Mapp closed the space between them and grasped her arms. "Tell me true, Mary, or it will go ill for you."

"Four drops, that is all I put in his wine."

"Four drops may have been enough to kill him," Thomas said. "Lyman was old and overweight. His breathing was bad. He should not have indulged himself as he did."

"And you would know all of this how?"

"It is who I am. You know it is. I am the most skilled physician in the three counties, and my daughter is the second most skilled. If the tincture did not kill Lyman one day soon his gluttony would have."

"But not on this day. Mary, go to your room. I will speak with you shortly as soon as Berrington leaves."

When the woman had gone, Thomas asked, "Who is to be Coroner now?"

"As deputy, I have assumed the position until told otherwise. I expect it will be confirmed eventually, but it will take time for the news of Lyman's death to travel."

"Can the Sheriff not appoint a new Coroner?"

"It is his right, yes. In the meantime I will perform the duty as best I can."

"Am I free to leave, or do you suspect me of having a hand in Lyman's death?"

"I am aware you could not have anything to do with it, and my thanks for confirming how he died. Take the Prior with you. I suspect he has nowhere else to go." Mapp smiled as if the thought pleased him.

When Thomas returned to the Coroner's bedroom, Bernard was sitting on a chair beside the bed. He looked up from staring at the corpse.

"What killed him?" he asked. "Was it foul play?"

"An accident, it seems. He and his housemaid indulged themselves with the help of Spanish Fly. They have been taking it for years, but today she opened a new bottle. I suspect the mixture was stronger than he was used to."

"It can be dangerous but is not something I am much familiar with, of course. I know of it but ... well, I am a man of God, so have no need of it."

Thomas wondered if the nuns at Elmbrook Priory or their clients had need of it. He suspected they might, and wondered if that was where d'Alston's housekeeper had sent away for it. He would ask Amal to speak with the housekeeper and ask where she had obtained it from. The questions would come better from her than him.

Bernard walked beside Thomas as they crossed the market square. He was dressed as an ordinary man and no one paid him any heed.

"You still cannot return to Lemster Priory," Thomas said. "Stay longer with us at Burway."

"I considered going to Wigmore Abbey, but Abbot Haylewith has taken up his position there. I am a man without a home, so my thanks. I will try not to get underfoot."

"Get as underfoot as you want. Amal may want to talk with you, though. She has started to show some curiosity about the Christian God."

"Then I will be happy to speak with her, but not alone. It would not be seemly."

"I think I can trust you, Bernard, but if you insist Bel will chaperone her."

"I would prefer that." Bernard stopped, and it took a moment before Thomas realised he was not at his side.

When he did he turned back. "What is it? Have you forgotten something, or changed your mind?"

"Over there," said Bernard, nodding his head to where the castle wall curved before the start of the descent to Dinham Bridge. "I am sure some of those men were with Amos Mapp when he arrested you earlier today. And can you see who is with them now?"

Thomas narrowed his eyes. "Madoc?"

"He is."

"He is not dressed in his habit."

"He is dressed like the warrior monks he stands alongside." Bernard moved to one side.

Thomas followed him until both were partially hidden in a narrow alley but still able to see the men.

"Now there is a man I could suspect of killing Lyman d'Alston," said Bernard.

"For what reason?"

"I believe Lyman may have been coming around to your way of thinking about the buried children. No doubt he would not want to, but the evidence you are uncovering makes it difficult to dismiss. And if he were, action would have to be taken."

"Do you believe Madoc may be involved in Lyman's death?"

Bernard shook his head. "I do not know. I admit to disliking the man, but that is not reason enough to accuse him. But he is with those pretend soldiers. And he is close to Felicia Hughden and Abbot Haylewith both."

"Was he also close to Ambrose?"

"They knew each other, of course, but no, not particularly. Ambrose was a different manner of man from Madoc. He had no ambition unless it was to perform his job to the best of his abilities. Madoc, on the other hand, is made of ambition."

"Can you ever regain your position at Lemster Priory?" Thomas asked.

"Not while he has control of it. He has placed a monk as head of the priory for the moment, but of course picked someone I would not have chosen. They are a cabal. Madoc, Felicia and Haylewith. Between them they have influence throughout both Herefordshire and Salop. Ousting Madoc would require guile, and that is something I lack. Whereas you, Tom..."

Thomas laughed. "What do you expect me to do — confront him and his soldiers?"

"Do only what you already have. If you uncover more about the buried bodies perhaps it will implicate Madoc in some way."

"That is not a plan, it is a hope."

"Then let me have hope."

On the edge of the castle wall, the group of men turned and started down the hill.

"Where do you think they are going?" Thomas asked.

"I have no idea. I suppose someone could always follow them and find out."

The look of innocence on Bernard's face made Thomas laugh.

THIRTY

Thomas knocked on the door of Emma's house.

When she opened it, he said, "Is Usaden here?"

Kin appeared and wound around Thomas's legs. He reached down to scratch the hound's ears.

Usaden came barefoot to the door. "Do you need me?"

"You and Jack Pook if you know where he is."

"Behind me somewhere," said Usaden. "I will fetch my boots and send him out to you."

"I am sorry, Emma," Thomas said.

She shook her head, blonde curls swaying. "He was getting itchy feet anyway, Tom. Take him off and let him do something dangerous."

"You do not fear for him?"

She laughed. "Usaden?" She turned and entered the house just as he came past and offered her a kiss. The sight of it confused Thomas for a moment, who had only ever seen Usaden offer affection to Amal and Will. But he supposed if Usaden could not offer affection to the woman whose bed he shared he would be the coldest man alive. And despite appearances to the contrary, Thomas knew that was not Usaden.

"I want you to track a man in the company of some soldiers. They were headed towards Dinham Bridge, but I did not see them cross it."

"Who are they?" asked Jack Pook. "And how much of a start do they have?"

"No more than a few minutes. I came directly here. Can you do it?"

"Of course we can. What will you be doing?"

"Madoc—"

Jack Pook interrupted. "Madoc is with these men?"

Thomas nodded. "Leading them."

"If it is Madoc you are after he will either be riding to Lemster, Elmbrook or Hindwell. Possibly Wigmore. But no matter. Between Usaden and me we can track a gnat. Can I borrow a horse from you?"

"Borrow whatever you need, Jack." Thomas looked at Usaden. "I want Will with us before we decide what to do. I will ride to Silva's cottage for him. Once you know where these men are going come for me and we will make a plan."

"What about Jorge?" asked Usaden, his expression unreadable.

"This is a matter for men of steel, not silk. He will stay to protect the house and the women."

Thomas turned to leave once Usaden and Jack ran off

to get horses, Kin loping beside them, but Emma called him back.

"Keep him safe, Tom," she said.

"Usaden keeps me safe, you know he does."

"He trusts you to do the same, I know he does. Both of you stay safe." She kissed his cheek before turning back into the house.

Thomas went to Burway for Ferrant. He rode south towards Croft Manor before ascending Leinthal Common, then on through the woods to where Silva's cottage sat in a clearing. When he reached it he was surprised to discover both she and Will sitting in bright sunlight on the edge of the slope looking west. Both were naked, and Thomas averted his gaze as he called out.

Will rose and came towards him, but Silva remained where she was.

When Will reached Thomas, he saw his son's pupils were blown wide.

"What did she give you?"

"She gave me nothing I did not ask for."

"I need you."

"And here I am."

"Naked, and not yourself."

Will shrugged. "Does this involve fighting? Because if so it may be several hours before I am myself again."

"Usaden will be with us."

"Then I will tell Silva that I ride with you if you can wait while I dress."

"What will she say?"

"Nothing. She knows my nature, as she knows yours and that of everyone she meets."

Words were exchanged, and when Silva approached Thomas he turned his head aside, but she gripped his face and turned it back to her own.

"Keep him safe." She echoed Emma's words.

"Of course."

"No of course, Tom. Do it."

He offered a nod. "You can continue what you were doing until Usaden and Jack arrive. I told them to meet me here once they know where Madoc is going."

"You are going after Madoc?" Silva seemed more in control of herself than Will, who was staring at a shaft of sunlight that came through the trees to dance against a patch of grass.

"He rides with a band of his warrior monks. I want to believe he had something to do with the Coroner's death but cannot make any link. Neither can I link him to my arrest earlier today. But I am convinced he and Haylewith are the key to what has happened."

"Lyman is dead? I did not hear of that. Nor that you had been arrested! On what charge?"

"No charge other than one in d'Alston's head. He died earlier today, and I am surprised nobody has accused me of murdering him. His housekeeper gave him too much Spanish Fly and it stopped his heart. She claims it was an accident, but I am less sure. I have told Amal to look into where the supply came from. I would dearly like to connect it to Madoc but so far he has been too clever for me."

"Or he is not as bad as you make him out to be. And Mary would not kill her master," said Silva. "She did not like him much, but she had a roof over her head and money."

"Accident or not, he is dead, and Madoc was in Ludlow with his men." Thomas was less disturbed by Silva's nakedness now, perhaps because she was barely aware of it herself.

Will's body jerked as he came back to himself. "I will go and dress," he said, making a conscious effort to control himself. "Then I will be ready when they arrive."

"You told me you have used the mushrooms in the past," said Silva. "Was it with a woman?"

"It was, but many years ago now."

"And was it good?"

"I thought so at the time, but it is a false lust."

"I agree, which is why we do not use it that way. We have sex, of course we do, but the mushrooms are unnecessary for that, only to enhance it. What it does for me is open my mind to the infinite. I am trying to teach the same to Will." Silva offered a smile. "But he is a poor student. He is too much in his own body to let go of it. Did you ever let go of your body, Tom?"

"Sometimes."

"Yes, I imagine you did." She smiled. "I would have liked to have known you thirty years ago. You are an interesting man, and not what I expected."

Silva turned away and walked to the house, leaving Thomas to wonder what she had expected. He tried not to stare at her but knew even if he had she would not have been concerned. He walked to the start of the steep slope where they had been sitting and took in the view. He tried to put his mind in a place it had once been long ago, but it was too far in the past. He wanted to know what they had seen in the rolling expanse of hills that faded into haze. Or rather, what Silva had seen. Thomas smiled at what she had told him. Yes, Will lived in his own body and would find it hard to let go. And if he did succeed he might no longer be the warrior he was destined to be.

Something in the distance caught his attention and he almost laughed.

A band of men rode a twisting track that climbed the slope a mile away. Thomas narrowed his eyes and counted. Yes — thirteen men. He could not make them out but knew they were who he sought. As he watched, two riders appeared closer. Usaden and Jack Pook. He could not see Kin with them, which was explained when the hound came bounding up the slope towards him.

"They are heading to Elmbrook Priory," said Jack when they arrived a quarter hour later. "What is the matter with Will?"

"He and Silva consumed mushrooms."

"Ah, that would explain it. He will return to normal soon enough if we need to fight, but I doubt it will come to that."

"Do you think they mean to avail themselves of its services?"

"Sure to be. Those soldiers pretend to offer protection to the priory, among other places, so believe they can lie with the nuns without payment. Though Felicia Hughden makes sure they take no liberties and do not impose themselves too often."

"You appear to know a great deal about Elmbrook Priory."

"Of course. The nuns are clean and in general pretty. Best of all, there are no repercussions and no need for words of love to be spoken. Though I have a woman of my own now so have turned my back on all such temptations."

"What do you think of the Prioress?"

"She is exquisite, but aloof. She is also exceedingly strange. She has unusual ideas for a woman of the cloth."

"Such as?"

"I think she and Silva would discover they have much in common if they could allow themselves to discuss their beliefs. Felicia will be preparing for the celebrations tonight. That is no doubt another reason those men ride west."

"What celebrations?"

"It is midsummer's eve, Tom, or had you forgotten?"

Thomas laughed. "I admit I have. Felicia follows the old festivals, does she?"

"She does. Which is why I say she is strange. In these borderlands many things are strange. The Christian God holds less sway here than in other parts of England. Here the people are more strongly linked to the land."

"As are you."

"Yes. As am I."

When Will joined them they rode on, coming to a halt

on the hillside where Thomas had first met Prioress Felicia Hughden. The soldiers rode into the courtyard of the priory. Nuns came out to welcome them. After a moment the Prioress joined them, and a horse was brought for her. It appeared the priory was not to be their final destination.

Felicia Hughden led them through the gate, riding ahead of the soldiers with Madoc beside her. Whatever argument they had had seemed set aside. A group of twenty-one nuns followed on foot. Which meant wherever they were going could not be far.

THIRTY-ONE

Madoc, Felicia Hughden, her select group of nuns and the warrior monks headed south for a mile before turning west.

"They are going to Hindwell Abbey," said Jack Pook.

"Or somewhere further west?"

Jack shook his head. "Hindwell is a few hours on foot, so the day will be drawing to a close by the time they reach the abbey. The midsummer celebrations start an hour before the day's turning." Jack glanced at the sky. "There is a storm to the west, but it should not arrive until morning. Besides, they will have a bonfire big enough to make it as light as day."

"You know a great deal about this celebration."

"I may have found myself out that way once or twice in my travels. Everyone around Hindwell knows what happens on Burfa Bank, but most want nothing to do with it. Men and women lock their doors on this night."

"Burfa Bank?" Thomas asked.

"The abbey lies hard beneath the hill," said Jack. "The remains of an ancient fort stand at the crest with an old quarry on one side. Most likely it is where the stone for the abbey came from. And there are caves. Some say people used to live in them, but I reckon they are talking out of their arses. Bears and wolves, more like. We still have a few this far west, for all the King in London claims they are driven out of England. The old fort is where they build their fires and celebrate the changing of the year."

"Now, not in January?"

"These are the old ways, Tom. Winter is when the Church decides the year starts. Midsummer is when the old gods set the year to turn, and it makes more sense. It is the most fruitful time but the start of a slow decline. Autumn comes. Fruit ripens then rots. The grass ceases to grow. Animals curl up and sleep, and men and women hunker around their fires."

"Who presides over these celebrations?" Thomas asked.

"The Abbot and Felicia Hughden. They have done so ever since they were appointed."

"And Madoc is the new Abbot at Hindwell." It was starting to make sense. Responsibility had passed from one Abbot to the next. "I take it Abbot Haylewith used to preside?"

"I expect he still will. It is not the kind of thing a man gives up willingly. But Madoc may get his share as well. He is younger and will no doubt take over one day."

"And Felicia Hughden?"

Jack smiled. "Wait and see, Tom. Wait and see."

They turned aside from the main track as Jack led them around the side of the hill. A narrow defile allowed them to climb the bank without ascending the precipitous slope on the south. At the summit, the defensive bank of the old fort surrounded a grassed hollow. Jack led them to where the bank was thick with trees and bushes which would allow them to view events without being seen in return.

They tied their horses to the trees a distance away before settling down to wait. To the west thunder clouds formed, framing the lowering sun and catching its rays in a brilliant display of colour.

"Are you sure the storm will not reach us before midnight?" Thomas asked Jack.

"I think not. The early hours of tomorrow I would guess. But it is hard to judge out here. These hills can direct a storm away from the path you expect."

"I will go down the far side of the hill and watch for those coming from that way," said Usaden. "I will return to tell you so we have time to hide."

Will stretched out on the ground and appeared to fall asleep, no doubt the remnant of the mushroom fading only slowly.

Thomas knew nothing would happen until after the sun had set so moved away to examine the hillside where the quarry had been carved. He found a small outcropping of rock from which he could obtain a better view. He saw the caves Jack had mentioned. They looked older than the quarry, and Thomas believed they may have been formed by nature; water, wind and frost. Only later would men discover the hillside was a source of stone for building. He looked to the west where the sun had already disappeared behind the high hills, but the last rays continued to illuminate the gathering clouds. The storm was a little closer. Occasional flashes of lightning showed, but no thunder reached this far. A curtain of rain drifted across the hills, a rainbow arcing through the sky. It would fill hollows and run off slopes to gather in streams and rivers. The headwaters of the Lugge lay in that direction, and come morning the waters at Lemster would have risen and coloured.

Thomas heard a sound from below, and it took him a while before he worked out it was singing. Someone played a drum, someone else a whistle, the sounds echoing back from the surrounding hills. He grasped the trunk of a young beech tree and leaned out. He saw a line of men and women following a twisting path up the side of the hill. The nuns still wore their habits. Felicia Hughden could be identified by her height, Abbot Haylewith from his white robe and long hair and beard. Following behind came a raggle-taggle group of men. Taking up the rear were the warrior monks, but of Madoc there was no sign. Most of the nuns carried bunches of flowers picked from the hedgerows, and it was their voices that rose in song, the words English rather than Latin. They were muffled by distance, but they carried a different lilt to the prayers and psalms they would be more used to. It was a song Thomas was sure Silva would recognise. It had a pagan feel to it. Thomas climbed back to the hillside and ran towards their hiding place, but in the growing darkness he tripped and fell hard. He rolled, then lay still as he checked to ensure there was no one other than him and his companions on the crest of the hill. He looked to see what had tripped him and saw a solid wooden post driven into the ground, a metal ring attached to the top. For a moment its purpose puzzled him, then he realised it must be there to allow quarrymen to descend the cliff face. He expected if he looked he would find others dotted along the edge of the quarry.

When Thomas reached the others, Usaden had returned. He lay on his belly beside Will and Jack on the edge of the hollow, watching as the celebrants arrived. As they came closer and fanned out across the clearing, Thomas caught sight of two familiar figures whose presence surprised him. Sir Thomas Cornwell strutted into the clearing, followed by Sir Richard Croft. Two men Thomas believed would never be seen in each other's company, yet here they were, and he wondered why.

As clay bowls were passed around, from which each of the celebrants drank, Abbot Haylewith picked up a long torch. One of the warrior monks used a flint to create a spark against a pile of wool. As soon as it began to smoke, slivers of dried wood were added until a flame built. When it was big enough, the Abbot thrust the head of the torch into it before raising it above his head.

The others had spread out in a horseshoe around the tall bonfire, the side above the quarry on the western side left open.

Abbot Haylewith turned to face the throng, the torch held high.

"We come to his place to offer penance for our sins, which exist in all the fissures and folds of our bodies. It passes to and fro through bodily orifices, from where it sinks into our inner being. From lip and tongue to tissue. From teeth to bone. From our sex to our very core. We are penitent because we have sinned. We are penitent because we are made of sin. We are penitent because we must sin. Let us sin then, to prove that it does not bind us, but we bind it."

Lightning flashed, and this time thunder followed but only long seconds after. The Abbot went to the bonfire and thrust the flaming torch into its heart before stepping back. The wood caught with a soft thump to climb hungrily through the pile until the entire bonfire was aflame.

It was a signal. The nuns let their robes drop away until they stood naked. Within a heartbeat men went to them, laying hands on the fissures and folds of their bodies.

"Do we have to watch this?" asked Will, who had come to lie beside Thomas. "We have come here on a fool's quest. There is nothing here but debauchery. We will learn nothing tonight."

"You are probably right. Go if you want, but I intend to stay."

Will rose and walked away.

Thomas glanced at Jack. "And you?"

"I too have a woman of my own these days, and agree with Will. This is wrong."

Thomas turned back to the events unfolding around

the bonfire. They had moved on apace. Few remained fully clothed and the debauchery was spreading throughout those lit by the flickering flames as more frequent cracks of lightning arced down against the westward peaks. Thomas considered it would be wise to move from their position before the storm arrived, but there was time yet, though it seemed for once Jack had misjudged nature.

Thomas saw Cornwell and Croft indulging themselves — a sight Thomas feared he would never expunge from his mind. Felicia Hughden pressed her naked body against Abbot Haylewith, whose hands explored every inch of her before he pulled her down on top of him.

"Will is right," Thomas said, disgusted. "There is nothing we are going to learn here." He slid back from the edge of the fort then rose and started away to find Ferrant.

"Thomas." Usaden's voice was a whisper but carried. "Something is about to happen."

"I have seen all I need. I have seen too much." But Thomas stopped, crouched and returned to his spot on the grass.

Usaden was right. Something was about to happen, but what he could not make out. Two of the warrior monks remained clothed. They had been standing to one side as if guarding events. Now they approached the bonfire. Between them, they carried something cloaked by the shadows. Only as they neared the fire could Thomas make it out. A length of heavy rope.

They came up to the Abbot and Felicia Hughden, who

straddled him, her head thrown back in real or pretended ecstasy. Abbot Haylewith gripped her waist in his hands and lifted her body, his strength greater than Thomas expected. As he did so, one of the men slipped a knotted noose of rope around her neck and tightened it. The move seemed to arouse Felicia Hughden even more, as if this was a normal part of the celebration. Except celebration it was not. Deviancy, more like, Thomas thought. The sight made clear to him how this western borderland had managed to slip so deeply into sin. The holy brothel — and he was sure Elmbrook Priory was not the only one. The burial of the children would be linked to what he was seeing. A pagan measure he knew nothing of. This midsummer celebration was the culmination and the binding of these people together.

Abbot Haylewith rose and moved away, staggering a little. No doubt the preparation they had all drunk roared through his veins, mixing the real and imaginary until it was impossible to tell one from the other.

The two warrior monks gripped Felicia Hughden by the arms, and as the Abbot moved away they dragged her after him.

Felicia Hughden cried out, but it was not a cry of fear but arousal.

Thomas watched as they approached the edge of the quarry and saw where their destination lay. The post he had fallen over. He watched Abbot Haylewith tie the rope to the metal ring and all at once knew what was about to happen. It had nothing to do with debauchery.

He rose to his feet.

"With me," he said to Usaden, knowing the man would come without question. "Try to cut the rope. I will provide cover."

"We do it the other way around," said Usaden. "You know I can keep you safer than you can me. Kin, with us."

They ran together, weaving through the writhing bodies, but Thomas feared they were too late.

Already Felicia Hughden had been pulled to her feet. Abbot Haylewith dragged her towards the edge of the quarry. She did not fight. Her body was slack from what she had consumed.

"Kin, attack," Thomas said, knowing the dog would cover the ground in an instant.

Kin streaked through the darkness and leapt.

His teeth closed around Abbot Haylewith's wrist and the man fell to one side with a scream. Kin shook his head, his jaws locked on the wrist until Usaden whistled and he released his hold. For a moment Kin started back towards them, but Usaden called out. "No. The others."

Whether Kin understood their words or not Thomas did not know, only that he did as asked most of the time. Now he turned, his head moving as he scanned the tangle of bodies in front of him. He ran towards one couple before stopping, then tried another, confused by the tangle of limbs, the flickering light from the bonfire.

Thomas ran on but knew he was too late.

Abbot Haylewith scrambled to his feet and staggered towards the slumped body of Felicia Hughden. He heaved her into the air, straining with the effort, then stumbled towards the edge of the quarry.

"Fly, witch!" he screamed as he tossed her over the edge.

Thomas flung himself at the uncoiling rope and caught it, only to have it snatched from his hands by the plummeting weight on the other end. He tried again, but before he could close his fingers around it the rope snapped taut. Then it went slack. Thomas knew exactly what had happened as he pulled the rope towards him. He expected at any moment to see Felicia Hughden's head appear, but when the noose emerged it showed nothing other than a slick of blood. Thomas rose and started towards the edge of the quarry, but Usaden grabbed his arm.

"We have to go, Thomas." He nodded at the warrior monks, some clothed, others naked, who approached them with drawn swords.

Thomas drew his own sword and backed away with Usaden at his side. Kin prowled the ground between them.

"You are a dead man, Thomas Berrington," one called out. "Here and now, or later if you flee. Stay and face us like a man. My master wants you dead. Let it be here. Let it be now."

"Why?" Thomas said, knowing there was no need to explain what.

"This is all because of you."

The speaker broke into a run, but Kin snapped at his ankles and he fell.

Two naked warrior monks knelt to help the man to his feet, but by the time they did Thomas and Usaden were running for their horses. Lightning flashed, illuminating the writhing bodies scattered across the hollow of the old fort. Few appeared to have noticed what had happened.

Thunder roared overhead. A second strike of lightning brought a scream as it cracked into the ground within feet of a nun and Sir Richard Croft.

At their horses, Thomas drew Usaden close.

"Make as much noise as you can when you flee. I intend to stay and need a distraction."

Usaden nodded but saw no reason to speak. He pulled himself into the saddle, clicked his tongue for Kin to follow, and turned away. Thomas slapped Ferrant on the rump, sending him after the two of them.

Thomas slipped away to the edge of the fort, then scrambled down the steep slope as the rain finally arrived as hard as if he had stepped beneath a waterfall. The darkness and rain cloaked him, but when he managed to reach the base of the quarry there was no sign of Felicia Hughden's body or head. Thomas crossed and re-crossed the ground but found no trace of either. Only when he heard voices as others descended did he turn and move away.

He found Usaden a mile distant. Or rather, Usaden found him, riding out from a copse with Ferrant's reins in his hand. He handed them to Thomas, who leaned against the horse for a while before gathering enough strength to climb into the saddle.

"Home?" asked Usaden.

"Yes, home."

The storm followed them, but of those on the hilltop they saw no sign.

Not yet, Thomas thought, but he knew they would come for him. Others had tried and now lay in the ground. Some consecrated, some not. Let them come. Unless he went for them first.

THIRTY-TWO

They rode a twisting route through the darkness that brought them eventually to Silva's cottage, a burning torch beneath an eave which kept the pouring rain from it. Thomas knocked on the door but did not wait for a reply before entering. He had not been inside the cottage before, surprised when he discovered only a single large room. At the far side stood a wide bed with crooked tree trunks at each corner, more branches twined above it, all laced with moss and rushes. A fire burned, little more than glowing embers, its smoke rising through a hole in the wall near the roof.

Silva sat up, but Will was slower, which worried Thomas. At one time he would wake immediately at any sign of danger. Unless he knew it was his father.

"What is it?" asked Silva. "Is something wrong?"

"I need Will at my house in the morning."

Thomas said nothing about the reason. He could explain when Will came. Let them sleep for now.

Knowing would change nothing. Thomas turned away, walked out into the downpour and mounted Ferrant.

It was the shortest night of the year, but when they arrived at Dinham Bridge below Ludlow the sky remained pitch black. How they had found their way was a mystery to Thomas, but Ferrant seemed to know each turn, and Usaden's instinct was uncanny. Thomas had spent the journey trying to work out what he had witnessed. The act itself was obvious and clear in his mind. The reason for it less so.

Had Madoc been present, Thomas would have suspected him of wanting Felicia dead, but he had not been. Which raised the question of why not. Did the debauchery disgust him? That would come as a surprise. Unless some remnant of religion remained in his soul. Some sense of good. If it did, he hid it well because Thomas had seen no sign of it.

Which meant Abbot Haylewith wanted Felicia Hughden dead. The reasons for this came only slowly to Thomas because he had to take down one tower of assumptions and build a new one. He needed to speak to Jorge. To Will, Amal, and most of all to Bel, who had lived in this borderland her whole life and would know its vagaries well. He also needed to speak to Bernard and hoped he remained at Burway.

"I will leave you here, Usaden," Thomas said. "You can climb into bed next to Emma, but may need to dry yourself first."

"I stay with you, Thomas. I expect we will ride out again tomorrow. It is what you do. You punish bad men."

"I can send for you."

"I know you can, but I can sleep under your roof just as well. I told Emma not to expect me. Jack Pook will have explained I am with you."

Thomas urged Ferrant into a slow walk for the last half-mile to his house.

"You are fortunate to have found her."

"And you to have Bel again. I loved Lubna and know nobody can ever replace her for you, but you and Bel have a connection like no other."

Thomas rode on, but a smile touched his lips. Yes, he and Bel shared a connection that went back further than any other, though there were times Thomas feared he neglected her when events conspired to fill his mind with intrigue. He could vow to change but knew he would not, and if he did he would no longer be the man Bel loved.

Thomas and Usaden bathed beneath the spout of hot water to drive the cold of the night from them, then Thomas climbed the stairs to his room while Usaden went in search of an empty bed. There were always several kept for visitors. Thomas let Bel continue to sleep. A single candle burning on a table in the corner threw a dancing light across her pretty face. To him, she looked no different to the girl he had first loved, but he knew they had both changed. There were lines on his own face, and his hair and beard were now streaked with grey. His body held scars that had not marked his thirteen-year-old body. But in his mind he felt no different.

He stared at the flickering candlelight, knowing he would not sleep.

"Tom, wake up!"

He mumbled and rolled his head to one side to discover Bel leaning over him, her loose hair almost touching his face.

"What is wrong?"

"Nothing, but I feared you were dead you were sleeping so soundly."

Thomas laughed. "No, you did not. What do you really want?"

Bel only smiled in reply. And no, Thomas thought, many years may have passed, but we are both still the same people beneath the weight of them.

He padded downstairs half an hour later to find Amal and Belia in the kitchen.

"Is Usaden still asleep?"

"Of course not," said Amal. "Will arrived and they went outside to practice, though there is little he can teach Will anymore."

"Does he still train you?"

"He does, and tells me I am improving."

"I hope you never have to use his teachings."

"As do I, but better to know them than face the consequences of ignorance. What is going on, Pa?"

"We need to all talk before I am sure, but we witnessed a death last night and know who the killer is. The question I have to decide is can the man be punished or not. Is Bernard still here?"

"He rose early and is out watching Will and Usaden."

"When did Will arrive?" Thomas knew he would need to tell his son the reason he wanted him.

"An hour since. He broke his fast then said he needed exercise, and Usaden offered."

"And Jorge?"

Belia laughed. "What do you think? Do you want me to go and wake him?"

"I will do it," Thomas said. "And I have a task for you later, Ami."

"What is it?"

"I will tell you that once I have woken Jorge."

Which took some time and persuasion, but eventually the man threw back the covers and stood.

"May I have some privacy so I can dress?"

"It has never bothered you in the past."

"We all grow older if not wiser." Jorge flicked his fingers at him and Thomas left the room.

Amal accompanied him as he crossed to his workshop. He saw Bernard sitting in a chair, his face turned up to the sky. Thomas took a moment to watch Will and Usaden train, if training was the right word for what he saw. It was closer to all-out war. Usaden was the faster, the more skilled, but Will was only a little less skilled and by far the stronger of the two, with a better reach. They used blunted swords, which clashed almost continuously. Will would prefer to use his axe, but Usaden always told him he could not. It would not be a fair fight. Will had stripped to the waist and sweat streaked his body. Usaden remained in the clothes he always wore. Dark jacket and trousers in the Moorish style, cut loose so they did not restrict his movements. His long hair was twisted into a knot at the back, which was slowly working loose.

"Who is going to win?" Thomas asked Amal, who also watched as she stood at his side.

"It is always a draw these days, but by next year Will is going to win every time. Usaden told me the same, but is not upset about it. He says if a teacher is good enough, the student should always exceed them." Amal reached for her father's hand. "Just as one day I will be cleverer than you."

Thomas laughed. "I think that day passed long ago." He tugged at her. "Come on, this will not take long."

In the workshop, he went to a shelf and scanned its contents before reaching up. He set a small bottle between them.

Amal stared at it before raising her gaze to meet her father's. "If you seek my advice about this I am the wrong person to ask."

"I believe not. I assume you heard the Coroner died?"

"Poisoned is the rumour."

"And in this case, for once in Ludlow, the rumour is true but also not true. He was either given an excess of this tincture — but clearly not this one — or the tincture itself was far stronger than he was used to."

"There is a fine line between too little, too much, and the right amount," said Amal. "I know all about cantharidin, Pa. You would expect me to. I appreciate it is called for in some instances, in both men and women, but it does not come without danger. Is this what was used?"

"It was. Spanish Fly, the housekeeper called it, which is the more common name. I doubt many people know of it as cantharidin or the beetles it is made from."

"Now you have shown it to me what is it you want me to do?"

"I want to know who in Ludlow or nearby might have sold the tincture to Mary, Lyman's housekeeper. She told me she ordered it on instruction from Lyman himself."

"I assume it was he who needed it. Who was the poor unfortunate woman?"

"The housekeeper herself," Thomas said, and smiled when Amal pulled a face. "She claimed to have taken two drops — to enable her to face the onslaught of Lyman's lust, I expect — and gave four to him in wine, as he always asked for. Except she used an older bottle for one drop of hers and the new bottle for his."

"Four is too many?" asked Amal.

"It is more than a normal dose, but not fatal. Four is what d'Alston asked for. Four is what she has given him in the past. See if you can find out who provided the bottle and whether they knew it was stronger than their usual supply. If you find the seller tell them to destroy any they still have or dilute it in spirit."

"I would ask Aunt Agnes if she knows where it might have come from but suspect she would not."

"Go to Emma and ask Jack Pook," Thomas said with a smile, which Amal returned.

Outside, Bernard now stood watching as the fight —

not training — approached an end. Neither man looked tired.

"Your son is a wonder," said Bernard.

"He is, but then so is Usaden."

"They are both so different. I would not have thought it possible they could match each other so equally, but they do. I am glad my fighting days are over. If I had come against their like in Spain or the Holy Land I would not be standing here now."

"I am glad they stand beside me in battle."

"What happened last night, Tom? Usaden said something about debauchery on a hill near Hindwell Abbey."

Thomas glanced at Bernard. "Are you telling me you know nothing about what they do there?"

"I am a simple monk at heart. You know I am. I care about Lemster Priory and those who used to be under my charge. What goes on in the outer world I allow to pass me by."

"I always thought you knew everything, Bernard."

The man smiled. "So did I at one time, but it is a falsehood to believe such about yourself. We learn nothing if we think we already know everything. I know you agree with me, which is one reason I like you."

"Only one?"

"That and your impertinence."

"Ah, I had forgotten about that."

"Do not worry, Tom; I will remind you often enough."

"What are you going to do now you have no place?" Thomas asked.

"That is a fine question but one I have no answer to. I am old, so perhaps I will die before I ever find one."

Thomas put his hand on Bernard's shoulder. "Try not to do that. I would miss you."

"And I you. Tell me about what you saw and what you intend to do about it."

So Thomas did, and when he was finished he saw tears in Bernard's eyes.

"Do not worry, I will take care. And I have those two at my back."

The fight had finished with no victor, which was only right. Usaden took both blades and returned them to Thomas's workshop where they hung from hooks on the wall.

"I do worry, Tom, but worrying does no good. So I will pray instead. For you and for Felicia, who had a good heart but a sinful body. I will pray for you all. May I offer you one piece of advice?"

"Always."

"If you have to punish people, try to punish only the guilty. Sin and guilt are not always the same thing, but it took me many years to work that out."

Thomas started across to where Will was washing the sweat from himself in the river. He needed to tell him what had happened on Burfa Bank after he left. Needed to know what must happen now, as soon as Thomas could work out a way of achieving it.

Punishment and retribution.

THIRTY-THREE

When Thomas, Will and Jorge reached Croft Manor, John Pryce, Sir Thomas Croft's stable hand, came out to inform them his master had not yet returned from business in the west. Thomas thanked him and turned Ferrant aside.

"I want to visit Silva while we are close," he said to Will. "I assume you have no objection?"

Will grinned. "I expect she will not object if we call on her. Why do you want to see her, Pa?"

"I need to ask her about what I witnessed last night. The celebration was pagan, not Christian, and Silva knows about such things."

"I should not have left as soon as I did," said Will. "You might have needed me."

"You were not yourself. Besides, everything happened so fast at the end, nothing could be done. Now I need to know how much Silva knows about what is going on around here."

"She has spoken to me about her beliefs and you are

right, she knows much about both the Christian God and what she calls the elder Gods. It is all mixed up with the land, trees, rivers. I believe Olaf worships pagan Gods."

"It is not something we spoke of much, but yes, he does. He wears Thor's hammer around his neck, and when he eventually passes from this life, which I pray will be many years from now, I hope he receives a Northman's funeral and feasts in Valhalla."

"So do I," said Will. "And if needs be I will ensure it myself." He glanced at his father. "What we witnessed last night, that was Pagan more than Christian. Silva has taught me enough so I could recognise it as such. Yet those there profess to be men of God."

"Jack said it best to me. This is borderland. Neither England nor Wales, neither Christian nor Pagan, but some mix of both. So yes, Haylewith is an abbot, but his beliefs may share much of what Silva believes in."

"You also told me he is a killer," said Will. "Why are we not perusing him? Punishing him?"

"Because he is the Abbot of Wigmore," Thomas said, "and I need more than simple proof before I can accuse him."

Silva had heard them approach and came out to greet them, dressed in a long, flowing robe that matched the colour of the leaves surrounding her cottage.

Thomas drew her to one side while Will showed Jorge the inside of the cottage.

"This feels serious, Tom," she said.

"Nothing too serious, I hope. A few questions is all. I

need information and judge you to be my best source. Do you celebrate midsummer?"

Silva frowned. "It is what Will and I were doing when you arrived yesterday."

Thomas had almost forgotten about the encounter.

"Am I right that it might involve altered states and nakedness?"

"You are. It brings us closer to nature, which is what my beliefs centre around."

"You are Pagan?"

Silva stared off to where wooded hills rolled like ocean waves into the distance.

"I have told you before what I believe in. Yes, I am Pagan, but I also believe in the God of the Christian Church. After all, it did steal most of its saints' days from our celebrations."

"I know about some of those," Thomas said. "But not about midsummer."

"Oh, they have the feast of St John, and it is celebrated with drinking and other forms of inebriation and pleasure. As Will and I would have pleasured each other had you not come."

Thomas wondered if her intent was to shock him, but if so she failed. Will was a full-grown man, as she was a full-grown woman. It is what men and women did, even if the Church often called it a sin.

"Have you heard of a festival celebrated on the hill above Hindwell Abbey?" he asked.

"I have, though never witnessed it myself. I prefer my pleasures to be taken more privately. Of course, we were not expecting company yesterday, but I was not ashamed of my nakedness, and neither was Will."

"What we saw on Burfa Bank was different, and it ended in death."

"Then it was not Pagan," said Silva. "Pagans celebrate life, not death, despite the Church pretending otherwise. Who died?"

Thomas had assumed she would know, but then remembered Will had only been told about it that morning.

"Prioress Felicia Hughden."

"Then I am sad. I know her and her nuns, as well as what she operates from the priory."

"Might that service have got her killed?" Thomas asked.

Silva gave the question some thought. She lowered herself to the grass with ease. Thomas sat beside her, grunting as he did so.

"Not for offering it, no, I do not see that. But then I am not a suspicious person. You are better at making such a decision than I am. The way you speak tells me her death was deliberate. Who killed her?"

"Abbot Haylewith."

Silva stared into space for a long time before speaking. When she did her words surprised Thomas.

"Does he know you witnessed the act?"

"I do not believe so."

"That is good. Haylewith is a man who makes harsh judgements. He makes a pretence of being Christian but also believes in older Gods and has melded them into something depraved. You surprise me when you say he killed Felicia, for she was also sympathetic to those Gods."

"What does the district think of his appointment as Abbot of Wigmore?"

Silva shrugged. "Those who are pious only see a new abbot and bend the knee. Other folk care neither one way nor the other. All they want to know is will the abbey still buy their wares. But everyone is upset about the eviction of Prior Bernard. They regard him as a good man. A holy man. I do not have to worship his God to see he is a man like you, Tom, who does what is right." Silva reached out and patted his hand. "I love Will because he is the same as you. You are fortunate that your children inherited your inner strength."

Thomas did not agree with her. He saw only the differences between himself, Will and Amal.

"If what you say is true about Haylewith, why would he kill Felicia? I admit many substances were used but do not believe they contributed to her death. It was a deliberate act and had been planned."

"Go speak with Madoc. Abbot Haylewith is the head of the Church in the district now but Madoc pulls his strings. He is the one hungry for power. He keeps Haylewith tied to him with promises of that which he seeks."

"If you mean the Grail then Haylewith is a fool to believe Madoc knows any more than he does. I spoke with the priest at Garway a few weeks ago and he told me much about Owain Haylewith, who preceded him. I also heard Madoc and Haylewith fought together in Spain against the Moors."

"Haylewith has always believed the Grail lies buried somewhere in Herefordshire. It fills his thoughts, and Madoc takes advantage of it. As for fighting together, I know nothing of that. You would be better to speak to Bernard, who also fought there."

"I will ride to Lemster and confront Madoc, but he was not at Burfa Bank last night."

"He would not be. He always gets someone else to do his dirty work. And he is no longer at Lemster Priory. I heard he rode to Hindwell to take up his position as Abbot there. But be careful if you do confront him. He always has those pretend soldiers around him, and it is said they show no mercy."

"The impression I have is they are not true warriors, even if one of them did stab me. And I saw only a dozen on Burfa Bank last night."

"There are three times that number at least, and more recruited all the time. Madoc wants his own army. What he intends to do with it is another matter, but one that worries me. As it should you. There was law here not long since, but the death of Prince Arthur changed everything. The Marcher Lords want to stamp their authority on this land before they strip it for their own benefit, but they fight each other instead of combining their forces. Which is fortunate for King Henry."

"Do you suspect Madoc works for one of these Lords?"

"I do not know. I believe Madoc may work only for

himself, but no doubt he wants them to believe otherwise. Take care, Tom. I would like to see you live a long time yet." Silva rose, then leaned down to kiss his cheek. "I would ask you to take care of Will, too, but know it is more likely the other way. I will think about what you have told me and see if I can tease out more that may be useful for you. I assume you will ride past this way again in the hope Sir Richard has returned."

Thomas watched Silva walk away, then rose to follow so he could fetch Will and Jorge. He was aware that if they were to ride to Hindwell Abbey later he wanted Usaden with him but not Jorge, so made a decision.

Sir Thomas Cornwell surprised Thomas for the second time in two days by inviting him and Jorge inside, but not Will, who stayed in the yard talking with his Steward. Sir Thomas led them into his study and offered them chairs and wine. Jorge accepted, but Thomas refused.

"What can I do for you, Berrington?" asked Cornwell. "I hope this is not some new spurious charge against me."

"I hope it is not, either, Sir Thomas. I was on Burfa Bank last night at midnight, as you were."

Cornwell stared at Thomas for so long it appeared he might refuse to answer. Then he shrugged.

"What if I was? I believe there is no law against attending a Christian celebration."

"If that was Christian then I have been sorely misled

my entire life. You were naked, and the last time I caught sight of you three nuns were pleasuring you."

"And you have a point to make regarding the law?"

"Did you know what Abbot Haylewith planned?"

"He planned a festival, a celebration, as he does every year at midsummer's eve. I attended last year and the year before that, and in both instances the events were the same as those you witnessed. A celebration of humanity in all its forms."

"Not quite. I assume you did not see what happened to Prioress Felicia Hughden?"

"Of course I saw her. Felicia is a most ardent celebrant, though has not attended of late. The last time I glimpsed her that was exactly what she was doing. Celebrating in the same manner as the rest of us. I admit I did not see you there, Berrington, but you are not much to look at, are you?"

"I was not partaking, I was watching."

"There is a word for men who do that, but I forget it for the moment."

"A gawper, I believe," said Jorge with a smile.

"Were you there as well?"

"Unfortunately not. I appreciate a beautiful body, male or female, as much as anyone. Probably more than most. But then I have seen the nubile women of a Sultan's harem, so my standards are undoubtedly high. I believe Thomas is talking of murder. To which you were a witness."

"I told you I saw nothing."

"Saw, perhaps. What about knowledge of?" Thomas

asked. "Did you know Abbot Haylewith intended to kill the Prioress?"

"Do you think I would have allowed it if I had? Felicia was a beacon of rationality in the Church. We need more such as her. If we did then priests would be allowed to take wives and father children, and fewer of their flock would suffer their predations."

Thomas sat back in his chair, stunned at what Cornwell had said. He disliked the man, with good reason, but believed he may have misjudged him in this instance.

"Do you have any idea why Abbot Haylewith might have wanted Felicia dead?"

"I do not," said Cornwell. "The two of them shared a special connection. I cannot believe he would kill her. I doubt you witnessed what you think you did."

"Doubt it all you like, I know what I saw. Perhaps now Haylewith is Abbot at Wigmore he wants the income Elmbrook Priory brings in for himself. I have seen the papers and it is significant, almost exceeding that of Wigmore itself. But does he believe he can get away with murder in front of eighty people?"

"Eighty people who will never bear witness against him," said Cornwell, allowing a slight smile to touch his lips. "Eighty people who, like me, were otherwise pleasurably distracted. As I have already told you, I saw nothing."

"You were there with Croft," Thomas said. "Perhaps he was more observant than you and can offer me something."

"Against Abbot Haylewith? I think you may be

confusing your powers as Justice of the Peace. Even the Coroner would be unable to investigate an Abbot of the Church, and certainly not this one. Any wrongdoing Haylewith may have done — and as I say, I did not see anything last night and suspect you will find no witness who will admit to doing so either — will be judged by the Church. An Archbishop at least, possibly to include King Henry as well. Croft will tell you the same."

"I called on him but he had not returned home," Thomas said. "I will ride there again once I leave here. Was it not unusual for the two of you to attend the festivities last night?"

"We are not friends, but neither are we enemies. What passes between us is a battle for power in the area, and no different to what has gone on for centuries. Richard and I have attended Burfa Bank together for several years, and he has done so for even longer. It is an important ritual in the area and we are expected to be there. Besides, Richard is a man of uncommon sensibilities. His wife spends most of her time in London, so what is he to do? He is no longer a young man but still has the passions of one."

"And your wife knows what you do?"

"Anne understands me. She too is away in Derbyshire at the moment. She dislikes summer here, just as Eleanor Croft, born a Cornwell, prefers life in London. We are a backwater here now the Prince is dead. Some of us do our duty and try to maintain law and order and hold back the Welsh." Sir Thomas Cornwell leaned over his desk. "Have you discovered who killed Lyman d'Alston yet?"

"I have been otherwise engaged, but I believe his death was an accident. He took too much Spanish Fly. It stopped his breathing and stilled his heart."

Cornwell smiled. "Then you are not as clever as people tell me. Amos Mapp took his master's place and arrested the housekeeper the evening d'Alston perished. All this while you were planning to spy on innocent men and women indulging their passions. The housekeeper was tried yesterday and hung this morning." Cornwell gave a shake of his head. "Mapp will need to find a new housekeeper, no doubt one who is younger and prettier. Someone able to measure tinctures more accurately. Though I doubt Mapp has any need for them in the same way Lyman did. He has shown decisiveness in the matter and I am minded to make his position permanent." Cornwell rose to his feet. "If we are finished, I have work to do."

Thomas glanced at Jorge, who offered a brief nod to indicate he needed nothing more.

Outside, Will was talking amiably with James Marshall, discussing the merits of stallions and geldings. Thomas said nothing until they had passed out through the gates of Burford Manor.

"What did you make of him?" he asked Jorge. "Was he telling the truth or not?"

"The truth, in the main, and what he hid was nothing important. It was to do with how much he enjoyed the coupling on that hill last night. And the fact he believes his wife has no inkling of what he does. But women are not as stupid as men believe them to be. I excuse those present from that judgement, of course." There was no need for Jorge to colour his reply with any doubt. He would have seen, as he always did, the lies men and women told. "He seems to be a changed man, do you agree?"

"He surprised me, I admit, but has he truly changed? I believe the news of Felicia Hughden's death shocked him. It may be no more than that."

"He had not heard of it, that was plain to see," said Jorge. "Do we ride to Croft's house now?"

"It is not yet noon, so yes. If we are fortunate he will have returned. If not we must decide whether to confront Abbot Haylewith or not. You heard what Cornwell said. Only an Archbishop or the King could judge him."

"What did you want to talk with Silva about?" asked Will. "I saw you with your heads together."

"What we witnessed on the hill. Paganism. The Church. We spoke a little but I want to ask her more yet. I need to know if what happened can be explained by the beliefs of those attending. I am hoping she has given more thought to it and may have something I can use. Some reason for what happened."

"Murder cannot always be explained, Pa. You know it cannot."

And Thomas did. This time he might have come up against a rock that could not be moved. Church and King combined.

THIRTY-FOUR

They called for Bel because she trusted in what Silva did, was familiar with both the mysteries of the Church and this borderland between England and Wales. Her opinion and insight would be valuable. They ate a little food and rested the horses before setting off with the afternoon partly gone. Thomas hoped it would be enough time for Sir Richard to have returned home, but in case it was not they climbed to Croft Ambrey. Silva came out to greet them again, stroking Kin's fur when he ran to her with his tail circling wildly. Bel slid from her usual position behind Thomas and embraced Silva. Words were spoken, and Silva walked with Bel back towards Thomas.

"Have you had time to think over what we spoke of before?" he asked.

"I have, but whether it will help, I do not know. Do you intend to arrest Abbot Haylewith?"

"I cannot do that. I have already been told it is a

matter for an Archbishop and the King. What I need is information. From both you and Bel."

"If it is a matter for Church and King then Haylewith is likely to die of old age before any decision is made, but tell me what I can do to help."

"Tell me more about the festival on Burfa Bank. You told me it is neither Christian nor Pagan. If so, what is it?"

Silva smiled. "I never believed I would hear such words from you." She glanced at Bel, who returned the smile.

"Tom has changed."

"Indeed he has. Do you know about what happens on the hill behind Hindwell Abbey, Bel?"

"Rumours, no more."

Silva looked back at Thomas. "Before I was born, my father would sometimes attend. He would tell me how it was in those days — a truly Pagan festival. We call that night Litha in our calendar. It celebrates a time when the distance between worlds grows thin, allowing our ancestors to cross over and speak with us." Silva waved a hand before Thomas could object, which he had not intended to do. "You do not have to believe everything I say, Tom, but you did ask the question."

"My mind is open," he said.

"Yes, I think perhaps it is." Silva reached out and took Bel's hand.

"From what you say the celebration is meant to be benign," Thomas said.

"Of course. And then it changed. Abbot Haylewith came and sought out Felicia Hughden. Madoc arrived a year later, a lowly brother at the time but one with ambition. The bordel at Elmbrook Priory had been operating for over a century. It was both well-regarded and well-used. I spent some time with Felicia because despite her position as Prioress she and I share some beliefs. I will miss her wisdom and her friendship. She bestrode the worlds between the Christian God and the older Gods, the Pagan Gods. I accompanied her the first time she climbed Burfa Bank. I had not been there in several years and immediately sensed a difference. The love was gone to be replaced by common lust. It did not surprise me, but I was disappointed. The festival there had taken place before the Christian God came to England, and it felt like the end of something important. You know me, Tom. I often walk these woods in a state of nature. That is what we used to do on Burfa Bank, but coupling was never involved. Our nakedness was pure. It was holy. What Haylewith turned it into was not."

"Was it all Haylewith, or did Felicia Hughden have a part in that change?"

"She worshipped both old and new gods, as I said, but it was Haylewith's doing. His and Madoc's. It grew worse after Madoc came. Much worse."

"When was that?"

Silva did not have to think about her answer. "Ten years ago. He came from Wales claiming he was a monk from an abbey there and had fought alongside Haylewith. He knew all the right words and prayers, but there was something wrong with him. Abbot Haylewith did not want to see it. They knew each other from when they fought in the Holy Land, so he took Madoc into Hindwell Abbey. Within a year he was his deputy. The man is both ambitious and ruthless."

"And the warrior monks?"

"Madoc recruited them from wherever he could find men willing to kill in the name of God. Some are ex-soldiers who returned from Spain or the Holy Land. Others are no more than men who like to inflict pain and bully others. Madoc used Haylewith's connection to Garway to spin tales to the men that they are the Templars reborn. Now they do his bidding, and often his bidding is not benign. If Abbot Haylewith killed Felicia Hughden then I believe Madoc was behind it. Why he wanted her dead, I do not know. Madoc wanted her as a man wants a woman, but Felicia told me there was something dark in his nature and rebuffed him."

"She did not rebuff Haylewith that night on the hill," Thomas said. "Far from it."

"Haylewith shares many of her beliefs, so they have more in common."

"Yet he threw her over the quarry cliff and killed her."

"Have you see her body?"

"I could not find it when I searched, so no."

"Have you thought about what you saw being an elaborate ruse? Some kind of twisted celebration?"

Thomas stared into Silva's eyes, uneasy at what he saw there. Something bright, also something of darkness.

"I felt the rope go taut then immediately slacken. If it was a ruse it had been well planned. Felicia is dead, I am sure of it, but must find her body to prove it."

Silva reached out her free hand and took Thomas's. Without thinking he did the same to Bel so all three were joined in a circle. Thomas tried to feel some flow of energy but failed.

"We followed Madoc half the day and he went for Felicia Hughden at the priory, but she was no prisoner. She went with him willingly enough, but by the time she was killed he was long gone."

"Madoc always sets himself apart from what he has plotted. I assume the participants were drugged?"

"Mushrooms mixed with Spanish Fly, I suspect. The same that killed Lyman d'Alston."

"If I know Haylewith, he would have indulged throughout the day," said Silva. "Madoc would have found the Abbot a willing subject."

"But he is not innocent. I watched. He knew what he was doing when he threw Felicia over the cliff."

"Who knows what ran through his mind? Madoc would have worked on him for days. Told lies about Felicia. Told him she was in bed with the devil. Whatever it took. The Abbot is not innocent in this, but it is Madoc who is the evil behind everything, as he has always been. Abbot Haylewith cannot be touched. As you say, it is a matter for the Church and the King. Haylewith might be protected by both, but Madoc is not." Silva squeezed Thomas's hand. "You have judged men in the past and dealt with evil. Is that what you intend to do again?"

"I do not know. I feel as if I have walked into a lake of pitch and cannot make headway. To act on these events is beyond my position. I spoke with Sir Thomas Cornwell and he warned me off. What I fail to understand is what caused Madoc and Haylewith to fall out so badly with Felicia that they wanted her dead. Madoc was assaulting her when Bernard and I last went to Elmbrook, and I wonder if that was the start of it or whether it had been going on for some time."

"Or Madoc hid his hatred well. He is more than capable of that."

"I must speak with Amos Mapp in his new role and ask if anything can be done."

Silva nodded her agreement. "Mapp is not a genial man, but he is at least competent. That is more than could be said of Lyman d'Alston. So speak to Mapp if you wish, he may have some advice, but I doubt it will be different to Cornwell's."

"Cornwell was on the hill last night," Thomas said. "So was Croft."

"I am not surprised about Cornwell, but Richard I am. Or perhaps I should not be. Despite his age, his lust is as big as that house of his. It always has been."

"Richard tried for me at one time, when I was married to John," said Bel. "I told him if he touched me again I would stick a knife up his arse and cut his cock off from the inside."

Thomas laughed. "I expect that was enough to cool his ardour."

"It was. He never tried again. But he never held it against me."

"He was the same with me when I grew to woman-hood," said Silva. "I like the man, but not in that way.

When his blood is not hot he is a pleasant enough companion. When it is, best to stay well away. So yes, I can see him indulging himself. But he is no killer."

"I do not suspect him, as I do not suspect Cornwell. I saw Haylewith throw Felicia Hughden over the edge of the quarry. But I want to know what Sir Richard knows, though what you have told me may be enough. I need to think about what action to take and need the advice of wiser heads than mine."

Silva smiled. "Where do you intend to find those in Herefordshire, Tom?"

"Bernard."

"Of course. Now there is a man admired and loved by all."

"But not by the Church at the moment. He is stripped of his position and living under my roof."

"Then that will make it all the easier to talk with him." Silva released his hand, and it felt like a loss. She turned and walked away.

"She is wise," said Bel.

Thomas leaned across and kissed her. "So are you, my love. Tell me what you think. You were quiet most of the time."

"There was no need for my words. I agree with all that Silva said. She knows more of the old ways than I do, but you cannot live around here all your life without tripping over them. Gifts left in hedgerows. Carvings over house doors. The Yule log my sons brought you last Christmas is one of the old traditions. They are many, and people around here follow the old ways as much as those of the Church."

"I always believed you pious," Thomas said.

She smiled. "Was I pious when I let you into my bed when we were young? I believe in God, and trust in His goodness, but..." She raised a shoulder. "... it does no harm to have a little extra assurance." Bel's smile faded. "What are you going to do?"

"Nothing hasty, I promise."

"I am sure I have heard that from you before, but am glad you said it. Are we to visit Croft Manor now?"

"We are, unless you do not wish to have your back-side pinched by Sir Richard?"

"If he does you will have to soothe it for me when we get home."

"I can probably manage that. Now, let us go before Will comes to find out what we are doing."

———

Sir Richard Croft had returned home but, like Cornwell, refused to see anyone but Thomas and Jorge, which no doubt came as a relief to Bel, also Silva who had decided to join them so she could ride back to Burway with Will.

Croft's face was sallow, his eyes bloodshot, and Thomas wondered if he had spent the entire night in debauchery. The man was not young and looked every one of his seventy-plus years.

"I hope whatever you want is worth my while, Thomas. I need to sleep."

"I saw you last night."

"Did you, by damn? I did not see you, but then I was looking at little other than the woman I was with. Did you enjoy yourself?"

"Did you see what happened to Felicia Hughden?"

"I did not even know she was there. I assumed she had fallen out of love with our celebrations. It is a shame, for she was once one of the most enthusiastic celebrants. And beautiful. Very beautiful."

"She was murdered by Abbot Haylewith," Thomas said.

Croft paled even further, and for a moment Thomas thought he might throw up. But the man reached to a small table at his side and picked up a glass of dark wine. He drank half the contents, holding it in his trembling hand ready for the next quaff.

"I do not believe you. They were close."

"You were all drugged, he more than anyone. I believe he was not in command of his senses and it was Madoc who was the cause of her death, if not the act itself."

"Madoc was not there. I saw him ride away as we climbed the hillside. He never attends." Croft's expression indicated he did not approve.

"Was he alone, or did he have those armed monks with him?"

"He had two, but the others came up the hill with us. They have more enthusiasm than their master. Now, if we are finished..." Sir Richard Croft started to rise but lost the enthusiasm halfway up. He had also forgotten he held a glass of wine in his hand and the contents spilled across his lap.

"Damn it!" he barked. "Send for Charles. Are we finished here?"

Thomas nodded at Jorge to go tell Charles his master needed a cloth and another glass of wine. When they were alone he leaned closer.

"I spoke with Felicia recently and she confessed something to me."

Thomas waited, watching Croft's eyes. He saw a change in them. An acceptance.

"Tell me what she told you. I may be able to confirm it or not."

"It concerns Ambrose," Thomas said.

"Then she told you true. She is his mother. I take it that was what she claimed?"

"Part of it. I asked who his father was and she said if I wanted to know that I must ask you. Are you his father, Richard?"

Croft was saved from answering by the arrival of Charles with a damp cloth and more wine. Croft rose and Charles removed his stained hose before helping him into a clean pair.

Jorge had not returned, so once Charles left, Thomas asked his question again, and Croft laughed.

"Oh, if only I was. To lie with Felicia would have warmed my soul these many years, but I never experienced the pleasure of her. No, I am not Ambrose's father."

"So who is? Haylewith?"

"You are far from the truth in your musings," said Croft.

"Do you intend to tell me who it is? Is it the reason Ambrose was killed?"

Croft stared into space. He reached for his wine and drained the glass. Thomas leaned over and refilled it.

"Do you want one?" asked Croft.

"Have you decided or not?"

"I have. When I heard Ambrose was dead it never occurred to me it might be because of who his father was, but now you have raised it, I see it makes sense. Ambrose was a threat. To this country and the man sitting in London as King." Croft raised his gaze to meet Thomas's. "Do you know I fought for the Lancastrians against the Yorkists when I was a young man?"

"I did not, but if that is the case why are you still breathing? And why a man of importance."

Croft smiled. "A man changes with the times. I crawled on my knees to Henry and swore my undying loyalty. If he knew about Ambrose he would have had me beheaded there and then. But he does not."

Thomas frowned. "You spin a tale of intrigue, Richard, but I have yet to hear anything that might explain why Ambrose died."

"Then let me tell you what happened over two days many years ago. What do you know about the battle of Mortimer's Cross?"

"Nothing other than the name. I was not in England when the Lancastrians and Yorkists fought their interminable battles. Is it significant?"

"Let me see if you consider it so. I fought alongside Edward, Earl of March, when we defeated Jasper Tudor in February 1462. After the battle I rode with him to Elmbrook where I had sent a man to tell them we wished to celebrate our victory. Edward was a tall, strong, handsome man. Felicia was a girl then, a novice at the priory, but she was even more beautiful than she became. She had fifteen years and Edward wanted her. I believe she wanted him as well." Croft smiled. "I will not bore you with the details, but nine months later Felicia gave birth." Croft waved a hand in dismissal. "Not significant in its own right, other than for who Ambrose's father became. The man who would be King of England twice."

"Was Ambrose a threat to Henry? How?" Thomas said, making Croft laugh.

"Everyone tells me you are a clever man. Yes, Ambrose carried the blood of a King, but only three of us knew that, and now two of them are dead and I am the only man alive who holds that knowledge. Of course, now you also know. No matter. Ambrose is no threat anymore."

"Is that the reason he died?"

Croft shrugged. "I cannot see that myself. As I said, nobody knew what blood ran in his veins, not even Ambrose himself. Whoever killed him did so for another reason. I leave it to you to discover what that is."

Thomas rose, aware he needed to consider everything he had heard. It changed things. Gave another reason for Ambrose's murder. Opened up a flow of suspects.

"Like Cornwell, Croft is a man of base lusts," said Jorge as they rode north. "Though I half admire him for

THIRTY-FIVE

Belia set food on the large table beside the courtyard, aided by her children. There was a fat capon, rabbit, beef, and a pie donated by Agnes, who had come to join them with her daughters. There was a festive air to the evening despite what Thomas had witnessed on Burfa Bank the night before and the information Sir Richard Croft had told him. The storm of the night had passed, leaving the air sharp and clear. Golden light washed the courtyard, the sound of the Teme beyond louder than usual as it ran high with stormwater.

Leila came and sat on Thomas's knee. He had to snake an arm around her to stop her from falling off as she leaned over to sample the array of dainty cakes and other delicacies. It was only as the air grew dense with the coming of night and the children were despatched to their beds that Thomas felt the time was right to discuss what their next steps should be. He knew Amal would have no problem with what they had to discuss, despite her lack of years. She had grown up through the fall of the Moors and the rise of Spain, with all the destruction wrought, and nothing could discomfit her now. Agnes's girls he was less sure of.

"We are going to talk about what some of us witnessed last night," Thomas said to his sister, "and what we intend to do about it. You can stay if you wish, but the conversation might not be suitable for Rose and Jilly."

Agnes looked at her daughters, pressed to either side of Amal as they all indulged in gossip, most likely about local boys.

"My girls are no innocents, Tom." She raised her voice. "Rose, Jilly, your uncle Thomas is going to discuss fighting and debauchery. Do you want to stay or return home?"

"Stay," said Rose.

"Yes, stay," said Jilly. "Can we sleep here tonight? Amal says there is plenty of room for us."

Agnes looked at Thomas. "May they?"

"Of course. So can you."

"My loaves will need preparing before midnight," said Agnes.

"Tomorrow is Sunday, sister. So stay."

Agnes laughed. "So it is. I lose track of the days there is so much to do."

"Then perhaps you need someone to help you."

"I cannot afford to employ anyone."

"And I have told you I can help; you only need to ask."

"And I have told you I will never take charity."

"Are we not family? And between family it is not charity. I have more wealth than I can spend in ten lifetimes. Half of it belongs to Jorge, but even he could not do so, hard as he tries."

"He loves his silks, does he not?" said Agnes. "I thank you, Tom, but we are managing as we are."

"You should charge more, Aunt Agnes," said Amal, the discussion over what manner of a boy made the best kisser now concluded. "Everyone else does."

"If I did, some would be unable to buy my produce. It would be a hardship on them."

"Then you should think about charging more to those who can afford it. You send produce to rich houses that are able to pay double or triple what you charge without even noticing. I will come and help work it out with you if you want."

"We will talk about this again, Amal. Your father wants a serious discussion tonight, not to hear about my problems."

"If you have problems," Thomas said, "they are also my problems. But you are right. We will talk again once this matter is concluded."

"Please try to avoid bloodshed if you can."

"I always do, sister. I never seek it, but it seems to seek me." Thomas looked around before setting Leila down and patting her on the backside. "Now you lot, off to bed. Belia will come and tell you a story in a while."

Once they had gone, Thomas looked around at the rest of them. He was still unsure about Rose and Jilly, but Agnes's daughters were older than Amal by three and four years so he supposed they could stay. Silva sat beside Will, and he needed to ask her to do something she might refuse. Belia remained with her hand in Jorge's. There was a frown of concern on her brow, but Thomas hoped she trusted him to bring Jorge home safe, as he had always done. Bernard sat opposite Thomas, next to the three girls. What he had made of their conversation would make interesting listening. Usaden had come down the hill with Emma and Jack, the three of them sitting at the far end of the table. Kin lay on the stone slabs beside the rill that ran the length of the courtyard because it was cooler there. The long, lean dog had more grey in his hair these days and slept more, but when called to fight he turned into a demon against those who confronted Thomas or the others. Kin allowed the children to tug at his ears and pull his long tail but would never react. He would protect those he regarded as his family with his own life.

"So what do you want to do?" asked Will.

"We go to Hindwell Abbey, but on the way I want to return to Burfa Bank and the quarry. They are tied together. It is where Felicia Hughden died at the hand of Abbot Haylewith. But tomorrow we rest. It is Sunday and would be unseemly to do what may be needed. We go the day after."

"Who will go?" asked Will.

Thomas glanced from his son to Silva who sat beside him. "Me, you and Usaden," he said. "Jorge, but only if he wants to come."

"You may need me," said Jorge. "Just promise to keep me safe."

Thomas laughed. "Will and Usaden can do that better than me, but I promise." He glanced at Silva. "I would also like you with us, but there will be no danger."

"I am used to danger, Tom. Say what you want of me and I will say if I am willing to come."

"You sense things others cannot. I was slow to believe in you but am now a convert. I want you to climb Burfa Bank with me to see if you sense anything there. Any power. Any evil. Even a body. I am sure Felicia is dead but Croft challenged me today because I have seen no body."

"It is possible she knew she was in danger and disappeared to evade it?" said Silva. "Perhaps Haylewith helped her to escape and it was all some mummer's distraction you witnessed."

"It was a strange way to affect her escape, to be tossed from the top of a cliff."

"Suppose Haylewith was part of it? You have told us Madoc is the evil behind what happened. What if Haylewith is aware of his growing power and helped Felicia escape?"

"Which is why I also want you with us. I accept your power now, but am I expecting too much? If Felicia died in that quarry would you be able to tell?"

Silva appeared to think for a moment. "I do not know, Tom. Death carries a resonance I might be able to feel, but I have never tried."

"I do not want you to do anything that makes you uncomfortable."

Silva smiled. "It will not, only that I do not know if it is possible. But I will come with you."

"In that case I want you to do the same at Hindwell Abbey. Have you visited there before?"

Silva shook her head, her long multi-coloured hair shimmering beneath the torchlight. "I never had the need nor inclination. I will do as you ask, Tom, but other than a sense of Felicia, what do you expect me to find?"

"If I knew that I would not need to ask this of you. I value your opinion. If you can, I would like you to tell me if there is evil there." Thomas turned his attention away from her. "And you, Jorge, when we visit Hindwell Abbey, I want you to tell me about the monks there and the new Abbot, Madoc."

"Why are we not confronting Abbot Haylewith?" asked Will. "You told us it was he who threw Felicia Hughden into the quarry."

"We will, but only when we have clear evidence of who else is involved. There are connections between all three holy houses: Wigmore, Hindwell and Elmbrook, and Madoc oversees two of those houses now, plus Lemster." Thomas glanced at Bernard sitting across from him. "Do you have anything to add about those places?"

"Elmbrook and Hindwell have been wayward houses for some time. I thought Wigmore was different, but the information in Ambrose's letter to you hinted that Abbot John might have been involved in what happened at Elmbrook and the burial of the children. I always considered him close to a saint, but I see now I was wrong. And now Abbot Haylewith is head of that place, matters can only get worse. I want to ride with you if you will have me."

"Are you sure, Bernard?"

"I am." Bernard smiled. "I am also glad I no longer have to chastise you for forgetting my title, for I am a man cut adrift from his calling. A man who perhaps needs a new one. Do you have weapons I can borrow? It is said once a man has been a soldier he never forgets how to wield a sword. If we are fortunate, I may never need to find out the truth of it."

"We have a surfeit of weapons. Will makes sure of that."

In that case I will go to my bed. My body still remembers the hours it used to keep at the priory. I expect it always will."

Bernard's departure seemed to be the signal for several others to leave the table. Belia rose to show Agnes where she could sleep. Rose and Jilly went giggling with Amal, no doubt to continue their earlier conversation. Emma rose and stretched. As she did so, Thomas took note of the slight swell of her belly. She had always been slim, slight of figure. Thomas glanced at Usaden, but his eyes were on his woman, a soft expression on his face Thomas had rarely if ever seen before. *The world turns*, Thomas thought, *and we grow old to be replaced by our children. Even Usaden.* He was sure he was right.

"How long, Emma?" he asked.

She glanced at him with a frown. When he said nothing else she looked down at herself and a flush coloured her cheeks. She placed her hand over the slight bump.

"How can you tell? No one else has."

"I was physician to the Sultan in Granada. Many of his concubines were as slim as you and I always knew when they were with child." Thomas glanced at Usaden, who he assumed knew of Emma's state, and received an almost imperceptible nod in return.

"Four months, I think," said Emma. Usaden told me he will ask Amal and Belia to attend me when my time comes."

"You should come here, it will be safer, and you are always welcome, you know you are."

"We ought climb the hill back to Ludlow," said Emma.

The words were meant for Usaden, but her eyes were on Thomas, who replied, "Stay. Belia will find you a room. You too, Jack."

"I will take you up on that," said Jack. "I would sleep in the woods but the ground is still soaked. My thanks. If you want me to ride with you, say the word and I am your man."

Thomas offered a nod.

Bel rose and kissed Thomas. "I am going to bed as well. Try not to be too late." She held her hand out, and Silva came around the table to take it before both walked into the house.

Which left Thomas, Will, Jorge and Usaden. And Kin, of course, who padded across to the table in the hope someone might pass him a morsel of the leftover food.

"What time do we ride out Monday morning?" asked Will.

"When Jorge decides to wake up, otherwise we leave him here." Thomas ducked as Jorge threw a capon leg at him. Kin leapt and caught it in mid-air.

"I will wake at dawn if you ask it, Thomas. I prefer not to, but I will."

"There is no need. We rest tomorrow, then ride to Hindwell Abbey and visit Burfa Bank on the way so Silva can try to sense if anything evil lurks there. Then we go to the abbey and confront Madoc. After that, if enough daylight remains we ride to Wigmore and do the same with Abbot Haylewith."

"Will Bernard be uneasy at confronting men of God?" asked Will.

"He may be, but he knows as well as we do they are not true men of God, otherwise they would not have acted as they did. But I will offer him the chance to stay behind if he wishes."

"I think he wants to come with us," said Jorge. "As some kind of redemption."

"He has nothing to be ashamed of," Thomas said.

"An apology for the Church as a whole, then," said Jorge, before rising. "Now, I will leave you."

"We are going to need him with us," said Will after Jorge had gone. "Confronting abbots is not without danger, and you are hasty sometimes. Leave the talking to Jorge."

"I would prefer for us to finish this the day after

tomorrow. If I let Jorge do the talking we could be there a week."

"Tell him to be succinct."

Thomas shook his head and reached for more wine. "Remember it is Jorge we are talking about."

THIRTY-SIX

"Yes, there is an evil in this place," said Silva when she rose from her knees. She and Thomas stood beside the remains of the bonfire on Burfa Bank, its damp ashes now cold to the touch. Silva had knelt and placed her palms against the ground, staying there for several minutes while Thomas waited. It was only the two of them, at Silva's request. The others remained beyond the raised banks of the old fort with the horses.

A whole day had passed since they had gathered in the courtyard at Burway and discussed what action to take. Thomas had spent most of Sunday resting, aware he had pushed himself too hard. His injured side ached, but not as much today as it had.

"Old evil or new evil?" Thomas asked, sure she would know the difference.

"Both." Silva frowned. "I have never felt such before and am surprised you know what to ask." The frown turned to a smile. "It tells me you not only believe in my powers but have also researched them."

"Amal did most of the work, as usual. She brought me three pages of her notes. I asked for the source books but she said there were none. Only folk tales told in the dark to scare children. Tell me about both the old and the new."

"Something lurks within this hill. You said there are caves?"

"I can show you if you trust me, but it is precarious."

"Of course I trust you, but there is no need yet. Besides, I do not believe the caves would welcome me. But you may be able to enter them."

"I am not sure if I can. They are scattered along the face of the quarry. It might be possible with a rope. Without one it would take a skilled climber, which I am not."

"It is the old spirits that reside within the hill. They are not evil of themselves, but they are old and care nothing for the men and women who scatter the surface of this world. We are less than ants to them. What is new taints the surface and is a corruption of the Christian God." Silva stared at Thomas. "Do you feel nothing at all?"

Thomas shook his head. "Nothing. I possess little in the way of imagination."

"Then perhaps you are the right man to explore the caves. Whatever resides there attacks the mind. It has no physical presence, only the ability to terrify. I feel it scratching inside my head but can ignore it while I am here in the fresh air." Silva looked beyond Thomas to the raised bank that surrounded the crest of the hill. "It may be worth asking Prior Bernard to perform an exorcism. He will have done so before and knows the rites. You should ask him, he is your friend."

"He will think I have gone mad."

"No, he will not. You and he go back a long way."

"We do, but there were over forty years when we did not see each other. He took me under his wing when I was a young lad eager to learn. Others did the same later, but Bernard was the first to teach me about the world."

"And Bel completed your education."

Thomas made no reply, but his smile was enough.

"Are you willing to come with us to Hindwell Abbey? It sits beneath this hill, and if there is evil here I want to know if it extends there as well."

"Madoc is Abbot there now?"

"He is."

"I detest the man, but if you ask it I will come, as long as Will is close to me. Madoc has hungry eyes, and it is not food they hunger for."

They walked back to the others, where Thomas asked Bernard about the exorcism, and Silva explained the reason.

"I do not believe it would help," he said. "I do not doubt what you say, Silva, but if you are right I would only be able to expel the Devil's demon. The Christian exorcism does not work on older gods."

"Do you believe in older gods?" Silva asked.

"I have lived most of my life in Herefordshire. I

would be a fool not to have seen evidence of something older than Jesus Christ in the worship that takes place here. One only needs to enter any church in the area to see the evidence. The Green Man carved over doors and altars, sprites and gargoyles to keep away evil spirits. They owe nothing to Christianity but to something far older."

"It surprises me to hear you speak this way."

"As I told you, I am no fool."

"He is not," said Thomas. "But Bernard does not need to make a decision yet. We visit the abbey first before deciding on what action to take."

"And if Madoc's warriors are there?" asked Will.

"Madoc knows nothing of our suspicions so has no reason to attack us. We are the only people in control of their senses who witnessed what happened."

They led their horses down the steep hillside as the afternoon faded. Thomas wanted to arrive at the abbey late in the day when the air softened and men's mind turned to thoughts of rest. The grey stone of the abbey glinted in the soft sunlight. Monks worked a small garden to one side, and in the surrounding fields sheep grazed. The small stream had been dammed to create a stew pond for fish. It was an idyllic scene, but Thomas felt a deep unease as they approached. Several monks had noted their approach and one ran into the abbey. As they neared the entrance, Madoc appeared with four warrior monks behind him. He nodded in acknowledgement of Bernard but did not use his name.

"I would say it is a pleasure to see you, Thomas

Berrington, but it would be unchristian to lie. What do you want here?"

"We have ridden all day and are tired. We ask for accommodation."

Madoc stared at him. Both of them knew the request could not be denied. Any traveller was entitled to seek lodging for the night, and if there was no space then other means would be offered. It was Christian charity, after all.

"We have no cots free tonight. We are a small abbey and at the moment have additional brothers housed with us."

"I take it you mean those men standing behind you."

"God's soldiers," said Madoc. "Fighting His good fight." His eyes latched onto Silva. "We might be able to find a vacant cell for the woman. There is a stable for the rest of you. The straw is almost clean and the horses will keep you warm."

"I will stay with my friends," said Silva, meeting Madoc's harsh gaze. "We thank you for your charity, Abbot."

"You may eat with us, my dear. I will send food out for the men."

"My thanks, but I have no hunger."

When Madoc turned away Silva moved to stand close against Will.

"We must watch he does not come back for me," she said. "Did you see the look in his eyes?"

Thomas saw Will tense and reached out to put a hand on his shoulder.

"If they come you know we can protect ourselves. It is better with us out here and they are inside the abbey. We set a watch."

"What if he brings a dozen of his armed monks to the stable?"

"Madoc is wicked but no fool. He knows we will be ready if he does. Besides, we have a reputation. He will not choose to confront us."

"How many of those warrior monks does he have in there? We are only seven." Will did not have to point out that one of their number was Jorge and another a Prior without a priory.

"But no doubt he believes we are all skilled swordsmen."

"Do you intend to fight your way into an abbey, Tom?" Bernard asked. "I did not agree to that when you clothed and armed me. I can have nothing to do with it."

"Even if the abbey is presided over by Madoc? You know he is evil. He usurped your position at Lemster and he was behind your dismissal."

"There are innocent monks in there," said Bernard. "Allow me to take a horse and I will ride to Wigmore and seek refuge there."

"Do you think Abbot Haylewith will be any more pleased to see you than Madoc?" Thomas smiled. "Besides, it will not come to a fight. We are a threat, and that is enough to stop Madoc from doing anything stupid."

"I hope you are right."

The stable floor was damp where holes in the roof

had let through rain. Thomas and the others dragged straw to a corner so they could rest in the dry, then sat against the wall, waiting. The promised food was not forthcoming, but each had brought bread and hard cheese, and the stream could provide water.

Will went to stand at the door, staring out. Thomas knew he would stand there all night if necessary. His axe hung from a leather strap along his back but would take only moments to release. He carried a longsword on one side, a shorter one on the other, and tucked into his boots were two knives, each honed to a wicked edge.

"If it comes to it," said Jorge. "Will can no doubt defeat whoever Madoc sends on his own."

"I do not doubt it," Thomas said. "If not we will send in Usaden and Kin. Tell me what you think of Madoc."

"I need more time with him for an accurate response, but even on such short acquaintance I can tell you he is arrogant, with an inflated opinion of his talents. Did you notice that beneath his habit he dresses the same as his warrior monks?"

"I did." Thomas glanced at Bernard, who sat with eyes downcast. "Tell me more about them, Bernard. Are they unusual, or not?"

"Monks have been known to fight to protect their houses and land. Many, like myself, served in God's army in the Holy Land and Spain. No doubt those men know how to fight, but how well is another matter. The majority of the monks here will not be like them, and the majority of priories and abbeys will house only men who would fare poorly in battle. There is nothing wrong with that. The life of a monk is spent in contemplation and prayer, which requires no knowledge of how to wield a sword."

"So why are those men here? We saw four, but I am sure there are more within the abbey itself."

"Or close by," said Bernard, "but I do not know their purpose. I told you they fashion themselves after the Templars, but those men were godly. These men are not."

"To me they look like recruits dressed up as monks and pretending a faith they do not follow," Thomas said. "But if they believe themselves descendants of the Templars that tells us something. Those men were reputed to be the guardians of the Grail." Thomas held a hand up as Bernard started to protest. "I am not saying I believe any of this nonsense, but Haylewith does. It is possible Madoc is using his obsessions to advance his own desires, or even believes in it himself."

"His warriors also pretend to have a skill with a sword they do not possess," said Usaden. "You will have seen it the same as me, Thomas. We have fought together long enough and can judge how a man will fight in the blink of an eye. These so-called warrior monks are not fighting men. They rule through threats against the weak, knowing they will not be called upon to prove themselves." Usaden's lips thinned in disgust. "They have not come up against fighters such as us." His opinion offered, he rose and went to stand beside Will, his hand on the hilt of his short Moorish sword. Kin lifted his head to watch them then laid it down again. No trouble. Not yet.

"We should try to get some sleep," Thomas said. "If anything happens the noise will wake us."

"I must pray first," said Bernard. "They will not let me inside the abbey, but God does not need the glory of a building to hear a man's words."

"You are not going to sleep, are you?" Jorge asked Thomas when it was only the three of them. Silva sat cross-legged on a bale of straw, her hands in her lap, eyes closed.

"I was planning on visiting the caves while the abbey slept. But I will need a torch or candle."

"There are candles over there." Jorge pointed. "And no doubt a flint to light them with as well. Do you want me to come with you?"

"Into narrow caves? Would you fit?"

Jorge looked down at himself and patted his belly. "Do you remember those tunnels in Alhambra, where I almost got stuck? I would not fit in them now, even if they had not been filled in. So perhaps best that you go alone, or take Usaden to look out for you."

"I think I can look after myself." Thomas rose and stretched. "But perhaps Kin will come with me." He clicked his fingers. The dog looked up, then rose to stretch hugely. When Thomas walked from the stable Kin followed.

THIRTY-SEVEN

Thomas stood for a moment in the gathering dark beyond the stable. Within the abbey the monks were at prayer, the sound of their chanting drifting out. Closer, Thomas saw Bernard on his knees, his own prayers more circumspect but no doubt more deeply felt. The peace that Bernard said came with his belief was unknown to Thomas, and he was unsure whether it was something he envied or not. Knowledge brought him peace, but sometimes it required work to unearth it.

Thomas turned away, his hand dropping to stroke Kin's slim head, and the dog leaned against him for a moment before trotting ahead. Both leapt over the stream where it was narrow above the stew pond and made their way around the side of Burfa Bank to where the quarry lay. Felicia Hughden's death continued to puzzle him. He was convinced she was dead but the shard of doubt planted by Silva still nagged at him. Felicia, Madoc and Haylewith had been close, so why had she been killed? Was it something she had done? Something she knew and threatened to reveal?

Thomas recalled a moment when, as they spoke together, she appeared to want to say more than she had. Did she hold secrets that put her in danger? Thomas wondered how close Felicia and Ambrose were. As close as mother and son? Did they talk together when he visited Elmbrook? And if they did had he revealed secrets to her he had discovered during his travels? Without knowing what they were Thomas knew he might never succeed in unmasking whatever evil had occurred.

The ground grew rough underfoot as he entered the base of the quarry, the pale rock wall soaring above him for hundreds of feet. In the last glimmer of light he could make out holes in the rock where men had worked it, using wooden posts to balance. They must have descended from the spikes above because there was no way to climb the almost sheer rock face. The openings of the original caves were set to the sides of the quarry but were too high to reach without climbing. Thomas surveyed them, unsure he wanted to risk attempting the climb in the dark. Which meant he had come on a fool's errand.

He turned to go back to the stables then stopped because Kin was pawing at the ground beside a growth of bushes. Thomas walked across. As he approached he saw Kin scratching at a bone.

"What have you got there, boy? Can I see it?" Thomas

went to his knees, knowing Kin would let him take the bone, which he did. It was old and discoloured, but unmistakable as part of a human jawbone. A few loose teeth still remained in place. He ruffled Kin's fur then examined the bushes, but the darkness beyond was dense. Too dense? He would have expected to see the pale stone of the quarry face but could not.

Thomas pulled the stub of the candle he had brought and sparked the flint onto a piece of oiled wool until it flared, allowing him to light the wick. He held the candle out and peered again into the bushes, working his head and shoulders into them until he discovered a narrow opening that disappeared into the hillside.

Thomas looked back. "Are you coming or staying?" he asked Kin, as if the dog understood his every word, which sometimes he believed he did.

Kin wagged his tail from side to side and opened his mouth so he appeared to be grinning, his long tongue lolling.

"I will take that as yes, shall I?"

Thomas pushed deeper, holding the candle at arm's length to avoid it snagging on the undergrowth. When he reached the opening, he discovered it was little more than a fissure and was unsure if he could enter. Kin came up beside him, glanced at Thomas, then padded into the space.

Thomas let his breath go and twisted sideways, pushing himself after the dog. He got caught once but remembered the words of a girl who had shown him the tunnels of Alhambra and let his lungs empty. One more push and he was through, the entrance opening into a wide chamber. As Thomas stood and held the candle high he discovered where the stolen skulls had been taken. They were piled almost to the rock ceiling, a haphazard jumble with no organisation, one skull stacked atop another. He knew that somewhere among these ... how many? ... a hundred, two hundred skulls, would lie those of his mother and brother. He also knew he would never be able to find them even if he held each of the skulls in his hands. Defleshed and worn with age, the skulls were all shapes and sizes, but it was impossible to tell what their owners looked like when alive.

Who had brought them here? Felicia Hughden? Madoc? Abbot Haylewith? Or had it been Ambrose, given the task of secreting the bodies of children in the graves of strangers? Had it been he who dug deeper to take a skull, as if in payment for the work, and brought it back here? But why? Was it to obtain the knowledge held within each skull, as Silva claimed? Thomas knew he had to talk with Bernard again. Knew he would have to talk with everyone. Including Madoc and Haylewith. It was beyond all reason that the men would not know of this cave.

As Thomas stared at the pile of skulls he saw something he had missed. Perched atop the pinnacle was another, more recent addition. The paleness of it had caused him to pass over it because it almost matched the stone behind. He felt a sadness fill him as the last hope that Felicia Hughden might have fled and remained alive was lost. Her head stared out at him, eyes wide, mouth caught in a scream. Tendrils of flesh hung down from her neck where it had been torn from her body. A year from now the head would be denuded of flesh and become just one more skull among many.

Thomas was drawn from the sight when Kin barked. He spun around, dropping the candle. It snuffed out, leaving him in pitch blackness. He went to his knees, his hands searching and failing to find the candle. He sat back and closed his eyes, waited, then opened them wide to scan the darkness all around. He saw a tiny glow from the snuffed wick. He retrieved the candle and relit it, only then recalling why he had dropped it.

"What is it, Kin?" But even as he asked the question, Thomas saw the answer. The headless, naked torso of Felicia Hughden lay discarded in a corner of the cave, tossed aside like carrion. Already insects worked to break down her flesh.

Kin turned and padded away, but not back the way they had come. Instead, he entered a wider tunnel to the right of the tower of skulls. Thomas rose and followed. Kin padded ahead as if he needed no light, and perhaps he did not. The tunnel was but a few inches higher than Thomas, so he walked stooping. Looking down he saw the dirt floor was hard packed from many feet coming and going, and suspected Kin must have sensed this other entrance. But as the tunnel went on he began to wonder exactly where it was leading him. Deeper into the hill? Was it a trap for someone who discovered the opening in the quarry? Would it end in a long drop into oblivion?

The tunnel descended then climbed again.

The candle Thomas held grew shorter, and he wished he had thought to bring a longer stub, but it was too late to change his mind now.

Ahead, Kin stopped. So did Thomas. An oak door barred their way. There was a catch on one side, but when he tried it the door would not open. Thomas went to one knee again and brought the guttering candle close. He knew if he could not get through the door the candle would die before he managed to find his way back. But Kin might, and he could hold on to his fur and follow. If he had to.

Thomas gazed into the narrow gap around the edge of the door and saw the reason for it failing to open. On the far side he glimpsed a length of wood. No doubt it would be fitted into brackets on either side.

Thomas drew his knife and slid it into the narrow gap below the barrier. He found a nub of rock and used it to lever the knife upwards. The wood moved, then stuck, and Thomas cursed. He shifted position and tried again, this time with more success. Slowly, the wooden bar rose. Once he judged it was clear of whatever held it, Thomas pushed against the door, relieved when it released. It opened more easily than he expected on well-greased hinges. He put a finger to his lips so Kin could see he wanted silence, then eased himself beyond the door. He found himself in a narrow passage constructed of the same stone as Hindwell Abbey. Which made sense if he was in its catacombs.

Thomas set the bar back in place and walked on, his

fingers burning from the melting wax. A chamber on one side offered a glimpse of more bones, but these were stored in the abbey's ossuary and could be expected. At the end of the corridor a set of steps led up. Thomas ascended, finally able to drop the stub of candle as light filtered from above. When he reached the top of the steps the light of burning torches made him squint after so long in the dark. Which was why he failed to see the figures approaching him until it was too late to hide.

"I thought I told you to sleep in the stables," said Madoc. "What are you doing here?"

"I went for a walk and must have become lost." It was weak, Thomas knew.

"Very lost, it seems." Madoc looked beyond Thomas. "There is nothing behind you but our catacombs. Were you down there?" Madoc made a motion to one of the men beside him and the man walked past Thomas.

Thomas measured those arrayed in front of him. Madoc plus six of his warrior monks.

"Are you coming from prayers?" he asked.

"We are, though my companions prefer to pray in their own way. We thought we might take this corridor out to the stable to visit your friend, Silva. She is particularly beautiful, is she not?" Madoc's expression changed, hardening. "She always ignores me. A man of my position. She thinks I am beneath her when it is she who should be beneath me. Which she will be soon enough."

"My son — he is the tall one — might have something to say about that."

Madoc smiled, but there was no warmth in it. "I

expect he might, which is why I despatched a dozen of my men to ensure neither he nor your companions can interfere."

"Only a dozen? Oh, dear."

Thomas heard footsteps approach from behind. The warrior monk knocked him as he came past and Thomas reached out to stop Kin from attacking.

"The door to the cave has been opened, master."

"Has it. Has it indeed. Your doing I take it, Berrington? Sticking your nose in again where it is not welcome. Well, you have done it one time too many." Madoc waved a hand. "Take him back to the chamber and remove his head. Add it to the pile beside Felicia's. They can rot away together."

Thomas tugged on Kin's ear. "Go. Fetch Will."

The soldiers advanced on Thomas. One of them reached for Kin and received a bite in return. The man staggered back, clutching his hand to his chest.

Now only five men, plus Madoc, and Thomas doubted he would be willing to fight.

He drew his knife, shorter than the swords the men advanced with, but in the confines of the stone passage more effective. He took slow steps backwards, not wanting to kill anyone, but not wanting to die either. He feinted at a man on his right, who jerked back so fast he stumbled and fell into Madoc, taking them both down. One of the other men took his chance and came at Thomas fast, but when he raised his sword to strike, it caught on a wooden beam in the roof and lodged tight.

Thomas took another step backwards. He wondered

if he turned and ran could he open the door to the cave and close it before he was caught? The problem was the door was barred on this side, and without any light he would never find his way back to the narrow cleft.

Two more men came at him, their swords held low. Thomas was unsure which to attack first, trying to work out a way to stop them without taking their lives. Then a voice sounded, loud.

"There is no fighting allowed in a house of God. Stop this. Stop this at once!"

Bernard stood behind Madoc, who was only now rising to his feet to confront him. Behind Bernard, a gaggle of ordinary monks jostled together.

"You are nothing here," said Madoc, his voice a snarl. "You have no position in the Church anymore. Leave us."

Bernard ignored him. "Your men call themselves warrior monks. How much are you warriors and how much monks? If even a small part of you remains as a monk then you know I am right. Sheath your swords. If you want to fight you can, but take it beyond the abbey grounds."

"Ignore him," said Madoc. "Kill Berrington, then kill those with him. I go to find Silva." Madoc turned and hurried away along the corridor which would take him outside.

Thomas looked beyond the men to Bernard, who stood tall, his stance that of the soldier he once was. The gathered monks behind had thinned.

"Well?" Bernard said. "Obey your master or obey your God. Burn in hell or ascend to heaven. The choice is yours, as it has always been." Bernard turned and walked away through the monks, who followed him to leave Thomas alone with the men.

Thomas watched them. Saw the moment they came to a decision. One man at first and then the others.

Swords were sheathed. The man who had fallen was helped to his feet. Someone went to help the one Kin had bitten. They moved away without speaking. After a short time, Thomas followed.

He met Will running into the cloister.

"Silva is gone from the stable, and Bernard told me Madoc intends to defile her."

"I do not know where she is." Thomas looked around, then ran past Will and grabbed one of the warrior monks and shook him. "Where did Madoc take the woman?"

The man pointed. "To his office. Take the corridor, turn right, turn left. The room is at the far end."

Thomas turned back, but Will had already heard. He ran. Thomas went after him but Will raced ahead.

When he reached the door it was open and Madoc lay on the stone floor, a look of surprise on his face and a pool of blood spreading beneath him.

Thomas pushed past Will but saw his son's knife remained sheathed. When he looked at Silva her face was pale. Her hand loosely grasped a short knife, the blade dripping blood.

"You did this?" Thomas asked, his voice soft.

Silva nodded.

"I knew what he wanted and let him think I was weak. He had six of his warriors with him and I couldn't fight them all. I suspected he would come for me. He is not the kind of man who can stop himself. When he did, I took the knife from his belt and used it on him."

"Will, take her out of here, then find Bernard and send him to me."

THIRTY-EIGHT

Thomas knelt in front of Madoc and drew the man's robe aside to reveal a deep wound in his side. The right side, which explained the quantity of blood. Whether through accident or design, Silva had thrust the knife into Madoc's liver and he was bleeding to death.

"They tell me you are a skilled surgeon, Berrington. Save me."

"I cannot. You are going to die."

"It hurts."

"It will. I have herbs that can help, but I brought none with me. Apart from which, why should I help you? Was it you who told Abbot Haylewith to kill Felicia Hughden?"

Madoc gave a shake of his head before grimacing.

Thomas glanced down at the wound where blood continued to pulse, but more slowly now.

"He told me to fetch her for the festivities, but I had no idea he would kill her."

"What did she know to have made him do that?" Thomas asked.

"Felicia knew everything. She kept a ledger with names and dates in it. Important men who came to her priory to lie with the nuns, together with their weaknesses. She showed it to me once. She wanted me to know of it. I think she considered it her protection. I told Owain about it and he asked me to take it to him."

"Where is this ledger now?"

"Gone." Madoc grunted the word. His face was paling and Thomas knew he would not last much longer. "However hard I searched, however many of the sisters I threatened, I could not find it. I can hardly ask Felicia where it is now."

"Did she have any suspicion when you took her that night?"

"She did not want to go but was too afraid to refuse." Even as his life bled away Madoc seemed incapable of acting with any degree of humanity.

"You took her but did not attend."

"I never do."

"Yet you came here to rape Silva."

"I make no pretence of being a good man. I—" Madoc broke off as Bernard entered the room. He had found a habit from somewhere. He held a Bible in one hand and a rosary in the other.

Madoc's eyes followed him as he came to kneel beside Thomas.

"Forgive me, brother, for I have sinned," said Madoc.

Thomas started to rise, but Madoc reached out to stop him, a hand around his wrist. "Stay. I want you both to hear my confession. I have sinned greatly, but it is all the fault of Ambrose. Of his birth and who is father was."

"I know who his father was," Thomas said.

"Felicia told me no one else knew. She teased me but never revealed a name. Who was he? One of the local Lords?"

"I will not tell you." Thomas stood.

Madoc's eyes went to Bernard. "I need to confess, Prior."

Bernard made the sign of the cross.

Thomas listened with growing anger and disgust as Madoc spoke. Both emotions may have grown even stronger, but Madoc breathed his last before he had completed his confession.

Bernard reached out and closed the man's eyes.

"We should leave his body here until we can work out what to do next," he said.

"I know a better place. Any brother might come here and discover him. Are you willing to help me?"

"As long as it does not involve any more killing."

"It does not."

Between them they dragged Madoc's body along the corridor, a blanket beneath him to catch any blood. Down the stairs. Through a wooden door.

Thomas lit a candle and held it up while he dragged one side of Madoc.

He watched Bernard's face when they came to the

chamber of skulls, waiting to see if he showed surprise. Fortunately, he did. Followed by disgust when he saw Felicia Hughden's head. Thomas felt a moment of guilt at doubting him, but he had seen too many men of God turn to corruption to trust any. Except in his heart, he knew of Bernard's goodness.

"What is this, Tom?"

"What it looks like. These are the skulls Ambrose took. I believe he did so for Abbot Haylewith. Silva told me a reason I think explains it, if you believe in degeneracy and magic. Which I suspect Haylewith does. Do you believe Madoc's confession was the truth?"

"What would it benefit him to lie when he knew he was going to his maker?"

"After what he admitted to? Surely the devil will take him."

"But he made confession, Tom. That wipes a man's sins clean."

"If only life was that simple. Here, put him in the corner so the skulls hide him."

"He will have to be buried soon."

"At the abbey?"

"Yes, at the abbey. I should leave him here to rot in hell, but that would reveal everything. He will have told the brothers where he should lie. All abbots do, even the newly appointed."

"He has been Abbot little more than a week."

"He was still the Abbot."

Thomas started back along the tunnel.

"Who will take his place?"

"No one until his death is announced, then the brothers will do what they should have been done at Wigmore and express their own preference. There must be one or two godly men left among them."

"It can only be hoped. Do you have any idea what he meant when he said everything was the fault of Ambrose?"

"I do not, and you should give it no credence. Madoc is a man who delights in spreading lies."

Thomas and Bernard climbed with the others through the dark to the top of Burfa Bank. No words were spoken until they reached the old fort, and then Thomas said, "We rest here where we are safe before moving on."

"I will arrange for Felicia's head and body to be taken to Elmbrook," said Bernard. "She has a place awaiting her there and should lie in it."

Thomas lay down and stared at the cloudless sky sparked by a million stars, each as steady as a hole punched through a velvet sheet. He was tired but knew he would not sleep until he worked through what Madoc had revealed. He wondered what remained unsaid when the man died, whether it would have made better sense of what he had heard. It mattered little. He knew enough. Knew what must be done next. He would need Bernard's blessing but expected it would be forthcoming because he had heard the same words as Thomas.

He had expected Madoc to be the guilty party in everything, but he was not. He had been weak, driven by anger and lust he could not ignore. Most of the lust was directed at Felicia Hughden, who had rebuffed him. Most of the anger at Owain Haylewith who had used Madoc as his enforcer. The anger because Madoc, for all his failings, had believed in the mystery of the Christian Church. Haylewith had not. His beliefs encompassed a bastard mix of the old and new. Pagan gods and ways. Templar stories. The Christian God, the legend of his son's death and rebirth. Blood and body, both male and female. And the submission to desire. Above it all loomed Haylewith's obsession with the Grail. The man convinced it lay hidden somewhere in Herefordshire. Madoc had revealed that Ambrose had told Felicia he had found it. The object men had searched after for centuries. Madoc had beaten the information out of her, convinced she also knew where Ambrose had hidden it. But if he had Felicia refused to say. It was why she had to die, so any knowledge she possessed was never told to anyone else. That had been Haylewith's doing, but Madoc had followed his orders without question.

"Haylewith will have to be stopped, but I know not how to do so." Bernard sat to one side of Thomas, his head lowered as if in defeat. He still wore the monk's robe he had taken from the abbey, as if it was some form of penance. "You cannot do it, Tom. It will have to be put before Archdeacon Webb. Perhaps even before the King, but you have a connection there if it needs to be done."

"And in the meantime? We cannot allow Haylewith to continue his corruption of the Church. It will fester, polluting every holy house in the area. And then it will spread. Perhaps over the entire land. Can you stand aside and watch if that happens, Bernard?"

"I will have to, because the alternative is against everything I stand for. Everything I am and ever have been."

"Then return to Lemster or Burway, and leave it to me."

"I cannot do that. My role is to prevent you from doing what you intend to."

"And allow Abbot Haylewith to continue imposing his deviant ideas on Wigmore Abbey, on Elmbrook and Hindwell? How long until he imposes them on Lemster Priory as well? He wanted Felicia Hughden dead, Madoc told us that."

"Then God will punish him even if man cannot. And I am no longer Prior at Lemster."

"You should be Abbot at Wigmore, and perhaps when I am done you will be. There is no more suitable candidate."

"Except I do not want the position."

"But you do God's will, I know you do."

"Is it God's will to exalt me to head the largest abbey in the Marches?"

"What the Marches needs now are honest men. You heard what else Madoc told us. Abbot John was drawn into the underworld along with everyone else. Wigmore is the centre of it. They shared secrets on secrets, not all of which have been revealed. Wigmore is where Haylewith now rules. If evil is to be destroyed it needs good men to do it. It needs you."

"I cannot impose myself."

"You will not need to. Felicia Hughden is dead. Madoc is dead. Soon, Abbot Haylewith will be dead, either at my hand or on a pyre lit by the Church. You should ride south to Hereford in the morning and speak with the Archdeacon. Tell him what we know and ask his advice."

"And if he is also involved? He voted for Haylewith to be Abbot, he must have."

"Did you vote for yourself?" Thomas asked.

"Of course not. It would be immodest."

"Do you think Haylewith voted for you?"

Bernard said nothing.

"I believe both Archdeacons voted for you. You received four votes, and I suspect one of them came from Felicia Hughden. Haylewith will have voted for himself. Who the fourth was I cannot say for sure. I doubt it was d'Alston, so most likely the brother invited to attend."

"I will leave at first light, Tom. Promise to do nothing until I return."

Thomas was about to refuse, but instead nodded, hoping Bernard could see it in the dark. "I promise to do nothing unless provoked." It was not the same thing, but Bernard seemed to accept it. He rolled onto his side, wrapped himself in his habit and pulled the hood up so only his mouth showed.

Thomas continued to lie on his back, aware of those around him. All awake. All waiting. He told them what they had learned and asked them to think about what it meant. He was most concerned about Will, knowing he relished a fight. So did Usaden, but he never sought one.

A figure approached through the dark and sat beside him.

"Tell me about the skulls," said Silva.

"There is not much to tell. They are piled three times the height of a man. There are hundreds of them. Some new, others old. They are skulls, there is not much more to say about them."

"Do you believe the skulls of your mother and brother lie in that pile?"

"Almost certainly, but if so they are lost to me."

Silva was silent for a time, a dark shape against the night. Then she said, "Perhaps not. Take me there. I have asked Will if I can go with you and he told me I can."

"It will do no good."

"I thought you believed in what I can do."

"This is beyond any talent you have."

"Perhaps, but I do not think so. I have never done anything like it before, but I believe it is possible. We will never know unless you take me there."

"I can tell you where it is. You are slim enough to slip through the cleft in the rock."

"You must be with me. They are your family, not mine. You must be close if I am to have any chance."

Thomas sighed. "Will this involve you taking your clothes off again?"

Silva's teeth flashed white in the darkness. "It will. But you told me it is too dark to see within the cave."

"We will need a candle to find our way."

"Then you will have to close your eyes. I need you with me, Tom. She is your mother."

"And Will's grandmother."

Silva glanced at him. "He never knew her. You did. It has to be you, however unsettling you might find it."

THIRTY-NINE

As Thomas and Silva descended the twisting track there was just enough starlight to guide them. Soon after they left the others Silva reached out and took Thomas's hand. He said nothing, but it seemed she needed to offer an explanation.

"I need contact with you, Tom. If it feels awkward I apologise, but it is necessary."

"It does feel strange, but I trust your judgment in this. It is far beyond anything in my experience."

"I need to warn you this may not work. It is hardly in my experience, either."

"If it does not I will have to let it go. I cannot allow the missing skulls to fester within me or I am in danger of becoming like Felicia and Haylewith. I have the rest of my mother's bones and that will have to be enough."

"You are strong, Tom. I like that about you. I like that about Will, too, but he is stronger in a different way and less strong in others."

"I do not understand."

"I think you do, but I will try to explain. I am sure you will not accept what I say, but for me it is what I see. What I sense."

The pale face of the quarry loomed ahead, each step taking them closer to the chamber of skulls. Thomas felt a tension rise within him and tried to dismiss it. He looked back to where the abbey sat, colourless in the night, and wondered what the brothers would be thinking and doing there. He had seen nothing more of the warrior monks, but if they came to find them it would come to a fight, he knew.

"What is it you see in us?" he asked.

"Will is as strong as a bear, but it is all physical. He tells me he inherits that from his morfar. I did not know what the word meant until he told me it is grandfather — his mother's father. He was a great warrior, is that right?"

"As far as I know Olaf Torvaldsson is still a great warrior, but where he is, I do not know."

"Will is strong. He can fight like no one else. I have seen it, and I have heard of it. Your friend Usaden is like him but is slight in comparison. Once Will told me if it ever came to a fight between him and Usaden he believed Usaden would win."

"So do I this year, but next year who knows?"

"But Will is less strong than you where it matters perhaps above all else. You are strong in spirit. Strong here." Silva punched her chest. "You have a good heart."

"So does Will."

"I know he does, but you are heart and mind combined. Like Amal. She is more like you than Will."

"Will had a different mother."

"He told me, though it only takes looking at them to know that. He also told me that you still miss Lubna."

Thomas felt his chest hitch, not speaking so Silva would not hear his emotion.

But she squeezed his hand and said, "I know, Tom. I know."

They walked on in silence, their feet making no sound against the grass.

Eventually, because he knew it needed saying, Thomas said, "For all his strength Will is still young. He will learn to listen to his heart in time. You are good for him in that way. I am glad you have found each other."

"So am I," said Silva. "I never believed I would commit to one man, but now I know I can. Will is my man, forever."

They reached the foot of the quarry and Thomas led the way to the stand of bushes, Silva's hand still in his. He had grown used to the touch. Welcomed it.

"I will go first and light the candle once I am inside. You follow when you see the light."

Thomas released her hand and went on hands and knees to push through the brambles. He found the cleft and eased through it on his side. Inside, in pitch darkness, he fumbled with the flint until it sparked, until the oiled wool flared, then lit the candle. Moments later Silva appeared.

She stood and stared at the towering pile of skulls.

Thomas saw Felicia Hughden's head had been removed, as well as her torso, and suspected that was Bernard's doing. Though he doubted Bernard had the power to do so anymore. Perhaps Haylewith had taken mercy on her soul.

"There are hundreds of skulls, Tom. I cannot help but think of all the children abandoned in the graves of strangers. There is a sadness here, and anger. But also ... something I cannot pin down. It is not hope, but is like hope. Perhaps they sense us and believe they will be saved."

"We cannot find out who each skull belongs to," Thomas said.

"Of course not, but they can be reunited with bones in an ossuary. Restored with other bodies. It is like our conversation as we descended the hill. A man is more than his mind, more than his body. It is the combination that makes him what he is. Not all men are like that. Madoc was all mind, his filled with hatred. Bernard is more mind as well, but his is filled with light and a love of God." Silva smiled. "Oh, I know you think me a Pagan, and I am, but I accept the Christian God as well as my own. That is one advantage of being Pagan. We are already used to the concept of many Gods in many places. I need to disrobe now. You can avert your eyes if it makes you more comfortable, but I do not mind if you watch. It might even help."

"You are my son's woman," Thomas said. "It would not be seemly."

"It is only flesh. The sight of it is not the sin. The

wanting to own it, to defile it is the sin. But do as you wish. I may be some time, but you need to remain close if this is going to work."

Thomas set the candle on a narrow shelf carved into the rock. As he did so he saw a gathering of wax there, telling him it had been used for the same purpose before. He wondered who of those now dead had come here to place the skulls. He suspected Haylewith. Felicia had hinted that it was he who had an obsession with them. He who had forced Ambrose to bring them to him.

As he turned away the candlelight caught on an object set on another shelf, and Thomas wondered how he had not seen it when he came to the cave before. With everything he knew of Haylewith's obsession he should have.

"Silva, come here a moment and tell me if you feel anything from this."

"From what, Tom?" But she came to stand at his side.

Thomas reached out, hesitated. The cup set in the alcove was small. Fashioned of gold and inset with jewels, it sparkled under the wavering light of the candle. He thought of the rumours, the legends. The goblet used at the Last Supper, which it was claimed the Templars possessed. And now, if it was here, Abbot Haylewith possessed the treasure he has sought for so long.

Thomas put his hands around it, half-expecting some kind of shock, but nothing came. He held it out to Silva, who took it without hesitation.

"It is heavier than it looks," she said. "Fine workmanship." She looked up at him. "What is it?"

"Do you feel anything from it?"

Silva closed her eyes a moment, her lips parted, her chest rising and falling. When she opened them she said, "Nothing. Not even a hint of its making, which means it is old." She held it out to Thomas who replaced it in the niche.

If it was the Grail he would expect Silva to sense something from it, but did the fact she did not mean it was not that prize? He stared at it, hearing Silva moving around behind him. The cup, whether the Grail or not, was valuable. The gold and jewels alone made it that. If it resided here in the heart of Burfa Bank he assumed Abbot Haylewith believed he had found what he had searched for over many years. Had Ambrose been brought here and asked to validate it? Thomas would have expected such to happen. And the skulls would be those brought here by Ambrose so he would know of the cup.

When he turned around Silva stood naked, her back to him.

"I am ready, Tom. Do you have another candle?"

He felt inside his robe and drew one out, lit it from the other and walked across to the other side of the cave without trying to look in Silva's direction.

He heard her laugh.

"If I was not with your son, and you not with Bel, I would be mightily tempted to make a pitch for you, Tom. You are so sweet."

"I am too old for you, " he said, still turned away.

"But when I sense you, you are not old. In your heart and your mind you remain as young as you have always been. Old men stop wanting to learn new things. They are content to sit by the fire and sink into a torpor. You are not that way."

"No, I am not. If I ever become so, you have my permission to tell Will to run me through."

"He would never do that. And do not worry, you are safe from me. You and Bel have always been meant for each other, even when you were apart for so long."

Thomas considered no reply necessary. He stood with his back turned, aware of shadows dancing across the rock as Silva moved. He heard the rattle of skulls being disturbed. Heard her climbing the tower of bone, and then silence reigned. It went on so long he grew concerned and turned around. What he saw would be seared into his mind forever. It was both beautiful and profane.

Silva sat at the peak of the pile of skulls. They covered her to the waist, exposing her breasts. Her hair stood out from her head as if she had been struck by lightning, and her eyes were wide but unseeing. She had no idea he was watching her. She had gone to another place.

She must have moved because a skull dislodged itself and bounced down to land at his feet.

"Your brother," she said, her eyes still closed. She did not need them to see. "I am still searching for your mother."

Silva thrust her hands between the skulls and began to speak, but it was in no tongue Thomas had ever heard, and he had heard many. It made the hairs on his arms stand up.

He knelt and picked up the skull at his feet and turned it over. He recognised it as that of a man. Male and female differed in tiny ways which he was familiar with. He held it up and looked into the empty eye sockets. He thought of his brother, John Berrington. Eighteen when he died of the sickness that took the lives of almost half of Lemster. He had never liked him, but would have preferred he had lived, married, had children. Had he done so he would no doubt still live in the house on Eaton Hill and Thomas would have had no need to move his family's bones. And none of what had come to pass would have happened because it would be John who went to France to fight. He stared at the skull, the bone seeming to ripple in the wavering candlelight.

He glanced up at Silva, shocked when he saw her sinking into the pile of skulls. Only her shoulders and head now visible, the strange words still on her lips.

Thomas dropped the skull in shock when he felt something. As if it had moved.

"John?" he said.

No. It was not possible. John had been dead for almost fifty years. But he had felt it move. For a moment it had become flesh and blood, even as he knew it must have been all in his mind. Thomas picked the skull up. As he did his fingers ran across the front along the nasal cavity and he felt something. He recalled Bel telling him how she had broken John's nose when he tried to assault her. Now, the slight raising on the bone to one side told him the nose of this skull had also been broken. It confirmed for him what Silva claimed. This skull belonged to John Berrington.

When Thomas looked again only Silva's eyes were visible, her iridescent hair spread across the skulls to either side. And then she was gone.

The tower of skulls moved, appearing to writhe as Silva burrowed through it.

And then she appeared as if emerging from being buried alive. She pushed a skull ahead of her, slid from the pile and slumped to the ground.

"Your mother," she said. "I am tired now, Tom. I have to sleep."

She lay her head on the hard ground.

Thomas stood, unsure of what to do. Then he knelt beside Silva and felt for the heartbeat in her throat, relieved when he found it. Slow. Strong. Steady. He found her cloak and laid it over her.

He sat back and picked up the skull she had retrieved, did what he had with the other and held it in front of him.

It was finer, lighter than John's. For a moment it occurred to him that Silva could have chosen any two skulls of the right size and weight, but then he glanced at her and knew his thought unjust. And there had been the sensation he felt when he held his brother's skull. He believed this was the skull of Catherine Berrington, his beloved mother. Tears welled in Thomas's eyes and fell as he clutched the skull to his chest. As he did so he felt arms enclose him and a scent fill his senses, a scent he had not smelled in half a century.

Thank you, Tom. You have become everything I ever hoped you would and more. Now I can rest again.

They were not words, but nor were they thoughts. They were something nestled within him. Some truth that had no need of words to express itself.

He had no idea how much time passed, but in the end he set his mother's skull beside that of his brother and dressed Silva in her robe. She did not stir, so he fashioned a sling from his shirt and placed the two skulls within it, then lifted Silva in his arms and carried her along the tunnel into the abbey. He would have to trust his luck to continue so he could pass through without challenge. Except luck does not always work that way. Sometimes it can only be pushed so far.

He made it as far as the oak door, which stood open, possibly from the last time he had come this way.

He arrived at the courtyard before his luck, like sand in an hourglass, ran out. As he knew one day it would.

"Berrington. How fortunate. This saves me the trouble of coming to kill you."

Abbot Haylewith stood in front of at least a score of warrior monks, all illuminated by wavering torches. In his hand the Abbot held a skull, and Thomas knew he had been coming to the catacombs to set it on those already there. Which meant it still went on. Would go on until someone stopped it.

"Did you move Felicia's head?" Thomas asked.

"I did. I was hasty in leaving it with the others. I have it now in a special place." He smiled. "I will set yours beside it so she can whisper her secrets into your ear. She told me she wanted to confess everything to you. Told me you were the kind of man who could be trusted. Which is why she had to die, of course. As do you." Haylewith glanced at Thomas's burden. "And yes, your witch, too, I fear. But I may allow my men to give her something to remember while she burns in hell."

FORTY

"They have been gone too long," said Will.

"It is not a loaf of bread they have gone to buy," said Bernard. "I suspect Silva has no idea how long it is going to take, or even if she can succeed."

"They have still been gone too long." Will looked at Usaden as if he would come to his aid, but as ever Usaden maintained his silence.

Will stood and walked to the mound surrounding the fort so he could gaze down at the abbey below. A quarter moon had risen behind him, its light falling across the pale walls. Will felt a vibration within himself, an urgency to take action. Any action. He knew his father would counsel patience, but patience was not in Will's nature. He wondered what Silva and his father were doing in the cave. Did they talk about what they sought? Will was jealous, but knew the jealousy irrational. That did not stop it from gnawing at him. He was aware Silva was trying to change him, to soften some of the hard edges, and he welcomed her attempt even as he was sure it would fail. As long as the failure did not change what lay between them. Will had been with women before. Plain girls, beautiful girls, young and old. He knew women liked him, and he liked them, but he thought if she would allow it he would never again be with anyone but Silva Taylor.

Will took a deep breath and let it go, misting the air. Through it, he caught movement and leaned forward even as he knew it would do no good. The approaching men were too far away to intercept before they reached the abbey.

Men were coming from the east, following the track that sat above the Hindwell brook, high now with the remnant of the storm running from the Welsh hills. Will narrowed his eyes, trying to count their number, but gave up at forty. They rode as soldiers, organised, steady. At their head came a man wearing a long white robe adorned with a red cross, the hood raised to cover his head, but long grey hair found its way out and his beard hung long on his chest.

"Abbot Haylewith is coming," he said, calling to the others.

Bernard rose and came to stand beside him.

"Yes, that is Haylewith." Bernard scanned the moonlit countryside. "I do not see Tom or Silva. Do you think they are still in the cave?"

"How am I meant to know that? I should have gone with them."

"There are two score men down there," said Bernard. "Too many even for you."

Usaden joined them. After a moment, he clicked his fingers and started down the hill, taking great leaps so he descended almost as fast as if he were falling. Kin ran beside him equally as fast.

"Stay here if you want, I am going down," said Will.

He could not descend as Usaden did, but he was fast enough until he stumbled and started to roll before coming up against a tree trunk. The collision knocked the breath from him so it took a moment to recover before he rose and went on, slower than before. Usaden had disappeared, but he glimpsed Kin racing along the far bank of the brook and knew the two would be close.

A sound from behind made Will turn, but it was only Bernard coming to join him. He carried no sword, so when he reached him, Will drew his own and offered it.

"What will you use?"

Will patted the axe hanging along his back. "I prefer this. And I have three daggers so you can have one of those as well, unless you prefer not to fight. In which case stay here because you will only get in the way."

"I still do not see Tom," said Bernard.

"He will come, but best we stop those soldiers before he appears."

"Two score against three of us?"

"Do not forget Kin. He is worth ten men."

"I have not fought in many years, and I no longer know if I can. It is not a part of me anymore."

"Then stay here. I will hold you in no less regard for it.

We cannot all be warriors." Will meant his words but saw Bernard did not believe him.

"They are splitting up," said Bernard.

Will turned. The soldiers behind Abbot Haylewith separated. Half turned south, fording the brook and continuing. The others went on.

Will smiled. "Only twenty now. This should be easy." He started down the slope again, taking more care.

After a moment he heard Bernard follow.

"Why did they split up?" Will asked.

"I suspect they are heading for Elmbrook, and from there to Lemster. Haylewith will have left more of his soldiers at Wigmore, I suspect. They are coming to claim all the holy houses of the district."

"For what reason?"

"Greed, I suspect," said Bernard. "The income of Wigmore is substantial. Add that to Elmbrook and you have a small fortune coming in every year. Add in Lemster Priory and Hindwell Abbey, and it comes to even more. Combined, the four of them become untouchable. Hereford would find it hard to close him down. Salop the same. Haylewith will be working with the Marcher Lords to lay a claim on all these lands. The rule of the King will become their rule, and I do not trust Haylewith to be a good master."

"Are you with me?" Will asked.

"I have no choice, but we wait until they reach the abbey and the others are well away and cannot hear the clash of swords."

Will grinned. "I will have to try for patience, then."

Which is when he saw his father come out from the abbey with Silva in his arms, and patience was abandoned.

Will ran hard.

Bernard tried to keep up but could not.

Usaden appeared and fell in beside Will. Then Kin came on his other side as Will reached back and grasped the hilt of his axe.

FORTY-ONE

Thomas saw movement beyond the abbey wall and tried not to look in that direction. He shook Silva in his arms in an attempt to wake her but she failed to respond. He suspected she would rouse only when she was ready. The search through the skulls had drained every drop of energy from her, and he knew he could not defend either of them while he held her. He turned away, intending to set her against the outer wall, but Haylewith motioned with a hand and four of his soldiers of God came to block Thomas's path. Without Silva in his arms Thomas was confident he could have dealt with them. With her, he knew they might both die.

So he whistled loudly, causing the men to look confused until Kin leapt from the stone wall and tore the throat from one of them.

Thomas darted to one side, set Silva down none too gently, and drew his sword. When he turned to confront them the remaining three were backing away with Kin prowling in front of them. If they attacked so would he. If they moved away he would let them go.

"One man and a dog!" shouted Abbot Haylewith. "You cannot take care of one man and a dog? Kill the witch. See how he likes that."

One man was brave enough to move towards Silva, but Thomas took him before he covered half the distance.

He turned back to Haylewith, who had moved so that his soldiers stood on either side of him.

"God is with you!" Haylewith cried. "That man is heathen. Finish him."

Thomas knew if they came at once he would be overwhelmed. He could take some but not all. But if Kin was here he would help. And if Kin was here then so were Will and Usaden. Against the three of them those remaining would stand little chance.

"Where are they, boy?" Thomas said.

Kin did not reply, which was to be expected, but he did growl deep in his chest. Two of the approaching men stopped in their tracks and others bumped into them. Which is when Usaden came running from one side.

His sword flashed and two men fell.

Then it was Will's turn, his axe swinging on a leather thong tied tight around his wrist. He took the head of one, the arm of another, and left them to bleed on the ground.

Beyond the group of men, Thomas saw brothers streaming from the abbey, woken by the noise. He was sure they would not join the fight, but they might get in the way. And he would prefer there to be no witnesses to what was about to happen. This evil had to end. It had to end tonight.

Abbot Haylewith pushed back through his men. He snatched a sword from one of them and went on. He emerged from the far side of the cohort and ran towards the gathering monks.

"Brothers, I am your master. Come to me. Protect me from these heathens."

The monks continued to mill around, confused and unsure. They had lost one master already. Some seemed as if they would obey Haylewith's order, others hung back clutching their rosaries as they mouthed prayers.

Bernard entered the courtyard and walked towards Haylewith, but his eyes were on the monks behind the man.

"You know me," he said, raising his voice. "And if you know me you also know I am an honest, God-fearing man." He raised an arm and pointed at Haylewith. "This creature is not. Decide, brothers, who you wish to follow. Him or me."

"Do not listen to him," said Haylewith. "He has no position anymore. He is defrocked."

"I served under Prior Bernard at Lemster," said one of the monks, stepping forwards. "There is no more honest man who walks this earth. Praise him, my brothers."

Abbot Haylewith lashed out with his sword and caught the man on the shoulder, causing him to stagger away and fall to his knees.

Bernard went to him and pressed against the wound,

which is when Haylewith saw his chance and came at him.

But he had not counted on the friendship of the brothers. They had suffered under Haylewith for years, then suffered again when he appointed Madoc as Abbot. Now with one of those dead, perhaps they believed they could free themselves of both. They recognised Bernard for what he was and came to stand around him to protect both him and their fallen brother.

Haylewith roared and struck out again, injuring more, but they were too many, coming forward as one, surrounding him so he had no space to strike out. Then Bernard rose and joined them. He pushed through their throng until he stood in front of Abbot Haylewith.

The brothers fell back to form a circle around the two men.

Thomas struck out at one of the soldiers between him and Bernard, but they were already pulling back now as they had when Madoc died. Cowards, all of them.

"Leave them," he called out to Will and Usaden. "Let them run if they want, they are a spent force without their master."

Will looked as if he wanted to object, but Usaden came to stand beside Thomas, his curved blade dripping blood onto the grass.

When Thomas turned back Abbot Haylewith and Bernard continued to face each other. He walked across, pushed through the brothers who parted to allow him through as if none wanted to be touched by him.

"In the name of King Henry, I arrest you for the

murder of Prioress Felicia Hughden." Thomas raised his voice so all could hear, noting the expression of shock on the faces of many of the brothers.

"You cannot arrest me. I am ordained by God to serve Him. Henry is not the legitimate King of England, and you are nothing. As is this man in front of me."

"Then let God decide," said Bernard. "I know you fought in the Holy Land. As did I. Let us fight now and see who God favours."

"You are an old man," said Haylewith. "It would not be a fair fight."

Bernard laughed. "Now you talk of fairness? Was it fair to throw Felicia Hughden from the top of a quarry and rip her head from her shoulders? Was it fair to bribe whoever you did to be appointed Abbot? We fight. You and I. Here and now."

Abbot Haylewith tried to flee but the brothers stood firm, an immovable wall even when he struck out and brought another to the ground. He could not kill them all, and those he did would die convinced of their place in Heaven.

"You do not have to do this," Thomas said to Bernard. "Will, Usaden and me can overwhelm him and take him for trial."

"He will not be found guilty," said Bernard. "He is the appointed Abbot of Wigmore. His position protects him. You do not know the Church as I do. He will never be brought to justice. So it has to end here. I must kill him."

"No," Thomas said. "If you say he must die then let me do it."

Bernard shook his head. "This is a matter for the Church. I have killed heathens before, and that is what Haylewith is. Stand aside, Tom, and let me do it."

Thomas looked out to where Will stood with Silva in his arms.

Will nodded. Let Bernard do it.

Thomas knew it was wrong but did not know what would be right, so he moved away and melted back among the brothers.

Bernard circled Haylewith, who raised his own sword and waved it about without purpose.

"Yes, I am old," said Bernard, "so fight me. Let God decide between us." He smiled. "I know who he will choose. Do you?" He feinted at Haylewith, who moved backwards so fast he fell, and Bernard laughed.

Haylewith climbed to his feet, and as he did so everyone saw a change in him. He had accepted what was happening and discovered courage from somewhere deep within. He grinned, convinced he would prevail against Bernard.

"All of you know even if I were to perish this is not the end, only the beginning," said Haylewith, his voice booming out so all could hear. "The Church must change. England must change and accept the old ways. To embrace them. We are a land blessed by Jesus Christ Himself."

He charged at Bernard. His sword came down hard, but Bernard deflected it with his own. He stepped aside and punched Haylewith in the side. But the man was filled with fire and turned fast, striking out again and catching Bernard on the side of his chest. Blood blossomed but Bernard ignored it. He let Haylewith's blade swing around, the blow so violent it unbalanced him. Bernard stepped closer and thrust his sword into Haylewith's belly. Bernard grunted and pushed harder.

Haylewith staggered back, the sword still embedded in him.

He fell backwards and lay still, his eyes staring up towards at a Heaven he would never attain.

Bernard turned away, but the brothers would not let him pass.

Thomas moved to stand beside him, making his face fierce.

Which was when the brothers uttered a great cheer and began to sing a psalm in Latin.

"Come pray with us, Abbot Bernard," said one.

They turned away and filed into the abbey, leaving Bernard and Thomas alone.

"Go with them," Thomas said.

"I killed him," said Bernard, looking down at the body of Haylewith. "I killed an Abbot. The Church will have me hung, drawn and quartered, then bury each piece in a separate county."

"Nothing happened here," Thomas said. "Go and pray with your flock. When you all come out there will be nothing to see."

Bernard looked into Thomas's eyes. "I will always know what happened. So will you, Will and Usaden. And the brothers. They are witnesses to my anger."

"Go." Thomas set his hand on Bernard's shoulder. "Go with your flock, Abbot Bernard."

When he had gone, Thomas called Will and Usaden to him and told them what they were going to do. It would take the rest of the night and much of the next day, but he believed the brothers would help. Order had been restored.

Thomas knelt and grasped Haylewith under the arms and dragged him to the abbey, along the corridor and down to the catacombs. When he reached them Will was behind him with two more of the felled soldiers.

"We leave them here and brick the entrances up," Thomas said. "There is plenty of stone scattered across the quarry floor. But first we take every skull out of here. Then we bring the dead in. If anyone asks, they all rode west into Wales when their plot was discovered. Bernard will vouch for the truth of it."

"Still you forget his title, Pa," said Will.

"Then Abbot Bernard will vouch for it. Now let us get to work."

It did not take as long as Thomas thought. Usaden carried as many skulls as he could out through the cleft in the hillside and set them in a cart from where they were taken to the ossuary in the abbey. All but those of the recent dead. Haylewith and his soldiers would fester to bones in the cave. When prayers were finished the brothers came, took more carts to the quarry and returned with irregular blocks of pale stone. The fallen brothers would be honoured with their own plot of ground within the confines of the abbey at Hindwell.

Silva woke and came to find them, still unsure on her feet, and Will took her back to her cottage. But not before she came to Thomas and embraced him.

"Thank you, Tom." She smiled, then reached up and kissed his mouth.

"It is me who must thank you. I have the skulls I sought. Without you I would never have found them."

"And without you asking I would never have discovered something about myself," said Silva. "You sparked a talent inside me that has lain dormant my entire life." She turned and slid her arm through Will's and they walked together to his horse.

Thomas watched them ride away. He was unsure how much to believe of what Silva claimed, but he had witnessed a power that had also changed him. He was a rational man, but rationality could not explain everything. And the wickedness he had uncovered and helped end owed little to rationality.

FORTY-TWO

Thomas rode to Elmbrook Priory alone while the others continued on to Burway. He was unsure why he needed to visit there, but Madoc had said something before he died that made Thomas want to ensure nothing had been missed. Felicia Hughden had lied to him. She claimed she kept no records of who visited the bordel at the priory. No names of who helped and who hindered her work. But Madoc said she kept a ledger holding names, dates, and monies exchanged for influence. The names of the good and the names of the wicked and corrupt. Thomas suspected her ledger might have been destroyed. Haylewith would have made sure of it. But there was a possibility, so Thomas rode the track familiar to him now and tied Ferrant to a post outside the priory wall. The day was early, but the sun shone in a clear sky, and the early low-lying mist was burning off.

Two of the nuns approached.

"You are early, sir, but one of us will entertain you for

sixpence if you wish it. Ten if you want us both." One put a hand on his chest. "You are a handsome man, so perhaps less than ten."

"I am not here for that. I need to see where Prioress Hughden had her rooms."

"All men are here for that, sir. Why would we show you where the Prioress lived? We are expecting a new Prioress at any time, as soon as Abbot Haylewith chooses who it should be." The nun smiled. "Perhaps it will be one of us. He knows us both and likes us."

"I expect he does. Her rooms?"

One of the sisters turned away. The other said, "Go find them yourself."

Thomas looked around. Sisters tended the herb and vegetable gardens. Three cast a net into the stew pond. Others strolled. None appeared to take any notice of him, so Thomas walked into the priory.

He tried to recall the way Bernard had brought him when they discovered Madoc and Felicia together. He followed the cloister to its far end, turned into a corridor and continued to the end where a solid elm door stood ajar. He expected to find Felicia's bedroom but instead entered a study. A large room lined with bookshelves, a sturdy desk, a table and chairs with another door on the far side. A heavy chest stood beside the desk with its top open. He went there first, but when he looked inside the chest was empty. Someone had come and taken whatever lay within. Had Felicia Hughden's ledger been among the contents? If, as he suspected, she wanted it kept private then most likely not.

He checked the desk, but it had no drawers. The door on the far side was shut, and when he tried to open it found it locked. He went to the table and sat, staring at the door. He wished Jorge was with him because he would have no trouble picking the lock. Thomas lacked the skill so would need a key.

As he sat there he heard soft footsteps approaching. He looked around, wondering if he should hide, but the steps were light, and there was only one set, so he stayed where he was.

A young nun entered the room and stopped abruptly.

"Oh, I did not know anyone was in here. Have you come for Prioress Hughden's things? Abbot Haylewith sent a message that she had been moved to another priory in the south."

Thomas was about to say what things, when he changed his mind.

"I have."

The nun smiled. "She will be much missed here, but Abbot Haylewith told us to expect someone and that her legacy will be maintained. I take it you have the note of permission?"

Thomas rose, patting his pockets. "Yes, it is here somewhere." He started to turn them out. Two in his jacket, one in his hose, the nun averting his eyes as he fumbled in it. He smiled. "It is here somewhere. Let me check my boots, I sometimes keep important documents there. I have only in the last two hours left the Abbots Madoc and Haylewith at Hindwell Abbey."

"They are well, I take it?"

"Sleeping when I left, and as well as can be expected." Thomas sat and started to work one of his boots off.

"Do not concern yourself, sir, I can see you are an honest man. I often mislay notes and items given to me for safekeeping. Prioress Felicia was always kind to me." Her expression changed as she recalled she would never speak with the Prioress again. "She saved my life."

"She is a good woman." Thomas made an effort to refer to Felicia as if she still lived. Clearly that is what Haylewith wanted her flock to believe. Though Thomas still found it hard to accept none had witnessed what happened on Burfa Bank.

"Indeed she is." The nun reached beneath her habit and drew out a heavy key. "The Prioress keeps all the most important items in her bed chamber." She came across and handed the key to Thomas. "I will leave you to study them in private. Can I fetch you something to eat or drink?"

"My thanks, but the Abbots have asked me to return with what I find as soon as possible. Another time, perhaps, sister..."

"Arabella. I look forward to your return, sir. You are not young, but you are handsome and strong."

When she was gone Thomas used the key to open the elm door and entered Felicia Hughden's bed chamber. He locked the door behind him, then stood and surveyed the room. He recognised it as the room Bernard had led them to when they discovered Madoc threating her. Now he knew the reason why.

A door on the far side led into the corridor which was

the way they had come that day, but when Thomas tried the handle it was locked.

The air carried a faint remnant of Felicia's scent; dark and musky, redolent of the woman's sensuality. Thomas suspected he had never seen the better side of her, and wondered if under other circumstances they might have become, if not friends, then at least acquaintances. If such was possible with her. With what he now knew he suspected Felicia Hughden had been corrupted by Abbot Haylewith and Madoc and turned to their will. Did her old self remain beneath the surface she showed the world or had it been completely destroyed? Had she resisted their deranged plans and that was why she had to die?

Thomas liked to think some of the goodness might have remained. She had maintained her ledger, after all, and that might offer some explanation for why she had become who she was in the end. If he ever found it. And to do that he would have to start.

He went to the bed first and lifted the mattress, but nothing lay beneath, not even dust. Next, he checked the drawer in the small table beside it, which was empty. A larger table set across the room had four drawers but those, too, were empty. There was nowhere else.

Thomas sat on the bed and thought. It was clear that the room had been cleaned recently, and the lack of anything in any of the drawers told him someone had come here and emptied everything out. The nun who had handed him the key? Except if it had been her why did she ask if he had been sent for Felicia's things? Unless she had removed everything and knew it did not matter if

Thomas gained access to the room. Except that would indicate Haylewith had corrupted every member of the holy houses under his control.

Thomas went to his knees, tapping every single tile on the floor, recalling other hiding places he had found in the past. But in this instance all the tiles sounded the same. Solid. Fixed. He surveyed the walls, but there was nowhere to hide anything.

Thomas unlocked the door, re-locked it and went into the corridor. He kept walking until he found a group of four nuns talking together.

"Are you lost, sir? If you seek the house of relief it is beyond the main building."

"I am looking for sister Arabella. I have a key for her."

One of the sisters came close. "I will take it for her if you wish."

"My thanks, but I would prefer to hand it to her myself."

"She will be in the herb garden at this time of day. Would you like me to show you where it is?"

"My thanks, but I saw it when I came in."

Thomas left them, aware of their whispers as he walked away.

There were several nuns on their knees tending the herbs, which looked healthy. He recognised sister Arabella and approached her.

"I am returning your key." He held it out, but she only stared at it. "Did you find what you wanted, sir?"

"Was it you who cleaned Prioress Felicia's room?"

"I did, sir."

"Did you take any documents from the chest in her office?"

"I was told by Abbot Haylewith to remove everything from it and burn them, which I did."

Thomas felt any sense of hope leave him. Felicia had known whatever she had recorded would be dangerous and Haylewith would covet it. Lists of names and favours owed. Lists he could turn to his own ends, had he lived. Thomas believed he had reached a dead-end and may never know the whole truth. Why Ambrose had taken the skulls. Why he and Felicia had to die.

There was one last possibility but Thomas did not hold out much hope.

"Did you remove anything from her bed chamber?"

"Only a few books, sir. I replaced them in the library where they belonged."

"I think one of them might have been lent to her by Abbot Haylewith. Would you be able to show me where you put them?"

"I think so, sir, unless someone else has taken them." She offered her hand, and Thomas helped her to her feet, uneasy at the casual sensuality she displayed.

He followed sister Arabella into the main building, then back along the cloister. She turned right to enter a tall room where five sisters crouched over desks, their fingers stained with ink: red, green and black.

"This gentleman seeks a book Abbot Haylewith loaned the Prioress," said sister Arabella. "It is the Illustratum, I suspect."

"It has been placed among the other profane titles," said the nearest sister.

It appeared that sister Arabella knew exactly where that was because she led Thomas through the room to a small chamber beyond. Here every inch of free space was lined with shelves, and every shelf was stacked full of papers, vellum and bound books.

Sister Arabella drew a small wooden ladder from an alcove and set it against a row of shelves.

"Steady me please, sir," she said, one foot on the bottom rung.

Thomas gripped her waist, but as she climbed higher he had no alternative but to move his hands lower. He knew exactly what she was doing and it amused him, even more so because she would think only of his reaction to her feminine curves. She reached high for one of the books, then as she came down fashioned a stumble so she fell into his arms.

Thomas took the book and eased her away from him.

Sister Arabella frowned.

"Do you not like me, sir?"

"You are very pretty," Thomas said. "But I was injured in battle and can no longer respond to a woman."

His reply seemed to placate her because her smile returned. "That is a pity, sir. I will show you the way out."

Thomas rode a mile east before easing Ferrant to a halt and dismounting. He sat in a copse of beech and examined the book. The cover was gilded, with fine script and small illustrations that would bring a flush to the face of most people.

Thomas opened the book and leafed through the pages. Each contained more detailed drawings and text, but it was not what he sought. He imagined some men would pay a great deal for what he held, but it did nothing for him. He had lain with some of the most beautiful women in the world and knew scratchings on paper could never compare. He supposed he was lucky. Most men would never have the opportunities he had been offered. Would never witness the lands and people he had experienced.

Thomas considered returning to Elmbrook Priory but suspected there was nothing there to find. He turned the heavy book over, admiring the quality of the work if not the content. He then noticed that the spine was thicker and deeper than it should be. He raised it close and ran a finger along the edge, where it caught on a raised metal bar. Thomas pushed a fingernail beneath and worked it around until suddenly the metal bar clicked away and the spine of the book lay in his hand, the rest of the book in the other.

He lifted it and noticed a narrow chamber created between the two. Deep within he saw a roll of papers. His fingers were too big to reach, so he found a twig and used it to ease them out.

When he unrolled them, he saw minute text written in Latin. At the top, it read: *Acta Abbatissae Felicia Hughden*. The journal of Abbess Felicia Hughden.

Abbess?

Had she possessed ambitions beyond her current position, or had she suffered a demotion? Or was being

Prioress even a demotion? Thomas knew he would have to consult Bernard yet again. He would also have to take the pages home to read. His grasp of Latin was not as good as it had once been, but what he could make out without fully understanding it was the nature of what was written there. Much of each page consisted of lists. A date, a name, and a short description of what that individual required in terms of satisfaction. Nine pages in all.

Here and there between the lists, Felicia Hughden had made her own notes. Thomas worked through one and knew he would have to decipher the rest because it said:

The one called Madoc called today and demanded three women. I made him pay more than they were worth, and after had to tend to their bruises. He will not be admitted again.

The date was six years previous, which meant Madoc had been granted subsequent admission and more. No doubt with threats of more violence. Thomas glanced rapidly through the pages, searching for names. He found that of Haylewith, but also Croft and Cornwell, the Archdeacon of Hereford and his precursor. Two other names stood out. Ambrose and Amos Mapp. He found references to the Grail, but much was no more than hearsay. Someone claimed to have known someone who might have seen something. Or perhaps not. And then he came to a page where a rough sketch of a bowl was drawn, beneath it a few lines written as if in haste.

Ambrose showed me his treasure today and allowed me to hold it. I felt the power and told him it must be hidden among the sheep.

Thomas stopped reading. He stared at the rough

sketch scrawled in ink, faint lines indicating the bowl might show some kind of pattern. He thought about Felicia's words. Could Ambrose have finally found what he had been searching for? Or was this nothing more than a false trail intended to guide a reader to a false destination? Thomas thought Felicia might have added both sketch and words in case Haylewith laid his hands on the notes. It would be her way of torturing him. Yes, both Ambrose and I know where the Grail is. And now we are dead at your hand, and you will never hold it.

Did Felicia mean it was hidden among the people? Would she refer to them as sheep in disparagement at their blind following of Christian doctrine, which she only half believed in? Once again Thomas was aware he was no closer to an answer. Too many people had died, taking their knowledge with them.

He slid the pages back into their hiding place. Another few hours and he would be home. These pages would have to be destroyed. Burned, their ashes crumbled and allowed to sink in the Teme. But only after he and Amal had read them and made notes.

He had done everything he could. Recovered the skulls of his mother and brother. Abbot Haylewith and Madoc were dead, as were Felicia Hughden and Brother Ambrose. Had any of them been innocent?

Their sins seemed too petty for what had occurred and the violence engendered. Men wanted to lie with women and were often willing to pay for the pleasure. Thomas had learned what happened at Elmbrook Priory was not unusual. It occurred throughout this land and had done so for many years. Centuries. The Church demanded celibacy even as it knew it was impossible, so had taken measures to keep the weaknesses of men under its own control. And to benefit from it. Elmbrook Priory would continue to serve the district. Nothing would change. Except people were dead who did not need to be.

Thomas rose, holding to the tree a moment as a wave of dizziness washed over him. He grasped his saddle and hauled himself up before allowing Ferrant to carry him home.

But as he approached Wigmore, an abbey once more without a master, he wondered if Bernard had returned there. A new Abbot. The thought brought Abbot John to mind, and memories of his passing. Thomas recalled leaving the room of the dying man to clear his head. He had met Ambrose on Tucknel Bank, leading his cart with the boxes on the back. Had they contained other bodies, or were they being taken to fetch them?

For a moment Thomas closed his eyes, swaying as Ferrant moved beneath him, Another memory surfaced of that day and he turned his mount away from the abbey and started to climb the track Ambrose would have taken that day.

FORTY-THREE

It was where he remembered. A pile of stones that had once been a place of refuge for a shepherd on winter nights. A place where sheep would gather.

Thomas dismounted and tied Ferrant to a branch of a tree that grew sideways from the constant wind. He stepped into the ruined hut and looked around. There was a place for a fire but the chimney, if there ever had been one, had collapsed. No fire had been lit for years, perhaps decades or even centuries. Most of the stones were moss-covered, some shattered by frosts.

Thomas sat as comfortably as he could and tried to still his mind. He imagined how Silva would approach the task, but knew she would have no need of preparation. If she was here, seeking what he sought, she would know at once whether it lay close or not. Thomas did not. Still, he stared into space and slowly the constant churn of thoughts in his head stilled. He recalled some of the times he had indulged in mushrooms and how, afterwards the same calm rose through him. His mind drifted, set free. No more thoughts for a while. His head fell forward and he slept.

When he woke he was falling in a dream, and then he was falling in life and threw out his hands, but too late. His forehead cracked against a fallen stone, sending shards of light through his vision. Thomas lay for a moment, hands on the ground as he tried to lift himself, but his wits were jumbled and he had no strength. He breathed hard, trying again, then rolled over. It felt better to be on his back.

He stared at the sky where clouds scudded across, a sign of more rain and he smiled at how he was learning the vagaries of English weather once more.

He sat up, rubbing at his head. When he withdrew his hand he saw a smear of blood, but as he examined further, he knew there was no permanent damage. He got to his knees and looked around, amazed he could have believed this was the place. He wondered if he had wanted to believe too much. And then, because he was Thomas Berrington, and even as rational as he thought himself to be, he began to search.

Thomas lifted stones and set them aside. There was nowhere in the remnant of walls for an object to be hidden. He thought of his own house where Silva had shown him where the family Bible had lain all the years he was away, but when he looked at this hut there was nowhere to hide anything.

He thought of St Michael's Church in Garway. Small, ordinary, yet not; in parts resembling something other-worldly. Had it been there Ambrose had finally found what he sought? But if so why had he taken it away? It must have been hidden well to avoid all those who had lusted after it over the years.

Thomas looked around again, thinking of the interior of the church. Of the heavy stone slab forming an altar with carvings scratched into it. He began to clear a place in the centre of the hut, throwing blocks out onto the grass until half the floor lay exposed and he saw what he had not believed might be there.

A slab of stone sat beneath the stones. Carved into its surface were crosses, stars, moons and crescents. Thomas knelt and laid his hands on it but felt nothing. No searing revelation struck him down.

He dug beneath one side far enough to get his hands under the slab and heaved but even as he put every part of his body into it, the slab remained as if set in stone itself. Thomas sat back, breathing hard just as the first spots of rain began to fall from a greying sky. He rose and went to Ferrant to search what he might use to lift the slab, but knew his sword or knives would break if he tried.

Thomas stood patting Ferrant's neck as he stared at the hut. He saw where he had flung stones out in his search and knew anyone passing this place would wonder who had done it, and what they might have been searching for. The hut was surrounded by young wood-land, but Thomas had taken the track up the hill that day he met Ambrose so others must also use it.

He considered the risk of riding down to Wigmore

Abbey and recruiting help. They would have stronger tools there, and many hands. But even as the thought came to him he knew it was impossible. What if the Grail lay beneath that slab? He could not risk others knowing of it. Word would spread and men would come to claim it. The battles he had already fought in Ludlow would pale into insignificance.

Thomas walked back to the hut and started to throw the stones back to cover the slab. He was still doing so when he heard someone call out.

"Pa! Where are you, Pa?" It was Will's voice, and a moment later the top of his head appeared. Then there were others. Silva behind Will. Amal, Jorge, Usaden and Kin. Thomas stopped his work and turned to wait for them.

"What are you doing here?" asked Amal as she slid from her saddle.

"Looking for something."

"What?"

"I am not sure I want to tell you."

Silva walked past him and stood on the edge of the hut. She turned her head to stare at him. She stepped across the wall and abruptly keeled over onto her side. Will was with her in a moment, followed by Thomas.

"Is she hurt?" It was Amal, who thought to ask.

Will lifted Silva and laid her on the grass beneath the paltry shelter of a stand of birch. Amal and Thomas knelt beside her. Amal brushed dirt from Silva's face. She had not hit her head but refused to wake or react when Amal slapped her face.

"Will, take her to her cottage. I believe she will recover there. Stay with her. I will send a message if I need you. If she does wake and wants to come back bring her. She will know not to step inside those walls a second time."

"What is in there? Poison. A gas?"

"Nothing that will affect the rest of us," Thomas said. He turned to Amal. "Go to Burway with Usaden and fetch something long and metal. I need to raise a stone slab."

"Let us do it now before I leave with Silva," said Will. "Between us all we can do it, I am sure."

Thomas was not, but he nodded. It was worth trying, at least.

Amal stayed to watch over Silva, holding her hand.

Thomas took them within the walls and they threw out again the stones he had put back. Then they stood with Will and Jorge at the short end of the stone slab, Thomas on one longer side and Usaden on the other.

"You will need to make a space for your fingers," Thomas said, kneeling.

"What do you expect to find under here?" Will asked. "More bones?"

That thought had not occurred to Thomas, but now Will had spoken of it, he thought it more likely to be what lay beneath the slab. Had Ambrose placed bodies here as well as elsewhere?

When they were ready, he counted down and each of them heaved.

Nothing happened. The slab remained as if part of the landscape.

"It can't be too heavy for four of us to lift," said Will.

"So why did it not move?" Thomas asked. He wondered if more than raw strength was needed here.

"Pa, Silva is awake and wants to come back." Amal stood beyond the ruined wall.

"Tell her to stay away."

"She says you need her, and that she is prepared now. She says you will not succeed unless she is with you."

Thomas stood and looked out to where Silva stood in the wind and rain, her hair tugged and twisted behind her. He stepped over the wall and went to her.

"Do you know what I seek?"

"I felt it, Tom, so yes, I know. I am ready now, I will not fall again."

She held her hand out and he took it and led her back, watching as she stepped into the remains of the hut, but she stood erect.

"You go there," she said. "Will, you on this corner. I will take the middle of the slab here."

Thomas did not believe Silva would add much in the way of strength but suspected it was not strength that was required.

"Where do we go?" asked Jorge.

"You are not needed, but you may lift on the long side if you want. You too, Amal. It will be good if we all contribute."

"Shall I count us down again?" Thomas asked.

Silva smiled and shook her head. "You will know when it is time. All of you will know."

She bent and slid her slim fingers beneath the centre

of the short side of the slab and took the strain. The others went where she told them, waiting until a certainty filled each of them and they heaved.

The slab came up, showering dirt and small stones into a cavity underneath that no one could yet see into. When the slab was vertical Silva said, "Lean it against the wall. We will need to replace it when we are done." She looked between them. "You need to do this next part, Tom. I can go no closer. When you bring it out pass it to Amal and she can take it out the other side."

Thomas looked down into the exposed cavity. It was three feet deep and empty, but the bottom was soil. He dropped down and knelt, dug with his hands and then used his knife. He found the first bone within minutes and felt a sense of disappointment. This was nothing more than another dumping ground for Ambrose. He cursed and started to rise.

"No, it lies beneath the bones," said Silva. "Go deeper, Tom. Amal, go with him and pass the bones out, they may also be significant."

Amal dropped down by her father and helped him dig the loosened soil. More bones appeared and she took it and passed them up to Will. Jorge stood off to one side, a look of disgust on his face. Usaden stood on the lip of the chamber, expressionless. Kin remained beyond the walls as if not wanting to approach any closer.

They uncovered bones but they were not a full set. All were small but not those of a child. Bones from hands and feet, one rib, one vertebra. There was no skull. And then, beneath them, Thomas's fingers found something else. He loosened it and drew out an object wrapped in oiled cloth.

"It is what you seek," said Silva, who stepped back as far as she could. "It is what all humanity seeks."

"Open it, Pa," said Will.

Thomas looked at the wrapped object and shook his head. "No, not here, not yet." He held it up to Amal, who took it. "Put it somewhere safe, my sweet. We need to lower the slab again, and then we need to go home. My bones ache and I am more weary than I have ever known."

It took time to set the slab back in place and to make it look as if it had never been touched. Between them they piled stones back over it.

Thomas was the last to turn away. He stood for a while looking into the ruined hut and knew this is where Ambrose had buried his most valuable finds. Where he had buried the most valuable of them all.

FORTY-FOUR

"Pa, wake up! I need to talk to you."

Thomas emerged slowly from some deep place where his dreams had been of caves, skulls, and something nameless that lurked in darkness.

"Is it safe?" His first thought was of what they had uncovered. He had shown it to all of them other than the children and Silva, who said she could not be in the same house as the object and had ridden to stay in her own cottage until its fate was decided.

"How can I know that?" said Amal. "Or do you forget that you left the house with it last night?"

Thomas closed his eyes a moment. The cup was slippery in his mind. He suspected it had not wanted to be found. Suspected before many months passed he would have no recollection of it. Which was for the best, because then he would have no recollection of where he had hidden it. Already it was starting to fade in his minds. A shifting memory of a place where it would be safe. Dark. Enclosed. Hidden in a castle that no longer served a purpose. Except now it did. Thomas knew the depths and chambers of Ludlow Castle and had chosen well. Alone. Except he had not felt alone. There were whisperings in his mind as he descended stone stairs, twisting and turning. The guards had admitted him without question and he wondered did they consider him Lord of the castle now its true lord lay dead.

When he opened his eyes again, Amal stood waiting, her arms crossed, and the cup squirmed away from his thoughts.

"You have slept a day and a half, and I need to show you something."

Thomas sat up, starting at his daughter.

"You cut your hair," he said.

"Bel did it. It was too long. Do you like it?"

"I am not used to it yet, but I expect I will."

Amal shook her head. "You are hopeless, Pa. I do not know what Bel sees in you."

"Neither do I. So what do you want?"

"Do you remember asking me to find out where the Coroner's housekeeper obtained the cantharidin from?"

"I told you to ask Agnes, but I assume you did more than that. Turn around while I get dressed, I have great hunger and we can talk as well at the kitchen table as here."

Amal turned her back after complaining there was little point because she had seen Jorge naked a hundred times and her father at least a tenth of that, so it was stupid to pretend modesty between themselves. Thomas let the words wash across him until she came to the point.

"Aunt Agnes told me there is a man in Hereford who supplies it. She also told me there are several people who pretend they can, but all they provide is a mixture of herbs that do not work. Though I admit neither do they kill anyone. The dosage can be dangerous, can it not?"

"It can." Thomas dressed in a long Moorish robe, which was enough to maintain his modesty, so he told Amal she could turn around. "I suppose you went to Hereford?"

"Yesterday while you slept."

"Alone?"

"Jorge came with me for protection."

Thomas was glad it had not been required.

"What did you discover?"

"I found the man. He has a small house hard against the cathedral in a narrow alley. He is an apothecary, and my impression is he is a good one, and Jorge confirmed it. He told me how he obtains his supplies from the east, how he mixes them and in what quantities. When I returned I checked your journals, and you would have mixed the ingredients in exactly the same way. This means either the housekeeper lied about how much she gave the Coroner, or someone distilled the liquor down after it was purchased. I bought a small bottle from him and tried doing that here, and it is possible."

"You did not try it yourself, did you?"

"Of course not."

They reached the kitchen, and after Thomas sat Amal

brought him a thick stew left over from the night before which was re-warming above the fire.

"Do you want me to tell you what I think, or not?" asked Amal.

"I do. You have done well."

Amal continued to stare at him, so Thomas said, "Go on, tell me what you think."

"That if the apothecary supplied the same strength of cantharidin for the Coroner he would still be alive. What I believe is someone distilled the tincture down to make it stronger. I did the same with what he provided and reducing it by half would be enough to kill him. You told me the housekeeper took one drop from the old bottle and one from the new, and that she gave four drops to the Coroner, all from the new one. It should not have killed him even if he was old and overweight. I asked the apothecary if he had supplied the Coroner before and he said yes, he had. He even showed me the order for his last provision and the one before that." Amal stopped, waiting.

"What?" Thomas asked, knowing she was doing it on purpose.

"The apothecary had sent all previous supplies with a boy he used. He had to charge extra because Ludlow is a long way from Hereford, but Lyman d'Alston did not mind paying. Except the last time someone called for the bottle in person."

"The housekeeper?"

Amal shook her head. "Amos Mapp. He told the

apothecary his master needed the tincture quickly so had sent him."

Thomas thought about what Amal had told him.

"Tell me what you think happened."

"Truly?"

Thomas nodded, and Amal smiled.

"What I believe is that Amos Mapp distilled the liquid until it was stronger than Lyman d'Alston was used to. Had there not been a little left in the old bottle then it is possible the housekeeper would also have died."

"Which she did anyway — when Mapp took her before a jury and accused her of murder."

"When it was he who murdered the Coroner."

"Why? Did he envy d'Alston's position so much?" Even as he spoke the words the real reason came to Thomas, and it made sense of what had happened. Not everything, but he suspected it would when he discovered more of the truth.

He rose and went upstairs, leaving a confused Amal staring after him. When he returned, he placed the papers of Felicia Hughden on the table.

"What are these, Pa?" Amal picked one up. "It is in Latin."

"Which you can read better than me these days. See if you can find mention of Amos Mapp in there." Thomas rose and poured himself a mug of spring water, then returned to finish his stew, which was excellent.

Amal scanned the pages as he ate, turning over each in turn until she came to the second to last. It had been third to last but Thomas had extracted the final sheet and burned it.

She set her finger on a block of text that he recognised as one of Felicia Hughden's commentaries.

"He is mentioned here, Pa, but only in passing."

"Read it to me."

"It says, 'Ambrose came to me this morning. He is worried about Mapp. He told me he is selling fake relics instead of destroying them. Ambrose fears for his life.' Then she has written another line. The ink is slightly different, so it was probably mixed later. 'Two more children sent with Ambrose. May they rest in peace and God's light.'"

Amal went back through the papers, backwards and forwards. She looked up at her father.

"She has recorded all of the bodies here that Ambrose took and buried. I will need to study the notes carefully, but there are dozens No, there are hundreds. Who were they, Pa?"

"Children born of the nuns at Elmbrook and elsewhere."

"She had them killed?" Amal's voice showed disgust.

"I do not believe so. The children Ambrose took away died from natural causes. You know the first year of life is the most dangerous. The first month even more so. Felicia Hughden could not bury them at the priory so she asked Ambrose to dispose of them in other graves. Consecrated graves."

"Why would he do such a thing?" asked Amal.

"We will never know, but I suspect Ambrose wanted

to honour the dead children. Another man might have simply disposed of them wherever they could, but not him. I can ask Bernard if he agrees, but he knew nothing of any of this or he would have put a stop to it. Did he return to the house?"

"He did, but a message came from Hereford and he had to leave yesterday while you slept. I want to believe he knew nothing of this, as you said. He is your friend, Pa. A good friend, yes?"

"He is." Thomas pushed his empty bowl away. "I need to confront Mapp."

"Do not go alone. You should take Will with you, but he has gone to Silva. Fetch Usaden. If what you suspect is true, Mapp has already killed one man."

"More than one. Many more than one. But I will do as you ask and go for Usaden."

Except when Thomas reached Emma's house, Usaden had gone hunting with Jack Pook, and the Coroner's house was only across the market square as he emerged from Raven Lane so he crossed to it and rapped on the door.

It was opened by a young woman, tall and slim, her face vaguely familiar and he realised where he had seen her before. It was sister Arabella. He would have recognised her sooner but she looked different dressed in normal clothing.

"Do you need to speak with the Coroner, Thomas Berrington?"

"I do."

"Come in then. He is in his study."

She led the way, opened the study door and let him in.

Amos Mapp looked up from a stack of papers on the desk in front of him.

"Welcome, Thomas. If I had known how much work was involved, I would have had second thoughts about accepting my new position."

"I would not worry yourself too much, you will not be Coroner long."

Mapp stood, his fists on the desktop. "Do you want the position for yourself? I expected you might, but I am Coroner now and there is nothing you can do about it."

"We will see if you are still Coroner after you are accused of the murder of Lyman d'Alston. I also suspect you of killing brother Ambrose but lack proof. It matters little because you can only be hung the once."

Amos Mapp laughed. "You are a madman."

"As we stand here my daughter is poring through Felicia Hughden's journal to build a full picture of what went on. The depravity. The corruption. The dishonesty. Ambrose discovered you were selling fake relics that were meant to be destroyed, and you killed him. You were there that night. I saw you."

"So were others. Abbot Haylewith, Madoc, the Archdeacons of Hereford and Salop. Prior Bernard. You. I could make a case for any of you killing Ambrose. In fact, that is exactly what I will do. I will have you arrested. It is you who will hang, not me."

"And your proof?"

"I am respected in this area; I need no proof. My word

is my proof. You come to Ludlow with your nose in the air making out how clever you are. How well travelled. How knowledgeable. But I have found you out, and you will hang before the month's end." Amos Mapp reached beneath the desk. When his hand emerged it held a long knife. "But hanging is too good for you. I will say you attacked me and I had to defend myself. Arabella will confirm all this."

"You intend to kill me?"

Mapp laughed. "No, I want to cut an apple. Of course I am going to kill you. Do not try to run. I knew you would come so Arabella locked the door after admitting you. I would promise to make this quick, but I would be lying. You have made things difficult for me. Made me kill when I would have preferred not to."

"You admit it now?" Thomas moved backwards, hoping Mapp would take it as cowardice. He reached for the door handle, but when he turned it the door remained shut. It had been worth trying. It might have been another of Mapp's lies.

"Ambrose told me he intended to expose me for selling fake relics."

"As he should."

"He brought it on himself when he asked me to dispose of the relics he had failed to authenticate. Except when I looked at them I could not tell they were false, and neither could the abbeys, priories and churches I sold them to."

"Except he found you out," Thomas said.

"Felicia Hughden gave me away. I did not know that

one of the relics I offered her was the same as the one Ambrose had confiscated. How could I? One toe bone looks much the same as any other. But she knew. Ambrose confronted me at the conclave and threatened to expose me. He also tainted me by saying he possessed an item I have searched for long and hard. I went to his cell to force him to tell me where it is but he refused, even as I cut into him. I have never seen a man suffer such pain without submitting to me."

"He is not the first you have killed, then." Thomas hoped Mapp's conviction might loosen his tongue, and it seemed he was right.

"Of course not. I was taught the skill when in the Holy Land. Owain used me to interrogate prisoners and I gained a liking for the work. In its own way it is pure; and those I killed were heathen in any case."

"But Ambrose was not. D'Alston's maid was not and you used the law to murder her."

"Because I had to!" Mapp raised his voice as his temper rose. "Everyone knows you have killed men. Women, too. Do not make a pretence you are a better man than me." Mapp struck the hilt of the knife against the desk. "Ambrose should have told me where he hid the Grail. Any other man would have."

"He knew you would kill him anyway, so why would he reveal it?"

"Because then his pain would end, of course. Men welcome death when their entire being is consumed by pain. But not Ambrose. He died with a scream on his lips. Just as you will do."

Thomas smiled, the expression causing Mapp to frown. "If I were you I would stick me hard and fast rather than slowly and painfully. It will make things easier for you."

Mapp came at him.

Thomas waited, then caught his wrist and twisted until the knife clattered to the floor, then twisted again until he felt bone snap.

Mapp screamed and backed away.

Thomas picked up the knife.

Mapp held his undamaged hand out in front of him. "I did not mean it. I only wanted to frighten you."

"People say hanging is a good way to die if the hangman knows his job. A short drop and a broken neck. Over in seconds. Or I can open your belly now and let you stare at your entrails while you bleed to death." Thomas shrugged. "Which is it to be, Amos?"

"Arabella!" Mapp screamed as he clutched his broken wrist to his chest.

She must have been standing on the other side of the door because it was flung open and she entered, also carrying a knife, but she held it wrong and when she swung at Thomas all he had to do was punch her on the side of the head and she fell unconscious to the slabs.

Amos Mapp tried to rush at him, but another figure entered through the door. Usaden caught Mapp and swung him around so his head cracked against the wall, and he too joined his companion on the floor.

"I thought you and Jack were out hunting," Thomas said.

"We were. Caught a fine bundle of conies, too. I'll bring a brace for your supper." Usaden glanced down at the figures. "Emma told me you came asking for me. She saw you coming this way so I thought I would join you. Looks like you would not have needed me in any case."

"Go find a constable or two and bring them back. I will tie Mapp so he cannot run."

"And the woman?"

"She can return to Elmbrook Priory when she wakes, or anywhere else she wants to go. She is not innocent, but then none of us are."

When Usaden had gone Thomas found a wooden box and filled it with all the papers he could find in the room. He set it on the floor in plain view, knowing nobody would question it and he could recover it later once Mapp had been taken away. There would have to be a trial, of course, but Thomas suspected all the proof he needed would be among the papers. Mapp was arrogant enough to believe he would never be caught.

Thomas had unanswered questions, but those answers might also be among the papers.

Why had Felicia Hughden stolen the skulls?

What was the involvement of Abbot Haylewith and Madoc? Were they drawn in by Mapp, or was it the other way around and he had been seduced by their evil? Thomas knew even if he did not find the answers it would not matter. Would not save Mapp from a long drop to oblivion.

FORTY-FIVE

Thomas stood on the slope beyond Linney Gate and looked across the verdant country spread below. Some was his land, some belonged to his neighbours, but most belonged to the Church. When he heard someone approach he turned and smiled to see Bernard.

"Why meet here, Tom? Are you the devil intending to show me all the world to tempt me with? If so you are too late."

"Are you Prior again?" Thomas asked.

"I am not."

"Have you done something to upset Archdeacon Webb?"

"I wish I had. I am now Abbot of the western region, which includes Wigmore and Hindwell Abbeys. I also control Elmbrook Priory but will have to find a suitable Prioress to report to me." Bernard wiped a hand across his face. "I did not seek this. I do not want this. But if it is God's will then I must obey."

"Or the will of the Archdeacon?" Thomas said.

"They are one and the same thing. I have been distracted, so tell me, what happened to Amos Mapp?"

It had been two weeks since his arrest, one week since his execution.

"He was hanged," Thomas said.

"Who will be Coroner now?"

Thomas said nothing.

"You?"

"Do you think me incapable?"

"No, I consider you *too* capable. The district has never had an honest Justice of the Peace, nor an honest Coroner. It makes my head spin to think of the ramifications of such. When?"

"Four days since. Cornwell and Croft came to tell me I had to take the position. It is meant to be temporary until a permanent man can be found, but both of them said nobody is going to look too hard for a replacement."

"Will you move into Lyman's big house?"

"It was never his. It is Church property, so you are its owner now."

"I do not think I am up to this task placed on me, Tom."

"You are what the abbeys and priories need, Bernard. An honest Abbot. I expect it is as strange a concept as an honest Coroner."

Bernard reached out and slapped Thomas's cheek, but gently. "Abbot Bernard, Tom. Try not to forget my title like you always used to. I am an important man now."

"You have always been an important man to me. Shall we walk?"

"To Burway?"

Thomas nodded and started down the slope. "You can stay and eat. I have much to tell you and a question or two."

"I cannot stay long, but I will answer what I can, and am keen to hear everything you have learned."

"Talk to me about Ambrose," Thomas said.

"What about him? You knew him. He was exactly as you saw him."

"Honest?"

"Sometimes painfully so."

"Weak?"

"I would say not. Neither physically nor in his soul. What was his involvement, if any?"

"He disposed of the bodies for Felicia, but you know that. He did it with love and with Godliness. I do not believe he was involved in any other way until the very end."

"He could be too hard on himself."

"Sometimes men such as that crumble in a moment of weakness."

"He did at times, but always rebuilt himself after. It must have been an enormous strain on him, but he fought as well as he could. I attach no blame to him."

"Nor do I. All the blame belongs elsewhere."

"With Amos Mapp?"

"Only partly. I would assign the majority to Abbot

Haylewith and Madoc. Mapp simply took advantage of Haylewith's obsessions. One in particular."

"Which was?" asked Abbot Bernard.

They had reached the low-lying land alongside the Teme and now walked through verdant fields where sheep grazed. Hawthorn grew thick in the hedgerows, small red berries growing plump. The orchards were heavy with fruit that would ripen in the autumn, mostly apples, but also pears. They would be stored for use over winter, a hundred different varieties, some small, some large, some sweet, some sour, but all would be eaten. It was a land outside of time, and Thomas wondered if he could see it one hundred or five hundred years in the future would it have changed at all?

"Haylewith was crazed but rational at the same time. A lunatic could not have done what he did, which was to almost overturn the rule of the Church in these border-lands. He recruited Madoc, who was a weak man but also a harsh man, not averse to killing or torture. Madoc was the worst of them. It was all in Mapp's documents. Dishonest as he was he kept meticulous records of his dealing, both real and fake. And the reason behind every-thing was there, written in ink on paper."

"What was it?"

Thomas hesitated a moment, wondering what Bernard's reaction might be, and whether he should tell him or not. But he had already set the seed and could not stop now.

"You know what Haylewith's obsessions were. Relics held by Christ himself. But I also discovered he knew

Ambrose's secret and wanted to use it to bring down King Henry."

Bernard slowed, turned to stare at Thomas. "Ambrose had no secrets. He kept nothing from me."

"I am not sure Ambrose knew of it himself. It concerns his father."

"A passing stranger, no doubt. I have never heard talk of it. Perhaps he was a foundling."

"It relates to who his father and mother were."

"If you intend to tease me then stop now, Tom. But if you mean to inform me then please do so."

"His mother was Felicia." Thomas watched Bernard's eyes widen, telling him he had not known. He had been unsure until that moment. "And his father was Edward, Earl of March."

Another widening of the eyes. "I met him once. No, twice," said Bernard. "The first time after the battle of Mortimer's Cross, the second when he was King and he passed through Hereford and Ludlow. If he truly was Ambrose's father, he must have set the seed on that first occasion."

"That is what Croft told me," Thomas said. "He took Edward to Elmbrook to celebrate their great victory after the battle, when all they had done was slow the ascent of the Tudors."

"And you said Haylewith discovered this?"

"He did. Croft claimed to be the only person who knew the truth but someone else must have. I suspect Felicia told Madoc, perhaps intending it as a threat, but if so it had the opposite effect. Haylewith intended to broadcast that a son of King Edward strode these border-lands. He recruited the Marcher Lords to his side and intended to threaten the King. But Ambrose's death stopped him from implementing any of this because Mapp was not made privy to his plans."

They had reached the Teme and Thomas stopped, staring into the clear water where pebbles and shards danced beneath the ripples.

"There was another reason Ambrose died. You know the legends as well as I do, as well as everyone does. There was one relic the Templars were rumoured to own. The most important in the Christian faith. Rumours abound in this region, many linked to Garway. Haylewith believed them. He claimed to have uncovered the Grail and held it in his possession."

Bernard stared at Thomas for a long time before shaking his head.

"Impossible," he said.

"You are right, it is impossible, but both Haylewith and Madoc believed it. They had possession of something. A cup of some kind. I saw it in that cave with the skulls. They claimed it was the Grail and used it to help recruit their army. Then they made a mistake. They asked Ambrose to authenticate it and he told them it was a fake."

"Amos Mapp wrote all this down?"

"He did, and his part in it as well. Ambrose told him of it. Mapp said he had wanted to take the cup from Hindwell Abbey but was told he could not. Haylewith refused to accept his judgement. For some reason, Mapp

481

also took it into his head that Ambrose was wrong and went to Abbot Haylewith and asked to see this wonder."

"He was allowed?"

"He was, because he had dealt with Haylewith many times, selling him relics both false and real. There are two pages of his reasoning which show he believed this cup was the Grail. He had even written in a value he could get for it. From King Henry. From the Pope." Thomas smiled. "I can show you the pages. Mapp estimated, crossed it out, wrote a higher value, did it again and again."

"If it were truly the Grail it would have no value. It would be invaluable. *Too* valuable. It would belong to the Church. To the Holy Father in Rome. If what you tell me is true then how can you claim everything that happened was Mapp's fault? It sounds to me as if he was also a victim of Madoc and Haylewith's madness."

"Which is what he wanted everyone to think. Mapp was bad to the bone, but clever. He could persuade people to his ends. And in the case of Madoc and Haylewith, all he had to do was reinforce the beliefs they already held. He told them the Grail was real, and it was their destiny to use it to create a new Church, one that melded the old with the new. Because he knew that is what both believed. Ambrose was to be part of this plan even if he did not know it. A new claimant to the throne of England."

"So why did Felicia die?"

"She was innocent of everything other than her duty to the Church. She discovered what they intended to do and confronted them, threatening to expose their plans to the authorities. She had to die. The manner of her death only demonstrates how angered Haylewith was."

"Is it ended now?" asked Bernard. "This false Grail is gone?"

"It will never be found. Just as Madoc and Haylewith will never be found. A rumour has been spread they left the country."

Thomas considered telling Bernard what else he had found and hidden again before deciding it was better the man remained ignorant. Such knowledge might erode his peace of mind.

"What will you do about Elmbrook?" he asked.

"Do?" said Bernard. "Nothing. I am not drawn to what is on offer there, but I am aware a great many men are. Sex is not a sin, Tom. I have never believed it is. I have indulged in the past but do so no longer. Elmbrook will continue as it always has, but I will ensure a Prioress with more steel is appointed. Things will have to change, and I pray I have enough years left to help that happen."

"As do I. I would miss you."

Bernard smiled. "Well, that will no doubt keep me alive."

Thomas put his arm around Bernard's shoulder, recalling how he would once have been unable to do so because many years ago Bernard had been a giant to him.

"You are thinking, Tom," said Bernard. "I can always tell. What about?"

Thomas looked into Bernard's eyes, feeling the love he had always possessed for this man. Love and respect.

"Nothing. I was thinking of nothing. I need to go away for a while."

"Back to Spain? I always thought one day you would. I will miss you."

Thomas smiled. "And I you, but I go only to London. The King has summoned me. He wants my advice." Thomas laughed. "*My* advice?"

"I can think of none better. On what matter?"

"Catherine. He does not know what to do with her. He has requested I talk to her, to sound her out regarding another marriage."

"In that case take your children with you," said Bernard.

"I intend to. The King has found me a house in London, close to where Catherine resides for all purposes as a prisoner. I have watched her grow from a babe to a strong young woman, and would see her find happiness while she can. I know she found it with Arthur but hope more may lie in her future."

Thomas embraced Bernard, holding tight to him for a long time. When he released him he reached into the pocket of his jacket and held his hand out.

"What is this, Tom?" asked Bernard.

"A final gift from Ambrose. When we lifted the bones behind my old house Amal found a small silver cross. After Mapp was executed, I went to the Coroner's house and discovered Ambrose's cart still there. Hidden in a box were these."

Thomas opened the bag and poured some of the

contents into Bernard's palm. Half a dozen small silver crosses.

"Ambrose set one around the neck of each of the children before he buried them. These remained unused." Thomas said. "The others were his final, godly gift to each child. I thought you might want them."

HISTORICAL NOTE

The Priory at Elmbrook and the Abbey at Hindwell do not exist but are based on real locations. Lingen, I have changed to Elmbrook, and Abbeycwmhir to Hindwell. Burfa Bank is a real place, as are the old fortifications at the top, but no quarry or caves exist.

The Grail is used in many books, and I have chosen it due to the real St Michael's church at Garway, which was one of the last redoubts of the Templars. If you ever find yourself in south Herefordshire, I recommend a visit as the church is strange and impressive, despite its small size.

To learn more about the Templars and Garway I consulted *The Knights Templar & Hospitaller in Herefordshire* by Audrey Tapper. Like the church itself, the book is small and impressive, as well as the very approachable *The Templars* by Dan Jones.

For details on life in Abbeys and Priories I used *A*

Medieval Monastery by Fiona Macdonald and Gerald Wood, and *Life in a Medieval Abbey* by Tony McAleavy.

The invention of Ambrose's father being Edward of March — later to become Edward IV — may not be such an invention. Edward fought at the battle of Mortimer's Cross in 1461, alongside Sir Richard Croft, who was then a much younger man than in this book. The idea they would have celebrated after defeating Jasper Tudor on the Lancastrian side is very much in line with Edward's reputation. Of course, it is a fiction, but I like the idea of a possible bastard heir to the throne wandering the borderlands between Herefordshire and Wales.

The initial conceit underlying much of the plot, that of the brothel at Elmbrook, I have based on *Medieval English Nunneries 1275-1535* by Eileen Power; in particular *Chapter XI: The Olde Daunce* which contains sections on the moral state of English nunneries, nuns and the celibate ideal, as well as some examples of where this broke down.

Information on the brothels (a word not in use until the mid-16th century, so I have used the earlier form of bordel or stew) which were set up under the reign of Henry II on the southern bank of the Thames in London can be found through several sources.

Southwark became the city's official red-light district by order of Henry II, which gave control of the Southwark brothels to the ecclesiastical authorities, which would allow the church to draw untold sums of money from them through the sale of licenses. At the time of the ordinance, there were eighteen licensed brothels in Bankside employing around a thousand prostitutes at any one time. As a result of the Church taking control, most of London's churches built during this period were largely financed by prostitution.

You can find more detail on this at the website dirty-sexyhistory as well as many other sources.

The Thomas Berrington Prequels

A Death of Innocence

Purchase 3 full-length novels for less than the price of two.

Thomas Berrington Books 1-3

The Red Hill

Breaker of Bones

The Incubus

Thomas Berrington Books 4-6

The Incubus

The Inquisitor

The Fortunate Dead

Thomas Berrington Books 7-9

The Promise of Pain

The Message of Blood

A Tear for the Dead

Unit-13: WWII Paranormal Spy Thriller

An Imperfect Future